MW00473313

"I KNOW WHAT SHOULD BE DONE WITH YOU, YOU LITTLE SPITFIRE!"

"If you kiss me, I'll scream!" she threatened. "I'll kill you! I swear I will!"

"Indeed." Alex growled as he pulled her into his arms. His lips covered hers, gently exploring, tentatively tasting.

"Let go of me!" She wiggled like a captured eel and tried to grab his hair. "I'm more woman than you'll ever have!" Stomping hard on his instep, she was free.

"You hellion!" he shouted, bending to rub his foot.

And then unexpectedly he chuckled. What a vibrant, beautiful tigress she was!

Other **AVON ROMANCES**

BELOVED INTRUDER *by Joan Van Nuys*
HEART OF THE WILD *by Donna Stephens*
SCARLET KISSES *by Patricia Camden*
SILVER AND SAPPHIRES *by Shelly Thacker*
SURRENDER TO THE FURY *by Cara Miles*
TRAITOR'S KISS *by Joy Tucker*
WILDSTAR *by Nicole Jordan*

Coming Soon

MY LADY NOTORIOUS *by Jo Beverley*
SURRENDER MY HEART *by Lois Greiman*

And Don't Miss These
ROMANTIC TREASURES
from Avon Books

THE MASTER'S BRIDE *by Suzannah Davis*
MIDNIGHT AND MAGNOLIAS *by Rebecca Paisley*
A ROSE AT MIDNIGHT *by Anne Stuart*

Avon Books are available at special quantity discounts for bulk
purchases for sales promotions, premiums, fund raising or educational use. Special books, or book excerpts, can also be created to
fit specific needs.

For details write or telephone the office of the Director of Special
Markets, Avon Books, Dept. FP, 1350 Avenue of the Americas,
New York, New York 10019, 1-800-238-0658.

Scoundrel's Desire

JoAnn DeLazzari

Vicke —
To romantic nights &
Scoundrel's delights — wherever
you find them!

Romance forever —
JoAnn DeLazzari

AVON BOOKS ◆ NEW YORK

2-13-93

If you purchased this book without a cover, you should be aware that this book is stolen property. It was reported as "unsold and destroyed" to the publisher, and neither the author nor the publisher has received any payment for this "stripped book."

To Mom—
who always knew I could

And Dad—
who taught me how to dream.

SCOUNDREL'S DESIRE is an original publication of Avon Books. This work has never before appeared in book form. This work is a novel. Any similarity to actual persons or events is purely coincidental.

AVON BOOKS
A division of
The Hearst Corporation
1350 Avenue of the Americas
New York, New York 10019

Copyright © 1993 by JoAnn DeLazzari
Inside cover author photograph © 1992 by Olan Mills
Published by arrangement with the author
Library of Congress Catalog Card Number: 92-90417
ISBN: 0-380-76421-0

All rights reserved, which includes the right to reproduce this book or portions thereof in any form whatsoever except as provided by the U.S. Copyright Law. For information address Pesha Rubinstein, 37 Overlook Terrace, #1D, New York, New York 10033.

First Avon Books Printing: February 1993

AVON TRADEMARK REG. U.S. PAT. OFF. AND IN OTHER COUNTRIES, MARCA REGISTRADA, HECHO EN U.S.A.

Printed in the U.S.A.

RA 10 9 8 7 6 5 4 3 2 1

Chapter 1

Boston
March 1845

Breanna Sullivan rubbed circles on the frost-covered bedroom window, clearing a path on the icy pane. Outside, pristine snowflakes fell from the steel-gray sky and added a new white mantle to the accumulated snow that already covered the city. Ordinarily she would have noticed that only the most hardy souls were venturing forth into the briskly blowing snow, but her mind was wandering to a warmer clime—back to her home in California.

Shivering in the cold draft from the window, she moved closer to the small stove in her room and raised her skirts to allow the heat to find its way beneath them. She preferred to exert her nervous energy pacing, but the chill of the room demanded she stay close to the source of heat. She tapped her small slippered foot in a rapid tattoo, her fingers gripping the latest letter from her sister.

"Heather . . ." She sighed, glancing down at the missive. "What can I do to help from here?" She had no ready answer, but maybe her cousins could help. It was too early for Garth to be home from his accounting firm, but she could speak to his wife. Tossing a deep auburn curl over her shoulder, she spun about and pulled open the door. A

1

startled scream escaped her at the unexpected presence of her maid.

"Millie! You scared me half to death!" she said, clutching her throat.

"Sorry, Miss Bree." The equally startled maid's brown eyes were wide. "I . . . I was just wonderin' if ya would like some tea?"

A shaky smile lifted the corners of Breanna's mouth. She was fond of Millie. Breanna had come to Boston last year to visit the few remaining members of her late mother's family, and Millie had been assigned to her the day she arrived to stay with her cousin Garth.

"Tea would be fine, Millie, but I'll take it downstairs." The two headed down the hall, anxious to get out of the draft. "Is Evelyn about?"

"No, miss," Millie replied with a shake of her head. "She's still taken to her bed with that cold."

Disappointed, Breanna sighed. "I was hoping to speak to her about . . ." She realized she was still clutching Heather's letter and slipped it into her pocket.

Millie regarded her mistress sympathetically. "I'd help if I could."

Millie seemed so genuinely willing, Breanna was ready to confide the latest news to her when a gust of frosty air swept up the stairs.

"Lord, it's cold out there!" came a muffled male voice as the front door was slammed against the wind.

"Better get another cup," Breanna instructed Millie as she hurried down the stairs to help her cousin remove his snow-covered coat.

"And have someone stoke up the fire," Garth said, shaking melting snow from his head.

In minutes the cousins were ensconced in parlor chairs, turned to the fire, their hands and feet facing the dancing flames.

"I can't understand why you stay in Boston

when you could be in that barbaric but warm place you call home," Garth said.

Breanna detected a note of envy in his teasing. "The cold is a small price to pay for getting to know you and Evelyn."

Smiling, Garth reached to squeeze his cousin's hand. "When you first showed up here, I was afraid you were going to be either a wild hoyden or a spoiled snob." He leaned his head back and recalled the tales his mother had told him about her sister. "Mama said Aunt Anna was headstrong. She wouldn't listen to anyone. She was determined to go west with your father to that godforsaken land, and there was no stopping her."

He saw a smile on Breanna's face that spoke of the fond memories she had of her mother and her home. There was a glow in her dark brown eyes, as if they reflected the California sun she often told him about.

"Instead, I find you are a lovely young woman, filled with genuine warmth and vitality."

Breanna grinned. "But still headstrong."

Thinking of her determination to travel across the country to meet her kin, he chuckled. "Perhaps a little," he mused, reaching to accept a cup of steaming tea from Millie.

Taking a cup for herself, Breanna said, "I'd always wanted to meet you, Garth. I thought if I waited too long, it wouldn't happen."

Garth realized that something was troubling Breanna. "What's wrong, Bree?" he asked. "Is there something I can help you with?"

Breanna rose, and the skirts of her heavy velvet gown brushed the stone hearth. "I received another letter from Heather today."

Heather sent so many letters that Garth often wondered if she started a new one the instant she posted the first. They came in such succession over so far a distance!

"More of her ramblings about that King fellow?" he inquired. Heather had made numerous references to someone who seemed to be involved in treason, swindles, or both.

"She isn't rambling this time," Breanna said, turning to face Garth. "She says Father has disappeared."

"Disappeared!" he exclaimed. He rose from the chair and took the letter Breanna held out to him. Frowning, he scanned the short note. "And she has mentioned this Alexander King fellow again."

"I know. It's almost as if she is accusing him of being responsible for Father's disappearance." Heather had told Breanna that King was close to the Americans who lived in the Mexican territory and hoped to control it, yet he was also in the good graces of the local Mexican authorities who wished to defend their land holdings. In these days of contention over California's future, it seemed suspicious to Breanna that one man could be allied with both sides. Heather had hinted that King was also involved in buying up large tracts of land just before the owners disappeared. Was there a connection? Was this mysterious man responsible for those disappearances? Was Alexander King behind her father's disappearance?

"I have to go home," Breanna announced firmly. She could see the concern on Garth's face and held up her hand to stop him from speaking. "It will do you no good to argue with me, Garth. Casa del Verde is my home. If Father is in trouble, I have to be there."

Garth wanted to ask her how her presence was going to make any difference, but he knew he would be unable to sway her. It was obvious in the determined tilt of her chin.

"I may be good at keeping straight the most complicated financial accounts, cousin," he said, "but I know better than to try and change *your* mind!"

Relieved that she would not have to waste time

arguing with Garth, Breanna smiled softly. "I appreciate that." She breathed a sigh of relief and settled back into her chair. "I have enough on my mind without having to worry how I'm going to slip away from you."

Garth grew serious. Breanna was about to return home to something that might be more than even she could handle. Although she was a resourceful, independent young woman, she had never had to cope with nefarious characters before. It was possible she was putting herself in jeopardy.

"We could hire an agent to check it all out," he suggested. Breanna grimaced. "It's just a thought," he quickly added.

"Don't worry, Garth. I won't do anything foolish," she assured him. "If things are out of control in California, I'll hire an agent of my own."

It wasn't the most comforting thought, but Garth knew it was the most he could hope for. "Want me to make your travel arrangements?" he asked, conceding to her plans. Her radiant smile was answer enough. "I could go with you," he offered.

Breanna shook her head. "That's sweet, Garth, but I don't think you really want to be away from Evelyn." His face reddened at her observation. "Besides, you'll be busy here trying to find a new maid. I'd like to take Millie with me."

Chuckling, Garth held out his arm for Breanna. "Have you asked her yet?"

"No." Breanna grinned coyly. "I thought I'd better check with you before asking, since she does work for you."

"And if I'd said no?"

Stopping in front of her bedroom door, Breanna wrinkled her nose. "I would have offered her more than you pay her." She slipped into her room as Garth's laughter floated down the hall.

* * *

"It ain't gonna be the same around here without you, Miss Bree," Millie said as she dragged a second trunk into the room and set it beside the first. She flipped open the lid and frowned at the lovely spring and summer dresses that filled it. "You sure you won't be needin' some warmer clothes?"

Breanna paused in sorting the contents of the first trunk. Sitting back on her heels, she smiled at Millie. "Within a week of leaving Boston it will get warmer with each mile we put behind us. There won't be any need for warm clothing again until we make the trip around the Cape. A few winter gowns and a good heavy cloak are all I'll need."

Unconvinced, Millie hunched her shoulders. "It don't seem right that this place you live in has no winter."

"We have winter!" Breanna laughed. "It's just not as cold as it is here and there is seldom any snow." Thinking of her home, Breanna gazed out the window to where the weak sun struggled to shine beneath a new gathering of storm clouds. "Our winter is milder, yet we get some terrible storms off the ocean. Still, there is rarely a frost."

Returning to her chore, Breanna decided this was as good a time as ever to test the waters with Millie. "You've never told me if you have family here in Boston."

"No, miss," Millie said matter-of-factly as she continued to fold garments. "My folks both died within a few years of each other before I was five. I have a brother in New York who raised me along with three of his own. It was hard on him, so I moved out when I found a job with Miss Evelyn's family."

Millie was a pretty girl, Breanna thought. She guessed her to be about eighteen, three years younger than herself. She lacked a delicacy of features, yet her healthy and jovial roundness was most attractive. Slightly taller than Breanna, she matched her in high energy and sunny disposition.

Sure she would be pleased with Millie's company in the four-month journey ahead, Breanna said, "Sit down a minute, Millie." She took Millie's hand and guided her to a seat on the bed. "How would you like to go with me to California?"

For a moment Millie simply stared up at her mistress. "Me?" she questioned. Breanna smiled brightly and nodded. "Oh, miss, I . . . I couldn't!"

"Why not? What's to keep you here?"

Millie began to chew on her lower lip. "Well, there's Mr. and Mrs. Mitchell. They've been awful good to me."

"Garth already said it would be fine with them if you like the idea."

"Then there's . . . there's . . ."

"Oh, Millie!" Breanna laughed. "Think of it as an adventure!" She dropped down beside Millie, her own excitement becoming contagious. "Don't you want to go?"

Millie sighed. "It ain't that, Miss Bree. It's just . . ." Rising, Millie returned to the trunk and knelt in front of it. She looked back at Breanna. "I only had four years of schoolin'. As much as I would like ta go with ya, I need this job."

Breanna had never considered that Millie would think her invitation was just a whim. "Very well, Millie. If you don't want to go, I'll have to post for a maid and traveling companion."

"Post?" Millie asked. "You mean ya want ta *hire* me?" The instant Breanna nodded, Millie squealed with delight. "Ya don't have ta post nothin'!" she announced. "I'll take the job!"

Delighted, Breanna embraced Millie fondly. "We'll have a great time. And when we get to my house, you'll see that California is all I said it was, and more!"

* * *

Breanna joined Garth and Evelyn for a farewell dinner.

"You've both been so wonderful, I hate to say good-bye," she told them.

Evelyn smiled. "If all of Garth's family was as special as you, Breanna, I would insist they move in with us." Thinking of her in-laws, she laughed. "Unfortunately they're all stuffy Bostonians!"

Garth cleared his throat. "I beg your pardon, my dear, but I, too, am a stuffy Bostonian."

"Quite so!" Breanna chirped in her best Massachusetts accent. As everyone laughed, Breanna became serious. Turning to Evelyn, she reached across the table to take her hand. "No one who could let a long-lost cousin impose on them for a year could be called stuffy. I can't tell you how much I appreciate your generosity."

Evelyn winked at Breanna. "Well, it certainly didn't seem like a year to me."

After the meal was over, they adjourned to the parlor. As they settled themselves, Breanna thanked them both for letting her hire Millie.

"She's a good girl," Evelyn said. "I'll miss her here in the house, but this is a chance I could never deny her."

Garth stepped close to the fireplace and lit a cigar after both women nodded their permission. "I feel better knowing she'll be with you." He puffed on the tobacco slowly, aware they were waiting for further comment. "I've been thinking about everything Heather has told us in her letters."

Breanna had too. Although she knew Heather had a tendency to dramatize, there was something wrong beyond her father's disappearance. She thought of Heather's references to secret meetings and the theft of several gun shipments. Heather could be fanciful, but surely not even she could make all this up. Breanna was about to tell Garth how she felt when he echoed her thoughts.

"It seems to me this Alexander King fellow is up

to no good." The sparkle in Breanna's eyes told him she agreed. "Don't trust anyone, cousin," he said. "And be careful."

Breanna rose and placed a gentle kiss upon his cheek. "I promise, Garth," she told him. "And I promise I'll get to the bottom of this mystery." A smile touched her lips at his groan. "I'm a Sullivan. I have Papa's Irish temper and Mama's stubborn streak." An impish delight seemed to radiate from her. "You might be wiser to warn Mr. King to be careful. He might be the one to need your concern!"

Garth was more tempted than ever to accompany his cousin back to California. He'd learned she had more spirit than was sometimes wise.

"At least your return trip should be more pleasant," he said. On her journey to Boston she'd had only the captain's wife as chaperone and companion. Not many women could have endured the long, arduous journey, let alone the less than comfortable accommodations. "I've booked your passage on a new clipper."

Intrigued, Breanna asked about the ship. Garth suggested she would better enjoy finding out about it for herself, but he did say it would accomplish the journey in only three-quarters of the usual time.

"Nearly a month less!" she exclaimed, whirling happily into her chair.

"I knew you would be pleased not to have to spend so much time on a ship," he said.

"Oh, it isn't the length of the voyage," Breanna explained. "It's how much sooner I will be able to face Alexander King and demand some answers."

Garth's gaze flew to his wife. He saw concern in her expression, yet also repressed humor. Shaking his head, he sent up a silent prayer for his cousin's welfare.

* * *

The newly launched *Rainbow* stood at her mooring ready to take on the first passengers for her maiden voyage. The spiraling maze of masts and riggings stood in dark contrast to the ghostly gray of the early April sky.

Garth had sent the trunks ahead the night before, leaving them little else to do before departing than share the remaining time amid the bustle of the busy New England port.

"We'd better just let them board, dear," Garth called to Evelyn, his lips close to her ear so she could hear him over the noise. She nodded, turning to embrace Breanna as tears filled her eyes.

"Godspeed, Breanna," she said.

"And may He bless you and Garth," Breanna replied, knowing she would miss them. Hugging Garth warmly, she smiled up at him. "Don't worry. I'll be fine." He nodded, yet she didn't think he was convinced. Deciding this was not the time or place to try to ease his mind, she turned to Millie, who was staring up at the swaying mast. "Time to go, Millie."

Pulling her eyes from the towering structure, Millie bid her farewells with more emotion. Before she succumbed to tears, however, Breanna was drawing her up the gangplank.

"You sure this thing can go so far?" Millie asked suspiciously as she glanced about. "It don't look none too big."

Breanna's melodic laughter floated on the breeze. "It's large enough! Besides, we'll have one of the six staterooms, thanks to Garth. We'll be traveling in style."

Not sure she was ready to believe Breanna, Millie stayed close as they moved onto the deck.

"You must be Miss Sullivan," a voice boomed from nearby. They turned to face a bearded man. "Captain Barrymore, at your service."

"Captain," Breanna acknowledged with a smile and a brief nod as he shook her hand. "May I

present my traveling companion, Millie Fortson."
Instantly elevated in station by the introduction,
Millie stood taller and extended her hand.

"I hope you ladies will find the journey pleasant," he commented, noticing the heightened interest his newest passenger was arousing among
the other passengers. His eyes sparkled in merriment. "I think you will enjoy it."

"I'm sure we will, sir," Breanna responded, unaware of the stir around her. "Your ship is most
beautiful, and I'm sure we are in good hands."

"That you are," declared a barrel-chested gentleman as he raced up to join them. "The *Rainbow* is
the finest ship to sail the seas." He looked lovingly
about the deck, as if caressing it with his eyes.
"Mark my word, you'll be seeing more clippers
just like her."

"You seem most pleased with her, Mr. . . . ?"

"John Griffiths is the name, miss, and I should
be pleased. I designed her. I've watched her grow
from a dream into the beautiful lady she is."

"I'm sure the young ladies would love to hear
all about her, John, but let's get them settled first.
We'll be getting under way in about"—the captain
checked his pocket watch—"fifteen minutes. You
can talk this evening at dinner."

Breanna paused long enough to agree to dine
with Mr. Griffiths and his wife before a young lad
led her below.

"I don't know about this sailin', Miss Bree."
Millie groaned as she looked around the small
cabin. It was all new, and the smell of fresh wood
mingled with the faint tang of resin.

Altering the course of the conversation before
Millie changed her mind about the trip, Breanna began to open the trunks. "If we're going to spend the
next three months together, don't you think you
could call me Breanna?" She bit back a grin at the
distrustful look Millie was still giving the cabin.

"Yes, miss," she mumbled, only half-listening until she realized what Breanna had said. Smiling sheepishly, she directed her attention to her new employer. "Yes, Breanna. If you want me to." Seeing the nod, Millie removed her bonnet and cloak, then hung them neatly before checking the bedding and accommodations.

After only a few minutes of unpacking, Breanna sighed heavily. "Let's leave this for now and go up on deck." She reached for her cloak, swinging it about her shoulders. "I want to see this ship get under sail."

Not as anxious to be on deck as Breanna, Millie told her she preferred to unpack now and insisted Breanna go on without her. Already aware that Millie was not going to be much of a sailor, Breanna made her way out of the cabin.

As she left the shelter of the companionway, a brisk wind whipped at her bonnet and tossed her skirts about her ankles. Her fellow passengers were lining the rail to wave good-bye to the friends and family who were seeing them off as the sailors scurried through the riggings preparing to sail.

Breanna clutched the long, rose-colored ribbons that fluttered wildly over her shoulder from the bow beneath her chin. With her russet hair parted in the center and drawn into a bun at the back of her head, she had tried to appear sedate and only mildly amused, but the promise of adventure sparkled in her eyes and was more obvious in the trembling of her gloved hand as she gripped the dark mahogany rail.

She was going home! There was no way to contain her excitement. As she scanned the faces ashore and spotted Garth waving frantically, she laughed and returned the gesture just as the first sail was set in the foremast and the ship pulled farther from the dock. A second sail and a third joined the first. In moments the faces of those ashore were a blur.

As the ship broke free of the harbor, Breanna felt the sting of snow flurries skittering in the stiffening breeze. It took a moment for her to realize that the other passengers had already sought the shelter of their rooms. Prepared to do likewise, she spotted Mr. Griffiths and paused to enjoy the expression on his face while he watched the *Rainbow* clear the bay and make for open water.

From jib to spanker, each sail was full and drove them through the water like a skater over the ice. Despite the swells, the ship rode smoothly, and a gentle melancholy seeped into Breanna's thoughts. Above her were man-made clouds of white sails that made her think of more natural ones dancing over the beaches of Monterey. Would that she could be as quick to reach home as the wayward clouds.

Stepping closer to the companionway door but not ready to go inside, Breanna thought of her home and the wonderful memories it held. A smile teased her mouth when she recalled the antics she and Heather had enjoyed. She began to wonder if in the last year her sister had become the beauty she had seemed destined to become. With their mother's thick red hair and their father's hazel eyes, she was an Irish rose ready to bloom.

Although the days of youth were pleasant to ponder, the image of her father's ruddy, laughing face filled Breanna's heart. She could almost feel the love that radiated from the depths of his eyes. Had she seen them for the last time when they parted?

Fighting a desire to cry and the sting of the blowing snow, Breanna decided to go below. As she opened the door, she saw Mr. Griffiths examining each nook and cranny, despite the cold. He certainly loved his ship, she thought with a sad smile, wishing she had something as important to keep her from dwelling on thoughts of home.

Rubbing some warmth back into her cheeks, Breanna entered the small cabin. "It certainly is getting cold on—" She stopped abruptly. "Millie!" The girl was seated on the floor hunched over a chamber pot. Racing to the commode, Breanna dampened a cloth and dropped to her knees at Millie's side.

"Why didn't you tell me you felt seasick?" Breanna asked sympathetically when she noticed how green Millie turned during each roll of the ship.

Gulping down a surge from her stomach, Millie looked up with watery eyes. "I . . . I didn't . . . I've never been on a . . . a ship before."

"Oh, you poor dear," Breanna crooned, removing her outer garments and setting them aside. She helped Millie to one of the bunks, chamber pot and all. "Well, my friend," Breanna said gently, "it looks like I'll have something to take my mind off home for a while after all."

Her remark was met with Millie's long, low groan.

It wasn't until they sailed into the harbor of San Juan in the balmy warmth of the Caribbean that Millie was able to make it to a deck chair to take some fresh air and sunshine. Fortunately, the voyage had been uneventful and the weather had turned kinder.

"Comfortable?" Breanna asked as she tucked a blanket around Millie's legs.

"I should be seein' ta you." Millie pouted, both loving and hating the attention.

Taking a chair at her side, Breanna sniffed. "Don't be silly. The best thing that could have happened was your getting ill." The surprised grunt from Millie made Breanna laugh. "I don't mean that I'm glad you got sick. It's just that I needed something to keep my mind off my worries about home." Smiling at the girl who was more friend than servant, she added, "Thank you."

Millie chuckled. "Well, just don't go thinkin' I'll get seasick every time you have a worry."

Relaxing in the warm sunshine, Breanna thought about how Millie's illness had had a second benefit. Confined, the two women had quickly formed an emotional bond. Despite the differences in their backgrounds, they found they shared many of the same dreams and fears. Normally a private person, Breanna had easily opened up in the face of Millie's genuine interest and concern.

"What you thinkin' about?" Millie asked when she saw that Breanna's eyes were closed. At first it had been difficult for Millie to think of Breanna as a friend, but Breanna's warmth and sincerity had broken down the last of the social barriers between them.

"About the time we've shared this trip."

"Me, too." Millie grinned when she caught Breanna's smile.

Settling more comfortably in the chair, Breanna gazed out over the calm sea. "What are your plans when we reach California?"

Never having considered the future beyond the voyage, Millie furrowed her brow. "I ain't . . . haven't really thought about it."

Millie's efforts to correct her speech by imitating her mistress's made Breanna smile. She sighed to hide it. She had never corrected Millie. All the credit for improvement had to go to Millie herself.

"Get married?" Breanna suggested.

"Maybe. If I can find somebody who cares for me."

"What about love?" Breanna asked, thinking of the love her parents had shared. "Don't you want to love a man?"

"If he loves me and is kind, I'll learn ta love him."

Recalling some of the men she had met in her lifetime, Breanna shrugged. "I want more than love and kindness." Rising, she stepped closer to the rail. "I need a man with pride and honor." She braced her hands on the rail and let the soft breeze caress her face. "He'll be strong yet gentle." As she turned to face Millie, her eyes were darker than usual with emotion.

"And more than all of that, he'll value his word more than his very life!"

Not sure how to respond to the conviction in Breanna's voice, Millie sat quietly watching her and wondering if she was still worrying about her sister's letters. Was she thinking about that rogue Alexander King she was going to have to face?

Realizing silence had fallen between them, Breanna forced a laugh. "Listen to me. I must sound like a lunatic." Not waiting for a reply, she resumed her seat. "Hearts are fickle things. I know it's just as possible I could fall for the least favorable of men."

Her words were light yet held an underlying fear. "Like Alexander King?" Millie asked carefully.

"Never him," Breanna said in a harsh whisper, thinking of what tragedies he might already have caused in her life. "Never him!" she repeated more firmly.

Yet Millie couldn't help thinking of the fine line that divided love and hate.

Chapter 2

The return trip to California was turning out to be more enjoyable than the journey to Boston had been. Breanna thought it was due in part to her desire to be home and in part to the considerably more comfortable accommodations, but she was also sure much of the credit had to go to Millie's presence.

Once her malaise passed, she was a delightful companion. She had a curious nature and there was much in the world she had never seen but was determined to learn about.

"What's the name of this place again?" she asked, never taking her eyes off the tropical coastline that was gliding closer to them.

"Recife," Breanna repeated. "And the country is Brazil. It's a Portuguese colony. I'm afraid my Spanish won't help us here so we'd better not go into town."

Millie frowned. "I haven't been off this bucket since we sailed. I was hopin' to place my feet on solid ground."

Breanna laughed brightly. "Don't you let Mr. Griffiths hear you call it a bucket!" A blush came to Millie's cheeks. She'd lost some weight with her illness, and her slimmer figure was very becoming. "All right, we'll get off, but we'll stay close to the ship," Breanna conceded.

Millie accepted the limitations less than graciously. "Too bad we can't just go across this country rather than around it."

Recalling the maps she had shown Millie, Breanna reminded her of a few choice facts. "Not only would we be unable to get through the jungles on this side, we'd never get over the mountains on the other. Believe me, Millie, this is the safest and best way."

"If you say so." Millie sniffed, still unsure.

The *Rainbow* was due to sail on the tide the next morning but didn't budge. Concerned that there was a problem and annoyed by the delay, Breanna asked several of the passengers if they knew why they weren't moving. She met with only conjecture until the captain announced that they were awaiting two new passengers.

"They must be awfully important to hold up the whole ship," Millie commented, echoing Breanna's own thoughts.

Accepting tea from a steward, Breanna smiled at Mr. Griffiths and his wife, who joined them at their table. The foursome turned their conversation to the unknown late arrivals.

"Do you have any idea who they are?" Breanna inquired. "After all, it is your ship."

Mr. Griffiths laughed mildly. "No, my dear, the *Rainbow* isn't mine. I only designed it for—"

"Look!" Millie interrupted, pointing out a small window toward the dock and the carriage that had drawn up there. "It must be them!"

Everyone made their way to the deck to see. Some of them were pleased and some disappointed when an attractive middle-aged couple alighted from the coach. Captain Barrymore was there to greet them personally.

"They don't look like anyone special," Breanna overheard one lady say. "Dressed fine, but nothing grand."

Breanna hid a grin. What were they expecting, royalty? Prepared to depart and allow the new passengers to board in private, she froze in her tracks. Slowly, she turned to stare at a man who was speaking to the captain as they both stepped onto the deck.

"I'm telling you, Barrymore, I've never known such genius! Who but King could make that old plantation pay like that? And in only two years!"

"King usually knows what he's doing," the captain replied, leading the couple below before the man could say anything else.

The color drained from Breanna's face. King! Was it possible they had been talking about Alexander King, the man she was so anxious to confront? An unexpected shiver ran down her spine. They were thousands of miles from Monterey, but somehow she didn't think it was a mere coincidence that King's name had been mentioned once again.

Breanna spent several hours in her cabin, torn between a desire to seek out the newly arrived couple in search of some answers and the need to sort out what she already knew about King.

It was obvious from the pride and admiration in the voices of the newcomer and the captain that King was someone they respected. If he was the same man Breanna was seeking, that respect didn't seem warranted.

Glancing at the bunk where Millie was taking a nap, Breanna decided she had to find out if the man she was seeking was the same one of whom they spoke. It was better to know your enemy, she thought. Should King prove to be the blackguard Heather hinted at, it would help to know in advance if he had a disarming, charming side.

Checking her appearance in a small mirror on the wall, Breanna set her chin to a pleasantly inviting tilt. If she was going to get any information from the new arrivals, it must come in the form of idle chatter. The last thing she wanted was to put anyone familiar with King on guard.

Despite her desire to meet the couple, Breanna had to wait until they were introduced at dinner that evening. She was pleased to find the captain had seated them at the same table with her and Millie.

Despite Breanna's fears, Kathryn and Lawrence Williams turned out to be delightful companions. Socially starved by the relative confinement of the plantation they had just left, they asked dozens of questions about the States and current affairs of everyone in the small dining room. Their interest kept the conversation moving and managed to include most of the passengers but prevented Breanna from making any of her own inquiries. Resolved to use the long journey still ahead to glean what she wanted to know, Breanna relaxed in their company until, quite unexpectedly, Lawrence turned to the topic she sought to bring up.

"If things go as King expects, you might find yourself building many more of these fine ships, Mr. Griffiths."

Breanna, seeing her chance, pursued the statement. "And what is it that this Mr. King expects?"

A condescending smile touched Lawrence Williams's face. "I wouldn't want to bore you with politics, Miss Sullivan," he said, rising to ask the other men if they wished to join him on the deck for a cigar.

"Not all women walk about with their heads in the clouds, Mr. Williams," Breanna stated firmly when the men rose. Male and female heads alike turned to face her. "I happen to take a great interest in politics. Especially if it affects California and my family."

Amusement danced in Lawrence Williams's eyes. "Don't worry your pretty head over it. Let the men take care of politics. You need worry about nothing more than running the household and choosing something pleasant to wear."

Millie's hand shot out to restrain Breanna before she could make a scene. Millie kept Breanna in her seat, but she could not silence her. Turning to face Kathryn Williams, Breanna spoke clearly enough to be heard by all.

"I'm sorry your husband is so narrow-minded, Mrs. Williams. It must be difficult to tolerate his treating you like a servant when you have a mind of your own."

A grumbling could be heard from the departing males, but Breanna was pleased to see some genuine humor and admiration on the faces of the ladies present. Realizing how rude she had been, Breanna rose to leave.

"I'm sorry, Mrs. Williams," she said sincerely as she placed her napkin on the table. "I had no right to say that."

Kathryn checked to be sure the men were gone, then grinned. "Perhaps not, my dear, but I must admit, you were very close to the mark."

Pleasantly surprised by the response, Breanna noticed the nodding of other heads.

"Mr. Griffiths won't discuss his work with me, either," the ship designer's wife said softly. "He thinks I can't fathom his trade even though I was raised with four brothers in my father's shipyard."

Another of the women joined in. "Jerome won't let me help him in his medical practice because it might offend my sensitivities, and I've had five children!"

It was not the direction Breanna had intended, but she found the conversation she had started with her outburst enlightening and entertaining. By the time the men returned it was obvious that a few more conversations were going to occur that evening when the group broke up. The women had found confidence in one another.

"This trip could prove very interesting," Breanna

commented as she and Millie were preparing for bed.

Millie scowled at her friend. "It could be downright dangerous."

"How so?"

Shaking her head at her friend, the independent troublemaker, Millie sighed. "You may end up swimming home if those men find out it was you who got those ladies riled."

"I didn't start this, Millie. The men did. All I did was listen to their wives' complaints."

Millie shrugged, unconvinced. "Whatever you say, but remember one thing ... I can't swim!"

By the time the ship sailed into Montevideo, Breanna knew no more about Alex King than she had before.

"I heard something about that man King you're interested in," Millie began when the two women were in their room one afternoon preparing for a short trip ashore the next day.

Breanna's head snapped about. "What? When?" she demanded.

Millie plopped on her bunk, scooting back until she could lean against the wall. "I heard Mr. Williams talking with some of the men. It sounds like your Mr. King made his fortune on his own."

"He's not *my* Mr. King!" Breanna snapped. "He may not even be the same man I'm looking for."

Patting the bunk, Millie made room for Breanna to join her. "I think he is the same, Bree." She waited for Breanna to sit before offering what she considered proof. "He was born in Pennsylvania but left when he was a boy. Seems he settled somewhere in California."

Breanna frowned. "That doesn't mean he's the one."

"This King is thirty years old."

Breanna shrugged, unaware of the age of the man she sought.

"And he has built up ... Let me see." She paused, touching her lip in thought. "What did Mr. Williams call it? Ah, yes! An empire. Said he had wealth and power."

It was very possible that this was the King she was going to investigate. "Anything else?" Breanna asked, already trying to sort out the new information.

"He said he is charac ... charis ..."

"Charismatic?"

"Yes! That's it!"

Slipping off the bed, Breanna tried to form an image of King. From this latest description, it sounded as if he was the sort of man her father would enjoy. A strong and powerful man. Probably very clever if he had made a fortune on his own. Patrick Sullivan was also a self-made man. He would admire such achievement, but would he be so foolish, or so blinded by such deeds, as to be easily manipulated?

"There's still no proof this is the man I'm looking for," Breanna mumbled aloud, not wanting to find anything admirable about the man she already considered a blackhearted miscreant.

"Even if this Mr. King owns half of Monterey?" Millie asked.

A knock on the cabin door interrupted Breanna's reply. To her surprise, it was Mrs. Griffiths.

"The ladies are meeting in the dining room to chat," she announced. "We'd like you and Millie to join us."

Breanna wasn't in the mood for small talk. She wanted to concentrate on one man in particular. "I have a slight headache," she said with a rueful smile, "but Millie might like to go."

It was obvious to Millie that Breanna needed some time to herself. "Tell the ladies I'll be there in a few moments," she called as she rose from the bunk. "Why don't you try and get some sleep," she suggested. "We have a lot of time to think about what we'll do when we get home."

A smile softened Breanna's tight lips. "So now California is *home* and it's *we*." Millie nodded, prompting Breanna to give her a hug. "Thank you," she said as she stepped away. "For the information and for wanting to help."

Millie grinned. "You said this was to be an adventure. I just figure it might be fun to help out."

"Two more stops and we'll be on the last leg of our voyage," Captain Barrymore announced to the exhausted passengers as they gathered for a dinner of fresh fruits and vegetables, the likes of which they hadn't seen since they had sailed from Montevideo over a month before. "We go from here to Callao, make a provisions stop in Acapulco, and then continue on to Monterey."

"Thank God." Millie groaned, surprised they had reached Valparaiso with only a few seasick passengers after such rough weather. Several similar praises went heavenward before someone asked when they would sail again.

"I expect to set sail in two days," Captain Barrymore stated. "We've made exceptional time and I'd like to see Mr. Griffiths' design set a record." Seeing the doubt on several faces, he smiled. "But I see no reason why you can't enjoy those two days ashore. This is a lovely town. You might find some trinkets for keepsakes and perhaps some fruit you can take to your cabins." At the mention of food, Millie groaned again. "Then you might prefer a rest on a calm sea for a while."

The passengers began to disperse, some to their rooms to catch up on lost sleep and some to the packet boat. Breanna decided she wanted to spend some quiet time alone, preferring the nearly empty deck with only a view of the town. As soon as she saw that Millie was comfortably resting, she made her way to the deck.

Taking a deep breath, she strolled toward the lee side of the ship. Sprawled across the landscape, as far as the eye could see in either direction, rose a ragged mountain range.

"Lovely, isn't it?"

"Oh! Captain Barrymore! I thought I was alone."

The captain smiled. "If I'm intruding . . ."

"No, not at all." She returned his smile before redirecting her gaze back to the coast. "I was just thinking how fierce those mountains look."

"They are," he told her as he leaned his arms on the rail beside her. "Many of the people in this land have lost everything they own to earthquakes and avalanches. Hundreds have lost their lives."

Breanna shivered at the thought of nature's violence. "Why do so many stay?"

"Why are you returning to Monterey? There are earthquakes and violent storms there. Sometimes the earth grows parched and dry. Sometimes sudden rainstorms flood it. Yet still you return."

"I see what you mean. If you love the land, you take it in its every mood, sometimes paying for it with blood, sometimes with sweat, but you stay."

"And you love Monterey, so you return." He saw her nod.

"Monterey and my family. We have a ranch south of town." The instant she spoke, she realized she wasn't sure of that anymore. If her father was truly gone . . . "Do you know the town well?" she asked, hoping to resume her search for answers.

Noticing the pause she'd made and the tension that seemed to be taking control of her, Captain Barrymore offered his arm and suggested they stroll around the deck.

"I'm quite familiar with the port," he replied. "The man who commissioned this ship lives there. You may even know him."

Breanna swallowed hard. She had no doubt who

that man was, but she asked anyway. "And who might that be?"

"Alexander King," he announced proudly until he perceived a tightening of her hand on his arm. "Is something wrong, Miss Sullivan?"

"N-no! No, nothing," she stammered, not wishing to make any comment that could reach King before she did. "I . . . I don't know him." She saw the captain frown. "I left Monterey over eighteen months ago. He must have arrived after that."

"Too bad," Barrymore said, wondering what had upset the young woman. "He's a genius at making money, and I believe the women find him very attractive."

It was all Breanna could do not to sneer her contempt for the unknown King. Her pledge to give him a chance blew away on the breeze that rustled her skirt. Gritting her teeth, she realized the captain was awaiting a reply.

"I'm sure he is all that and more," she finally remarked.

Still baffled by her apparent dislike of a man she professed not to know, Captain Barrymore was ready to pry just a bit when he was called away.

"Perhaps we can speak again sometime," he said, bowing over her hand.

"Perhaps," Breanna agreed politely, but in her own mind she expected to find the real answers to her questions only once she arrived in California.

Chapter 3

"**T**hese are wonderful!" Millie exclaimed before taking another bite of the meat- and bean-filled tortilla Breanna had insisted they buy when they reached Acapulco.

Sighing in apparent rapture, Breanna licked her lips and fingers. "I forgot how much I love these." She watched Millie finish her second. "Want another?"

"Lordy, no! This is the most I've eaten at one time since we left Boston."

"One more with a *vaso de cerveza?*"

"A what?"

"A cool glass of Mexican beer." Millie grinned, and Breanna placed the order. Once a smiling peasant woman served the food, Breanna suggested they stroll along the beach to enjoy it.

They found a large rock to use as a chair. Breanna stared out at the *Rainbow* riding at anchor. With the sails down, it resembled the skeletal remains of some great sea monster.

"Mexico is not a wealthy country. Most of her people are very poor, but there are some who have great wealth," she said.

"That's the same in the United States, isn't it?"

"Yes, but in the United States they don't keep taking from their poor, nor do they force families to pay far beyond what they can afford." Gazing skyward, she closed her eyes. "The Mexican government imposes tax after tax to help pay for the

27

troops that roam from California to Texas. We don't need those troops. There is no threat to the people who live there, except the threat of looting by the very soldiers who are supposed to be our protection."

"And that's what makes you mad?"

"No!" Breanna said sharply, setting aside her drink to stand. "What makes me furious is that no one has the courage to make them stop!"

Millie didn't understand much about politics, but she could understand what Breanna was implying. "Bree, are you sayin' ya want ta see a revolution?" The impact of the thought made her forget all her attempts at proper speech.

"Yes! No! Oh, I don't know." Breanna rubbed her brow to try to clear her mind. "I just wish we could have some say in what goes on in the land we live in."

"You mean you want the freedom and government the United States has."

Sitting down slowly as she digested the simple statement, Breanna turned to gaze at Millie. "That's exactly what I want." Relieved to have it out in the open, Breanna explained.

"I was not born in California, but Papa moved us there when I was five. Mother died just a year after that and our ranch became my life. I love it." Her eyes began to tear with the passion she felt for California. "I hate seeing Mexico take and take from the land when they never even come and see its beauty, or give us a chance to decide on its laws."

"And do others feel the same?"

"I think so. Unfortunately, the one thing they do like about the Spanish rule is keeping their women in the dark, too."

Millie fought a grin that threatened. "So you try to change that."

"I suppose I do," Breanna admitted with a shrug. "I've always been headstrong. I guess I can't seem to stay out of things I have an opinion on." The sun slipped behind a fluffy cloud, cooling the breeze coming in off the water. "I guess we'd better start back to the ship. We wouldn't want to miss dinner." Laughing at Millie's groan, they retraced their steps back to the boat.

Clutching her shawl tightly about her shoulders, Millie watched Breanna's expression as they neared her homeland. The long voyage had been the adventure she was promised, but her emotions paled next to the look on her friend's face. Love, admiration, pride; they were all there, mingled with the gentle memories only she could see.

It was as Breanna remembered. The jagged islands of Point Lobos ascended from the sea, golden in the late afternoon sun. The granite crests were lined with the dark silhouettes of a thousand gulls. The sound of barking sea lions rose above the crashing surf.

As they neared the docks, Breanna could see many changes. Buildings stood where none had before and many appeared only recently finished. She could also see that now the city's streets were lined with wooden walks. A large building looking out over the town seemed to be a new hotel.

"It isn't very big, is it?" Millie said softly, not sure what she had expected.

Breanna laughed. "But, Millie, it's twice what it was when I left!"

Gazing at the rolling hills about the countryside and the expanse of undeveloped area, Millie shook her head. "It's not Boston, but it is pretty."

"Believe me, Millie, once you see this country and discover its beauty in your soul, you'll never dream of seeing Boston again." Breanna leaned close and added, "And as soon as you settle in a hot bath of fresh water, you'll think you're in heaven!"

* * *

A number of people milled about on the docks when the *Rainbow* tied up in its berth. Mr. Griffiths hadn't broken the record for speed, but his ship had accomplished the journey within an impressively short time.

"How far is the ranch from here?" Millie asked, checking to be sure all their trunks were accounted for.

Breanna looked up to see an already darkening sky. "Too far to travel to this evening," she announced. "We'll take a room and go out tomorrow." She signaled for a lad with a cart and ordered their things to be taken to the hotel.

"The King Arms or the old one?" the boy asked.

"The old one," Breanna stated through clenched teeth.

The boy looked perplexed. "The King Arms is a lot nicer, lady. Most everybody stays there unless they ain't got much money." His sidelong glance would have amused Breanna under other circumstances. He was obviously wondering if she had the funds to pay him for his services.

Breanna considered the new hotel. It was possible she might discover something about King there or even meet him.

"All right, the King Arms will be fine." His immediate grin went unnoticed as the two women followed him to the edifice she had already determined must be the hotel.

While Millie absorbed the local sights, Breanna's eyes were focused on the number of King Company signs hanging about. Almost every new building in town bore his name. A large curly "K" was even emblazoned on the arch over the hotel desk. She felt sickened by the ostentatious display.

Despite her annoyance with the man's obviously inflated sense of himself, she could find no fault with the accommodations. They were as up-to-date as anything in Boston. And the service was even better, she thought as she eased into a tub of

pleasantly hot water. On the other side of the
screen set between them, Millie was cooing like a
child with a special treat.

"This is heaven," she crooned, the water running down her arm from a cloth she was squeez-
ing above it. Breanna didn't reply, and Millie
frowned. "Isn't it?" she called louder.

"Isn't what?" Breanna replied.

Sitting up in the tub, Millie sighed. "It's started,
hasn't it? You're already thinking about this King
fellow."

It was useless to lie. Millie was learning to figure out which way Breanna's thoughts were going. "Yes, I was thinking of him and how powerful
he must be." Absently washing, she added, "This
whole town looks like he owns it. If, of course,
those flashy replicas of the King of Diamonds everywhere mean what I think they do."

Millie sniffed. "So he's rich. Does that make him
bad?"

"No, but it might make him suspicious and hard
to get to."

"So hire someone to get to him for you. He has
to have friends you might also know, or maybe
even enemies who are just as powerful." The room
grew silent. "Bree? Did you hear me?"

"Yes, I heard you." Hire someone! Even Garth
had suggested she get an agent to approach King.
What neither he nor she had thought of was that
the agent could be an enemy of King's, an enemy
who would be her ally! Should King prove to be
the scoundrel she suspected he was, she might
need such an ally.

Satisfied that Breanna was considering what she
had said, Millie again relaxed. "I'm hungry," she
muttered when her stomach growled unexpectedly, "but I don't know if I ever want to get out of
this tub again."

Breanna arched a brow. She didn't want to
waste a moment before finding out all she could

about the man she had traveled so far to meet. Possibly much of what Heather had said in her letters was imagination, but if any of it was true, facing him might prove a challenge.

"I think I'll go down to dinner," Breanna said gaily, suddenly looking forward to learning what she could before she met Heather.

It was just the start of the dinner hour, and few patrons occupied the dining room. Greeting two couples they knew from the ship, Breanna and Millie entered, marveling at the richly appointed room. It was luxurious. A crystal chandelier hung from the ceiling and amber sconces lined the brocade-covered walls. Fine linens graced the tables, and the place settings were of the highest quality. Alexander King was still an enigma, but he definitely had very fine taste.

They were led to their table by an impeccably dressed young man of Spanish descent. A second came to take their order, and a third brought wine.

Dinner was a sumptuous affair. Both women chose Mexican fare, relishing the spicy dishes and pungent sauces. They turned to a simple pot of tea at the end of their meal. They were sharing recollections of the journey they had just completed when their attention was suddenly drawn to a commotion in the hotel lobby.

A group of men entered the dining room. When the staff began rapidly preparing a private table for them, Breanna realized that they must be well-known to the establishment. It occurred to her that the ruckus could be a result of the owner's arrival. Her interest was piqued.

"Shall we go?" Millie asked, not sure she cared for the curiosity burning in Breanna's eyes.

Breanna shook her head. "I'd like more tea," she said, pouring out a cup she didn't really want.

Too tired to try to change Breanna's mind, Millie excused herself with the knowledge that Breanna couldn't get into too much trouble with so many people about.

Breanna was seated with her back to the door, and it would have been too obvious if she had risen and changed places, so she tried to catch reflected images in the darkened windows. The sound of rich male voices came nearer, then seemed to be passing. Disappointed, she strained to overhear what they were saying from the table they selected on a draped riser.

The soft roll of Spanish met her ear, but the words were not discernable. Rumbling male laughter made her glance sideways surreptitiously. Her breath caught. A man, clad all in black except for a pristine white shirt, was staring blatantly at her. The look that flashed in his icy blue eyes made her swallow hard and fast . . . and begin to choke.

With catlike grace, he rose to his feet and moved to her side. As she struggled to breathe, she became aware of his high black boots directly in her line of sight. She raised her eyes, intending to wave him away. Instead, she could only stare in wide-eyed distress at the towering height of him. Without a word to her, he called for water. It was instantly delivered, and she felt his strong, deeply tanned hand cup her chin and press the goblet to her lips.

Struggling to regain her composure, she pushed the glass away and took a deep breath to still her racing pulse. Feeling as if she was now fully recovered, she turned to the stranger to thank him . . . and was struck dumb for the first time in her life.

Never had she seen such a man. His thick, ebony hair curled over the collar of his white silk shirt. His skin was richly bronzed and made his blue eyes look like crackling ice. The white ridge of a scar curved over his cheekbone in a perfect crescent. His wide shoulders were covered with a black, well-fitted jacket that stopped at the slender waist wrapped in a black satin cumberbund.

His polished appearance and arrogant stance gave him the look of a Castillian don, yet she suspected he was not Spanish. A crooked grin played at his lips, as he seemed to be allowing her to inspect him. Momentarily stunned by the man, she had no way of knowing he had been examining her just as closely since entering the room.

He had detected her curiosity even before he noticed her beauty. Her russet hair reflected the lights while her gently tanned skin seemed to absorb the amber glow. There had been a provocative pout on her lips when she frowned slightly while trying so hard to see him and his guests in the window. He had wondered if she was merely curious about them or if she was seeking someone and suspected one of them was the one she sought.

Standing close to her, he was amazed by a sudden tightening in his groin. The rise and fall of her full breasts beneath her soft green gown, the fragrance of wild roses, her very demeanor excited him. His desires must have shown in his eyes because hers began to crackle with a fire all their own. He wondered if the fire was a matching passion or a show of angry temper.

Lifting one side of his mouth in a crooked grin, he leaned his palm on the table, trapping her in her seat. "I hope you have recovered," he said in a low, rumbling growl.

His comment did not sound sincere, nor did Breanna think his move to hover over her was meant to be solicitous. Placing her hands in her lap, she stiffened her spine. "I'm fine, thank you."

With difficulty, he restrained his laughter at her attempt to dismiss him. "Are you sure?" he questioned, his eyes dropping to the hint of soft flesh revealed above her neckline. "You still seem to be having trouble breathing."

Breanna gasped. "My breathing is perfectly normal!" she said between clenched teeth.

"Too bad," he teased, his eyes sparkling wickedly. "I was rather hoping you were responding to the attraction between us."

"There is no ..." Breanna realized she had spoken loud enough to draw the attention of everyone in the room. Dropping her voice to a rigid whisper, she continued, "There is no attraction between us. I don't even know you!"

Though softly spoken, the words had lost none of their vehemence, which further amused him. She was a little spitfire, this beautiful redhead. "Oh, there's an attraction, my dear," he said, straightening to his full height. "And I wish I had time to prove it to you. Perhaps later I can—"

"Señor Rey, your dinner is being served and your guests are waiting," a waiter said.

"*Gracias.* Tell them I shall be right there," he answered without breaking eye contact with Breanna.

"You may leave this instant," she said with all the authority she could muster. She attempted to turn her shoulder to him, but he took her hand and drew her almost out of her chair before he bent over and pressed a kiss to her fingers.

Her skin began to burn where he touched it and she was filled with sudden apprehension. It felt as if this man were branding her! His lips lifted, but she gasped when he turned her hand palm upward to kiss her again.

"Mr. Rey!" she exclaimed, yanking free of his grip.

He remained standing over her. She had turned away, but he wanted to leave a more lasting impression. Cupping her chin, he turned her face toward him while his eyes danced with sultry humor.

"The next time I kiss you, it will be on your tempting lips." Her next gasp parted her lips, and he smiled. "And I'll want you to open them in just the same way." Arching one dark brow, he gave her a curt bow as she immediately closed her mouth, then he turned away to join his guests as if she no longer existed.

Torn between the desire to give him the slap he so richly deserved and the urge to flee, she chose the latter and returned to her room. In truth, she didn't think she could endure facing the man again, even to lay him low for his cavalier treatment of her.

She had reached her room before she decided she should have dressed him down then and there, after all. Should they ever chance to meet again, he might think she would again accept his rude attentions. But any action now was too late, she thought as she began to undress.

Once clad in her nightgown, Breanna sat on the bed to brush out her hair. No matter how hard she tried, she could not keep her thoughts from the dark stranger and the disturbing effect he had had on her. She wished Millie were still awake. She needed to share what had happened.

The mere image of the man in her mind made her feel warm all over. She had never before experienced the fever and chills that had racked her at his touch. Was that normal, or was she getting ill? Possibly it was nothing more than a reaction to his bad manners.

Sighing, she lowered the brush and gazed down at the upturned palm on her lap. Suddenly she could feel the touch of his lips there. Making a fist to quell the thought, she closed her eyes, hoping to shut him out completely. Unfortunately, his image was printed in her mind. He was there, leaning toward her. She could see his eyes, all fire and ice, devouring her.

"Damn!" she said, standing quickly and tossing her brush on the nightstand. Furious at herself for behaving so childishly, she blew out the lamp and climbed beneath the downy quilt. Plumping her pillows, she plopped down on them and stared at the ceiling.

After long minutes, she sighed heavily. She was tired. She should be sleeping. Tossing back the covers, she decided the air seemed suddenly hot and heavy in the room. Perhaps a fresh breeze would help her fall asleep.

She rose and went to the window, pushing it wide open. She took deep breaths to still her nerves. More relaxed, she perched her hip on the sill and looked up at the moonless sky. Millions of stars glittered overhead, offering solace to her frayed nerves.

She was being foolish. Her fatigue was creating illusions and magnifying everything out of proportion. She was overreacting to a simple gesture of assistance and some flirtation that was bolder than what she had experienced in Boston.

Ready to return to bed, Breanna felt as though something or someone was calling her into the darkness. Her eyes darted about the street below. At first it seemed deserted, then she tensed. Someone *was* watching her! She could see the tip of a cigarette glowing and the vague outline of a man lounging against the wall in the shadows between two buildings.

Some unknown power held her frozen as she watched the shadowy figure move out into the light cast from the lower floor of the hotel. Before she could see his face, she knew it was he, and she knew he was watching her, calling her from her bed with some silent force she seemed powerless to ignore.

It had been difficult merely to sit and watch as she rose to leave the dining room. He had known many women. He had used them to fulfill his natural urges, but he had never desired one as he did this fiery-haired beauty. He remained outwardly cool when he faced her, but a fire raged inside him. He felt he could drown in the dark depths of her eyes. Doe eyes, he thought. Large and deep brown, fringed in long, dark lashes. She was like a wild creature, one he wanted to tame.

As surprised as he was by his reaction to her, it was nothing compared to the shock of learning who she was. He'd sent a waiter to inquire at the desk. He had almost chuckled aloud when the man had returned with her name. Patrick's girl! No wonder there was that touch of fire in her.

He'd been told that Heather was in touch with her sister, and he had to wonder now if Heather had written something that had made her sister return or if her arrival was mere coincidence. Either way, the timing might prove to be bad. Heather knew little of what was going on, yet it might be enough to cause a problem, especially if her older sister got involved. Patrick always said Breanna was the more stubborn of the two, and Heather was bad enough.

He'd almost been ready to follow her when he'd finished dinner with some of the local Mexican hidalgos, but he'd thought it best to find out first exactly why she had come home. She obviously didn't know who he was since he'd been addressed by his Spanish name. If Heather had mentioned him, it might not have been in a good light. Not knowing all the details, she would tend to paint him in dark colors.

Telling his guests he wanted to find out something about the woman who had so amused him, he excused himself. Once he was sure he had not been followed, he stepped into the shadows.

"Evening, Alex." A low voice broke the silence, not unexpectedly.

"John," he responded. "I have only a few minutes. The others are waiting, and Guillermo will be joining us shortly."

"What do you have for me?" the voice asked from a darkened doorway.

"No new troops are scheduled for these parts. General Guillermo is confident that the Mexican army can hold its own for now. The only time we will have to worry is at the end of the year. They'll be changing troops then and doubling the forces here and at the fort in Sonoma for a few weeks. After that it will be back to one company."

"That helps," John replied, knowing any information leaked from under General Guillermo's nose was a gift for his own gathering force of Americans in California. "We'd be wiped out if we had to face twice the number of troops now. We're not strong enough for that yet."

"Yes," King agreed. "That's all I have this time. Guillermo's been a bit tight-lipped recently. But tell Pat that Breanna is here from Boston. I don't know if it's in response to something Heather wrote or mere coincidence."

"Do you think she'll cause trouble?"

"I don't know yet," came his reply, then a pause. "But I'm going to find out." Without a farewell, Alex moved toward the street and took out a cigarette. Looking up, he nearly burned his fingers before lighting it and tossing away the offending match.

Like a dream, she was standing in the window. The soft folds of her nightgown were pressed to her curves by the night breeze that lifted her long tresses into a wispy halo about her head. It was too dark to see her face, but he knew she had yet to spot him.

He suddenly wanted her to know he was there. He wanted her last thoughts before sleeping to be of him. As he moved slowly into the light, he saw her stiffen in recognition and had to struggle not to laugh. She had felt his power as his body called to hers. There was something bound to come between them. He knew it as surely as he knew California would one day be free.

Chapter 4

Breanna rose early and roused Millie. She had a desperate need to see Heather and feel the familiar things of home around her. They breakfasted quickly and were soon in a hired carriage heading out of town. As they rocked silently aboard the conveyance, Breanna's thoughts filled with the events of the previous night.

Anger renewed itself when she thought of the mocking bow the stranger had made before tossing aside his half-smoked cigarette and moving toward the hotel doors to disappear from her sight. What audacity! She had pulled back and slammed the hotel window so hard she guiltily checked Millie afterward. Fortunately, she had not awakened her, but the knowledge did not cool her temper.

Flouncing down on her bed, she realized it wasn't all his fault that he was caught looking at her in her dishabille. She had put herself on display by sitting on the windowsill. Anyone could have seen her! After that, sleep was not within her grasp. There was too much anger and something she couldn't name disturbing her.

Now, in the light of day, she was irritable and had yet to get over her realization that she had searched the sea of faces that morning for a man she prayed she would never meet again. She was relieved when he was nowhere to be seen, but she sensed that he was near. It annoyed her further that she could not forget him. Mentally shaking herself, she turned her head to look at Millie and saw her eyes darting over the surrounding landscape.

"Beautiful, isn't it?"

"I don't think I've ever seen anything so pretty!" Millie was awed by the land through which they were traveling. Hundreds of acres of gently rolling hills were dotted with grazing cattle and lush vineyards. Purple mountains rose in the distance as they followed the pristine waters of the Carmel River.

Breanna related the history of these parts as she knew it. The Spanish had settled there hundreds of years before, and their influence on the land was everywhere. Red-tiled roofs gracing white stucco buildings could be seen a distance from the dusty road they traveled. Each hacienda had a small chapel of its own, announcing the Catholic influence, with its spire high above the cool walls surrounding each complex.

"You'll be able to see Casa del Verde soon," Breanna told her wistfully.

"What does that name mean?" Millie asked.

Laughing lightly, Breanna explained. "It means 'house of the green.'" She saw Millie frown. "It isn't actually green," she went on, "but you'll understand why it was given that name when you see it. Of course, the name was also chosen as a family jest. What better name for an Irishman! It's my father's own piece of the Emerald Isle right here in California."

Millie chuckled. "Your pa must be something." She saw all humor fade from Breanna's face, forgetting her concern over his possible disappearance. "Bree, I'm sorry. I wasn't—"

"It's all right, Millie," Breanna said hopefully. "He might be there waiting when we arrive. Heather does tend to exaggerate sometimes." Needing to push her fears aside for a while, she forced a smile. "Anyway, he'll be thinkin' ye're a fair lass and be likin' the looks of ye, Millie, me darlin'!" she rolled out in her best brogue to relieve Millie's apprehension.

They finally neared the land Breanna called home. Her feet had raced over these gentle hills many times. This soft breeze had caressed her in her youth and had stayed to caress her now. It was difficult not to let her mind wander back to the days gone by, but she had to concentrate on what was ahead.

The stone wall that announced Casa del Verde to anyone on the road stretched out before her. There was no gate, just a large arch beckoning strangers and promising a welcome. This time, however, the welcome was not what she expected. The scene was almost as she had pictured it in her mind during her absence but for one heart-wrenching difference. Propped against the wall was a large sign that brought a snarling growl from deep inside her.

"What's wrong?" Millie asked at the sound. Without replying, Breanna climbed from the carriage and stood before the intricate monogram she was beginning to hate.

"This is impossible!" she fumed as she read the announcement that Casa del Verde was the property of Alexander King. "I'll show him what he can do with his sign!" she screeched, gripping the fragile board savagely and sending it to the dirt at her feet. Grinding her heel across the message, she tried to fathom how this had happened.

Satisfied she had wreaked enough havoc on the sign, she scurried back into the carriage. Her face red with rage, she snapped the reins. Despite the sign, she felt sure her family was still within. At least, they'd better be! she fumed, determined to get to the bottom of this.

Millie held on for dear life. Breanna was in no mood to be reminded she should be careful. She was too busy mumbling about this being *her* home and *he* had no right. She was all the furies rolled into one small, explosive package.

Despite their rapid approach, Millie was able to appreciate the beauty of Casa del Verde, if only briefly. It was obvious the lush green trumpet vines covering the stucco walls of the courtyard were the real reason for its name. Within the walls, the air was cooled by the verdant greenery and a softly bubbling fountain.

The house immediately caught Millie's eye as they neared. She stared at its simple beauty. It was two stories high and white, like the walls. The roof was layers of sloping red tiles. Black iron grills covered the windows on the lower floor and matched the railing of a balcony above the main door, toward which Breanna was heading.

"Heather!" she called, praying her sister was still there. "Heather! Where are you?"

"Bree!" came a shout from the top of the stairs. In a flutter of skirts, Heather launched herself into her sister's arms. "Oh, Bree! What a surprise!"

"Surprise?" Breanna gasped, stepping back to glare into the face of her smiling sister. "You send me those damned letters and you're surprised?"

"The letters," Heather groaned, biting her lip.

"Yes, Heather! The letters!"

Heather spotted Millie standing in the door. "Who's that?" she asked, straining to peer around her sister, obviously stalling.

Breanna knew she was not going to get any answers until Heather was ready to give them. Lifting a hand to her brow to keep her temper, she made the introductions. Heather ushered them all into the salon, ordering lemonade from a young maid Breanna had never seen before. She was ready to begin asking her questions when Millie spoke.

"You sure have a fine-looking house, Breanna."

She cast admiring eyes on the tiled floor and brightly colored rugs scattered about.

Accusingly, Breanna faced Heather. "If it still is our house," she said.

Heather had grown up. She was now almost as tall as Breanna, and her long hair no longer hung in wild disarray but was tied neatly back at her neck. Its golden red enhanced the hazel of her eyes to nearly green, reminding Breanna of their father.

Heather squared her shoulders and lifted her chin. "No, it isn't ours, Bree." She saw the pain and sighed. "It seems Father owed a lot of back taxes. He couldn't pay and ... and someone else did."

"King!" Breanna seethed as she drew her hands into fists at her sides. "So he is the unscrupulous brigand you hinted at."

"No!" Heather cried in surprise. Seeing the confusion Breanna was struggling with, she decided she had better tell all she knew. "Sit down, Bree," she said, taking a chair herself.

Feeling like an intruder, Millie excused herself to find the maid and get settled. She wasn't sure what her future held now that Breanna was apparently a guest in her own house, but she didn't think she needed to burden Breanna with it now.

Once alone, the two sisters sat quietly for a moment. Breanna took a calming breath and began to ask the questions she had traveled thousands of miles to have answered.

"What's going on here, Heather?" she asked, her tone brooking no delay.

Heather stared at Breanna, suddenly wishing she had stayed out of the whole thing. When Alex King and her father became friends, she had thought he was the sort of man her headstrong sister should have for a husband. Spinning romantic tales in her head about uniting the two, she recalled that Breanna hated to be told what to do and would stubbornly refuse to listen even if it was good for her.

Deciding to make King sound a little suspicious to intrigue Breanna, she had begun the letters. Unfortunately, things began to become truly suspicious. At some point she was genuinely afraid of the secrecy enveloping their father and King. It wasn't until Patrick explained what was going on that she agreed to go along with their plans. Drawing a deep breath, Heather opted to avoid the part about her desire to play Cupid and gave Breanna only what facts she could.

"King came here from somewhere up north just after you left. Some say from Sonoma, others say San Francisco. Well, it doesn't matter." She rose and paced, a family trait for sorting things out. "Within six months he had purchased a number of haciendas for back taxes and some large tracts in town. He started building as soon as the ink was dry."

"Yes." Breanna nodded. "I've seen his mark everywhere."

Ignoring the disdain in her sister's voice, Heather went on. "The locals enjoyed the growth, but suddenly there seemed to be a lot of strangers showing up to run these new enterprises. It was as if King was using only his own men."

Not wishing to dwell on the unknown King until she had more facts, Breanna interrupted. "Since Father hasn't shown himself, I assume he is still missing?"

"Yes, but I've—"

Breanna didn't let her finish. "And you suspect King is responsible!"

"Bree!" Heather snapped, forcing her sister to pay attention. "Will you let me tell this!" Contrite, Breanna clamped her mouth tightly shut and nodded. Blowing out the breath she was holding, Heather went on with the tale she had been instructed to tell anyone who questioned Patrick's disappearance. She wasn't sure that it included Breanna, but she couldn't take any chances. She'd given her word on the matter.

"Papa met King a few times at Mr. Perkins's place and in town, mostly socially. After a few months, they began to meet here."

"What were the meetings about?"

"I don't know," Heather said. "Some men would come late at night. I was usually in bed, but I could hear them below with Papa and King."

"And they took Papa away?"

Heather shook her head. "No, he didn't go with them." Frowning, she began to chew on her lip. "I . . . I'm not even sure Papa didn't go somewhere on his own."

"What!" Breanna shouted, coming to her feet.

"Don't shout at me, Bree!" Heather roared, coming to her own. The two sisters squared off, one furious and the other undaunted. "When I wrote you I had no idea where he was or why he'd left!"

"But you know now, don't you?"

Heather grimaced. "Kind of."

"Heather, please." Breanna threw up her hands in frustration. "Will you get to the point!"

Striking an indignant pose, Heather sniffed. "Just because you're a few years older than me you think you can—"

"Heather!"

The younger woman pouted for a moment, then continued. "As I told you in one of the letters, Papa would go off with King sometimes. He never said where he was going or why. He only told me it would be safer if I didn't know."

"Safer? Safer for whom?"

Heather shrugged. "I don't know that, either. That's why I was so frantic when I wrote that letter."

Breanna thought over the letters and what she had just heard. She still had many unanswered questions, but at least she knew Heather hadn't merely been spinning stories to get her back home.

"If Papa lost Casa del Verde to King, why are you still here?"

"Papa told me before he left that I was to stay no matter what happened. With Rosa here to chaperone, and having nowhere else to go, I've stayed."

"And the rest of the staff, are they here, too?"

"Some. Some must have left with Papa. King—" Heather saw the tightening of Breanna's lips. "He sent out some help within days of their leaving."

"How thoughtful," Breanna sneered.

Heather rolled her eyes. She could see she had given Breanna too many negative hints about King to get her to think of him kindly. Hiding a grin when she thought of any confrontation between the two before Breanna knew the truth, she went to her.

"There's one more thing you should know, Bree. King is very close to the local authorities," she said, adding fuel to the fire. "Despite his close association with the Americans living here."

"What's wrong with that? Most of the people here are Spanish! It would be foolish for him to alienate them." She watched Heather hesitate. "What else?"

"You'll find out soon enough," Heather said, her shoulders seeming to slump. "So I might as well tell you. Four other ranchers are missing, too." She paused for impact. "All of them are Americans." Before Breanna could speak, she added the last bit of daunting information. "There has been talk of a revolt to free California from Mexican rule. I think Papa and King are involved, and probably the missing Americans, too."

Breanna needed a few minutes to think over what she had just heard. It would come as no surprise if her father became involved in a revolution to free California. He'd often spoken of the possibility. What she found perplexing was how King fit in. Was he on the side of the Americans or using them to make himself more valuable to their foe?

"In your letters, you mentioned stolen guns," Breanna said, trying to decide what she believed. "Whose were they, and did the authorities find out who took them?"

"The shipment belonged to King," Heather replied, wondering if this was the last of the damning evidence she would have to place at his door before discovering where Bree stood. "They never caught the perpetrators."

"So he might have done it himself," Breanna mused, beginning to believe King a traitor possibly to both sides. Raising her chin, she stared at Heather. "You say the man is very wealthy?" Heather nodded. "An opportunist?"

"Yes, but—"

"And Americans are disappearing but the authorities are doing nothing about it?"

"No, but—"

Breanna drew her fists to her hips. "I think we have a mercenary in our midst," she declared. "I think King is trying to undermine both sides to make a profit."

It was getting out of hand. Heather knew she was supposed to discourage Breanna from nosing about, not cause her to be more suspicious.

"Bree, what are you going to do?" she asked when she saw the determined gleam in her eyes.

"I'm going to find Mr. King and warn him to stay out of our lives!"

"You can't!" Heather cried, wishing she had simply minded her own business for once.

Surprised by Heather's vehemence, Breanna frowned. "Why not? As an American, I have the right to help fight for a free California, don't I?"

"Yes, but you don't—"

"And if King isn't an ally, he's the enemy."

For a bright girl, Breanna was jumping to all the wrong conclusions. Of course, her own vague comments and innuendos hadn't helped. "Listen, Bree," she implored. "This could be dangerous. I just got you back. I don't want to see you harmed."

Pleased by her emphatic plea, Breanna smiled. "Before I left Boston, Garth suggested I find someone to act in my stead. That's all I plan to do for the time being."

"Garth!" Heather was glad for the chance to change the subject. "How is he?"

Breanna frowned. "Not now, Heather. I have to get back to town to see if I can hire someone to help me find King."

Blanching, Heather moaned softly. In trying to make him sound disreputable enough to keep her sister away from him, she had managed to paint him the villain. Breanna's sense of justice was probably screaming for retribution. To the devil with it, she thought. Let King sort it out!

"The carriage will take too long. Would you like me to have a horse saddled?"

"Yes." Breanna smiled, glad Heather was no longer going to argue. "And I'll need to borrow one of your riding outfits." She mentally measured her sister. "We're close enough in size for me to get by."

Falling into stride beside each other, the two sisters started for the stairs. Heather thought about informing Rosa of what Breanna was going to do, knowing the woman would put a stop to it, but she decided she really did need to speak with Alex. Once he saw that Breanna could be trusted, the truth could be told. Appeased, Breanna would then join her at the hacienda to help the cause in whatever way they could. Then, when everything was back to normal, she would work on getting Alex and her sister interested in each other.

Breanna galloped toward town. At any other
time she would have relished being on the back of
a strong steed while racing over the countryside,
but her mind was totally absorbed with Alex King,
and finding someone who could delve into King's
life.

A man of his power must have enemies. Even
Millie was astute enough to figure that out. And a
man with enemies was a man who had things to
hide. She planned to find out what those things
were. If they included treason against a people
destined to rule a free California, she would see
him stopped. No matter what it took.

Realizing what she was implying, she decided
the man she hired should be able to defend himself. King could quite possibly be devious enough
to resort to murder to keep his empire safe. She
didn't want anyone's life in jeopardy because she
hadn't considered her hired man's need to defend
himself. It occurred to her suddenly that maybe
she needed to hire a gunman.

Pressing the horse into a canter, Breanna wondered if what she was doing was right. She had no
proof King was a lawless rascal. All she had were
some impressions from Heather. Biting her lip, she
decided a gunman was a good idea, just as long as
he realized he was to investigate first and act violently only if he was in danger.

Not sure how to find a hired gun, Breanna returned to the only building she was comfortable
with in Monterey. She wanted to avoid the soldiers
in town and deemed the new hotel a safe starting
point. Once her horse was secured to the post out
front, she entered, drawing off her riding gloves to
slap the dust from her clothes.

The dining room seemed busier that evening.
She supposed many of the passengers from the
Rainbow had recovered sufficiently to dine out.
Wishing to avoid meeting any, she went straight to

the desk. En route she came up with a plausible reason for being there.

"Excuse me," she said sweetly to the clerk who beamed at her. "I stayed here last night and—"

"*Sí, señorita!*" The lad grinned. "I remember you well."

Realizing his eyes kept falling to the snug fit of her jacket, Breanna tilted her chin to project dignity and demand respect. "Did anyone find a gold locket I might have left behind?"

"A locket? No, señorita." He frowned. "There was no locket found."

She shrugged lightly. "I must have left it on the ship. I'll have someone check for me. Is it safe to ride at night, señor?" she asked, sounding somewhat nervous with the thought.

"*Sí!*" He grinned widely, revealing surprisingly good teeth. "We have no trouble here."

Sighing for effect, Breanna maintained her edginess. "I think I'd feel better if I had a pistol. I suppose most of the men carry them." As the clerk shook his head, she urged him on. "Are there many who are good with guns in these parts?"

"There are many who are fine with the pistol, señorita, but none are as good as Señor Rey."

The familiar name made her shiver. She already knew he was a rake, now she had to consider if he might be the man she needed to investigate King.

"And you know this man?" she asked, trying to sound duly impressed.

"But of course. He stays here often and is here even as we speak. He has a regular room we hold for him on the second floor. It's the best the hotel has to offer," he declared proudly.

"Then I am sure I will be safe on my ride to the ship," she said, flashing him a smile. "With men like that about, I doubt anyone harmful is close." Prepared to leave, Breanna had another idea. "Has the room I used been let again?"

Checking the keys, the boy shook his head.

"Then could I go see if my locket is possibly still there? It won't take me but a few minutes, and it could save me checking the ship."

Seeing no reason the lovely lady shouldn't be allowed to look for her locket, he handed her the key. She thanked him and started up the stairs.

Breanna glanced back to make sure the boy didn't see her turn in the opposite direction at the top of the stairs. If Mr. Rey had the best room, it would look out over the water, not the noisy streets of the town. To her relief, there were only three doors along that hallway. Rather than play a guessing game, she would merely try them in order.

At the first there was no response. Possibly it was his room and he was out. In front of the second door, she could hear movement inside. Gathering her resolve, she tapped firmly on the door.

A deep, muffled voice bid her to enter, and she turned the knob. Pushing back the door, she could see a small, well-appointed parlor. She entered but saw no one, and started to close the door. Thinking better of it, she left it ajar. There was no doubt that Mr. Rey had unnerved her at their first meeting. Even though she was capable of telling him exactly what their relationship would be this time, she didn't trust him. He seemed to be the sort of man who got what he wanted, and she wasn't going to help stack the odds in his favor.

"I'll be right out," a deep, husky voice called from the other room.

Breanna swallowed hard. She definitely had the right room. No two men could use that rich growl for a simple statement like that! She removed her hat from where it hung about her neck, and set it on the table along with her gloves and crop. She wanted to appear calm when he entered, so she chose to stand at the window, apparently patient and unaffected by him, despite the nervousness she was feeling.

The view was definitely superb. There was a door opening to a balcony that, under other circumstances, she would have loved to stand on. The room was far enough from the shore to prevent damage in a storm, but close enough to hear the surf as it broke on the rocky shore.

For a brief moment, she felt her tension dissipating but a decisive click made her instantly wary. She turned slowly to see the man she had come to find leaning against the closed door.

Chapter 5

The instant she saw him Breanna decided she had been foolish in seeking this man out. Some inner sense warned her that he was more than even she could bargain with. He braced one shoulder against the door with an easy grace, yet there was a raw energy lying just beneath the surface. A burning intensity filled his blue eyes, even though his face revealed no emotion.

That was not true for Breanna. She knew her face was turning a deep crimson as she gazed at him. It wasn't his nonchalance as he leaned against the door; it wasn't even what she saw in his eyes. It was the cream-colored shirt that hung open as if he had just slipped it on. The dark, curling hair on his chest looked damp. She suspected that he had come directly from his bath, and that made her uneasy.

Amused by the attention his bare chest was drawing, Alex straightened and moved slowly in her direction as he broke the silence.

"I'm delighted to see you again, Miss Sullivan," he said with the same soft growl he had used the night before.

Breanna backed up. "You . . . you know who I am?" she stammered.

"I make it a point to know all strangers in town." He kept moving closer until he had her backed up to the wall and stood within a foot of her.

She had been on his mind all through the night. Even when he was supposed to be subtly questioning Guillermo, her image had wavered in his mind. He had no idea why she was there, but he wasn't going to miss a chance to get to know her better.

She could feel the warmth emanating from his bare chest and grew frightened of his looming presence. "You ... I ... I made a m-mistake coming here. I think I'll ..."

He blocked her flight with his arms and looked down at her. Her eyes darted about, looking for a route of escape, but there was none. She would have to use bravado to extricate herself from this situation.

"Move!" she demanded firmly. "I wish to leave." She stood quite still, her eyes fixed on the squareness of his chin to avoid noticing anything else about him.

Fighting a grin, Alex backed off one step but still stayed close enough to prevent her from running. "But I would be a poor host if I didn't inquire into your reason for coming." His eyes raked her from her dusty boots to the neat twist of hair at her neck. "Perhaps there is something I can do for you ... or with you."

Breanna swallowed the lump in her throat. She fervently wished Heather's outfit had been a bit larger. As it was, the deep wine jacket strained to remain buttoned and the split skirt hugged her hips and thighs. It was no wonder he thought she might be there for some reason other than business!

Aware that she was close to bolting hysterically, he eased off in his teasing. If he wanted to discover why she was there, he had to keep her with him.

"Would you care for some wine? Or perhaps you would like me to ring for something else?"

"No. No, nothing," she barely said, turning to

reach for her hat. A strong hand covered hers and stopped her. He was so close she could feel his breath against her ear.

"You aren't thinking of leaving, are you?" his deep voice rumbled, sending a chill down her spine he could hardly ignore. "You haven't told me why you've paid me this visit. I assume you did have a reason." She hadn't moved. Still holding her hand, he drew her toward him. "Maybe you just want to spend some time with me." His lips played with a smile and revealed the humor he saw in her situation.

That revelation angered Breanna. This wasn't funny! She tried futilely to yank her hand away. She realized she would either have to tell him her reason for being there or allow him to imagine his own. Raising her chin, she relented.

"I wanted to hire you, Mr. Rey," she said firmly.

He released her immediately, the name she used reminding him of her misconception. He walked toward a decanter on the buffet against the wall. After pouring out a glass, he moved to a chair, stretching out his long legs when he sat. "Wanted to, Miss Sullivan?" He sipped his drink. "Have you changed your mind?"

Trying not to become angrier over his apparent disregard for manners, Breanna looked at him, then lowered her eyes, her cheeks turning a soft pink. The dark hair on his wide chest disrupted her thoughts as she noticed the way it tapered to his waist. She squirmed in agitation.

"Mr. Rey, if you would fasten your shirt, perhaps I could better talk with you."

He grinned devilishly. "My apologies," he said with a ring of insincerity. He placed the glass aside, stood, and began to finish dressing. "I didn't mean to offend you."

"You didn't offend me," she replied too quickly. "You just . . . I mean I . . . Oh!" She hated the way he made her feel like a floundering child. She meant for this meeting to be a mutually satisfying business venture, not the seduction he seemed bent on making it.

He was deeply amused and rather intrigued by her behavior. He didn't think she was pretending to be embarrassed, nor did he think she was being coquettish, but he could be wrong. After all, she was no child. Patrick had told him she was nineteen when she left. That would make her twenty-one or close to it. Surely she had experienced *something* by now! Finished with the buttons of his shirt, he wondered if she was merely feeling the same attraction he felt.

"Please, sit down." He motioned to a chair to make her feel less conspicuous. Resuming his seat, he braced his arms on his knees and picked his glass up again, palming it in both hands. To alleviate the tension and get to the reason for her visit, he grew more serious.

"Now, Miss Sullivan, how can I be of service to you?"

Staring at her hands, Breanna drew a settling breath. She had to go through with this now or look the fool. "I want to hire you to investigate someone for me," she finally said. "I want to find out all I can about a certain man."

"And who might the lucky gentleman be?" he mused.

"I doubt he's that," she said, her distaste for the man she sought obvious. "In fact, I don't know what sort of man he is," she admitted honestly. "That's what I want you to find out."

Returning to the decanter, with his back to her, he prodded. "Who is this . . . this man you want me to find?" He tucked his shirt in and picked up a belt from a chair near the bedroom door.

"Alexander King," she said coolly. "Do you know him?"

"I know him," he said as he finished dressing

without turning. "But I can't help wondering what you want with him."

Breanna rose and paced. "I want to talk to him. I want to find out what he and my father are involved in. I need him to explain some rather odd events to my satisfaction."

"And if he won't tell you, what then?"

Breanna froze, staring out the window without seeing a thing. "If he won't tell me, then it must be because he is guilty of some treachery," she reasoned aloud. "He must be held accountable if he's done wrong. He must pay!"

Her fury was almost tangible. She had an odd sense of honor, this woman. How much honor, he was about to discover.

"By pay, do you mean you want me to kill him?" His voice was deeper, almost threatening in its intensity.

"Yes! No! Oh, I don't know," Breanna said, her shoulders slumping. "No, I don't want him killed," she said just above a whisper. "Just find him so I can talk to him."

If she had been watching him, she would have seen his shoulders drop slightly in relief. For a moment, he had thought he might have pure mayhem on his hands. Shaking his head, he turned to look across the room at her.

Though filled with worry, she was exquisite. As refined as a perfect gem, she stood there, more beautiful than any other woman he had ever seen. She was proud and courageous, ready to fight for what she believed. It was time to reveal his identity, and he found himself hoping it would not destroy any chance he might have with her. She could be an asset to the cause if she sided with her father, and she could be something for him as well.

"I'm glad you don't want King dead," he said. She raised her head to look at him. He moved closer. "You see, Miss Sullivan, I know him better than anyone, and I have no penchant for suicide."

Breanna was confused. He wasn't making sense. The only way killing King could be suicide was if ... Her eyes darted about, searching for evidence of the possibility haunting her when they were drawn to him by a pronounced movement.

He had hooked his thumbs in his belt and circled the silver buckle with his fingers. Almost hypnotized by its shiny brilliance, she didn't move as he walked toward her.

She was mesmerized by the light flashing off the beautifully engraved "K." When he was well within reach of her, she snapped out of her stupor and would have run, but he grabbed her arm. Swinging her around so her back was pressed to his chest, he crossed his arms beneath her breasts to hold her fast.

"Let me go!" she cried, trying to reach over her shoulder to rake his face. With his exceptional height advantage and superior strength, he easily avoided her nails. She grew more furious with her frustrated efforts.

Seeking to calm her, he tightened his arms, restricting the breath she could draw until, finally, she ceased her struggles. Although she was near exhaustion from all the blows the day had dealt her, he was not even winded.

"You really should have brushed up on your Spanish, Breanna, or paid closer attention to the translation. You would have known all along who I was," he said against her temple.

Damn him! He was right. She had allowed some primitive desire he awakened in her to blind her to the task she had traveled so far to complete. Oh, how he must have laughed at her when she called him Mr. Rey without realizing *rey* was the Spanish word for "king"!

Struggling to breathe, she spoke icily. "Let me go this instant!" To her surprise, he complied at once. Without looking back at him, she moved toward the door and gripped the knob in preparation to leave.

"I thought you had some questions for me, Breanna," he said in a husky whisper that stopped her in her tracks. "It seems this would be a perfect time to ask them."

Again he was right and she hated him for it. That he had to remind her of her quest galled her, but she knew she had to take advantage of this meeting, for it would most likely be the only one they would have. At least she hoped it would be. The man unnerved her. Letting her hand fall from the knob, she remained facing the door and did as he suggested.

"What have you done with my father?"

"You'd be more comfortable if—"

Before he could finish, she spun like a raging fury. "Damn it! Where is he?"

Alex had to struggle with his desire to laugh. He hadn't expected any of this mission to be so enjoyable. There she stood, braced for battle, and all he could think of was the way she had felt when he held her tightly against him. Disciplining his wayward thoughts, he poured out another drink and sat down.

"I don't talk to bad-tempered children," he scolded, wondering what her reaction would be. "Sit down and behave yourself."

"I'm not a child, Mr. King!" she flared, flouncing indignantly into a chair.

"Well, you're behaving like one. You came here to seek news about Patrick, yet you run off the moment you feel threatened. Even Heather is braver than that." He saw her sniff and fold her arms across her chest, reminding him of the firmness of her breasts when they had pressed against his arm. "But I agree, I cannot think of you as a child."

Breanna ignored his attempt to pacify her. "Where is my father?" she asked again.

"I can't tell you that, Breanna," he replied without pause.

"Can't or won't?" she demanded.

"Both. I can't because I'm not sure right now of his whereabouts, and I won't because I won't jeopardize his safety by telling anyone, not even you."

"But he's my father!" she cried, growing more animated. "I don't understand what gives you the right to—"

"No! You *don't* understand," he interrupted fiercely. "You don't understand at all!" He slammed his glass down and stood. She flinched as he stepped toward her. "There is more at stake here than you can imagine, and we've decided it would be better for everyone if you and Heather know as little as possible until it's necessary."

"You mean you decided!" she shouted back, standing up.

"No, damn it! I mean exactly what I said!" Alex drew a deep breath and blew it out, trying to maintain control of his temper. Never had he met an adversary with Breanna's tenacity. Raking his fingers through his hair, he tried to make her see how important it was that she take his word.

"Look, I admit Patrick and I are involved in something together." He placed his hands on her shoulders, and she was listening so intently she did not object. "Something very serious and very dangerous. The more you delve into it, the greater the risk to your father." Blue eyes locked with brown. "I swear to you, Breanna, your father is doing what he wants to do, and he is in no danger from me." He slid one hand up to her neck and gently caressed her jaw with his thumb. "You must believe me," he said softly.

"Prove it," she said to keep him from taking control of her senses. His touch was devastating. She couldn't allow him to think he had any power over her or she would never find out the truth. "Take me to him."

Alex sensed the effect he was having. Under ordinary circumstances he might have been amused by her attempt to divert his attention from herself as a woman, but this time he felt compelled to challenge her instead.

"All I plan to prove to you is that I make the rules, and you will live by them." She tried to push him away, but he merely grinned crookedly. "You are no match for me, Breanna." She began to struggle again. He brought her arms behind her back to hold her still. "Whatever I decide to do with you, you will be unable to stop me."

Infuriated by the way he was manipulating her body as well as her choices, she tried to kick him while snarling an unsavory oath. "Let me go, you miserable wretch!"

Alex laughed. "I think I know what should be done with you, you little spitfire! You need a good spanking!" Her head shot up as she stilled. His smile faded. "But I think I have a better way to tame you." He began to lower his head.

Breanna leaned as far back as she could to avoid the kiss he seemed intent on giving her. "If you kiss me, I'll scream!" she threatened. He kept coming. "I'll kill you! I swear I will!"

"Then best you do it now," he growled, his long fingers circling her chin to hold her still. "And open your mouth the way you did in the dining room, the way I knew you would."

She gasped at this reminder, and Alex took full advantage.

What nerve! she thought, trying to push him away when his lips covered hers. What audacity! her mind cried as his tongue touched hers. What madness! her body screamed as she felt that kiss jolt the entire length of her. He was her enemy! He had to be stopped! She could not surrender to his will!

"Ow!" Alex yelled, leaping back while testing his tongue for blood. "Damn it! What did you do that for?" There was blood on his fingers when he examined them. "I'm bleeding!"

"You're lucky you're still alive to bleed!" she shouted, putting as much distance between them as she could. Trembling from the kiss despite her anger, Breanna struggled to think of something to make him take her more seriously.

"I don't know who you think you are, Mr. King, maybe California's own Alexander the Great, but anyone who steals his own gun shipments and meets with both sides of a conflict certainly has no say over what I do!"

Alex groaned. There was no doubt where she had gotten her information. What the hell did Heather think she was doing? The problem was she wasn't thinking at all! Arming Breanna with such facts could be explosive. If she was making connections, then Guillermo might get wind of the information, which could put King's own life at risk. He needed to divert Breanna's attention from the details she sought.

"Let me explain," he offered.

Breanna glared at him. "Go on, then. Explain."

Alex considered whether partial truth or her own confused conclusions were more dangerous. Unwilling to divulge too much information until he spoke with John Frémont, his superior in all this, he stared hard at this russet-haired beauty. Focusing on the determined pout of her luscious lips, Alex came up with a solution.

"I'll answer every question you ask," he said with conviction. "But each question will have a price."

"I'll pay no price for the truth!" she snapped. "If you won't tell me, I'll go to the authorities." She spun about to leave.

"And be responsible for your father's death?"

Was he bluffing? she wondered. Could she afford to take the chance? "What price?" she asked in a mere whisper.

If his plan worked, she would ask very few questions. "A kiss for every answer to every question."

This was beyond mere madness! She turned to be sure she had heard him correctly. The smug look on his face was answer enough. "This is absurd," she blurted.

"Absurd or not, Breanna, it is the price I am exacting for each question. Either leave and chance destroying the very person you seek to protect, or stay and pay my price." He saw her hesitation and thought to up the ante. "Decide now or the price goes up."

The memory of his lips covering hers brought warmth with it. She felt as if she couldn't draw a decent breath. "Don't d-do this, I beg you," she pleaded.

"A kiss and—"

"All right!" she cried, stopping him before he gave her an ultimatum she would have to refuse. There was no doubt in her mind he was definitely capable of making excessive demands. "A kiss for a question, but nothing else!"

Alex nodded when he would rather have laughed aloud. "Agreed." He moved to the settee and patted the vacant spot beside him. "Come, sit down, Breanna. We might as well be comfortable while we settle your mind."

"There?" she nearly squeaked, when she realized how close they would have to sit through the coming ordeal.

A smile touched his lips. "That was a question, Breanna, and the answer is yes, here." Relaxing back, he placed an ankle on the opposite knee. "Come here and pay me."

"Surely you don't think—" She saw his brow arch. "I didn't finish it!" she exclaimed, growing wary of the man with whom she had made this pact.

He conceded the last with a nod. "But you still owe me a kiss."

Breanna wished she had left when she had the chance, before he could warn her about her father, before he had made this ridiculous demand, before she actually had to kiss him! Now that she had agreed, she refused to break her word, especially to him.

"Very well," she said, squaring her shoulders to maintain a certain amount of dignity. She walked calmly to the settee. Placing a hand on the back of the small sofa, she leaned forward. Without touching him anywhere else, she placed her closed, dry lips on his for a quick peck.

"That wasn't much of a kiss." He grinned teasingly.

"It wasn't much of a question," she retorted as she turned to sit on the edge of the couch, her hands folded demurely in her lap. Feeling a bit smug that she had beaten him in the first round, she said, "Shall I begin?" The instant the words left her mouth, she knew she had made another mistake.

"Indeed," Alex growled quickly, pulling her back into his arms. He wasn't going to give her a chance to place another chaste kiss on his mouth, and he wasn't going to let her have time to prepare for a distraction.

His lips covered hers. They were not demanding, but neither were they passive. It was more like a gentle exploration, a tentative tasting. Her hands, trapped between them, closed over the silk of his shirt. She wasn't sure if it was an act of anger or if she was holding on to keep from floating away.

"Now, what's your next question?" he asked, still holding her in his arms.

It took Breanna a few moments to clear her

head. There was a slight buzzing she couldn't explain. She opened her eyes and saw a hint of a satisfied smile lifting one corner of his mouth.

"You weren't supposed to do anything but kiss me," she reprimanded in a breathy voice.

Alex flexed the arms that held her. "This is part of a real kiss, Breanna."

Swallowing to give herself more time to think, she considered how to phrase her next sentence so it was clearly not a question. "The kiss is over. You can let me go." She released his shirt and sought to push free.

"Was that all you wanted to ask me?"

"Very well," she said. "But you must answer each *before* I pay." He agreed, releasing her slowly. Once out of his arms, she contemplated how to get the most information from each question. She didn't think she could stand too many more of these payments.

"Why are you playing a role on both sides of the interests in California?"

Clever question, he thought. The way it was asked, he would have to reveal a considerable amount of information unless he was very careful.

"I believe in what your father and the others are doing, yet I own much in this territory and can ill-afford to antagonize the authorities."

His reply made sense, but offered very little. She turned to ask him to clarify himself, but he was already waiting for another kiss. Chafing at the delay in asking him another question, she said, "Can't we wait until I'm done with my questions to do this?"

A sensual smile was his reply. She breathed deeply as his arms drew her to him. This time, however, he leaned back, forcing her to lay atop his chest.

This kiss had more impact. Not only did he slowly stroke her tongue with his, but he rubbed his chest firmly against her sensitive breasts. She found the restraining tenseness of her body giving way to a certain lassitude. She wanted to believe it was due to the strain she had been under, yet she knew that wasn't quite true. It was the discovery of the unknown that was tapping her energy. It was his kiss.

Alex felt her resistance ebbing. These kisses were meant to take her mind off her questions. To his delight, they were changing his thoughts, as well. She was responding. He didn't think she wanted to, but she was beyond choice. Her small, lush body was taking control of her quick mind, and his, as well.

Slowly, Alex drew back enough to gaze at her. She already owed him another kiss, and he planned to make it one that would scare her into forgetting the entire game, until he saw her face. Her eyes were closed, her lashes brushing her cheeks. The tempting sweetness of her lips beckoned for more. He could feel her panting little breaths brushing his chin.

A jolt hit him hard in his masculine parts. He was filled with a desire so intense, it was he who wanted to run. Suddenly he had to wonder if the change in her was intentional. Was it possible she thought to get what she wanted from him another way? He had never bothered to delve into the minds of women, yet he had heard enough to know they could be conniving and manipulative.

Breanna's head began to clear with his delay. She opened her eyes, wondering what had happened to make him stop. He had been so gentle, she was prepared to admit she might be wrong about him until she saw the dark scowl on his face. Had she done something wrong? Was he angry with her? It wasn't until the scowl was replaced by a raw flare of desire that she realized his playful manner had turned more threatening.

"Growing tired of just kisses?" he snarled, his painful need making him testy. He ignored her

wide-eyed surprise. He didn't want to see innocence. He didn't want to hear her denial. All he
wanted was to take them both over the edge to
blessed relief.

"No," she whispered, suddenly afraid of him.
She tried to push herself off him, but his arms
tightened. He shifted his body, rolling to press her
down on the seat.

"You still owe me," he rasped while his fingers
drew out the pins that held her hair. She shook her
head to stop him, but her arms were trapped between them, making her defenseless. "Another
kiss and more."

His mouth no longer teased gently. He was taking full possession of hers in a savage kiss, a kiss
that demanded total surrender. While his hands
entwined in the thick auburn mass he had freed,
his mouth claimed, his tongue invaded.

Breanna began to tremble anew. It was a combination of her body's response to his kiss and the
terror welling up inside her, the terror of losing
control of herself. He was a master puppeteer, manipulating her to respond to his touch. A fearful
whimper grew in her throat and finally escaped.

Alex heard the sound. To him it was a moan of
passion. He growled in response, wanting more of
her, wanting *all* of her. Dragging his lips from
hers, he traced her chin with his tongue. "You are
all fire, Breanna," he whispered against her throat.
He could feel her racing pulse beneath his lips.
"You are a living flame, burning me."

His words had no meaning for Breanna, but she
understood the searching hand that fumbled at
the buttons of her jacket. He wanted to touch her;
she wanted to feel that touch. Her young, healthy
body was aching for it and more, but there would
be a price. With him she felt there would always
be a price.

"Stop!" she cried, shoving at his shoulders. She
glanced down to see him untying the ribbons of

her camisole. "No! Kisses!" she exclaimed. "You said just kisses!"

Her distress reached into his brain, clouded with the rage of desire they had kindled. He felt the cold knife of frustration plunge into his vitals. For an instant, he wanted to pursue the path they were taking, to force her to admit she wanted him as badly as he craved her, but the madness passed.

Using all his restraint, he moved back from her. It was nearly his undoing when he saw the rosy tip of her rigid nipple peeking out from beneath a scrap of lace on her camisole. Closing his eyes, he struggled to gain control of his body.

"Get up!" he said sharply, grabbing her arm to assist her. "Get dressed and get out of here."

Scowling at the harshness of his tone, Breanna felt anger began to simmer inside her as her shaking fingers tried to button her jacket. What right did *he* have to be upset?

"What about my questions?" she asked, her own tone surly. "You promised to answer them."

Alex had moved away from her to try to tamp down the mayhem he was on the verge of committing. Her words, her question, nearly lost the battle for him. To keep the upper hand, he resorted to harsh words of his own.

"Another time. I grow bored with your pitiful kisses." He heard her gasp from behind him. "Perhaps, when you grow up a little more and understand what it is to be a woman, we'll resume this amusing chat."

Alex flinched when the brandy decanter smashed against the wall near him. He whirled to face her, her defiance the one challenge he could not resist. "Damn you!" he shouted, already en route to her. Before the amber liquid could slide down the wall, he had shackled her arms with his hands.

"Let go of me!" She wiggled like a captured eel and tried to grab his hair or rake his eyes. "I'm more woman than you'll ever have!" Stomping hard on his instep, she was free.

"You hellion!" he shouted, bending to rub his foot.

Breanna seized the opportunity and made her escape. She shoved against his unbalanced form and sent him sprawling to the floor. "You bastard!" she screamed as she grabbed her things and flung open the door. "I'll see you rot in hell for this!"

Alex sat up and grimaced at the slamming door. He wanted to go after her, but thought better of it. Patrick probably wouldn't like it if he gave her what he really thought she deserved!

Unexpectedly, he chuckled. What a vibrant, beautiful tigress she was. She had a bad temper and a waspish tongue, but she intrigued him. He was sure she would be as entertaining in his bed as she was out of it. Maybe more so. He laughed, recalling the passion she had struggled so hard to mask.

Rising from the floor, he also recalled her parting words. Would she cause trouble to revenge herself against his insults? She was clever enough and had just enough information to see him damned. All he could hope was that she realized if he fell, so would her father.

Not relishing the responsibility of Breanna Sullivan, Alex went for his jacket. Maybe he could find John. He could face the entire Mexican army, but he didn't think he had the strength to handle one little girl. Girl? Hardly! As she had said, she was probably more woman than he could handle.

Slowly he grinned. Someday he would enjoy finding out.

Chapter 6

$\sim\!\!\mathcal{O}\!\!\sim$

Breanna leaned against the wall around the corridor from Alex's room and tried to still the trembling in her legs. She wanted to put as much distance between herself and that conniving womanizer as possible, but found herself unable to move. Anger rose like bile in her throat at the contempt she felt for him and herself.

For an instant she thought of returning to his room to lay a litany of expletives on him, the likes of which he'd never heard, but only for an instant. A greater fear held her rooted where she stood. The fear of the unknown longings with which he had tempted her.

Concentrating on the fiasco of their meeting instead of the emotional turmoil he had caused in her, she tried to figure out what she would do next. She wanted to go to the authorities to enumerate his crimes, yet she needed concrete proof. Plus, she had to think of her father. King was right about one thing. If he fell from grace, her father and the others involved would surely tumble with him.

Perhaps the only thing she could do now was go home and think it all through. With her questions remaining unanswered, she was right back where she started. Her lips tingled at the thought, still sensitive from his kisses. His kisses! Would she ever touch a man's lips again and not recall the earth-shattering effect of them?

Pushing away from the wall, she forced herself to move down the hall. The instant before she was at the top of the stairs, she realized she couldn't go down looking the way she did. Her hair was unbound and mussed from his hands. Her jacket, though buttoned, was badly wrinkled from the weight of his body pressing against her own.

Stepping back, she reasoned there had to be another way off the floor. The maids didn't march up the main staircase to see to the rooms. Moving toward the room she had occupied the night before, she saw another staircase, darker and narrower than the others, and made her way down.

At the bottom she heard some voices and belatedly recalled the key she still had. She thought of calling to someone but instead she set it on a stair, sure it would be discovered and returned to the desk.

The night air was considerably cooler. Perhaps it only felt that way because her skin still burned from the memory of what had just passed, but it could be from the lateness of the evening. Slipping down the alley, she made sure there was no one about before making her way to her horse.

Once astride, Breanna turned the steed toward home. She gave the horse its head, anxious to flee the effects and affrontery of Alex King. In all her life she had never been treated so ... so ... Her mind refused to believe the only crime he had committed was to treat her like a woman. She had believed he was a threat and, as far as she was concerned, he had just proved it.

She couldn't recall a moment of her ride home. The landscape had gone by in a blur. She never noticed the brilliant stars or felt the cool night air whipping through her already tangled hair. Not until she saw the house loom up before her, did she realize in what a dreamlike state she had been riding.

After handing the reins over to a groom who

seemed to appear out of nowhere, Breanna raced to the house. She threw open the door to her father's den and, without a second thought, poured out a large quantity of whiskey and took a swallow. The burning fire that traveled down her throat to sit in her stomach made her eyes water as she choked and gagged. This, however, did not deter her from finishing the glass.

Drawn by the ruckus of banging doors, Heather ran in to find her sister pouring a second drink in the almost dark room. "Breanna! My God! Where have you been?"

Breanna almost dropped the glass at her outburst. She spun around and grimaced. The last thing she wanted to do was talk. "Go away, Heather. Just leave me be and I'll talk to you tomorrow." She shivered, picked up the bottle, and made her way to a chair.

"But Bree, at least tell me where you've been these last hours," Heather said, going to light the fire. Her jaw dropped when she turned around and spied her sister's total disarray. "Good Lord! What's happened to you?"

Breanna stared silently into her glass. Heather came to her knees beside the chair. "Bree, you haven't been . . . nobody's hurt you, have they?"

Breanna swallowed more of her drink and shook her head. "No, Heather. I'm all right."

Sighing, Heather reached to take her sister's hand and gasped. "Your hands are like ice!" She rose and added another log to the fire. "You need something to warm you. I'll get some hot tea and—"

Breanna burst into laughter before Heather finished. "For heaven's sake, Heather. If Papa's Irish whiskey can't do the trick, nothing can."

Heather placed her hands on her hips and tapped her toe in agitation. "Breanna Sullivan, you're drunk."

"Not yet, little sister, but I'm working on it." Breanna poured out more of the magic elixir.

"Are you going to tell me what set you off on this . . . this foolishness? For goodness sake, Bree, you don't even drink!" She sat in the chair opposite her sister's.

After a moment, Breanna raised her glass to toast her sister mockingly. "My dear Heather, tonight I have had the pleashure"—she giggled at her slurred word—"the pleasure of meeting the mysterious Alexander King."

Heather groaned. She had never dreamed they would have an encounter so soon. Glancing suspiciously at Breanna, she wondered just what had occurred.

"He's clever and diabolical." Breanna closed her eyes. "And he's very attractive." She missed the grin on Heather's face because she was imagining him lying over her. The thought was sobering and her eyes flew open. "And he's a tricky, no good rogue!" she exclaimed, sloshing her glass with emphasis. Noticing the glass, she emptied it as if she were drinking water.

Heather was speaking, but Breanna couldn't be bothered to listen. She had something more important to consider. She began to poke at her nose with a shaky finger and trace her lips in deep thought.

"Are you listening to me?" Heather demanded.

"My nose is quite numb," Breanna mumbled. Her head began to bob. "And I'm tired, Heather." The glass dropped from her fingers to the floor. "I'm so tired."

Heather stood. "Come on, Bree." She gripped her sister's arm and hauled her from the chair. "You win. We'll talk tomorrow."

Noises began to penetrate Breanna's dreamless sleep, and she stirred. Peeking through her lashes, she could see the room was still dark. Great thirst made her throw back the covers and attempt to get up. Swinging her legs to the floor, Breanna cried out. Thundering drums beat out a rhythm in her temples to match her pulse. She grimaced and clutched her head between her hands.

"So you're finally awake!" Heather said vivaciously. "I was beginning to wonder if you were going to sleep the day away to avoid my questions." Refraining from laughing at her sister's obvious pain, she went to the drapes and yanked them back.

"Damn it, Heather! Shut those drapes!" Breanna yelled, then groaned at her folly.

Heather laughed and closed the drapes, returning the room to darkness. "You better watch your tongue, Bree. If Rosa hears you she'll wash out your mouth." She was rewarded with a pillow aimed at her head. "And your temper isn't getting any better, either."

"Shut up, Heather. I'm in no mood for your good cheer." Breanna set her feet on the floor and swayed. She held her head to slow the pounding and finally managed to reach the basin and pitcher after several false starts. Gripping the edge of the commode, she steadied herself to pour out some water and splash it on her face. She could hear Heather humming brightly while she put the room in order.

"Must you be so cheerful?" Breanna moaned, pushing her tangled hair out of her face. "Here I am, wishing I was dead, and you're singing. Have you no heart?"

"You know, Bree, Papa always said the best cure for a hangover was a glass of what gave it to you." Heather grinned mischievously. "Shall I get you some more whiskey?"

Her question was met with a growl, in part from a failure to see the humor of the situation and in part from a wave of nausea that crept through her at the mere mention of whiskey.

"What you can do is get me a pot of strong, black coffee," Breanna ordered. "And do it quietly!"

Laughing, Heather bobbed a curtsy and left to do as her irritable sister bid.

When Heather returned, she found Breanna looking relatively composed. Neatly dressed in a long dark skirt and a prim, soft pink blouse, Breanna was wrapping her hair into a knot on her neck.

"Why don't you just let it hang, Bree? It looks so pretty that way."

Breanna thought of the way King had slid his hands into the long mass and shivered. "No! I'll wear it how I wish!"

"I see your mood hasn't improved any, despite the improvement in your appearance," Heather retorted as she handed Breanna a cup of steaming coffee.

Breanna was ashamed of taking out her anger at King on her sister. "I'm sorry, *chica*. I shouldn't be blaming you for my foul mood." A tentative smile went with the apology.

Heather's eyes filled with tears and she smiled. "You haven't called me that since we were children." She extended her hand and Breanna took it. "I'm glad you're home, Bree."

With a gentle squeeze, Breanna managed a full smile. "I'm glad to *be* home. Let's go out on the patio for our breakfast. We can talk there, and I'll see if I can atone for my bad behavior."

"I'm dying to hear what happened last night," Heather said, "but I think Carla is preparing lunch."

"Lunch! Good Lord, you don't mean it's that late?" Breanna was generally an early riser, and the thought of sleeping half the day away astounded her.

"It's past one." Heather giggled. "And I've been dying of curiosity all morning."

"We have at least that much in common," Breanna teased. "I've been doing a little dying of my own!"

Their trip to the table was delayed when a bubbling Rosa embraced her older charge and demanded to hear everything. Fortunately, Heather was able to get them away with a promise that they would have a great chat later that afternoon.

"She still thinks we're children." Breanna laughed, sitting in the lovely garden-encircled patio. "But she is a dear, isn't she?"

"You didn't think so when we used to try to sneak off to the shore and she would catch us, insisting we learn something more valuable, like sewing."

"I'm older and wiser," Breanna admitted, "but I do wish she had taught us something I could use now, like history and politics." She saw the interest flash in Heather's eyes but wasn't quite ready to discuss the night before.

"I haven't seen Millie yet today," she interjected to keep Heather from asking any questions. "I hope she doesn't think I've abandoned her."

Buttering a roll, Heather paused. "Thanks to me, she feels like one of the family." She saw Breanna's smile of appreciation. "She's very nice and she thinks the world of you, though why I'll never know."

"Because she's a very bright girl," Breanna explained as she reached for more coffee.

Noticing that Breanna was avoiding any of the food on the table, Heather began to nibble on her roll. "She is bright and eager to learn, so I sent her out to look over the place with Paul."

"I don't remember anyone named Paul. Is he new?"

"He's one of King's men," Heather said, observing the flinch of Breanna's hand. "He's a likable fellow and works very hard," she added to see if it was the unknown Paul or King that upset her sister, and since Breanna began to fidget with her spoon, paying no attention to what she had just said, Heather realized it was King.

"Bree, what's wrong? What happened last night between you and King?"

Breanna slammed down her spoon and winced at the noise. "Nothing happened!" she snapped.

Heather waited. Breanna was lying. It would take her a moment, but she would eventually confess.

Almost on cue, Breanna began. "Alexander King played me for a fool last night. The night we arrived, I met him but thought he was someone else." Sniffing, she added, "A mixup on my Spanish translation." She stood up and began to pace. "He could have corrected the mistake but chose, for some amusement of his own, to let me go on believing it." She came up behind her empty chair and gripped the back. "Can you imagine how I felt when I hired him to investigate himself?"

Heather held a grin in check. Alex didn't do anything without cause. If he wanted to keep Breanna in the dark, he must have had a motive. It went without saying that he had known who Breanna was, for he was also very careful. She almost wished she could hear his side of this. Heather pushed her plate away. "What happened then?"

"Then I demanded answers," Breanna said, leaving out the part about the payments he demanded for them.

"And did you get them?"

Breanna sighed heavily. "No. I . . . we . . . we just didn't get along. We couldn't talk."

It wasn't like Breanna to let the opportunity to grill Alex slip by. There was more to this than Breanna was admitting. "Bree, I can't believe that's all of it. You're too distraught. For Papa's sake, I have to ask you to tell me everything."

Breanna raised her head and looked down at her sister. "You've known all along about Papa and King, haven't you?" Heather's face reddened. "And you let me race into town to interrogate him." Her temper was beginning to simmer. "You know all about the men working secretly to liberate California from Mexican control, yet you wrote those letters anyway."

"No, Bree!" Heather exclaimed. "When I wrote I didn't know. I was truly scared."

Breanna forced herself to sit and face her sister. "All right, Heather. Let's have the truth." She saw Heather frown. "All of it."

"I can't tell you, Bree," Heather said. "I made a promise to Papa and Alex." She could see the disappointment in her sister's eyes and relented slightly. "All I can say is that Alex is a good man. Everything he's done is for the benefit of California."

Considering the way he had used her the night before, she shook her head slowly. "And for the benefit of Alex King."

"You're wrong, Bree," Heather scolded. "Papa and the other Americans who have gone north to train an army couldn't have done it if Alex hadn't come up with a way to protect their land." She knew she was revealing more than she should, but she didn't want Breanna causing trouble for Alex for the wrong reasons. "He came up with the tax idea to free them without having to find excuses about their leaving."

"And his friendship with the authorities, is that a way to help?" Breanna asked, not convinced of Alex's good intentions as Heather was.

"Our men need to know things, troop movements, convoys, if they are to remain out of sight. Alex gets that information."

It made sense. There was even a possibility in

Breanna's mind that it was true, but Alex's behavior the night before kept her from accepting it blindly.

"You may see him as a paragon, Heather, but I assure you he is not. The man likes power. He expects things to go as he wishes. I can't trust him with the life of Papa and the others the way you do. Not until I have proof."

Heather was suddenly frightened that Breanna would do something foolish, jeopardizing what had already been done. "So what do you plan to do?" she asked, hoping she wouldn't have to warn Alex.

"I don't know," Breanna admitted. She rubbed her forehead to try to ease her headache. "I need to think some more." She rose and paused. "I think I'll take a ride down to the beach. It always helped me to think when we were children."

Watching her leave, Heather fell back in her chair with a breath whistling from her lips. This was not the Breanna she knew so well. Something else had happened. She was refusing to see the good in Alex, no matter what she heard. There was only one reason for that. He'd done something to make Breanna mistrust him.

Thinking back to her original plan to see the two matched, she wondered if there was something brewing between them that neither expected. The volatile Breanna would be a challenge to Alex, and his arrogance would certainly spark her independent streak. It was just possible that Alex King was more than Breanna could handle.

Smiling slowly, Heather pulled her plate back into place. She was suddenly famished.

The surf and sun were working their healing properties on Breanna's tensed muscles. Needing to be alone to sort out her feelings, she had ridden to the beach as soon as she changed. She had kept all disturbing thoughts at bay during the hour-long ride to reach her destination. She had merely enjoyed the surrounding beauty of the land until she could see the deep blue water sparkling along the horizon.

After dismounting, she tied her horse on the grassy hill above the beach and stood looking over the place where land and sea merged peacefully.

Clad in the black skirt and jacket of her own riding outfit that had been unpacked for her the night before, she sat on a piece of driftwood to enjoy the view. The sun was very bright and very warm and made her drowsy. She decided to walk off her lethargy before setting her mind to thinking, and pulled off her boots and slipped off her short black jacket.

Stepping gingerly through the debris of the tide line, her feet found the cool, wet sand. It was soothing, and she wiggled her toes. Removing her flat-brimmed hat, she sent it sailing back to where her horse stood grazing and turned to face the water. Still feeling confined, she rolled up the sleeves of her gray silk shirt and pulled open the thin black ties at her throat.

The beach was deserted as far as she could see. Searching for the freedom she had known as a child, she unfastened the buttons on her shirt. The warmth of the sun penetrated her thin camisole as she bent to place her shirt on a stick protruding from the sand. A cool breeze caressed her warm skin, and she felt like laughing as she drew the pins from her hair to ease the tautness of the severe style.

All at once her problems seemed like gulls on the wing. She felt unfettered and refused to ruin her peace with thoughts or worries. For a short while, she would be mindless, running with the tides and as free as the wind. Throwing her pins high into the air, she moved to the edge of the sea to enjoy running in the surf.

After covering a long stretch of beach, Breanna

stopped to catch her breath. She looked back over the span and began to retrace her steps slowly, kicking up scoops of sand and leaping aside to avoid the incoming tidal surges. So intent was she in her play, she neglected to see a pair of riders stop atop a hill not far from her who watched and enjoyed her play.

"I should have known our nymph was Breanna." Alex laughed.

"That wisp of a child is the one causing you all the trouble?" John Frémont teased.

"Child! You must be getting old, John." He watched Breanna toss back her hair and bend to investigate a small tidal pool.

"Not so old I can't detect a more than casual interest on your part." John caught the side glance Alex cast him and opted to change the subject. "Anyway, Jessie doesn't complain."

Alex chuckled. "That wife of yours doesn't complain because you're here and she's in the East having the time of her life acting as your father-in-law's hostess."

"Yes, the senator is a hard man to compete with in her eyes. In fact, the only reason I accepted President Polk's appointment to lead this mission was because of her." His serious side was replaced by his natural good humor. "Yet, as it turned out, I think I owe her my appreciation. I would never have gotten the opportunity to know you, my friend, or been involved in this adventure if she hadn't pushed me. Besides"—he laughed—"at thirty-two, how many more chances will I get?"

"Since I'm just two years your junior, do you recommend I make every moment count?" His eyes had returned to Breanna.

"By all means!" John smiled, having heard about only parts of their meeting, he was sure. "Can I be of any help?"

"As a matter of fact, you can." Alex made a few suggestions, then turned his horse toward the sea.

Feeling better than she had since receiving Heather's first cryptic letter so many months before, Breanna allowed the natural splendor around her to lull her into a false sense of privacy. She didn't consider that anyone would disrupt her peace, so she was doubly annoyed when she sensed some invasion. She couldn't explain it, yet she seemed to feel the tranquillity of the day was over.

Sighing, she turned back to her horse in time to see a rider pick up her things and gather her horse's reins. She called out for him to stop and began to run after him, but it was useless. He was too far for her to identify him or make herself heard above the surf. Slumping, she watched him ride off with her property.

Her first impulse was to stand there and scream at the thief, yet she knew it would be a waste of the energy she would need to walk back home. With any luck, Heather would send someone out to search for her if it got late. If not, she would merely return home on foot. It was a long walk, but one she had made several times in her youth.

Realizing she had left her shirt back on the beach, she decided to get it and see if she could find any of her discarded pins. Turning to scan the beach for the stick holding her shirt, she gasped in surprise. Silhouetted against the lowering sun was another horse and rider.

A knight in shining armor, she thought as the sun cast a golden glow around the dark rider. There was a magnetism, a strange aura emanating from him that seemed to encompass her, a sense of raw power. The sensation was familiar. She had felt it the night before. Drawing in an unsteady breath, she knew who the rider was even before he spoke.

"It seems you are in need of assistance, Breanna." His voice rumbled like a gathering storm.

"Go away!" she cried. "I don't need any assistance from you!" She spun around and began to walk away. She had no destination in mind; she just refused to stand and listen to him.

Staying on his horse, Alex rode up beside her and leaned on his thigh. "That wasn't your horse being led off, was it?" He grinned at her stiffening spine. Predictably, she turned furiously toward him.

"You know damned well it was!" she flared. "And even though I am unable to prove another of your sins, I'm sure the loss of everything I own is all your doing!"

"As I recall, Breanna," he mused, "you own very little. In fact"—he pushed his hat back off his brow and let his eyes roam over her—"just your personal things. But, if you aren't careful," he said, drawing her shirt from inside his own, "I'll have more of even those than you."

"Give me that!" she demanded. She watched him finger the silk and lift it to his nose.

"Smells like roses. Are you partial to roses?"

"That's none of your business! Now give me my shirt!" He held it out to her and she moved closer to take it. Again she had underestimated him and would pay for the mistake. Before she touched the material, he grabbed her wrist and pulled her close enough to feel her chin pressed into his thigh.

"Like last night, you're in no position to give orders, only to take them, doe eyes." His own eyes smoldered as they fell to her heaving chest. She had been in his thoughts all night and day. He still wanted her; perhaps here, on the warm sand, he could have her. He was beginning to believe it was the only way he could exorcise her from his thoughts.

"Don't call me that!" she snapped in anger, hating the intimacy it implied. "And stop looking at me like ... like a hungry wolf!" She tried to pull free of him and hang on to the shirt at the same time.

Alex released her then, sending her to the sand. He threw back his head and laughed. "You are a joy, Breanna! That so much fight can be put into such a beautiful little package is pure delight." Bending one knee around the saddle horn, he grinned at her. "You should save it, though, for the cause instead of me."

His comment was met with a face full of sand. "*Bruja!*" he growled, throwing his leg over the horse to dismount. He spit out the grit and tried to clear his eyes.

If she were a witch, she thought as she ran down the beach trying to increase the distance between them, she would cast a spell on him and turn him into the snake he was! Surreptitiously glancing over her shoulder at him, she gasped. He was only a few yards behind her and gaining with each long stride.

Running with all the speed she could muster, Breanna was pulled up short and spun around. She lost her balance and fell facedown in the sand. Sputtering, she tried to free herself from his grasp. When he let her go she grabbed at her shirt. In her frustrated anger, it never occurred to her to let go of the shirt and resume her flight.

Hand over hand, he pulled her closer. When she was within reach and pulling furiously, he let her go to send her sprawling again.

"Oh! You ... you blackguard!" She rose and dusted the sand from her bottom. "I hate you!" She needed something to throw at him and, without thinking, threw the shirt.

Alex caught it and raised a brow in amusement. "Don't you want this?" he teased. "Or are you hoping I will exact a price for it?" She screeched and began to stomp away. She kept walking until she heard the sound of tearing fabric.

As she whirled to glare at him, her jaw dropped in surprise. "What are you doing?" she demanded, racing back to see him holding half of her shirt in each hand.

Alex looked innocently from one half to the other. "It wouldn't have fit me." He grinned mockingly. "And you weren't in the mood to bargain."

"I didn't need to bargain!" she cried. "You bastard! That shirt was mine!"

In an instant the gray silk fluttered to the sand, and Breanna felt the grip of his hands on her arms. He pulled her to his chest, twisting her arms behind her back so she was arched close to him.

"I don't mind being called names when I've earned them, *mi amante*, but I've yet to give you cause. Anything I've done until now, you've instigated." He had drawn her so far back, her only means of standing was his strength. "Or is that what you have in mind, to instigate this?"

Before she could utter a single word, he lowered his lips to her exposed throat. She felt his tongue in the hollow at its base. She struggled, wanting to scream at him to stop, but he pulled her hair when she made the effort.

The sun was suddenly hotter, brighter than her eyes could stand. Her head was beginning to pound to the same beat as her heart. She heard him chuckle and opened her eyes to find him looking down at her.

"You're a fraud, Breanna." His lips turned up on one side in a half-grin. "You're a sensual woman under your facade of independent fury. You hide your wanton nature beneath a waspish tongue and a shrewish mind, but I know the truth." He set her free and watched her rub the blood back into her arms. "What are you afraid of, Breanna?"

"Not you!" she snapped, and he chuckled anew.

She was running out of scathing things to say. Nothing seemed to put a dent in his arrogant hide. The only thing she could think to do was put distance between them. Without another word, she turned and started to walk away with as much dignity as she could muster.

"Breanna!" he called after her. "Don't be a fool! You can't walk home. I'll take you." She kept walking, and he shook his head in exasperation. Damn, but she was stubborn! She would do something foolish rather than give an inch.

He shouted out her name and gave up. Returning to his horse, he mounted. He could see her climbing over some scattered driftwood, trying to gain access to the grasses beyond. He began to ride toward her as she gingerly stepped over the broken ground. With the sound of the horse's hooves muffled by the sand, he came up behind her undetected.

In the last seconds, her weary mind heard him, but she was too tired to run and too late to react. She merely clutched at the arm that circled her waist and pulled her up. He drew the horse to a halt so he could settle her before him.

Alex sensed her fatigue and temporary truce. She wasn't giving him the war, but was relinquishing the battle. Deciding to wait for another time to scold her for her temper, he silently started their short journey back to Casa del Verde.

Chapter 7

They were nearly halfway to their destination before either spoke. She was silent because she had nothing to say, and Alex because he was too busy enjoying the feel of her in his arms. He had glanced down at the chestnut head beneath his chin when they started the ride and had been enchanted ever since.

From his vantage point he could watch the rise and fall of her breasts above the neckline of her lacy camisole without being reprimanded. She hadn't bothered to look at him, but he knew she was aware of the pressure of his arms against the sides of her breasts by how hard she tried to keep herself from touching him.

They might have remained silent if a breeze hadn't carried a wisp of her hair against his cheek. He swallowed a threatening groan and took hold of the strand to draw it down over her shoulder. The heat coming from the rounded softness of her body was greater than it should have been. Disregarding her indignant draw of breath, he laid his hand fully on her shoulder.

"Take your hand off me!" she ordered stiffly.

He halted the horse and turned her enough to be able to examine her more closely. "How long were you running around the beach half-naked?" He began to pull his shirt from the waistband of his pants and undo the buttons.

"What are you doing?" She didn't think she

could endure another romp with him. It was all she could do to remain upright in his arms as they rode. Between the steady beat of his heart against her back and the rhythm of the horse, all she wanted to do was curl against him and sleep.

As he finished removing his shirt, Breanna tried to leap from the horse's back. Alex grabbed her and held her tightly to keep her from falling.

"Sit still! I'm not about to ravish you on horseback!" He chuckled and began to wrap her in his shirt. "Although, if you don't stop wiggling that firm bottom of yours, I won't be responsible for what happens."

Breanna ceased her struggles immediately. "That's the second time you've accused me of something I haven't done and I don't like it! If you think—"

"Shut up, Breanna," he ordered. "I'm only trying to help you. You've taken too much sun today. You're starting to burn."

She had felt the tightening of her skin, but had never thought about sunburn. She became more receptive to his ministrations after that and slipped her arms into his shirt when he told her to. It hung in great folds, and she had to struggle with the sleeves to free her hands.

"Better?" he inquired, resuming the forward motion of the horse.

Breanna nodded tersely, ashamed of herself for her earlier thoughts. "Yes. Thank you, Mr. King. I . . . I'd forgotten how long it has been since I've enjoyed the sun. I should have been more careful."

Alex leaned forward until his mouth was at her ear. "Don't you think you could call me Alex after all we've been to each other?" he teased.

Forgetting her concession to civility, Breanna tried to pull free of his arms. She would have fallen if not for his quick reaction but, this time, she intended to remain angry.

"If you don't hold still you'll—"

"If you would stop making innuendos I'd—"

In her indignation, Breanna had twisted her body so that her hands were spread on Alex's bare chest and his were pressed to her back. The tremor that ripped through his mighty frame clearly conveyed the effect she had on him.

Wishing they were anywhere but on a well-traveled road, Alex broke the trance between them. "You really should think about joining our cause, Breanna. You're a natural-born rebel."

"I've always believed in a free California, Mr. King," she said icily as she turned to glare ahead. "It's you I won't join!" She felt his arms tense. Her voice remaining brittle, she said, "Now if you will take me home, I will not give you any more trouble."

She had thrown up her defensive wall again. It sent a flash of anger surging through him. He knew he would get nowhere antagonizing her, but he couldn't resist one last comment.

"Trouble is the last thing you're going to give me, Miss Sullivan!" He knew his tone implied a dual meaning but he suspected she would refrain from asking him to clarify it. For the first time, she did exactly as he expected.

Not another word was exchanged until they entered the courtyard of Casa del Verde. Alex dismounted and offered his hands to Breanna. She wanted to refuse but, not being astride, her only other choice was to jump. Atop the huge mount, she knew she could harm herself if she tried. Reluctantly, she placed her hands on his bronzed shoulders and felt his hands circle her waist.

It was too much for Alex to resist. Rather than lower her to the ground, he held her high against him. He looked up and saw the fire in her eyes, and gave her a slow, crooked grin as he let her slide down the length of him.

Breanna could feel the muscles in his shoulders

bunching beneath her hands even as the corded strength of his thighs brushed her own. There was a sensual quality to the slow movement she couldn't deny. Their eyes met. For one shameless moment she found herself wanting him to kiss her, touch her, return her to the world of sensation she had found only in his arms.

Alex knew her thoughts. They were evident in the way she stayed pressed to him despite the fact that her feet had touched the ground. Proof was in her rapid breathing and the quiver of her lips. Lips that were begging to be kissed!

He responded to her silent plea before she could change back into a spitfire, and took full possession of her mouth. For a brief moment he tasted her surrender and reveled in the wonder of it, but it didn't last.

As his tongue traced the inside of her lip, he touched a chord of passion that brought back her fears. He was capable of controlling her if she gave in to that passion. Stiffening, she tried to break the spell he was weaving.

"That was the kiss you still owed me, Breanna," he said calmly to cover the frustration raging in him. "And I'm still not sure if I'm dealing with a woman or a curious child."

Breanna flashed him a contemptuous glare and tried to walk away, but he wrapped his fingers around her arm to haul her back.

"I'm not through with you yet, *mí amante*."

Breanna tried in vain to disengage his hold. "I'm not your lover!" she cried out and sunk her nails into his hand. Her reward was to be yanked hard against him to receive a punishing kiss, one that proved his superior strength and his possession of her.

"So far you have succeeded in making promises of passion you have not kept," he said in a gravelly voice when he lifted his mouth from hers.

"Someday, Breanna, I will not stop until you keep them."

Stepping back the instant his hands loosened their grip on her, she wiped her lips with the back of her hand. "The only promise I make you, Mr. King, is that you'd be the last man I'd let make love to me!" Tipping her chin defiantly when he sniffed in reply, she felt her distress intensify when she saw the smirk on his face.

"I'll be the *only* man to make love to you, Breanna."

"Damn you!" she cried and ran to the house.

Heather sat perched on the side of Breanna's bed. She was thinking of the scene she had witnessed earlier. She'd give anything to know what was really going on between Breanna and Alex.

"Life has certainly become exciting since you've gotten home, and it's only been two days."

"You mean a rebellion and Papa's absence weren't enough for you?" Breanna replied as she ran a soapy sponge over her tender shoulder.

"Well, that was nothing compared to thinking you were lying hurt or dead somewhere, then seeing you ride in with Alex, and both of you are only half-dressed!" She saw Breanna flinch but went on. "Why, if Rosa had been home and seen you, you'd be preparing for your wedding this very moment."

The sponge splashed in the tub where Breanna threw it. "I told you, Heather. It wasn't what it looked like."

Heather thought of the way Alex held Breanna after helping her off the horse. She had seen the look on his face when he kissed her and witnessed Breanna's attempt to flee. Then there was that second kiss and their exchange. Oh, it was exactly what it looked like. Alex was trying his best to seduce Breanna and she was weakening, even as she fought it.

A knock at Breanna's bedroom door forestalled Heather's next question. She opened it to see Millie standing there.

"Good timing, Millie." Heather laughed. "You've finally caught her where she won't go running off!"

"Millie!" Breanna smiled, waving her in. "I'm so sorry I've been so neglectful. I—"

"She's been too busy being chased over the countryside in her undergarments."

"Heather!" Breanna threw the wet sponge at her sister. "Go away!"

Millie laughed at the exchange and watched Heather make a hasty retreat. "Does she always tease you like that?" she asked, taking a chair in the corner of the room after handing Breanna her sponge.

"Unfortunately, yes." Breanna chuckled, glad to see her friend. "But I mean it, Millie. I do owe you an apology. I drag you halfway around the world, then abandon you without even seeing to your comforts."

"My comforts have been seen to very well, Breanna," Millie said. "And that's why I wanted to see you." She was a little nervous, but the matter needed clarifying. "When you asked me to come with you, you said it was a job, but you've treated me more like a friend than an employee."

Breanna smiled warmly. "You are my friend, Millie."

"Thank you, but ... well, I don't know if I'm supposed to work for you here or if I need to look for work someplace else."

"Good Lord," Breanna said. "I certainly have messed things up for you, haven't I?"

"Oh, no, Breanna!" Millie exclaimed. "The trip was wonderful. My room here is a regular guest room. I've met Paul. There's been—"

"Paul?" Breanna interrupted. "Oh, yes. The young hand." Her smile faded, alarming Millie.

"Don't you like Paul?"

"What? Yes, I . . . Millie, I don't even know Paul," she said, relaxing when she saw the relief on Millie's face. "I was thinking about someone . . . something else." Shaking off the effect the momentary thought of Alex was having, she continued, "Now, let's get one thing settled. You tell me what you want to do. You have a hundred dollars coming for the trip." She saw Millie's eyes grow wide. It took her six months to make that much in Boston.

"Then, if you don't mind, I'd like to help out in the stable."

"The stable?" Breanna nearly choked.

Millie nodded. "Paul takes care of the animals, and he said he could teach me about them."

So, Breanna thought, it was Paul who was keeping her at Casa del Verde! "Then, by all means, you have the job."

"Oh, thank you!" Millie beamed, leaping to her feet. "I'll go tell him right away." She ran to the door and turned back. "You've made my life wonderful, Breanna. I'll never forget it, and neither will Paul."

In a flurry, she was gone, leaving Breanna alone with her thoughts. Would that her life was as easy as Millie's. A simple task and a man who was kind; was that so much to ask for?

Leaning her head back on the rim of the tub, she thought of King. The man was proving to be more than she could cope with. He was infuriating. No matter how she defended herself, he looked upon her as no more than a conquest. Of course, the way she responded to him gave him the idea she would be an easy one.

Closing her eyes, she conjured an image of him. Though very attractive, he certainly wasn't the handsomest man she'd ever seen. In fact, he rather reminded her of a Spanish pirate with his darkly tanned skin and scarred cheek. All he needed was a cutlass and a ship beneath his feet. A chuckle escaped her. He already had the *Rainbow*. What better proof that he was a blackhearted pirate.

In her mind's eye, she saw him standing on its deck, his feet braced, the wind ruffling his black hair. He would be raiding the coast, perhaps even carrying her off . . . She sat up, shaking off the image. She didn't need fantasy to make him a rogue. He did well enough on his own.

By his own admission he was playing a dangerous game. What bothered her was why he felt it necessary to keep her from becoming involved. He'd told her at the beach she would make a fine rebel. Why couldn't he see she really would? Was it the old masculine problem of dealing with a capable woman? Maybe he was trying to seduce her, hoping to scare her off.

The water had cooled considerably, and she stepped out of the tub. Once dry, she slipped on a soft shift and sat before the mirror to brush out her hair. As she removed the pins, she thought of the way Alex looked at her. She couldn't help wondering if it was all an act or if he did desire her. Slowly she examined her image in the glass.

She was attractive, but certainly not a beauty. She was too short to be statuesque and too tall to be petite. Her eyes were too big, she thought. They failed miserably at being coy and tended to reveal her emotions to any observer. Had King known from her eyes that he touched some chord of her womanhood yet undiscovered? He'd called her a fraud, accused her of teasing him, yet in her innocence she could not fathom why.

The only thing she could conclude was that she was as great a threat and a challenge to Alex King as he was to her. That alone would make them attractive to each other, but it wasn't enough. When she found someone to love her as she was, only then would she give herself to him. Alex might stir her passions, but he would never have her heart.

"How'd it go?" John asked when Alex joined him later that day near the deserted mission.

"Not bad, John." Alex grinned, rubbing at the nail marks on the back of his hand. "But it could have been better."

John laughed. "That's obvious! You weren't gone long enough!"

Grinning good-naturedly at John's teasing, he shrugged. "There'll be another time, I promise you." He settled on the ground at John's side and poured a cup of coffee from a battered, blackened pot. He would have liked to lean back and think over all that had transpired between him and Breanna, but he knew there were other matters that needed attention.

Actually, Alex respected John's primary role in the mission. He had been given a great task by President Polk and was determined it would be successful. John had been dubbed the Pathfinder on previous mapmaking expeditions, and even the Mexican government knew and respected his exploits, but this time his expedition was just a cover. His real mission was to unite the Americans in California while charting the movements of Mexican troops and their forts. In the event that the Mexicans refused to relinquish the disputed land holdings for a fair price, the well-informed American forces would be prepared to act. To protect himself and the mission, it was imperative that no one know of John's connections to the gathering rebels. It could mean war before Polk was ready.

Alex was, therefore, a crucial link between John and the Mexican authorities and was one of only a handful of men who knew John's real purpose for being there. He'd been groomed to align himself with the local Mexican powers to facilitate

John's invitation to map California. With his holdings in the north and Monterey, he had cause to move about without arousing suspicion.

Another in the network of Americans making preparations was Breanna's father, Patrick Sullivan. He'd been assigned to train men in the north so they would go undetected for as long as possible. It was Patrick's letter that was the reason for this meeting.

"Everything is going well with our troops in Sonoma but Patrick said he could use a few more of those guns you had stolen."

Alex nodded. "I'll contact Hank as soon as possible and see he gets them."

John scratched the bridge of his nose and chuckled. "That was quite an idea you had about burying them in coffins to be dug up later. I'll have to remember to write that into my report."

"Don't do it on my account." Alex laughed. "I don't need any more ribbing about 'ghost' rifles!" The two men relaxed a moment, then Alex asked if Patrick had anything else to say.

"Well, he did mention his daughters. He hasn't received word yet that Breanna is back, but he said we could do anything we felt was necessary to keep them from interfering. All he asked was that we use good judgment." He looked at the shirtless Alex. "You do have good judgment with Breanna, don't you?"

Alex lowered his eyes. "I'm not sure. One minute I want to take her in my arms and the next I could beat her!"

"You could just marry the girl. That way you could haul her north to your ranch and hold her there with no repercussions, no matter what you did to her."

"Marry! No, thank you! I like my freedom. I don't want to be shackled to anyone, but, even if I did, it wouldn't be to a fury in skirts!" Pausing a moment to digest something else, he grinned. "But, as to hauling her off, I'll keep that in mind."

John sighed. "Just remember we all have to make concessions in war—and there will be a war."

"No one knows that better than I," Alex replied seriously. "And you know I'd take any risk and give all I have to see this territory free."

"Then you would marry her?" John asked, his own grin hidden. He didn't want Alex to know he thought it was a good idea. It would start him worrying, but the girl was volatile. She could be a problem. In fact, if she endangered the mission, it might be their only alternative, if Alex was willing.

"I'll cross that bridge when I come to it, John," Alex answered noncommittally. All John could do was nod in agreement.

While Alex went north to see about getting the guns to Patrick, Breanna was left with time on her hands. For several days she was content to rest and spend time with Heather and Millie. She was introduced to Paul and found him a pleasant-looking young man who was obviously enchanted by Millie. That she was sweet on him, there was no doubt.

Breanna even managed to spend time with Rosa and fill her in on the highlights of her trip. It had been difficult, since the older woman kept dozing off. Hers was a token position of respect now that Heather and Breanna were grown, as was obvious by the amount of time she spent in her room resting, but she still was a dear.

However, very soon Breanna began to feel restless. She spent hours strolling about the land that once was her heritage and now was only a place for her to stay until her father returned. She hadn't really realized that until after she told Millie she could have the job with Paul, and was later informed it was all right with Alex!

Thoughts of Alex soon turned to thoughts of the pending rebellion and the role her father played in it. If only she knew where he was, she would go to him and have her questions answered. Maybe then she could feel useful and less frustrated.

After several days of contemplating what must be going on around her without her knowledge, she knew she had to locate her father. With so many of his old friends gone, too, she didn't know how to proceed, but decided to start in Monterey.

"There you are!" Heather said, striding briskly toward her sister. "I was looking for you."

"News?" Breanna asked.

"No, just thought you seemed edgy and might want to join a few of us on a picnic."

Breanna shook her head. "No, thank you. I was just thinking I might go into town."

An alarm went off in Heather's head. "Why?" she asked, uneasy with this sudden decision.

"I just thought there might be someone who knows something about Papa."

"Bree, stay out of it." She saw Breanna's eyes flare. "Alex told you we have to wait."

"Alex isn't my master!" Breanna snapped.

"But he is Papa's friend. He knows that your snooping would be dangerous to him."

Breanna whirled about in frustration. "A daughter's concern for her father isn't snooping."

"It is if she's doing it because she's too stubborn to believe Alex King."

Breanna winced. Heather had hit a very sore spot. It was her distrust of Alex and his motives that made her want to find their father. She needed to hear from his own lips what she suspected was the truth.

"I promise you, Heather, I won't cause any trouble." Heather rolled her eyes, knowing better. "I'll just look around and listen. What damage can that do?"

Heather knew all too well the trouble Breanna could get into with her sharp tongue and sharper wit. "I'll go with you," she said, hoping she could keep Breanna in line.

"No," Breanna said firmly. "Two of us would cause more attention. Besides, I've been away. It will seem natural that I'm in town to see the changes and to see old friends."

There was a certain logic to that which Heather feared. Whenever Breanna had a logical solution, there was bound to be a snag. "All right, Bree, but I swear if you get into anything, I'm telling Alex it was all your fault!"

"Thanks a lot, *chica!*" she snapped. "I'm delighted to see you trust him more than you trust me!"

"He wouldn't be going into town if he was told otherwise."

Not wanting to waste time arguing, Breanna swept past her sister to prepare for her outing, leaving Heather shaking her head in frustration.

Breanna met a few old acquaintances as she strolled along the town's wooden walkway. She had to admit it was much nicer than dragging her skirts through the dust the way she used to. Another thing she had to admit, albeit grudgingly, was the fact that Alexander King had been good for Monterey.

It was prospering. She saw it in the enlarged general store and the addition of a new dress shop. Where there had been a handful of merchants before she left, now there were dozens. Of course, all the growth meant many new faces, faces she didn't know if she could trust.

Deciding it was a fool's errand to come into town after all, she headed for the dress shop. Heather had been right, and a peace token was needed. In fact, she thought, it might be nice to buy a few things for herself and maybe a gift for Millie.

A commotion at the end of town drew her attention before she could slip inside the shop. She strained to see if she could distinguish what the problem was. Several of the people strolling the streets began to find doors to enter. It occurred to her they were hiding.

Within mere minutes, the streets were empty but for her and a half-dozen soldiers in Mexican uniforms. Or so she thought until she saw an old man trying to rise from the ground. One of the soldiers intentionally tripped him, arousing Breanna's sense of justice.

Since no one was around to help she realized that if anything was to be done, she would have to do it. Spying a buggy, she made her way toward it as quickly as she could. The old man who had been tripped cried out just as she was reaching for the horsewhip.

"Stop it!" she ordered, cracking the whip over the head of the nearest soldier.

Six stunned faces whirled to face her, several even drew pistols to use against the threat, but the faces soon dissolved into varying degrees of smiles. Several crude comments were exchanged before they returned to their amusement.

"I said stop!" she cried again when one soldier kicked the old man. It was apparent they were going to ignore her, deeming her more of a joke than a threat. Drawing a deep breath, she snapped the whip again, circling the raised wrist of one soldier. With a firm jerk of her own, she spun him about.

"Get away from him!" she demanded of the others. She cracked the whip on the hand of one who was reaching for his pistol, eliciting a yowl. Their faces sobered. They realized she knew exactly what she was doing with that whip.

"Step back, all of you!" she said in perfect Spanish. There was a pause she didn't like. "I said back!" The whip whizzed close enough to cut the sleeve of one without touching his skin. Immediately, the six formed a line several paces from the old man. She moved cautiously toward him.

"Are you all right?" she asked, never taking her eyes off the soldiers.

"*Sí*, señorita," the man said, slowly gaining his feet.

"What has he done wrong?" she inquired of the soldiers.

"I did nothing, señorita," the old man replied, "but get in their way when they left the saloon."

Breanna scowled at the soldiers. "So you stoop to beating old men, do you?" She was pleased the men looked ashamed of their deeds. "How do you think your superiors would feel if word got out their troops were drunken ruffians?" They began to shuffle their feet. "Go on! Get out of here!"

The men left, falling over one another in their haste. She was tempted to snap the whip one more time, just for effect, but thought better of it. She was already drawing a crowd. Coiling the whip, she turned to the old man.

"Go home, señor." She smiled kindly. "Everything will be all right now."

The old man took her hand and bowed over it. "*Gracias*, Madonna," he said, bestowing an honor upon her with the name. "*Muchas gracias!*"

Still smiling, Breanna watched him run to several people who were surely his family. They beamed at her, and she waved at them. Turning to go back to the buggy to return the whip, she stopped and stared.

A large number of townspeople stood watching her. As she prepared to move away from them, someone began to applaud. To her stunned surprise, the entire gathering started in. She could hear calls of "Madonna" above the ruckus. Her face went red. For someone who was not going to make any trouble, she certainly was the cause of this scene.

Chapter 8

The gray sky and falling rain matched Breanna's mood. She had spent the last three days since the fiasco in town worrying about someone relaying the tale to Heather. She was sure her sister would be furious at her for drawing so much attention to herself, but she couldn't have helped it. There was no way she could have ignored the situation.

Of course, the greatest part of her agitation was in wondering what King would do when he returned. Through the grapevine she knew he had left town shortly after their encounter on the beach. Afraid that same grapevine would let him know about her escapades, she'd spent several sleepless nights.

It wasn't that she was afraid of King. She wasn't! She just didn't want him thinking she had made another childish mistake. For some reason, she hated his thinking of her as a child. Not that she really wanted him to think of her at all. It was simply a matter of her Sullivan pride that he respect her as a mature, intelligent woman.

"Bree, are you in there?" Heather called from the hall into the dark library.

"Yes, *chica*," she replied.

Heather entered, frowning at the darkness, and walked toward a lamp in the corner. "What are you doing in here?" she asked, spying Breanna at the window.

"Just watching the rain," Breanna said with a small smile. "It's soothing."

"This just came for you," she said, turning on the lamp and holding out a letter. As Breanna approached to take it, she added, "It bears the seal of General Guillermo."

Breanna's hand stopped in midair, then she took the missive. "I don't know the general," she immediately announced to ease Heather's furrowed brow.

"Then why would he be writing you?"

Shrugging, Breanna broke the seal and unfolded the single sheet of heavy linen paper. "It's an invitation!" she exclaimed. "He's having a ball to celebrate his birthday and wants us to come."

"Us? Why would he ask us? I don't like it, Bree," Heather said, biting her lip. "He's up to something. I've only met Guillermo once. He joined Papa and me when we went to town to dine. He's a very attractive man, but Papa told me to stay away from him. He has a reputation with the ladies."

"Surely that's not enough to distrust him," Breanna said with her usual fairness.

"No, but there's more. We think he suspects Papa's involvement with the rebellion."

"We?"

Heather nodded. "Yes, Alex and I."

Breanna stood, needing to move far enough from her sister to hide her reactions. "How well do you know Mr. King?" she asked, keeping the hint of dismay she felt from her voice. It wasn't jealousy, she reasoned, just concern for her sister's safety.

A grin lifted the corners of Heather's mouth, but it went unseen. "Not as well as you seem to," she teased, "but well enough to have spent some time listening to him and Papa."

The goading was not lost on Breanna, but she chose to ignore it. "So you think we've been invited because of something the general suspects," she mused, trying to get back on track.

"Why else would he invite us? He's never met you and I'm not his type." Heather noticed there was no reply, and she turned in her chair to glance back at Breanna. "Bree, *is* there a reason he might want to meet you?"

"No! I . . . I mean, I can't imagine any."

She was too nervous. Heather knew she was hiding something. "When is this ball?"

"The middle of September," Breanna said, her voice sounding distant.

"And will we go?"

Breanna sighed, wondering if this was a good time to tell Heather about what had happened in town, yet still hoping the ruckus was forgotten by now. Choosing to take her chances, she smiled and shrugged her shoulders. "Yes, *chica*, we'll go because I don't really think we have a choice!"

"I'm going to wring that pretty neck of hers!" Alex fumed as he paced the confines of his room. "How could she have been so incredibly stupid?"

"Take it easy, Alex," John said as he poured two drinks. "From what I've heard she's become a veritable heroine." Handing Alex his drink, he took a sip of his own while Alex continued to glare. "They've even been calling her the Madonna."

Alex groaned and gulped his drink in one swallow. He slammed his glass down the instant it was empty. "All she had to do was stay at the hacienda," he seethed. "Keep out of sight and out of mind, but no! Not Breanna! *She* has to go and save an old man from six—*six* of Guillermo's soldiers!"

John shrugged. "Seems to me you should be proud of her for what she did."

"I am proud of her!" Alex said harshly. "I just want to beat her for drawing Guillermo's attention to herself!"

Taking a chair, John rubbed the smile off his

face. So that was the real problem. Alex didn't like the idea of the handsome young general knowing about Breanna. Alex was jealous.

"There will be lots of people at the party, Alex. You and I included. Surely he won't notice her among so many."

"Huh!" Alex snorted, raking back his hair with splayed fingers. "You can bet that since the tale of her antics is all over town, he'll make damned sure he meets her." Stomping to the buffet, he poured another drink.

"If I didn't know you better, Alex, I'd say you're jealous," John said in an amused voice.

Alex glared back at him. "What the hell are you talking about? I'm not jealous! It's just that she's Patrick's daughter. I'd worry the same about any of the men's kin." He took a slim cheroot from a tin and lit it.

Watching Alex roll the thin cigar back and forth between his fingers, John coughed to disguise his mirth. "I'm sure you would," he finally said when he could sound serious.

"You're damned right I would!" Taking his cigar and drink with him, he sprawled in a chair, yet he didn't relax. "The only reason this has me so upset is because of the trouble she can cause. She has a knack for it, John." He brooded a moment, then proceeded to list her flaws. "She's stubborn to a fault and too proud of her intelligence to think of the consequences of what she does."

He rose and paced. "Patrick must have been mad to teach her how to use a whip."

John stood and placed a hand on Alex's shoulder, stilling him. "Even women need to be able to protect herself, Alex," he said gently, trying to make him see that it wasn't such a sin for her to wield a weapon.

"Herself, yes," Alex agreed, "but not the world, John. She might well have done more damage than good with this one."

"Surely you don't think anyone is going to think a woman is involved in our politics?" John asked, his tone one of surprise. "Why, it would be preposterous!"

"It would be right up Breanna's alley," Alex said. "If she's allowed to get away with this, she'll be insisting on joining the troops next." John laughed heartily. "I mean it, John. You don't know how stubborn she can be. If she takes it into her head to help the cause, there'll be no stopping her."

John sobered. "*You* could stop her."

Alex thought of the idea they'd already discussed. It seemed most likely that he would have to intervene, and soon. Breanna was overstepping her bounds. If he didn't stop her, she could bring the entire Mexican army into California either to protect themselves from her or to court her!

"I'll speak to her the night of the party," Alex said after some thought. "Should she appear to be a problem, I'll take care of it."

"And in the meantime?"

"In the meantime, I'll speak with Heather and keep an eye on Breanna."

John was convinced Alex wanted to keep more than an eye on the beautiful vixen. It was possible her antics could do more to bring them together than anything else could. Alex loved a challenge, and there was none better than Breanna Sullivan.

The night was exceptionally warm, and Breanna's sleep had been troubled. She rinsed out a cloth in cool water to bathe her face. With the heat of summer lasting into the night, she frequently found herself strolling through the garden for some cool air.

Wearing only a soft shift, she wrapped a shawl about her shoulders and left the room for the patio. She found great pleasure in the lush gardens at night. In fact, it was the only real peace she'd known since those moments on the beach before Alex intruded on her solitude.

Once again, he invaded her thoughts. She was sure he was to blame for her restlessness. He was still an enigma. There was no black and white where he was concerned. Everything was shades of gray that seemed to haunt her. One thing she was relatively sure of, though, was that he knew about the incident in Monterey.

It occurred to her the first time she asked for a horse that she was being followed. After that, there was always someone close by. There was no doubt in her mind that the orders to watch her came from *him*. The only times she felt truly alone were when she made these late-night strolls.

Wishing to hold any thoughts of Alex King at bay, she sighed and sat beside the fountain, trailing her fingers in the cool water. To occupy her mind, she tried to recall the dream that had awakened her many of these past nights. No matter how she tried, she couldn't remember details. All she knew was that she would awaken feeling restless; her skin would be damp, her breathing rapid. She rather thought it was some sort of nightmare, intruding in her sleep and leaving her anxious for something.

A rustling in the foliage behind her disturbed her, and she tried to peer into the dark to discover the cause of it. There seemed to be an insufficient breeze to stir the leaves. Besides, it sounded more like dry leaves being stepped upon.

"Who's there?" Breanna called, standing and drawing her shawl tightly around her to still her sudden trembling as a shadow moved away from the trees.

"Can't you sleep, Breanna?" The familiar voice seemed to fill the night as Alex stepped onto the granite patio.

"What are you doing here at this hour?" she whispered harshly.

Alex placed a foot on the fountain wall and leaned his arm across his raised thigh. "Just checking my men." His eyes caressed her, taking in her long, wild tresses and the thin cover of her shift. "And the rest of my property."

Breanna could almost feel the raspy quality of his whisper and looked at the ground in confusion.

"You didn't answer my question, Breanna." He straightened and stepped closer to her, enough so he could see the vague outline of her features in the dim moonlight. "You should be snug in bed." He placed a finger beneath her chin and forced her to look up at him. "Preferably my bed."

There was a dreamlike quality to this whole scene, Breanna thought. She could feel a pleasant tingling on her flesh where his fingers touched her and she knew he had to be an illusion, a phantom of the night. There were no thoughts of distrust, no words of dissension, only a gentle closeness. It had to be a dream!

Breanna lifted her hand slowly and tentatively touched the line of his jaw. His arm dropped to his side. He was letting her explore him without hindrance or threat. Tipping her head, she moved to lightly trace the scar on his cheek.

"You're really here," she said softly. "This isn't a dream."

"No, Breanna." Alex took her hand from his face and placed it on his chest over his heart. "I'm not a dream. I'm a flesh and blood man. A man who desires you terribly." His voice rumbled from deep in his throat, and his hands moved up her arms to slip beneath her hair and caress the slender column of her neck.

Breanna swallowed hard and pressed her cheek against his outstretched arm. "But if you are real, we'll argue and I'll have to hate you," she reasoned, feeling herself drawn to him. "I'd rather you were a dream for a little while." It was madness and she knew it, yet she had to steal this moment to discover what it was about Alex King that haunted her.

"So be it, doe eyes." His lips brushed her brow and lingered at her temple to inhale her sweet fragrance. "And you will be my dream come true." Alex drew her into his arms, holding her tenderly and brushing his fingers through her hair. He wanted her to take the initiative, to be the aggressor so she would have no regrets.

Breanna leaned back over his arm and looked into his eyes. She wanted him to kiss her. Why didn't he? Maybe since it was her dream, she had to tell him.

"Please," she whispered, willing him to understand.

"No, *mí amante*. If you want to be kissed, you must do it." There was a teasing tremor in his words, and he hoped he wouldn't break the mood with what he was making her do, but he soon knew there was nothing to worry about. She slipped her soft hand up to circle his neck and draw his lips to hers.

The tides of passion roared in her ears and the stars became blinding behind her closed lids. Never had she felt such wonder, such exhilaration from a single act. She stood on her tiptoes to get closer to the source of her pleasure and to press up against his raw strength. She felt a growing hardness against her stomach. She didn't exactly know why, but it thrilled her and gave her a sense of power over him at last.

Alex sensed her exaltation and reveled in the way she shyly touched her small tongue to his lips. He couldn't explain the change in her, nor could he believe it was more than an experiment for her; all he knew was that he was becoming desperate with the ache to possess her.

Drawing his lips from hers, Alex pressed his mouth to her throat and groaned. "Breanna." He swallowed hard. "Unless you wish me to take you to your bed to finish this, we must stop now." His breathing was harsh to her ear and, regrettably, reality returned.

She carefully disengaged his arms and stepped back slowly, avoiding his eyes. "All dreams come to an end." She sighed softly. Turning from him, she paused. "Good night," she whispered, and walked away.

Gripping his hands into tight fists, he turned his back so he didn't have to watch her. "Yes, Breanna," he rasped. "Go quickly to your safe bed or, as God is my witness, I'll not be responsible for what happens."

When she heard such pain in his voice, she turned and looked back at him. There was magic in the night, but the light of day—and the consequences should she allow him to go further—would come soon enough.

"Good night," she said again, returning to the house. She didn't know he had turned back to watch her flight, or that he remained there for long minutes after she was gone.

"Good night, doe eyes," he said softly in the empty night. "I don't know what your game was, but you must have won because I am in agony."

He rejoined the shadows, wondering why she had felt the need to experiment with him this night. She had so distracted him, he'd forgotten how angry he was with her. But who wouldn't have forgotten? Breanna was a beautiful woman. A moment in her arms could confuse the strongest of men.

An image of her in General Guillermo's arms appeared unbidden in his mind, making him come up short. Would she stoop to playing one of these charming games with him? Would she go further if it was to save her father or herself? Rage took over where desire had been.

"Not if I can help it!" he whispered angrily into the darkness.

Sleep came quickly once she found her bed. She had stood watching him from her window until long after he was gone, wondering why he had paused. Once he was out of sight, she wondered if he had ever really been there. Carefully, she touched her lips with trembling fingers. They were moist and sensitive. Yes, he'd been there and he had kissed her.

Her mind rebelled against the half-truth. It was she who had kissed him. He had given her the chance to refuse, but she hadn't. In truth, she had wanted to kiss him. She had wanted his arms around her, keeping her safe and warm, even if it was just for a few brief moments.

For those moments he was not an antagonist. He was just a man. She was not his adversary. She was just a woman. She couldn't explain it; she didn't want to try. She just wanted to close her eyes and remember.

The day of Guillermo's ball arrived, dawning bright and clear. Breanna felt it was a good omen. She woke early and stretched like a cat on her bed. The house was still quiet and the air cool. It felt good to be alive, she thought, rising to greet the day.

A quick wash would suffice for the morning. She would bathe later before dressing for the fiesta. She was filled with energy this morning and thought to dress so she could get in a brisk walk before the others rose.

When she reached for her shawl at the end of the bed, her hand froze upon it. There was a vibrancy to it, as if it held some secret. Closing her eyes, she wrapped it about her shoulders. For a fleeting moment she was wrapped in warm, strong arms.

"Enough!" she cried aloud, forcing the memory of the night before from her mind. Dawn had restored her sanity. She'd been foolish in the darkness, but everyone was entitled to be a fool sometimes. It wouldn't happen again, she was sure, yet there was a lingering doubt deep inside her.

The brightening sun dispelled her apprehension and restored her to peace. Dew kissed the foliage and left it clean and fresh. The air smelled sweet. It prompted her to take full strides across the garden to the lush pasture beyond. It dawned on her as she strolled that she wasn't being followed.

She'd grown accustomed to someone shadowing her on her morning walks. It was almost disappointing to know she was alone. Recalling Alex's comment that he had come to see his men, she wondered if he had told them it was no longer necessary to watch her. Perhaps after their interlude he considered her less of a threat.

A grumbling stomach announced it was time to return to the house for breakfast. Dismissing thoughts of Alex or what motivated him, she made her way back. As she neared the barn, she heard a giggle from within. Curiosity made her pause. It sounded like a low voice, some more soft laughter, then silence. Realizing she was intruding, she continued on.

"Breanna!" Millie called as she passed the open doorway.

"Morning, Millie." Breanna smiled, waiting for the other woman to catch up to her. There was a softness on Millie's pretty face she hadn't seen before. She looked almost as if she had just risen, yet that wasn't possible unless she'd taken to sleeping in the barn. "What has you up so early?"

A light flush covered Millie's cheeks, and Breanna noticed a piece of hay in her unbound hair. Nonchalantly, she reached to pull it from her tresses. "Whatever have you been up to?" She laughed at the higher color that touched Millie's face when she held up the straw for her to see.

"Do you remember when we talked about the kind of men we would like to marry someday?"

"Yes." Breanna nodded. "I remember."

Millie smiled shyly. "Well, I've met mine."

Whirling to face her, Breanna laughed brightly. "Millie! That's wonderful!" she said, hugging her tightly. "I assume the somebody is Paul?"

"Oh, yes!" Millie said dreamily.

"Is he kind, like you wanted?"

"Very kind, Breanna," she said, her dimples flashing in her cheeks.

Breanna's face softened. "And do you love him, Millie?"

"With all my heart," she replied with no hesitation.

"When is the happy event to take place?"

"In two weeks," she said. "Will you come, Breanna? Will you stand up with me? I'd be terribly proud if you did."

Breanna smiled warmly. "I'd be honored, Millie." They hugged again. "Come on, let's go tell Heather the good news."

Millie pulled her hand free and gazed back at the barn. "You tell her." A wistful smile showed the path of her thoughts. "I'll go tell Paul you know."

Breanna chuckled and waved her hand. "Go ahead. I suppose if I was in love I'd rather be with him than with two women!" She stood for a moment watching Millie disappear into the barn. When the sound of male laughter reached her, she moved on.

Nearing the house, Breanna wondered if there was a man out there for her to cleave to and love. Would strong arms ever reach out for only her? Icy blue eyes filled her thoughts and strong hands seemed to caress her.

"Breanna!" Heather called from the door, driving away the illusion.

"Coming!" She pushed her fantasy aside. Alex King was not for her. They struck more sparks than flint. "You really are dreaming, girl," she said to herself.

"What?" Heather inquired, hearing her mumbling as she entered the patio.

"Nothing important, *chica*." She smiled. "Just a touch of the blarney."

Heather merely shrugged at the cryptic words and poured out two cups of coffee while listening to the happy news Breanna had to share.

The late afternoon was hectic with their preparations. It seemed this ball would be the social event of the year, according to Rosa. Everyone who was anyone for miles around would be there. Heather might have originally objected to going, but she was bubbling with excitement now that the prospect was at hand and chattering incessantly about who would be there and what they would be wearing.

Millie entered when Breanna had all her undergarments on, ready to do her coiffure. Drawing Breanna's hair up from a center part, she coiled it into a crown about her head and wove a strand of creamy pearls through the auburn tresses.

Since the coming evening would apparently be cool, Breanna chose a gown of soft hunter-green velvet. Ivory lace underlined the full cuffs of the tapered elbow-length sleeves and showed beneath the split front of the full skirt. She had always loved this gown but found herself scowling when she caught her reflection.

Never before had she realized the expanse of exposed flesh the deep, square neckline revealed. From the shoulders it dropped to trace the fullness of her breasts and hint at the shadowy valley between them.

Heather caught her unsuccessfully trying to pull up the suggestive neckline and couldn't resist teasing her.

"Are you planning on making a conquest tonight, Bree?"

"Of course not!" Breanna snapped, still yanking on the front of her bodice. "What ever made you ask that?"

"Well, you were going to discreetly look around Monterey and you used a whip. I just wondered if that gown was your weapon tonight."

"Who told you?" Breanna asked, her cheeks burning at the memory.

"Does it matter?"

Shaking her head slowly, Breanna sighed. "No, I guess it doesn't, but I hope the subject doesn't come up tonight. I'd rather everyone forget it."

Heather grinned wickedly. "Trust me, Bree. If you wear that gown, no one there will be thinking of the plight of an old man. They'll be much too busy trying to get a closer look at you!"

The expression on Breanna's face was anything but amused. "With your fascination with men and their appetites, why aren't you married?" she snapped, fastening a strand of pearls about her neck. She frowned deeply. They seemed to want to curve to the very spot she wished not to draw attention to.

Good-naturedly, Heather ignored her caustic sarcasm and smiled sweetly. "Because you're older and should be married first. Of course," Heather mumbled, "at the rate you're going, I'll be an old maid."

"Honestly, Heather!" Breanna turned from her reflection, deciding she didn't care how she looked. "It's not that I don't want to marry someday. It's just that I haven't found the man I want."

"Oh, I think you've found him. You just spend so much time fighting, you can't see what's right before your eyes." She blissfully left the room before the inevitable protest was forthcoming.

Breanna ran after her, refusing to let the issue lie. "You're mad!" she called after Heather. "I wouldn't have Alex King if he was the last man on this earth!"

Heather stopped and whirled to face her. "Then how did you know I meant Alex King?"

Breanna's mouth moved but no sound came out. Flustered by the logic, she was preparing a retort when Millie called that the carriage was ready. It saved her from arguing with Heather, but gave her cause to vent her fury in another direction. Emblazoned on the door of the carriage like a royal crest was the familiar "K."

Stomping to within inches of it with clenched hands and teeth, she turned to the driver standing by the horse. "I don't know who ordered this carriage, but get rid of it! I won't ride in . . . in *his* carriage!"

"Yes, you will," a deeply amused voice said from behind her. It brought her about in a huff.

Breanna was ready to wail her anger at his overbearing arrogance but her mouth closed with a snap when she caught the seductive exploration in his eyes. Like a caress, they touched her, and she splayed her hands across her chest to block his view.

"I have an excellent memory, Breanna. Your gesture is quite wasted." His mouth turned up at one corner. "I assure you there is no more exposed than when you wore only your camisole on the beach."

Warmth suffused Breanna's cheeks and she wanted to slap the lecherous grin from his face. She took a step toward him to do just that but was interrupted by Heather's bright voice.

"Alex, what a surprise to see you! What brought you out here?"

"I happen to own the place," he said with a

crooked smile. Heather's wide grin and Breanna's groan told him he was on the right track. "But I came to escort you and Breanna to the festivities."

"How thoughtful!" Heather said.

"I'm not going!" Breanna said and started back toward the house.

Grabbing Breanna's arm to stop her, Alex continued to speak to Heather as if hanging on to a struggling wildcat was nothing unusual. "I thought you would be more comfortable in my carriage."

Wanting to chuckle at Breanna's predicament, Heather also pretended nothing was amiss. "I'm sure we will be. Thank you."

Holding Breanna far enough at arm's length to avoid her foot, Alex offered his free hand to Heather and helped her to step into the carriage. She settled her aqua skirt and nodded her thanks.

"Breanna." He motioned for the door and swung her toward it. "Your carriage awaits."

As she tried futilely to pry her arm free, Breanna's fury grew. Still fuming over Heather's earlier remarks, she wanted to lash out at someone, and Alex was convenient.

"Go to hell!" she seethed. "I won't—"

"Tut, tut!" He shook his finger at her. "Try to remember you're supposed to be a grown lady tonight." His implication caused her to draw in her breath quickly. "Now, be a good girl and get in." He checked his pocket watch. "Or we'll be more than fashionably late."

"No! I told you, I'm not—oh!" Breanna cried out as Alex scooped her into his arms and deposited her aboard. He braced a strong arm across her thighs and gave her a stern look when he saw her eyeing the exit on the other side.

"Shut up, Breanna," he ordered firmly before she could say a word. He grinned at her slack jaw. Calling to the driver to begin their journey, he cast a sidelong glance at his guest. She had clamped her mouth closed and stiffly stared out the window, her body rigid in an effort to avoid any unnecessary contact with him.

Looking across to Heather, he winked.

It was bound to be a very entertaining night, Heather thought as she turned to see Breanna's barely controlled fury.

Chapter 9

The carriage cleared the boundary of Casa del Verde, and Alex decided it was time to have a few words with Breanna before they arrived at the party. With Heather as an ally, he was hoping she would listen but, considering her mood, he rather doubted it.

"I understand you made a spectacle of yourself in town while I was away," he began. "I meant to speak to you about it last night, but—"

"Last night!" Heather interrupted in surprise. She looked at Breanna and bit her lip. Her sister's cheeks were flaming. Seeing Alex's scowl, she remained silent, her grin in check.

"As I was saying," he went on. "Last night, I—"

"I didn't make a spectacle of myself!" Breanna spoke sharply, not wanting Alex to discuss the previous night.

Turning to face her, he shouted, "Then what would you call wielding a whip against a dozen soldiers?"

"Six soldiers, and there was no one else to help the poor old man."

"But a whip?"

"Would you have preferred that I took a pistol and shot them?"

"She could have, you know," Heather offered, receiving two warning scowls for her efforts.

"Don't you have any idea what you've done?"

122

Alex asked, resuming his conversation with Breanna.

Breanna sighed heavily. "I just don't see why everyone is so upset about this." She crossed her arms over her chest in a huff. "All I did was help someone, and you're making an issue out of it."

"All you did, my hot-tempered vixen, was to interest Guillermo in you. How long do you think it will be before the subject of Patrick comes up?"

Fear flashed in her eyes, but she refused to let him bully her. "If you think that I was invited tonight because of that little incident, you're mad. Besides, I'd never say anything that would harm my father."

Alex rubbed his brow. "You don't have to say anything, Breanna. If Guillermo decides you're an interesting conquest and, believe me"—his eyes fell to her bosom—"he will, he'll find out all he can about you." Leaning toward her for emphasis, he added, "And that *will* harm your father!"

Alex's words truly scared her. She had never dreamed that her escapade would lead to such a mess. Chewing at her lip, she tried to find some way to extricate herself from it. A thought took root, and she tried to consider it from all angles before airing it. She might have made an error in judgment once, but she wasn't going to let it happen again. Satisfied she had come up with a logical solution, she lifted her chin.

"I could turn the tables on him," she announced, proud of her plan.

Alex felt the blood rush from his head. He was afraid he knew what scheme she was hatching, but preferred to hear it from her before he reacted.

"What the hell does that mean?"

"It means I could get information from him instead of giving it to him."

Heather couldn't resist a stunned gasp, but it was nothing like the sound that rumbled from

Alex's throat. Undaunted by either of them, Breanna went on to detail her idea.

"It seems to me that no one would consider a woman capable of spying." She hunched her shoulders. "Look how shocked everyone is over my using a whip! They'd never expect—"

"Woman, are you out of your mind?" Alex asked in angry disbelief.

"You claim you're gathering information!" she shouted at him. "Why not me?"

Rolling his eyes, Alex fell back against the seat, his hand bracing his head. She was giving him a headache! He took a deep breath to still his desire to throttle her, then slowly blew it out.

"Breanna," he began carefully, "you are to stay out of this." Without looking, he knew she was not receptive to his order, but he refused to let her bad temper stop him. "This is not a game. We are not playing here. Men's lives are at stake, as is the future of California."

Rage, hot and roiling, flowed through Breanna's veins. He was doing it again. He was treating her like a child! Utterly indignant, she glared at him.

"From the first time we spoke you have given me no credence, but I know I am not incompetent. I can help and I will!" Though spoken softly, every word was enunciated clearly, causing Heather to flinch and Alex's face to go florid.

He knew it was useless to argue with her. Her stubborn streak could never respond to logic. He would have to handle it another way, another time. The last thing he needed was to be at odds with her when she met Guillermo. The general would like nothing better than to think it was a lover's quarrel and would have no qualms about solicitously offering his support to her.

"Very well," Alex said, hoping she would believe what he was about to say. "I'll speak with John, and we'll see what we can do." He caught the stunned expression on Heather's face and motioned carefully that she go along with what he was saying. To his relief, she understood and complied.

"Who's John?" Breanna inquired, a bit wary of his apparent concession to her plan.

"You'll meet him tonight." He looked out to see how close they were to Guillermo's hacienda. "He's my superior."

A shiver of excitement went down Breanna's spine. He really was considering her help! "I'll look forward to it," she replied, not wanting to give him an excuse to change his mind.

A glow that caught her eye appeared on the horizon. It was the light of a hundred lanterns. Within moments they joined a stream of carriages that led to the palacelike structure illuminated in the darkness. Pleased by the turn of events, Breanna was more generous in her opinion of the house then she might have been had things not gone so well.

When the carriage had its turn before the massive doors, she even allowed Alex to help her down without coercion. She didn't realize he knew exactly what was going on in her mind and was wisely letting her believe it for the time being.

When Alex spotted John in the throng of people, he beckoned him forward to meet Breanna, without telling her exactly who he was.

"My pleasure, Miss Sullivan," John said, bowing over her hand.

"The pleasure is mine, Mr. Frémont." She smiled brilliantly.

John cocked a brow in Alex's direction when Breanna was distracted with straightening her skirt.

"Later," Alex told him, offering his arm for Breanna to take. He'd decided it would be more beneficial if Guillermo thought he had a former claim on the fiery beauty. To his delight, she placed her slender hand upon it.

A bit of nervous apprehension touched Breanna as they neared their host. She heard deep rich laughter and could see his dark head above those in front of them. Suddenly, she began to wonder why he really had invited her.

"Relax," Alex leaned down to tell her. She gazed up at him, causing his breath to catch. Shaking off the effect she was having on him, he smiled crookedly. "And don't look at our host like that, or you'll never get out of here alive."

Breanna couldn't explain the pleasure she felt at his words. In his way, he was complimenting her. Unable to resist the gentle teasing, she cocked her head. "But think of all I could learn if I stayed."

His smile vanished. His eyes glittered dangerously. "Don't play with me, Breanna. You'll find I am more than even you can handle." He turned to stare straight ahead, his face devoid of expression.

Disappointed that their rapport had dissolved so rapidly, she lifted her chin to mimic his stance. The man was a boor! He liked to tease but couldn't take it. Well, she didn't need to impress him. The only person she had to win over was his superior. When she met him, she would explain how she could help and he would accept. Then Alex King could go to the devil!

Alex stepped forward, and Breanna realized they were to be presented next. "Good evening, general," he said familiarly. "It looks like you've put together quite a party."

The general nodded, but his eyes never left Breanna. When it was clear Alex wasn't going to introduce the vision on his arm, he reached for her hand.

"And who is this?" He smiled, impressed by the large brown eyes raised to meet his. In truth, he was impressed by the entire package!

Unable to avoid an introduction, Alex turned slightly, slipping his arm about Breanna's waist. "General, this is Miss Breanna Sullivan." He saw the immediate spark of recognition. Alex bent close to Breanna and smiled warmly down at her. "Bree, my love, this is our host, General Felipe Guillermo."

Sensing Alex's attempt to brand her as his possession in the general's eyes, Breanna turned an exquisite smile toward their host. "Your excellency," she breathed, dipping low in a graceful curtsy.

Enchanted by the beautiful woman who also had the audacity to face his troops, Guillermo stepped closer to her and was rewarded with a tantalizing view of her cleavage. "Please, señorita, you must call me Felipe."

It was all Alex could do to remain civil when he spied the pleasure on Guillermo's face and the way Breanna was playing the coquette. Fortunately, the line behind them began to grow restless, forcing Guillermo to usher them on and resume his role as host.

"Please, enjoy my hospitality." He bowed over Breanna's hand and kissed it. "And perhaps we can speak later, Madonna."

Stunned by what he had called her, Breanna was easily drawn away to a somewhat secluded spot beneath a flowering tree.

"He knows!" she gasped, finding her voice at last.

"Of course he knows!" Alex snapped, still unhappy about her effect on Guillermo. "I told you, he's no fool."

Glancing back, Breanna nodded. Their host was, indeed, more than she expected. He was handsome, but it was the polish of his Castillian upbringing that made him attractive. He'd been groomed to be suave and autocratic through generations of selective marriages. It was in his stance and innate arrogance.

As he noticed her lingering gaze, Alex's temper simmered. He never recalled losing it as often or as readily as he had since meeting Breanna. Deeming it a flaw in his character to let her influence him so easily, he waited for John and Heather to join them. At the moment, he didn't trust himself to speak to Breanna civilly. In fact, there didn't seem to be anything civil he wanted to do to her!

"Here come John and Heather," he said, his voice hard.

Breanna ignored his apparent brooding, and smiled as they approached. "You're right, *chica*. Our host is attractive," she said sweetly and loudly enough to antagonize Alex further. He deserved it for the way he had so blatantly claimed her earlier.

John saw the chips of ice crackling in Alex's eyes and knew this was not the time or place to start a war between these two. He had to act quickly.

"Heather tells me you have recently returned from Boston," he said to Breanna. "Did you enjoy it?"

Breanna breathed normally for a moment to calm her flaring temper. Decorum had to be observed, and he really was being kind. They began to chat, and he offered to escort her to the refreshment table. They excused themselves, and John hid a grin when he spied Alex's still smoldering anger.

"That wasn't very clever, marking her as yours the way you did," Heather commented to Alex when they were alone. "She'll find a way to get even."

"She already has," Alex grumbled, seeing Breanna become the center of attention.

Heather heard the jealous note in Alex's voice and couldn't help thinking about her original plan to bring the two together. It would be a volatile relationship—that was already clear—but they would never be bored with each other.

"Give her tonight, Alex." She smiled at him.

"Once the party is over, you can pull in the reins. Or better yet, try your charm. I gather it worked last night."

Her perky grin and tilted head made him relax with a smile of his own. "Not a bad idea, Heather." He looked back at the glowing woman laughing lightly with the small group around her. "In fact, it could be quite entertaining to see if I can ruffle her feathers."

That hadn't been exactly what Heather had in mind, but she had to admit it would be fun to watch Breanna pursued by the general while tempted by Alex.

"Then shall we join the party?" she asked mischievously.

"Indeed!" He smiled crookedly, extending his arm.

Much to Breanna's relief, her escapade in Monterey was a source of neither amusement nor shock for its citizens. She was surprised to find them genuinely impressed with the exploit. Many expressed a need for the people to insist that the Mexican soldiers be less aggressive. Her actions had shamed them into realizing they had let things go too far.

"You have shown us such courage," one silver-haired gentleman said kindly. "We have written a petition to the general, asking him to see that his men are better controlled."

"And that nothing like that will be allowed to happen again!" another stated emphatically.

Breanna smiled warmly until she felt a pair of strong arms slip around her from behind. Not wanting a scene, she froze.

"You see, *mi amante*," Alex breathed against her ear. "I told you not to worry about it." He raised his head and smiled at the gathering and the tender regard he saw in their eyes for Breanna. "She feared she had overstepped her bounds but simply could not ignore the problem."

Bounds! she thought. He made her sound like some sort of servant! Laying her hands over his, she looked back over her shoulder at him and smiled. "Actually, I was hoping it wouldn't be necessary to damage any of the soldiers permanently to prove my point," she said sweetly while digging her nails into his flesh.

Alex's jaw tightened to keep from yelping. To prevent a spectacle, he began to tighten his arms about her middle. He was impressed with her fortitude but, eventually, she had to relinquish her attack or face fainting from lack of oxygen. When he knew she was surrendering this round to him, he returned his attention to the others.

"Now, if you will excuse us, I think we'll get something to eat." Keeping an arm about her waist, he turned them away from the group.

"Will you stop pulling me around like I'm your . . . your pet?" she whispered harshly through clenched teeth as they approached the buffet table.

"Will you stop behaving like a wildcat?" he returned, sounding amused. Looking down at the furrows on his hands, he grinned. "You seem set on your pound of flesh, Breanna, yet I find it difficult to figure out why."

After grabbing a plate at the buffet table, Breanna pierced a slice of beef, wishing it was Alex instead. "The reason you keep getting what you deserve," she said softly as she moved down the line, "is that you keep insisting on making me look as if I belong to you." She glanced back to find him grinning. "Well, I don't!" she said more sharply than she intended, causing the woman in front of her to turn around inquisitively.

Smiling weakly at the curious woman, she dropped her voice low and leaned toward him to be heard. "You are not my keeper, so leave me alone!"

Alex enjoyed her fury. It not only kept her from considering her scatterbrained idea about spying, it made her breathe more heavily, making his view of her bodice even more pleasing.

Annoyed by his silence, Breanna glanced up at him. The spoon she held stilled in midair. There was such primitive fire in his eyes, she wanted to run. He was consuming her in the heat of his gaze. She might have stood there forever if someone hadn't asked her to move on. Still flustered, she did, but she had no idea what she was putting on her plate.

She snatched a napkin and fork at the end of the line, then made a hasty retreat to a flower-strewn table. She wasn't a bit hungry, but her legs were shaking badly and she needed an excuse to sit. To her chagrin, but not her surprise, Alex joined her.

Though they ate in silence, he destroyed any chance she had to relax. All she could do was push her food around on her plate.

"You should try some," he finally said. "It's really very good."

Not trusting his solicitous behavior any more than she trusted his barbs, she placed her fork across her plate. "I'm not hungry," she said, her voice still chilled.

Alex leaned forward. "You might need your energy later," he said, hinting at another confrontation. "You'd better eat."

Annoyed at the authority in his tone, she was preparing to leave him sitting there when Heather floated up with her dinner.

"Mr. Frémont was just telling me the most fascinating tale," she exclaimed, moving so John could join them. "He's a topographer," she said. "That's a mapmaker. He's making a map of California."

"I know what a topographer is," Breanna replied sharply, resenting Heather for preventing her escape. Hearing Alex's chuckle, she recalled her manners. Forcing a smile, she turned her attention to John Frémont. "So, Mr. Frémont," she began.

"Actually, Miss Sullivan," he said, "it's Captain Frémont but I would prefer you to call me John."

"Captain?" she inquired, her mind beginning to sort through some new information.

"Yes, I'm a captain in the United States army. I'm here on special assignment." John saw the wheels turning in her head. Alex was right. She was bright.

Breanna's brow arched slightly, and she glared at Alex. He nodded once tersely and she clenched her jaw. So this was his superior. She wondered if he had planned to let the entire night pass before giving her that bit of information. Turning her attention back to the captain, she was about to speak when Alex stopped her.

"Not here, Breanna," he cautioned, indicating the number of people around who might overhear. "You can talk to him later. We'll be giving John a ride back to town tonight."

She didn't wish to waste the time, but she could see the logic. "Very well," she said with a smile in John's direction. "We'll talk later." Standing, she held her hand to keep the men in their seats. "If you'll excuse me, I think I've spilled something on my dress," she lied. "I'll be right back."

Alex knew he would look foolish if he followed her now, but he cast her a warning glance. "Hurry back," he ordered.

Sorry she hadn't thought of this ruse to get away earlier, Breanna whirled without a word to leave them all behind.

He watched her walk regally across the patio and disappear inside the house. He noticed that she had also caught Guillermo's attention. Alex started to rise when John stopped him.

"Don't," he warned gently to keep him from following. "Guillermo will find a way to speak with her, Alex. Don't make her more of a challenge."

Sighing, Alex knew he was right, but it didn't sit well with him to imagine the general fawning over Breanna and Breanna playing up to him. She failed to see Guillermo as a threat. To her, he was a means to an end, a way to help the cause. What she didn't realize was that she was in over her head. The general would have no qualms about enjoying her, then turning her over to his men. He'd done it before, and Alex suddenly wished he'd told her that.

"Alex," Heather called to him when she saw the strain on his face. "She may be headstrong and stubborn, but she is bright enough to know what the general is interested in where she is concerned."

A muscle twitched in Alex's cheek at the mental picture of her in Guillermo's arms. His hands clenched into fists, but he remained seated.

"He can be very charming and convincing," he said, his eyes scanning to see if he could catch sight of either of them.

"More charming than you?" she asked, her mouth lifting in a grin.

Alex felt the heat of a blush and fought it by chuckling. "What's that supposed to mean?"

"It means if she fought you, she'll never give in to him."

It took a moment for Alex to figure out what she was implying and, even when he did, he wasn't sure he believed it. Heather believed Breanna was attracted to him. The thought was pleasant, yet he also knew they struck sparks. Too many, perhaps, to ever allow them to share a relationship.

Deciding it was better if he only concentrated on Breanna as far as the mission was concerned and ignored his romantic interests, he forced himself to relax.

"All right," he conceded to John and Heather. "I'll leave her alone for now but, if I think she's

going to cause trouble, you won't be able to stop
me."

Breanna couldn't stall too much longer in the
room that had been set aside for the female guests.
If she didn't appear soon, she was sure Alex
would send someone after her. Frowning at her reflection, she wondered why he felt he had to be
her guardian. She could take care of herself. She
certainly didn't need him at her side when she
spoke with General Guillermo—and speak with
him, she would.

Not only was he her host, he knew things she
was sure could be useful. Of course, there would
be no way of probing for information at the party,
but she could lay the groundwork. Patting her already neat hair, she decided this would be the perfect opportunity to see him.

She gasped when she exited. The very man she
was about to seek out was standing there, presum-
ably waiting for someone. To her surprise, that
someone was she.

"Ah, señorita." He smiled, extending his hand
for her to take. When she did, he tucked it in the
bend of his arm. "I was hoping to have a moment
to talk with you."

Even though she had wanted to speak with him
as well, Breanna felt a nervous flutter in her stomach. The man was certainly smooth, she thought
as he led her away from the hallway and into a
private salon, so adroitly that she didn't have time
to object. Swallowing her apprehension, she withdrew her hand and strolled to the far side of the
room.

"What did you wish to speak to me about?" she
asked, her tone sounding only slightly interested.

Felipe smiled. She was going to be great fun to
seduce. There was a sensuality lying just beneath
the innocence she projected. He had no doubt she
was nervous in his presence, and that added to the

excitement of her. He moved closer to her and indicated she should sit. When she chose a chair over the settee, his lips twitched with amusement.

"I wanted to tell you how disturbed I was when I heard about what my men had done." A becoming blush rose up from the swell of her breasts. He moved to stand beside her chair to better enjoy the vista before him. "They have all been reprimanded and for a long time will have to endure the teasing of the other men."

Breanna winced slightly. She had most assuredly made six enemies. They were not likely to forget they had been bested by a woman. "They were drinking, general," she said, hoping to offer an excuse for their behavior.

"That does not condone what they did, Breanna," he said gently, using her name familiarly without asking permission even though she had refused to use his. He reached into her lap and took her hand as he squatted down at her side. "I want nothing to occur that could cause a grievance between your people and mine."

She kept her eyes on the hand that held hers and shrugged lightly. "I . . . I'm sure it will soon be forgotten if it hasn't been already." She lied badly and knew full well from her reception that it was still the topic of the day.

Felipe knew it, too, but he let her think he believed her. "Then, if the Madonna deems it forgotten"—he smiled silkily and placed a finger beneath her chin to turn her face toward his—"it is forgotten."

He was going to kiss her! She could see it in the way his black eyes caressed her slightly parted lips. "Shouldn't we go back with the others?" she blurted, unwilling to let him think she was an easy conquest.

For a moment, Felipe wanted to ignore her plea. He wanted to see if she would resist should he force an intimacy, but he recalled the houseful of people.

"Of course, my dear," he said, turning his mouth into a smile he didn't feel. Standing, he helped her from her chair and began to lead her back to the festivities. "I would like to see you again, Breanna," he said when they were stepping out onto the patio. "Perhaps we can go riding some afternoon."

"Perhaps," she said, but there was little enthusiasm in her voice. All she wanted to do was put some distance between her and this man. She had the feeling he had the ability to look inside and know her thoughts before she did.

Music began and she was afraid he might ask her to dance, but she was saved from that fate by none other than Alex.

"I've been waiting for you, *mi amante*," he said, once again claiming her with an affectionate kiss on her brow. To his surprise, she didn't seem annoyed. Was it possible she wanted him to take her away from Guillermo? And, if so, why? "I believe this is our dance."

Breanna nodded. "Good evening, general," she said tersely and started for the dance floor.

"You are very fortunate, *mi amigo*," Guillermo said before Alex could follow her. "She is quite unique." He turned his attention from Breanna to meet Alex eye to eye. "She could be capable of things no other woman would attempt."

Was that a warning? Alex wondered. Had Breanna somehow tipped her hand? "I wouldn't worry, *mi amigo*," he said with the same strained tone. "I plan to keep her too busy to get into any trouble."

Felipe bowed his head slightly and excused himself to join the other guests, leaving Alex to follow Breanna.

"What happened?" he asked, pulling her closer than was necessary to waltz.

"Nothing!" she snapped, her nerves still on edge. "And don't hold me so tight!"

"Breanna," he warned, easing his hold on her. "Either you tell me what went on between you two or, so help me, I'll—"

"You'll what?" she challenged, needing to regain some control.

Alex glared down at her. Did she know how magnificent she looked when she was angry? Was she aware how she tempted him to ravage her every time she dared him with those dark brown eyes of hers?

"Someday, Breanna," he said, his voice a gravelly rasp, "I'm going to accept your challenge. Someday, I'm going to see if you really are the woman you profess to be."

His words were not a threat. She could see it in his eyes. He was promising her that he would someday make love to her. A strange ache filled her, one that was more terrifying yet also more exciting than anything she had ever experienced. Tearing her eyes from his, she decided this wasn't the time or the place to examine it.

A small smile of victory played at Alex's mouth as he twirled her around the floor. He knew the impact of his words on her. They tempted her, but she didn't want to admit it. The music ended, and he took her hand when she would have fled.

"Do you still think you can handle Guillermo?" he asked, needing one last bit of information before he made up his mind about something he and John had discussed with Heather when Breanna had left them.

Forcing a bravado she didn't feel, she yanked her hand free. "I can handle him," she said, presenting her back the instant it was said.

So the die was cast. He sighed heavily. Following her to the table, he nodded a secret signal to John and Heather that he had made his decision.

Chapter 10

Breanna was glad when Heather suggested they go home. Although they had been at the fiesta only a few hours, it seemed like an eternity. Her nerves were taut from the silent battle that raged between Alex and the general. They seemed to be sparring, with her as the prize. Passed back and forth between the two on the dance floor, she was sure she had drawn the attention of everyone there.

Finally, refusing to dance another step with either man, she sat sipping wine with John Frémont and several local couples. The result was a headache and fatigue. It took all the social skills she had ever learned to get through the remainder of the evening. Now, settled in the carriage, she knew her resources were tapped.

Resting her head on the back of the seat, Breanna half-listened to Heather and John, engaged in some conversation. Alex was quiet. She suspected he was probably upset with her again, but she didn't care. All she wanted was to sleep. She was tired of the cat-and-mouse games they had played all evening.

As she was dozing, she heard her father's name, and her eyes opened. In all the turmoil of the evening, she had almost forgotten her desire to speak with John. Sitting up quickly, she drew everyone's attention.

"Did Alex mention my plan to you, John?" she

asked, ignoring the sound that escaped Alex's throat.

"As a matter of fact, he did," John replied, sorry she hadn't fallen asleep.

"And?"

"And I'm afraid I can't enlist your help until I've had a chance to speak to Patrick."

"But I could be of great assistance," she exclaimed, desperate to have a part in the events unfolding. "I might even learn something before you see Papa, if given the chance!"

"I'm sorry," John said firmly. "It's my way on this, Breanna, or no way. I would never risk your safety unless your father knew and did not object."

Breanna realized it was senseless to argue. She also realized he was right. Her father would want to know, and she rather thought his approval would be forthcoming. Of course, she could begin without any of them knowing it. The general had suggested they ride some afternoon, and possibly she could make it sometime soon. Prepared to let them think she agreed, she smiled.

"Then I hope you see my father very soon."

"And I hope you never see him," Alex said softly, but everyone heard.

"I don't care what you hope!" she retorted, wishing her headache would go away, and him with it. "I have as much right as you to help the cause!"

The carriage stopped and three others sighed collectively, afraid this exchange could have become a full-blown battle. When Breanna opened her door to step out, Alex's arm snaked about her waist, drawing her to his lap.

"Good night, Heather," he snapped, his tone indicating she was dismissed. "See her in, John," he added sharply, ignoring the squirming bundle he held.

"No! Don't go!" Breanna yelled, trying to pull free of the steel bands that held her.

"Sorry, Bree," Heather said, her humor barely contained. John only shrugged and the two left the carriage hastily.

"Let go of me, you oaf!" she cried, wiggling about until she could pound her fists on his chest.

Alex gripped her wrists and shook her. "Shut up!" he roared, making her cease immediately. "Now, young lady, I have one question for you. You'd better think long and hard before you answer it. You won't like the consequences if you give the wrong answer."

Stubbornly, she glared at him. "Ask your question then."

"Will you wait until John speaks with your father before going on with this harebrained scheme?" She did not reply. "Well?"

"I don't have to answer to you!" she said vehemently.

Her statement was answer enough. "No," he said softly, "I suppose you don't." He released her, and she was ready to step from the carriage when he spoke again. "Don't you want to know the consequences?" he asked, making her pause.

"No!" she answered quickly. "I really don't think it matters!"

"Afraid?" he challenged, seeing her tense.

She completed her exit and turned to glare back into the carriage at him. "I'm not afraid of you, Mr. King, no matter what you think."

He responded with a deep chuckle. "Well, Miss Sullivan, you should be." She turned in a huff and headed for the house. He was still chuckling when John joined him.

"Then it's settled?" John asked. "You're going to go through with it?"

"She has left me no choice, John. The instant she can, she'll go to Guillermo and try to get any information she can put her hands on."

"And what he only suspects, he'll be able to prove," John sighed and shook his head. Digesting the import of that thought, he leaned forward, bracing his arms on his thighs. "So how do you want to go about it?"

"I'll have to go home to make arrangements while you and Heather keep her here."

"Thanks." John laughed, rolling his eyes at the prospect.

"I should be back in no more than four days." He sighed and stretched out his legs on the seat across from him. "Think you can handle it that long?"

"I don't have a choice, do I?" John countered. Alex shook his head. "You know, Alex," he mused. "It's possible this one little girl could ruin all the months of planning and hard work we've done."

"It's probable, John," Alex said. "That's why we'll go to whatever extremes it takes to prevent it."

The tension within the walls of Casa del Verde mounted steadily. As Breanna entered the house after the party, Heather had been foolish enough to mention that it was best if Breanna awaited their father's permission before getting involved, and it set Breanna off.

"I'm old enough to make my own decisions, Heather! I don't need a nursemaid!"

"Father is hardly a nursemaid," she replied. "Regardless, you don't know anything about being a spy. Perhaps Alex could give you some training while you wait to hear from Papa."

"I don't want anything from Alex King!" Breanna said with a snarl and pushed past her sister to go upstairs.

Heather followed her, unbidden, into her room. "You know, Bree, you're not behaving rationally where Alex is concerned. In fact, you've got me worried," Heather continued as Breanna unhooked the clasp of her pearls.

Speaking to Heather's reflection in the mirror, Breanna asked, "Worried about what?"

Heather came up behind her and began to unfasten her gown while Breanna started to remove the pins holding her hair. "I've never known you not to be fair. Despite anger or hurt, you were always fair. But with this one simple man, you've become irrational."

"One simple man!" Breanna laughed without humor. "Alexander King is anything but simple!"

"All right," Heather conceded with a grin, "so he's not simple, but that isn't cause to hate him as you do."

Breanna frowned as she examined her feelings. "I don't hate him, *chica*," she finally said truthfully. "It's just that he infuriates me."

"Why?" Heather asked, hoping she could force her sister to search her heart for the answers.

Why, indeed? Breanna thought, slowly stepping out of her gown. "Maybe because he tries to run my life. You know how I feel about being my own mistress."

Heather smiled. "Or maybe because he's hinted he would like you to become his?" She watched Breanna whirl to face her. "Surely you don't deny he desires you, Bree." Her skin darkened with a blush. "And I think, if you were honest, you'd admit you desire him, too."

"Heather Sullivan!" Breanna gasped, feeling she was too close to the truth. "How dare you speak like that! Why, I would never! What do you think I am?"

Going to her sister's side, Heather smiled sweetly. "I think you're a grown woman, Bree, who is fighting a feeling that scares her because she's never experienced it before."

Her indignation failed and she sighed, relaxing

her defensive stance. "And I think I don't want to talk about it anymore."

"Okay, Bree," Heather agreed. "But, sooner or later, you're going to have to come to grips with how you feel about Alex." She leaned and kissed her cheek, bidding her good night.

The instant Breanna was alone, she completed her toilette and slipped beneath the cool sheets of her bed hoping to find sleep before she could begin thinking, but it wasn't to be.

How did she feel about Alex? There was no denying she found him attractive. In fact, there were times she thought she could lose herself in his arms. Then he would say something condescending or contradictory to her own beliefs and she would find herself furious with him.

If only he would realize she was a capable person. If he would treat her as his equal and place a higher value on her thoughts, then maybe her feelings would deepen. Perhaps then she could even come to love him.

She rolled to her side and snuggled into her pillow, not wanting to think about *that*. There was simply too much to settle before she could even *like* him to consider anything more.

The trip was more successful than Alex could have hoped. He stood on the deck of his schooner, his dark hair blowing in the wind as they tacked ever southward. He had made good time. Even with the delay of zigzagging the ship to catch the prevailing winds, he had been gone only three days.

"You seem awfully pleased with yourself," his ranch foreman observed, joining him at the rail.

"I am, Eric." He grinned. "And you'd be smiling, too, if you knew the job I have for you." He went on to explain how he wanted Eric to run Casa del Verde and protect the women in the house.

Eric emitted a mock groan. "A whole houseful, and I bet not one is under forty!"

Alex laughed. "That's the part that you're going to enjoy." He described Heather Sullivan to him. "But remember, young man, she is Patrick's daughter. I don't want you to do anything that might cause him to shoot you. You're a damned good foreman and I would hate to lose you for an indiscretion."

Eric's face grew warm under the teasing. "Can I look?"

"Look all you want, my friend, but leave the idea of touching to Heather."

They stood quietly, thinking of what they faced in the next few hours.

"Alex?"

"Yes?"

"Alex, are you sure this is right? I mean, taking the other one up north, ain't that kidnapping?"

"Um-hm," Alex said seriously. "But if I'm going to hell for helping to start a war, I might as well have some fiery company!" Eric turned to gape at him and saw the humor in his eyes. Shaking his head, he joined Alex in his laughter.

Heather slipped into the barn, checking to see that she was not followed, before hurrying to the tack room. She knocked softly and was admitted quickly.

"I got your note, but I don't see why you had to be so secretive."

"I needed to know if she's left the grounds since the party."

Heather shook her head. "No, she's been—" Heather's words ceased as a tall stranger moved to Alex's side. "She's been moping about the house," she finished slowly.

"Heather Sullivan," Alex said, "I'd like you to meet my foreman, Eric Wilson."

Heather nodded a greeting and offered her hand

to the younger man as he stood clutching the brim of his hat as if it were a lifeline. At that moment, he knew he would do whatever Alex asked, especially if it concerned the beautiful girl before him.

Taking her hand, he smiled. *"Con mucho gusto."*

"The pleasure is mine." She smiled back.

Alex cleared his throat and brought them out of their mutual reverie. "We don't have much time. I have everything ready up north, but I wasn't able to get in touch with Patrick." Heather shrugged, and he felt he needed to clarify the ramifications of what he was going to do.

"Heather, without Patrick's permission to do this, I'll be kidnapping Breanna." She stared at him. "That's breaking the law."

A slow smile touched her face. "So is starting a revolt, isn't it?"

Alex chuckled. "Yes, I guess it is."

"And they can only hang us once," she said soberly.

The thought of hanging wasn't as frightening to Alex as imagining Breanna at the mercy of Guillermo. "They have to catch us first." He grinned to ease the worry on Heather's face. "And, with Breanna out of the way, our chances of avoiding a noose are infinitely better."

Heather appreciated his attempt to ease her mind, but there were still things she wanted to settle. "Speaking of Breanna, what are you going to do with her?"

Alex knew what he wanted to do, but he didn't think it gentlemanly to tell her. "I'm going to see that she stays out of trouble, Heather." He could see the concern still on her face. "I won't hurt her," he said gently. "I swear to you."

"I know." Heather sighed. "It's just that she's so damned proud and stubborn, I keep thinking she's going to hate me for this."

Alex placed a finger beneath Heather's chin and lifted her saddened face. "Better that she hate all of us than end up in Guillermo's hands. He would use her, both as a hostage and ... well, you understand." She nodded slowly. "Where would her pride be then?"

"You're right, of course. I guess I need to keep that in mind."

Grinning broadly, Alex continued, "And keep in mind that your father would have my hide if I let anything happen to her." He hoped he had made Heather feel better about her part in his scheme. "Now, let's work out the last of the details. I'm sure I'll need help. I don't think Breanna is going to give us any."

Heather slipped the latch on the door and let the two men enter. She still wasn't completely convinced she wasn't betraying her sister, but she knew it was the only logical thing she could do. Breanna simply wasn't going to sit idly by and let things develop around her without taking a dangerous and potentially damaging part.

"She's asleep. I just checked," Heather whispered. "Is everything ready?"

"Yes. Paul has the horse out front," Alex explained. "I'm only taking one. I can't trust Breanna to follow my lead, and I don't have time to chase her all over the countryside should she break away." Heather was chewing nervously at her lip. Taking her hand in his, Alex smiled down at her. "This may seem unorthodox, Heather, but it is the only way."

Heather nodded and motioned for him to follow her up the stairs to Breanna's room while Eric remained in the foyer. Outside the door, she rose on her tiptoes, placing a chaste kiss on Alex's cheek.

"Good luck." She smiled shyly. "I have a feeling you're going to need it." She left him standing in the hall and went back down to the kitchen to secure the house. She didn't want to witness the coming event, even though she agreed it was nec-

essary. It occurred to her that she had linked
Breanna and Alex in her mind months before, and
she grinned at the possibilities that could arise between them in the following weeks.

Eric entered the kitchen in hopes of finding
some refreshment. He saw her smile and paused.
"I wasn't sure you liked Alex's plan," he said
when she spied him. "Yet you're smilin'."

"It does seem funny, doesn't it." She sighed at
his perplexed expression. "It's just that I was
thinking of the two of them together. You've never
met my sister, but I assure you, it will be interesting."

She poured him a mug of still-warm coffee and
took one herself to help quell her nerves. "She
isn't going to cooperate," she commented as she
joined him at the table. Glancing up at the ceiling,
she grimaced. "In fact, you'd better be prepared
for the worst."

Eric frowned, unsure of what to expect, but it
wasn't long before they heard a shattering crash, a
shriek, then a full scream. Wincing, they expected
more, but there was only silence. Unable to resist
checking on the situation, Heather raced from the
kitchen with Eric close behind. He found her looking up the stairs, her hand clamped over her
mouth.

Alex was descending with a squirming bundle,
wrapped in a blanket and tossed over his shoulder. Alex signaled them to silence, tipped his head
in farewell, and started out the door. The entire
time his cargo was crying out muffled oaths.

"Oh, Lord!" Heather exclaimed as she lowered
her hand. "She's going to kill him!"

"Alex can take care of himself," Eric said, enjoying the laughter in Heather's eyes.

Heather glanced up at Eric. It occurred to her
that she would be spending a few weeks or more
with the handsome man at her side, and they were

standing in the foyer in the middle of the night alone. Her cheeks turned pink, and she grew shy.

"I . . . I'll show you where your room is," she said, motioning him back toward the kitchen. "It's . . . it's back here."

Eric reached to touch her arm gently, his own face slightly flushed. "Miss Sullivan," he said softly. "Don't worry. You and your sister will be okay."

Nodding and giving him a weak smile, Heather could see he was as nervous as she about spending time together. "I know." To ease their tension, she smiled more fully. "But how am I going to explain to Rosa why you're here and Breanna isn't?"

Chuckling, he shrugged. "Maybe she won't notice."

Thinking of the forgetful old woman, Heather realized she had slept through the entire ruckus. Suddenly she laughed. "You know something, maybe she won't!"

How could this be happening? Was it a dream or reality? The pressure against her stomach as she rode facedown across the saddle of a horse belied the dream, yet she was sure it had begun as one!

She had been dreaming of a garden and a dark stranger. She wanted him to hold her, protect her. She was unafraid as she slipped her arms about his neck and invited his kiss. It was gentle and sweet, and she found herself responding to the warm, moist lips. Suddenly the tender arms became bands of steel and the lips began a demanding kiss that drew her soul from her.

Her eyes fluttered open when she realized the shadowy figure had followed her into wakefulness and was standing in her room! Only one man would have the audacity to invade her room in the dark of the night. Alexander King!

She was suddenly fully awake, with eyes wide and arms that were ready to do battle. She began to struggle fiercely to gain freedom from the man above her. She bucked like a wild creature, her fists pummeled his back, and her nails sunk savagely into his shoulders. A large hand covered her mouth, and she sunk her teeth into the fleshy part of it.

"Damn you!" Alex roared, pulling his hand away to survey the damage.

It was the opportunity she needed. By rolling to her side, she was able to gain her feet, only to be cornered between the bed and the wall.

"Get out!" she demanded, but he came closer. In desperation, she grabbed the pitcher from her bedside and hurled it at him. Missing her mark, she watched it crash uselessly to the floor.

"Settle down, *gatita*," he murmured. "You're not strong enough to fight me, and I assure you, I am the more determined." He yanked a quilt from her bed and drew nearer.

Trapped and in a blind rage, Breanna kicked at him, crying out when her bare foot made contact with his boot. "I'll kill you, you bastard!" she wailed, drawing back a fist, but he threw the quilt over her head before she could make contact. A piercing scream echoed through the house as he bundled her up like a sack of laundry and hoisted her over his shoulder. With her arms trapped at her sides, she was defenseless and could only kick out her frustrations. A solid whack to her bottom stilled her momentarily.

"Quiet, love," he growled. "If Heather wakes, she will have to be dealt with, too."

His threat stilled her. She wasn't in a position to bargain, so she rode subdued through the hall and down the stairs. Her thoughts were so clouded with anger and hatred at that moment, she didn't realize Heather would have already heard the noises and come to investigate.

The cool night air drifted up the stairs to brush her bare feet. He was taking her from the house!

She resumed her violent struggles, but it was to no avail. She was tossed none too gently over a saddle, and she felt him mount. His hands moved her effortlessly until she was secure, then the horse surged and her unknown journey began.

Thankfully, the ride wasn't a long one. She tried to attune her senses to which direction they headed, but soon knew it was impossible from her upside-down position. All she could distinguish was the sound of the hooves, first on the compact road, then the softer thuds of open ground.

Her dreams of a black pirate loomed up to haunt her. She could smell the sharp tang of the ocean and hear the slapping of the waves as they made contact with the silencing sand.

The instant the horse ceased moving, she struggled to slide off the saddle. Forgetting the height of the huge steed, she fell less than gracefully. She found herself on her back in the sand, the quilt tangled around her.

"Damn you! Get me out of this!" she cried from the folds.

"In time, *gatita*." He pulled her to her feet. "In time." His arms wrapped about her thighs and hoisted her over his shoulder once again.

Breanna's muffled cries ceased when she heard him speak to someone. Ready to scream, she realized the unknown man was one of his, and there would be no help forthcoming. They began to move, and she heard Alex's boot strike a wooden surface. She remained still until she felt a gentle rocking. Comprehension dawned and she tried to pitch herself from her precarious perch.

Alex's strong hands lifted her in one fluid motion, holding her tightly against his chest when she squirmed. Through the cover she heard him speak, amusement in his voice.

"Unless you want a dunking, Breanna, you will hold still." Tightening his arms to squash any attempt to escape, he added, "I neglected to bring you a change of clothing. Though I might enjoy you naked in my arms, you'd best think of my men. They are far from saints."

She ignored the humor, but the words sunk in. She went still, sure he was not jesting. The oars began to cut through the water, and she counted each stroke to keep herself from screaming. Rage churned in her like the inky water against each dipping oar. She could think of a hundred curses to rain down on his head, but she knew if she uttered one sound, she would be lost to her own hysterics.

Like a bag of grain, she was tossed up to a pair of waiting arms and set on her feet. By the gentle roll beneath them, she knew she was aboard a ship. Several voices reached her, along with the squeal of winches and lines.

Obsessed with escape, she decided she would rather face the cold, dark water than remain passive. Lunging forward, she screamed. Someone grabbed the quilt and her hair in a single move and brought her up hard against his chest.

"You weren't thinking of leaving my company so soon, were you, my love?"

She could visualize him preening before his men with his captive in tow and refused to reply. She was too angry at him for leaving her standing in their midst with a blanket still over her head. He would pay dearly for this humiliation, she thought.

Without warning, the quilt was lifted from her. She was immediately assailed by the cool night air, but Alex quickly wrapped the blanket around her shoulders. The light was dim, with only a few scattered lanterns about, but it was enough for her to see the face of her abductor.

"You miserable vermin!" she rasped. "I'll never forgive you for this!"

Alex looked at her strangely and she thought, for a split second, that his eyes looked troubled, almost sorry, but the moment passed and she was sure she had imagined it when a spark of devilment lit his eyes.

"I wish I had time to prove you wrong, Breanna." His fingers brushed her cheek tenderly until she jerked away. Grinning, he added, "But I've a ship to sail." Sweeping her into his arms despite her protest, he carried her into a small cabin and tossed her into a bunk. "Get some rest." His eyes slid over her bundled form and his lips twisted in a crooked grin that he knew she wanted to slap off his face. "You're going to need it."

With a huff, she presented her back to him. She heard him laugh as he left the cabin. Instantly she struggled to get free of the weighty quilt and ran to the door. She heard the lock slip into place before she could pull it open.

Shaking the door fiercely to be sure it was secure, she screamed out her frustration and heard his laughter fade as he made his way up on deck. Fatigue finally displaced her anger. The last few days had been long and restless, the night tense and exhausting. The impotence of her situation was suddenly more than she could endure stoically.

A tear slipped from her lower lashes and fell to her chest. With quivering lips and a deep, ragged sigh, she moved back to the bunk and sat down dejectedly. Her mind refused to ponder the whys behind her abduction. All she could think about was how chilled she was and how soft the mattress beneath her felt.

Scooting back, she drew up her cold feet and tucked them beneath the quilt. Huddling into its folds, she found a comfortable spot and let herself relax. She would need her strength, she reasoned. Within moments, she was nodding off and soon slept.

Alex braced his arm against the lowered ceiling over the bunk and looked down on the sleeping woman. How could anyone appear so angelic in sleep and be such a fiery hellion awake? Her hair was loose and wild across the pillow. She was huddled against the wall in her sleep, leaving most of the bunk unused.

He was suddenly too tired to wake her and endure another tirade. Slipping off his boots and shirt, he lifted the corner of the cover and slid in beside her. In her sleep she moved toward his warmth, and he smiled. It felt good to lie with her peacefully, and in moments he joined her in slumber.

Chapter 11

Breanna stirred but refused to open her eyes. She knew it had to be late in the day; the warmth of her room indicated the sun had been up a long time. Her covers seemed to be weighing her down and she pushed them away, but there was little relief. She still felt confined.

Yawning and stretching out her curled body, she tried to sit up, but her hair was caught on something. She opened her eyes to free it . . .

"Good morning." Alex smiled softly, sleep still heavy in his eyes as he held her hair wrapped around his hand. "Are you always so restless in the morning, or were you just anxious to wake me and insist I make up for my neglect last night?"

Although he was hinting at something more intimate, the actual events of last night came back in great waves. She wasn't safe in her own bed, but aboard a ship in his! "Let go of my hair!" she ordered, giving it a painful tug.

"And so sweetly charming," he sarcastically replied as his hand released her auburn tresses. "What's the matter, *gatita*, upset because I have foiled your plans?" He rolled to his feet and stood looking down at her. "Sorry you didn't get a chance to test your wiles on Guillermo?"

He knew he wasn't being fair snapping at her the way he was. He hadn't planned on it. In fact, his last thoughts before falling asleep were of waking her gently with a kiss. Each time they ended

154

up in each other's arms, they got closer to consummating their desire for each other. He was hoping this morning, catching her unaware, he might succeed in discovering all her secrets.

"You're disgusting!" she finally managed to say.

He picked up his shirt and began to put it on. "Why? Because I speak frankly? Honestly, Breanna, any woman who is willing to spend time with a known rake can't be that innocent."

"I didn't ask you to bring me here, you pompous ass!" she exclaimed, tossing aside the cover to wiggle to the edge of the bunk. She was so anxious to be on her feet and facing him, she didn't realize how much leg she had exposed.

"I was speaking of your desire to be with Guillermo," he said, his eyes appreciating the way she looked. From her tangled russet hair to her bare feet, she was a tempting morsel.

Seeing his interest in her limited attire, Breanna crossed her arms over her chest. "That's none of your business!" she declared.

"I've made it my business!" he retorted harshly, hating the way she seemed bent on denying him what he reasoned others must have had.

From the first time she had brazenly faced him, there had been blushes but her actions had belied their purity. It was easier to attribute them to fury. Thinking of the trip she'd taken East alone and the cousin in Boston, who Heather informed him was a similar age, made him wonder. Breanna was a passionate woman. She showed evidence of being a free spirit. Hadn't she tossed off some of her clothing on a beach where anyone could come along? Wasn't she willing to use her feminine wiles to seduce Guillermo into revealing information?

It was possible she had more experience than he originally thought. It was also probable that her refusal to fall at his feet was because he was the controlling force. Breanna was strongly independent in nature. Every time they kissed, he had forced the issue, and she fought him. Except once. Once in the dark gardens she had offered her lips to him. It wasn't until he was close to losing control that he demanded she give over or leave. The moment he made the order, she cooled toward him.

Breanna threw her hands in the air impotently. "Why can't you just leave me alone?" she asked with a groan, hating him at that moment.

Sitting, Alex drew on his boots. "Because you're more trouble than you've been worth." He stomped hard to make sure his boot was in place. "You act before you think and you refuse to listen to those more experienced than you are."

"That's not true!" she yelled back at him.

Alex's own temper boiled. He stepped close and towered above her. "Tell me you weren't going to see Guillermo even when John and I asked you to wait." He saw her flinch at the volume of his voice and, he was sure, because of her own guilt. "Swear you were going to comply with our wishes!"

Breanna couldn't do that. It would be a blatant lie. To avoid the prevarication, she glared back at him. "I could have helped! I could have gotten useful information if you hadn't interfered!"

Enraged by her stubbornness, Alex gripped her arms and shook her. "You little fool! All you would have gotten was tossed on your pretty backside!"

"No!" she cried, trying to wrench herself free.

"Yes!" he roared, pushing her easily to the bunk. Dropping on top of her, he gripped her chin, making her listen. "See how easy it would have been, Breanna?" he asked, still furious. "He would have tossed up your skirts and had his way with you." She was shaking her head violently in denial. "And, if you were lucky, all you would come away with was a Spanish bastard in your belly!"

Tears were streaming down her cheeks. Never had anyone talked to her the way he just had! "How dare you!" she seethed, struggling to keep from erupting into hysterics. "You kidnap me! You abuse me! You accuse me of . . . of . . . Oh! I hate you!" She began to thrash and pummel him unmercifully.

Surprised by the level of her violence, Alex leaned back but didn't try to stop her from hitting him. He was too stunned, both by the pain he felt in hurting her and by the sight of her tears. He felt as if he deserved her punishment.

"Breanna," he called softly, trying to reach her troubled mind. "Breanna!" he called more firmly. Her flailing ceased slowly, but it was more from fatigue than because of his soothing murmurings. Finally she was breathless and spent.

Alex had never before experienced the tenderness he was feeling at that moment. It made him uncomfortable because he wasn't sure what to do. Gently, he began to brush back her hair. She hiccupped and sniffed, making him smile.

"Better?" he asked, hoping she might forgive him for causing her such anguish if he pretended it had never happened.

"Get off me," she said without conviction in her voice.

Alex rolled to her side but would not leave it. Perching on an elbow, he looked down at her. He noticed her spiky lashes were wet where they laid upon her cheeks. Slowly, he lowered his lips to kiss them gently. Breanna didn't move. Encouraged by her silence, he brushed the tip of her nose with his lips. He wanted to cover her trembling mouth, but felt she needed time to get over her hurt.

"I'm sorry," he finally forced out. Her eyes opened slowly and he almost hated himself for causing the deep sorrow he saw in their dark depths. "I didn't mean to be so harsh. I only wanted you to realize why it was foolish to do what you wanted."

Breanna tensed. For a moment she had softened to him. "Foolish?" she asked, dismay in her tone. "Why is it foolish for me to want to help?" She saw him frown. Was he sorry he'd spoken at all? "Why can't I believe in this cause as deeply as you and want to be a part of it? Because I'm a woman?" she demanded more strongly. "Because I should be meek and obedient instead of involved?"

Regretting the loss of their tender interlude, Alex rolled off the bunk. He ignored her questions and finished dressing.

"Answer me, damn it!" Breanna called after him when he reached for the door.

Without turning, Alex spoke. "I'll see about getting you something to eat." And then he was gone.

Outside the door, Alex paused. He heard her cry out in exasperation. Rubbing the back of his neck, he tried to reassess Breanna Sullivan. Which was she? The not-so-innocent firebrand or the woman-child with tears in her eyes he'd held in his arms moments before? Befuddled by the many aspects of her, he shook his head and went to arrange for her breakfast.

Alex returned to find her seated, her hands folded in her lap. She had used his brush to restore some order to her hair and had donned one of his shirts over her gown as a robe. He had no way of knowing she was waging the same battle of confusion that he was.

After he had left her, she sat up, still trembling from her outburst of tears. She hadn't cried like that since her mother died. Sniffling, she tried to recall the things he had said. Was it possible she wasn't thinking clearly where Guillermo was concerned? Could her overzealous desire to help have clouded her judgment?

Not wanting Alex to see her so vulnerable again, she tried to regain some composure. She thought she would eventually have lots of time to think things over but very little time until he came back. When she faced him again, she wanted to make sure there was no evidence of her childish behavior.

"Here," he said, sliding a tray on the table. "Come eat this."

She rose and moved silently to the table. She wasn't very hungry but didn't want him to think she was going to refuse food out of petulance. She picked up the mug of coffee and began to sip it. It was bitter, but she didn't want to ask for sugar. In fact, until she figured out just how she felt about him, she didn't want to ask him for anything.

She broke off a piece of the sliced bread onto a plate and took it back to her chair. "Is Heather all right?" she asked, her voice bland.

"She's fine," he answered tersely. He had removed a leather pouch from a drawer and seemed to be reading something. He glanced up to see a barely perceptible nod. He didn't think she believed him. Sighing, he explained the facts.

"Breanna, Heather really is fine. I left more men to make sure she stays that way." She dropped her eyes without indicating her feelings. Annoyed, he returned his attention to the reports he had received when he was home.

"Did she know what you were going to do?" she asked after a few minutes.

Alex set aside his papers. He simply could not ignore the timidity in her voice. Going to her side, he dropped down on his haunches. She continued to stare into her coffee.

"Yes, she knew," he said, grimacing when he saw the pain on her face. "She helped because she knew it was the only way to ensure your safety."

Breanna shrugged lightly. "So she didn't think I could take care of myself, either."

There was nothing he could say to her comment without sounding patronizing, so he said nothing. Raking his fingers through his hair, he was ready to rise when she spoke again.

"Where are you taking me?"

It was the first logical question she had asked since coming aboard. Or at least the first he didn't mind answering. "We're going to my ranch. It's up the coast, north of San Francisco. It's beautiful. I think you'll like it there."

"And how long will you make me stay?" she asked, not appreciating his pleasant chatter.

He stood, and looked down at her. She seemed awfully small sitting there in his large shirt. He almost wanted to cradle her in his arms. Shaking off the image, he replied. "As long as I deem it necessary."

She didn't care for his tone, nor did she savor the idea that he was still acting like her guardian. Straightening her shoulders, she couldn't resist a retort.

"I hope you don't expect me to just sit there obediently, waiting for you to release me. You'll be sadly disappointed in me . . . again!"

Alex couldn't restrain his desire to chuckle. "The only thing I expect from you, Breanna, is the unexpected." She cocked her head and looked at him. Her guard was down. She was vulnerable, and he was drawn to her. Not only to her body, but to her very essence. Taking a step away to break the spell she was weaving, he withdrew behind his own protective wall of arrogance.

"I'm sure you'll try to escape, but there is nowhere for you to go, and no one to help you." He refused to look at her and see the effect of his words. "You will be my prisoner, but you will not be uncomfortable."

"How thoughtful," Breanna said with a sneer,

wondering why she thought she had detected some tenderness in his eyes only moments before.

"And I'll tolerate your bad manners to me, but not to the people who work for me," he added sharply, ignoring her remark. "They don't deserve it."

Breanna stood. "And I do? I deserve to be dragged from my home, hauled about like a rag doll, and imprisoned?" Her temper was beginning to simmer again. He didn't answer her. Going to his side, she grabbed his arm, yanking him hard so he would look at her. "You're a hypocrite, Mr. King!" she told him bravely. "You claim to fight for freedom yet deny me mine!"

He couldn't believe her. Here she was, totally at his mercy, and she was blatantly antagonizing him. She was either the bravest little thing he'd ever seen or slightly mad.

"Your loss of freedom is necessary in this fight, Breanna," he explained patiently, though his patience was wearing thin. "The needs of the many outweigh the needs of the few." Glancing down to the hand that still held his arm, he quirked his lip. With a small tug, he was free. "Now go sit somewhere and be quiet until we get home."

Breanna watched him turn from her, apparently thinking she would blindly obey his mastery. "Alex?" she called softly. She watched him try not to respond. "Alex?" she called again, her tone mysteriously questioning. He blew out a deep breath and turned.

"What, Breanna?"

Her hand cracked hard against his cheek, snapping his head back. "That's some of my temper you said you would tolerate!" She whirled and headed for the door.

Alex stood stunned and watched her go. The very last thing he expected was that slap. Thinking of what he had said about the unexpected, he began to chuckle. He placed his hand over the imprint of hers, feeling the heat of the stinging blow. The chuckle turned into rumbling laughter. When one of his men ran in, there were tears of merriment in his eyes.

"Sir, ya better come up, quick!"

Wondering what chaos she was causing on deck, he followed the disgruntled sailor who kept muttering something about the old whip that had hung near the mast.

"I said turn this ship around!" she yelled, cracking the whip too close for comfort at the hand on the wheel.

Looking over her head, the sailor spotted the ship's master. "Sir, what should I do?" he asked, genuinely stymied.

"Maintain your course, Mr. Lyons," Alex said firmly without taking his eyes off the termagant wielding the whip. Breanna whirled, bringing the whip to a ready position in his direction. "Give me the whip, Breanna," he added, stepping forward.

"Stay away!" she ordered, pushing the overlong sleeve back up her arm. "This ship is going to turn around, and you can't stop it!"

"Can't I?" Alex asked, striking a relaxed pose. He seemed amused by her actions, but his mind was trying to figure out how to get the damned weapon from her hands before she hurt somebody.

He spied one of his men working his way up behind her. A few more steps and he would be able to yank it from her hands. To make sure her attentions remained on him, Alex took another step.

Alex's nonchalance gave him away. He was fully aware she knew how to use the weapon. She realized that the only reason he was not on guard was that he was planning something. Considering what she would do in his position, she whirled around in time to spy the sailor stalking her. With surprising accuracy she snapped the thin leather coil, catching the unsuspecting sailor across the thigh.

His pants were cut smoothly, as was the skin beneath. He yowled and fell back. Spinning around to face Alex again, she stared blankly. He was gone! She glanced around the deck but saw only the stunned faces of his men. She screamed when someone swept down upon her from above.

The whip sailed into the air. Breanna grabbed Alex's neck as she was lifted off the deck. They swung out over the water on the lowered mainsail rigging before being caught by his men on their next pass. Safely on deck, she realized she was defenseless once again and tried to move away from Alex, but the arm he had wrapped around her waist tightened.

"Let's see how much damage you've done," he said, his voice chilled. He drew her along until they stood before the wounded sailor. Another was cleaning the blood that oozed from the neat slice on his thigh.

"How are you, Billy?" Alex asked.

Still stunned that the little female at his captain's side was responsible for the stinging cut on his leg, Billy stared. "It's okay, sir. Just hurts a little."

Breanna swallowed the tears that threatened. "I . . . I'm sorry," she stammered. "I didn't mean to . . . I just didn't want you to . . ." She tore away from Alex's side and raced for the companionway.

Alex heard the door to his cabin slam and glanced at his men. There were varying degrees of surprise still on their faces. He was ready to mete out her punishment for disregarding his warning about his people when Billy spoke.

"She's pretty good with that whip, ain't she?" he asked, his amazement clear in his tone.

"Damned good!" Alex said quietly. Deciding not to stall any longer, Alex headed for his cabin but was stopped once more by the man at the wheel.

"What ya gonna do ta her, cap'n?" he yelled across the deck, aware the others were just as concerned.

Alex paused and rubbed the back of his neck. He looked back at his men and shrugged. "Damned if I know!"

Curled up on the bunk, Breanna hugged her knees close to her chest. She felt awful. She had hurt that sailor purely on instinct. He became a threat, and she attacked. Now, looking back, she shivered at the thought.

Perhaps Alex was right. Maybe she did always act without thinking. Maybe it could cause trouble. She was filled with self-recrimination when the cabin door opened.

There was no hint of how angry Alex was when he entered. Wondering what her punishment was to be, she remained huddled where she was while he returned to his papers. She decided she would at least face him with dignity.

After a few minutes, her nerves were stretched. Punishment was one thing, but waiting for it was another. She stirred, hoping to draw his attention, but he continued to ignore her. Not wishing to prolong the agony, she spoke.

"I'm sorry," she said softly. "I . . . I just had to try!"

Alex looked up from his reports to see her chewing her lip. His delay had worried her and it was punishment enough. Sighing, he gave her a small smile. "I would have tried, too," he told her.

Wide-eyed with surprise, Breanna released her knees and sat up. "You . . . you're not angry?"

Shaking his head, Alex placed the papers on the table and made his way to the bunk. Sitting beside her, he replied. "No, Breanna. I'm not angry. How can I be when I goaded you into acting."

This was something she had never expected. Sincere understanding and compassion! And it was coming from Alex King! Confused, she wrinkled her brow. Slowly he raised his hand to stroke his fingers over the furrows.

"I'm not the ogre you make me out to be, Breanna," he explained, his voice soft. "I'm just a man with an important mission. I do what I must to accomplish it successfully."

Her eyes softened. Why hadn't he talked to her like this from the beginning? Perhaps because the first time they met, she had tried to hire him as a possible gunman, she thought, suddenly ashamed.

"I won't hurt anyone else," she said, her chin lowering to hide her shame.

Placing his finger beneath her chin, he lifted it. "And will you give up this idea of escaping?"

Breanna closed her eyes, not wanting to witness the disappointment she expected. "I can't."

Alex shook his head ruefully. "I didn't think you could," he said as he released her.

She watched him go to the door. "Alex."

He turned to look over his shoulder at her.

"Thank you for understanding."

He stared for long moments, surprised how proud of her he felt. She had a strong set of convictions and she was willing to fight for them, yet when treated fairly, she could humble herself. Unwilling to break the tenuous threads of peace between them with words, he smiled and winked before leaving.

Breanna returned the smile, but didn't think he had seen it. Wondering why she had done it, she realized it was because she had enjoyed their last encounter. They had spoken to each other as equals. For the first time, he had listened. Continuing to smile, she made her way to the tray he had brought in earlier. Suddenly she was hungry.

Alex stood at the rail and watched the rugged coast slide past, but he really wasn't seeing it. His mind was filled with the woman in his cabin.

Their relationship had changed in the snap of a whip. Where he once saw only stubbornness, he now found courage. What he used to see as defiant obstinance, he now saw as the same determination and will he had. And, the biggest change of all—he no longer saw her as a child.

From the first time he saw her, he had craved her body. He couldn't deny that. Yet each time he held her, he felt that, like children, they were playing games. But he had realized that was no longer true when she called out to him before he left the cabin earlier. It was why he couldn't speak to her. If he had, he would have returned to her side to take Breanna the woman in his arms.

Although it was often painful, he'd been able to put the thoughts aside. He didn't think he had the strength to shun them much longer. He had too many responsibilities, too much was at stake for him to become involved with any woman, and Breanna wasn't just any woman!

Drawing a deep breath, he decided that to continue the mission he would have to avoid the temptation she offered. He would see she got settled at the ranch, then send word to John that he was ready to get back to work. The worst he should have to face was a week with her. Reasoning he could find enough to do around the ranch to keep them apart, he started back to the cabin.

Almost to the door, he paused. The cabin had seemed so much smaller with her in it. If he was going to keep the peace successfully, he thought it best he return to the deck. He was an honorable man, but he was certainly not made of stone.

The ship sailed into Bodega Bay just before sunset. Within an hour, Breanna would be in her velvet prison. No matter that she was given all the comforts, she was still going to be Alex King's prisoner.

She considered giving him her word that if he

returned her to her home she would cause no trouble, but she knew it would be a futile gesture. He had no reason to believe her, and she didn't know for sure if she could keep such a promise. The more she thought about the secretive goings-on, the more she wanted to be a part of them.

At first she thought it was the excitement tempting her, but after her encounter with the Mexican troops in Monterey, she began truly to consider the plight of California if it remained a Mexican territory. As more Americans poured in, more troops would be sent to keep them in line. Eventually there would be conflict, no matter who began it.

Pacing the cabin, Breanna wondered if she should try to convince Alex that she had changed just to secure her freedom. The thought tasted sour. At one time, she could have, but not now, after they had achieved a certain peace between them. She discovered she enjoyed that peace. It gave her a chance to get to know the man who had perplexed her since they met.

Perhaps "perplexed" was too tame a word, she reasoned as she passed the time. He had rattled her on more than one occasion. Not only had she achieved the height of anger in his presence, she had also known an unexplainable bliss.

Heather had hinted that Breanna cared for Alex. Was it possible she did? She had once told Millie she would only have a man who kept his word. Alex had warned her she would regret disobeying him, and here she was, his prisoner. The man she wanted would be strong yet gentle. Alex had revealed both those traits. Her chosen mate had to be proud and honorable. Well—she smiled—Alex was proud!

Wondering if she should start thinking of Alex in a different light, she was distracted by a tap at the door. "Come in," she called, sure it couldn't be Alex. He wouldn't knock.

"The cap'n says for ya ta come on out," a lad with reddening cheeks said, seemingly in awe of her.

Smiling gently, Breanna rose, holding a laugh in check when the lad backed up immediately. "I assure you, I am not some sort of witch!" she exclaimed in amusement.

"But the whip!" the boy said, wide-eyed. "I ain't never seen a woman use a whip like that!"

Careful not to frighten him, she moved closer. "My father taught me how to use a whip when I was ten, and I practiced a lot." He seemed to relax a bit. "You should see my sister wield a knife."

"Really?"

Breanna nodded. "Yes, really." His awe changed to respect. "Now let's go up, all right?" He nodded and led the way.

Alex stood facing the cliff, his hands folded behind his back, his feet braced. Breanna thought of how at ease he looked on the deck of a ship, but he should, she reflected. After all, hadn't she imagined him a pirate on more than one occasion?

Forcing her eyes from his form, she saw the rugged cliffs. "It's beautiful," she said, moving close to his side.

Alex swallowed hard. He had decided it would not be wise to encourage friendship with Breanna. He didn't want to hear her talking softly or to enjoy the rippling sound of her laughter. Of course, he didn't think he could handle her rage again, either. All that remained was a distant acquaintance, and that's what he had chosen.

"I like it," he answered tersely. He was sure that if he turned to her that instant, she would be frowning, and probably wondering why he was suddenly withdrawn. Well, he thought, let her wonder. He didn't have to explain anything to her. She was his prisoner. That was all of it.

Leaving her standing there, he joined several of

his crew to see to some lines. It wasn't necessary, in fact it was quite unusual, but no one mentioned it. No one but the lad.

"He ain't never done that!" he mused, not aware he had said it aloud.

Breanna winced. He *was* avoiding her! Why? Their last encounter had been pleasant, and she hadn't exchanged a word with him or even seen him since. Deciding he might be tired or troubled by something, she would let the matter drop. They would soon be rowing ashore. She was sure he would speak to her then.

Chapter 12

Breanna stepped from the small rowboat onto the shore, still puzzled by the sudden change in Alex. He had ordered someone to help her into the craft, joining her only when they were ready to depart. He sat at the opposite end, preventing any conversation. Even when they came ashore, he ignored her. It was only when a single horse awaited them that she heard him speak, and that wasn't pleasant.

"Damn it!" he said with a snarl, gripping the reins of the large black steed prancing at the base of the path that led to the ranch. "Why is there just one horse?"

"You told me ta bring only one," the stable boy said, unused to seeing the man so angry.

Recalling his orders, Alex nodded. "So I did, Tommy," he said more kindly as he swung himself onto the back of the horse. He reached down to ruffle the lad's hair. Having wasted all the time he could, he moved the horse toward Breanna.

"Give me your hand," he ordered, but she shook her head.

"I'll walk, thank you," she replied, already picking her way over the rocky terrain.

He would have preferred she walk. He would have preferred anything but bringing her up to sit in front of him. It would be more temptation than his resolve could bear. But as he prepared to let her walk to maintain his sanity, he saw her stumble.

"Breanna!" he called, prodding the horse close to her.

"Leave me alone!" She held up the hem of her nightgown and began again. Keeping pace, he reached a hand out before her, but she was still smarting from his earlier treatment. It was possible he could change his feelings in an instant, but she couldn't. Slapping away his hand, she continued to move more quickly up the path.

Alex knew it was safer for her, and for his sanity, to let her climb the steep path. She might fall if he interfered. He stayed close behind, however. As she moved ahead of him, he thought he was losing the battle. He had always wanted her, but now he liked her. With the growing respect and fondness he felt, it was becoming more difficult to stay clear of her. In fact, it was damned impossible! He gave up and reached down for her unsuspecting form.

"I told you I'd walk!" Breanna snapped while hanging from his arm.

"And I'm telling you that you will do as I say," he said ruefully, feeling the fates were against him.

Sensing another change occurring, Breanna exclaimed, "You're a devil, Mr. King!"

Her hair blew back to brush his cheek. He felt her softness pressing against his hardened groin. "And you're my own private hell, *querida*," he rasped, tightening his arm. He heard her quick indrawn breath, then a soft denial as he set his large, strong hand upon her tender thigh and groaned her name.

"Please," she begged softly, trying to make him see the people gathering ahead.

Some urgency in her voice forced him to notice. Reining his raging desire for her, he forced himself back under control. Leaning toward her, he whispered near her ear. "Let's go home."

His home was incredibly beautiful, yet Breanna had to struggle to examine it. She was too caught up in the feel of him behind her, but she knew nothing could develop between them. He'd made it clear she was only of interest to him when they touched. She turned her attention to the house, refusing to dwell further on its master . . . and hers.

The setting sun had cast the stucco hacienda in a deep pink light with mauve shadows. It sat in a large clearing against the base of a rugged hillside. Lush green trees seemed to lean protectively near it and offer cool shade against the heat of the day.

Farther along the bluff was the stable and fenced corrals where a number of exquisite horses pranced, but none as magnificent as the one they rode. Several smaller houses could be seen along the far side of the clearing. She wondered if perhaps someone in them could help her.

"Do you like it?" Alex asked, scattering her thoughts.

She thought to ignore him, but didn't want to play his game. "Yes, it's beautiful," she told him honestly.

Alex was torn. He wanted to hold her, to be tender and gentle, yet, if he gave in to his desires, he would lose himself to her, and California had first claim on his heart. He was prepared to explain that to her when he heard a familiar call.

"Hey, Alex!" A weathered old man hailed them as he limped closer. He grinned warmly. "Good to see you back, boy. You stayin' awhile this time?"

Alex felt Breanna squirm and struggled to sound unaffected. "For a while, Hank," he said, dismounting before he ravaged her on the horse. He handed the reins to the old man, then turned to place his hands around Breanna's small waist. "Take care of Satan for me, will you?"

"Sure thing, Alex!" Hank grinned, leading the horse off with a wave.

Alex reluctantly set Breanna on her bare feet. He

noticed how she refused to look at him. He was sure she was having as much trouble figuring out his moods as he was. Pushing the brim of his hat back with a thumb, he sighed.

"Listen, Breanna, I want you to—"

"Alex, my boy!" came a cry from the front door. "Hank said you were home and I came right over to—" The woman's face froze along with her voice. "*This* is Patrick's daughter?" she asked, stunned by the beautiful little woman standing there clad in her nightgown and Alex's huge shirt.

She glanced up at Alex and saw his eyes on the girl. What she saw in them made her heart break. There was love . . . and terrible regret. Hating his pain, she reached for the girl's arm. "Come on, dear," she said kindly, noticing a sadness in her, too. "Let's get you settled." She whisked her away before Alex could introduce them and took care of the matter herself.

Alex watched them go. He had a feeling he was making a terrible mistake by having Breanna in his home. His memories of her were already enough to cause him pain. What would they do to him when he had images of her under his roof, at his table, and only one bedroom door away.

After Hilda bustled out to find her some clothes, Breanna moved about the room she had been given. The tiled floor was covered with brightly colored woven rugs. The bed seemed small for the spacious room, but it was covered with immaculate linens. The cold hearth finally drew her attention, and she imagined it crackling on a damp winter night.

She moved toward the window and gazed out in awe. From it she could see the ocean spreading out to disappear on the horizon. The sun was almost gone, but its reflection turned the water gold.

She felt that the blackness of the coast mirrored the darkness in her heart. She drew her lip between her teeth to keep it from trembling. She couldn't stay in the same house with him. Her nerves were already on edge, and they had just arrived! Backing away from the window, she was filled with the need to run.

Run from the turmoil in her heart! Run from the desire to be in his arms! Run from Alex King, the man!

"So that's Patrick's daughter!" Hilda said again as she sorted through a chest of clothing left by a housekeeper who had run away one night with one of Alex's men. She held up a skirt, shook it out, and nodded. "This'll do," she mumbled to herself. Shifting back to her conversation with a pacing Alex, she went on. "Sure is a pretty little thing, isn't she?"

Alex paused and looked down at the short, plump woman kneeling beside the chest. She and Hank were the closest thing to loving parents he'd ever had. They had opened their door and their hearts to a boy, and the man he had become would never forget.

"Very," he said absently, not wanting to bring up her image in his already tormented mind.

Hilda heard the pain in the single word. Sitting back on her heels, she looked up at Alex. He had been a handsome lad, but he'd become devilishly attractive as a man. He had built an empire in this rugged land and beyond. He was self-educated; success followed his hard work and dedication. He was all this and . . . he was lonely.

He needed someone to share the world he had created. The veneer he'd hidden behind needed to be stripped away, to reveal the sensitive, loving man underneath. At fifteen, when he had come to their door, he had cried in his sleep though he acted tough and resilient in the light of day. Perhaps this girl was what he needed.

"Want ta talk about it, Alex?" she finally said, sure his thoughts were on his guest.

"There's nothing to talk about," Alex said stiffly. He headed for the door, wanting to avoid a conversation.

Hilda rose to her feet and stopped him with a gentle hand on his arm. "When you want to," she said kindly. "I'll be around."

For a moment, Alex was tempted to wrap his arms around the woman who had almost raised him and open his heart, but he didn't know his own feelings, and examining them was a terrifying thought.

"Thanks, Hilda." He smiled, bending to kiss her brow. "But I have to work this out myself." And he would, he thought, making his way down the hall toward Breanna's room. He was no coward. No one was going to disrupt his life, especially a woman! He'd done fine on his own so far; he certainly didn't think it was necessary to change at this late date.

With that settled in his mind, he stopped outside her door to reinforce his decision. She was just a woman—a bit more troublesome than most, but just a woman, nonetheless. He desired her, but there were other women who could satisfy his needs; it didn't have to be she. In fact, if she would give her word not to try anything, he would let her go home so his own life could return to normal.

He opened the door and stepped inside, sure he had the matter under control. "Breanna, I'm going to—" Large brown eyes lifted to glance back at him, stopping him dead in his tracks.

"I want to go home, Mr. King," she said with trembling lips. "I won't do anything to interfere, I promise."

Alex's blue eyes burned with rage. How dare she want to leave him! "You're not going anywhere, Breanna," he said, all his resolve to release her going up in the smoke of burning desire. With long strides, he was at her side.

"You aren't going anywhere," he repeated firmly, his hands gripping her arms. He intended to exert his power over her, intimidating her into becoming submissive to his wishes, but the instant he touched her, the fires flared anew. "Breanna," he breathed, drawing her into his arms.

His mouth fell to hers, claiming all she had to offer. He couldn't fight his passion for this woman any longer. The mission be damned. California be damned! She was here and he wanted her more than anything in his life.

Breanna tasted his desperation on his lips. She felt his hands moving slowly over her back to slide down the roundness of her hips. She could feel his urgency in the thickness pressed to her belly. Her heart skipped and accelerated. Her blood heated. Nothing mattered but the feel of him in her arms.

Alex moaned into her mouth when she surrendered. Her arms circled his waist; her hands worked the tense sinews of his back. His tongue slipped into the warmth of her mouth, and she made a tiny mewling sound that drove him ever more mindlessly toward making love to her.

Slowly, he inched them back toward the bed, the whole time his hands seeking the softness of her body. Finding the fullness of her breast, he held it poised, ready for the exploration of his mouth. Moving his mouth from hers reluctantly, he glanced down at the lightly covered mound. He could see the rose tip through the thin gown. He flicked the pad of his thumb over it, eliciting a drawn breath from her.

"I want you, Breanna," he said, his voice a harsh whisper. "I have from the moment I first saw you." Her head had fallen back and her eyes were closed. He couldn't resist kissing the pulse in her throat. "Let me love you," he begged huskily. "Let me have you."

His words, the sensuousness of his movements, were setting her afire with a need she couldn't define. Her young, virgin body knew only Alex could fulfill that need. Her hands rose to take his head and hold him as his mouth slipped lower. The heat of his breath touched her first, and she arched closer to the sensual teasing.

"These ought to—oops!" Hilda gasped, spying the intimate embrace of lovers. "I'll come back," she said and quickly departed.

It was enough to bring the pair back to their senses. Breanna released him and brought her shaking hands to cover her mouth, preventing the gasp that threatened. Alex raked his dark hair with a none-too-steady hand. Both realized how close they had come to surrendering completely to raw passion and to each other.

Stepping back, Alex saw the inevitability if he shared a house with her. He would make love to her. He couldn't help himself. In fairness to her, he had to remove her from the threat of his presence. She was the daughter of a friend. She deserved better than a few weeks of sharing sexual pleasure, and that was all he could give her now.

"I have a friend nearby that you can stay with until I tell you to go home," he said, not realizing his frustration was making his voice sound remote and cold.

His words cut like a knife. He was sending her away. Wondering how he could turn his passions on and off, Breanna reasoned it was because he felt purely sexual attraction for her. There was no caring, no desire for her as a person. She was a convenient woman in a not-too-convenient situation.

"Fine," she said softly, wishing he would leave her alone.

"I'll arrange it," he called back as he walked out the door.

Breanna squeezed her eyes closed in anguish. When he had kissed her, she realized her feelings for him. She was falling in love with him! Despite his arrogance, despite how little he took her seriously, she was falling under his masculine spell. Suppressing a sob, she sniffled and lifted her chin.

If she let him make love to her, she would be lost. Nothing would be left to her. Her pride, her self-worth would be gone in exchange for a few weeks of being his lover. Oh, it would be exquisite, she was sure. The stolen moments had been splendid! But in the light of day, she would be left with nothing.

Moving toward the door, she made up her mind. She couldn't bear to see him again. She would find Hilda and request asylum until she could leave. If she needed to explain, she would simply tell her the truth. Alex and she were attracted to each other, but there was no future for them.

It was nearly dark. Breanna paused outside the front door, wondering which of the small houses belonged to Hilda. Shrugging in an effort to appear nonchalant, she stepped off the porch to make her way toward them. Surely someone would be around to direct her. Her bare feet left a clear track in the dirt as she went in search of sanctuary.

Hilda was still feeling embarrassment over her interruption of Alex and Breanna earlier, but she was delighted by what she had seen. He did care for the girl! And it appeared she cared for him as well.

Pleased by the turn of events, Hilda had retreated to the storage room down the hall to see if she had missed anything Breanna could use. In her wake, Alex stomped past. A few moments later, Breanna slipped silently down the hall. Tossing her bundle on a chair, Hilda decided to interfere. Something was wrong!

"She left the house," Hilda declared the instant she spied Alex at the kitchen table.

He leaped to his feet. "Left! Where?"

Hilda shook her head. "I don't know. I saw her go out the front door and—" Alex was in pursuit before she could finish. A satisfied grin started to blossom on her face. "That's my boy," she said. "Go get your woman."

Alex swung his head left and right, trying to catch a glimpse of her, but she was nowhere in sight. The evening was darkening. Shadows fell everywhere. The woods that arched around three sides of the house could hide an army! Deciding he could cover more ground on horseback, he called out, "Blackie!" The shaggy head of his blacksmith appeared from the barn. "Get Satan!"

Alex leaped onto the bare back of the horse. Riding for the highest ridge above the ranch, he scanned the landscape below him.

It was all dark shadows and lush growth. If she had gotten into the denser woods, he might not easily find her. He considered returning to the house for help before total darkness fell when a flash of white caught his eye.

Sighing, he leaned forward to pat the powerful neck of his horse. "Come on, Satan. Let's go get her."

The horse snorted, sensing his master's anxiety. Obeying the tug of the reins, Satan started back down the hill, unaware of his part in the destiny of the would-be lovers.

Breanna felt the earth tremble before she heard the thunder of hooves against the hard ground. A few more minutes and it would be dark enough to slip back into the house and find Hilda. She hadn't meant to run into the woods, but when she glanced back and saw Alex exit the house, it had been an automatic reaction. Now she was trapped by her own foolishness. He would think she had planned to run.

Ducking behind a tree to avoid him until she could find help, she ventured to look to see if he had spotted her. A startled scream nearly choked her when she saw him. The last ray of light was reflecting in the eyes of both horse and rider, casting them in menacing shadows.

The image was so frightening, she turned and fled. She knew she was safer staying still, but her fear was pushing her into action. The thundering of her heart grew louder. It took a moment to realize it was the sound of Alex on horseback riding toward her. By the time she realized it, he was leaping to the ground before her.

"I'm not running away!" she cried, defending herself before she was accused. She stepped back as he advanced. "I only wanted to go to Hilda and . . . and you scared me!"

Alex stopped. He was facing his destiny and could no longer fight it. Slowly, he extended his hand, "Come, *pequeña chica*," he said softly, his voice like velvet. "Let me take you back."

She didn't think that was all he was offering, yet she couldn't refuse. It was useless to fight the attraction she felt for him. Despite the logic of staying away from him, she stepped forward and placed her hand in his, but not without one small act of independent defiance.

"I'm not a little girl," she mumbled.

Alex lifted her up on Satan's back, swinging up behind her. Once settled, he wrapped his arms about her. "No, *querida*," he murmured against her ear. "You are no child." There was no need to speak further. He had all night, he thought, all night to prove she was a woman. She had given herself into his keeping, and he was going to take full advantage of it. He couldn't wait anymore.

The horse headed back for the house. Breanna, exhausted and emotionally spent, was surrendering. She knew instinctively what was going to happen this night, but she was powerless to prevent it.

They stopped before the house. Alex dismounted and lifted her into his arms. She was ready to tell him she was capable of walking, yet his arms felt so strong about her, so protective, she remained silent. He paused just inside the door.

"Hungry?"

She nodded.

"Would you like a bath?"

She nodded again more firmly.

A slow smile twitched at one corner of his mouth. She had no way of knowing he was thinking of satisfying all her appetites. "Then you eat while I see to having a bath readied for you." He put her down but didn't let her go.

"Breanna," he began, his tone growing serious. "There will be no turning back." Her eyes widened, then she lowered her head. "Do you understand?" he asked, his hand cupping her chin.

Breanna nodded slowly. "Yes, Alex," she said softly. "But there is something you have to know."

Alex didn't want to know anything if it prevented him from having her. "Tell me later, *querida*," he said, turning her around and gently shoving her toward the kitchen.

A dinner of chili and cornbread sat on the table, but Hilda was nowhere in sight. Sniffing the spicy aroma, Breanna ladled out a bowl, buttered the bread, and settled down to eat. It was delicious, and she finished every drop. She was licking the crumbs from her fingers when Alex came in.

"Your bath is ready," he said, trying to keep his eyes from her. He prepared a serving for himself and turned to find her still seated. "Go on, *querida*. Go take your bath."

Breanna's tongue slipped out to moisten her suddenly dry lips. She was nervous and it gave her pause.

Attributing her hesitation to a prelude of denial, Alex set his bowl on the table sharply. "You said you wanted a bath, now go take it."

His mood wasn't going to be conducive to talking. Biting her lip, she decided it was easier simply to obey him for the time being. Once she had bathed and he had eaten, she would tell him she couldn't go through with it.

As she started down the hall to her room, she gathered resolve. She had never actually said she would go to him. It was true she had not said no, but she hadn't said yes, either!

What they both needed, she reasoned, was a good night's sleep. Then they wouldn't be so tense, they would be clear-headed and they could work everything out. It never occurred to her that no amount of sleep was going to ease the sexual frustration tearing them apart.

Alex stood at her door. He could hear her humming softly. He closed his eyes, imagining her in the tub. "Fool," he mumbled, realizing he didn't need to fantasize. All he had to do was open the door. He reached for the knob and saw his hand shaking. That a wisp of a female could do this to him made him snarl and open the door more sharply than he intended.

"Oh!" Breanna cried as she clutched the edge of the tub when the door hit the wall behind it. It took seconds for her to notice his shirt was hanging open and his inky hair was still damp from a bath of his own. The fact upset her more than the noise the door made.

Alex flinched, seeing the fear. "I . . . I . . ." He stepped inside, hating his sudden shyness. "I thought you would be done," he said more firmly, once he cleared his throat.

"Well, I'm not!" she exclaimed, tensing at the flame that seemed to come to life in his eyes. Careful not to reveal herself, she turned her back to him. "If you'll wait outside, I'll come out when I'm through. Then we'll talk."

Talk! They were past talking. Didn't she know that? He thought that he'd made it clear and that she'd accepted it. Striding toward the tub, he glared down at her. For a moment he was distracted by the curves of her breasts above the water. The pinkness of her knees then caught his eyes. It was only when she tried to slip deeper beneath the water that his attention returned to her face.

"We have nothing to talk about," he said, dropping to one knee beside her. His hand reached out gently to run a finger along her bare shoulder.

"We do!" she squealed as a shiver racked her from his touch. Alex slowly shook his head, his finger sliding lower to trace the waterline across her chest. "Alex, please! I . . . I'm tired! I want to go to bed!"

Blue fire leaped into the eyes he turned on her. "At last you're being sensible," he breathed.

She placed her hand over his to still it. "Please, Alex. This is insane! We'll only regret—"

"I won't regret it, Breanna." Then he claimed her mouth before she could utter a sound.

If only he hadn't touched her. If only he hadn't kissed her. If only . . . She felt his arms drawing her from the cover of the cool water. Her breasts met the matted hair of his bare chest, and she moaned a sound of pure pleasure. She felt his hands circling her waist until she was standing naked in his arms.

Floating in a sensual sea, Breanna felt the pins drawn from her hair even as his mouth pillaged hers. In the morning she might hate herself, but tonight she was going to discover all the secrets of her womanhood.

Her hair tumbled down over her back and his hands relished the heavy tresses, while his body felt the warm wetness of her skin and pressed intimately to it. He dropped his head to her shoulder and lathed the beads of water from it with his tongue.

"God, Breanna! You are so lovely, so perfect." His tongue moved to the curve of her breast. "You make me forget everything when you're in my arms." He found the tight bud he sought. Slowly he ran his tongue across it, making her gasp in delight. After teasing it a moment longer, he could hear the huskiness of her breathing and knew she was as lost as he.

He straightened to full height and swept her lush nakedness into his arms. Her hair curtained some of her delights, but he didn't care. Soon, very soon, he would savor every inch of her.

The time had come. Breanna knew she was about to become a woman . . . his woman! She did not resist when he lifted her into his arms, or when he began to carry her damp body across the room, but when he reached the door, she stiffened.

"Someone might see us," she said, hugging him closer as a shield.

"No one would dare," he said. They slipped into his dark room and toward the bed.

"You forgot my nightgown," she said, her apprehension growing as the night air cooled her body.

Alex paused beside the bed. "You won't need it, Breanna. I'll keep you warm." He started to deposit her on the bed, but her arms tightened around his neck.

"Wait!"

Standing, he frowned down at her. He didn't want to waste time talking! "What now?" he said more harshly than he intended.

Breanna winced and lowered her head. "I told you I needed to tell you something first," she said in a whisper. She realized how ridiculous it was that he was standing there nearly dressed and she was stark naked in his arms. Glad for the darkness, she went on. "Could I have a robe first before we talk?" she asked shyly.

"Oh, Lord!" Alex said with a groan, unable to believe she was trying to delay their union in the most childish of ways. "You don't need a robe!" He tossed her on the bed and shrugged out of his shirt, throwing it down beside her. He turned to sit and remove his boots and heard her moving around. "You'd better not try to leave," his voice rumbled. "I want this to be pleasant for you, too, Breanna, but I won't tolerate any games."

Biting her lip, Breanna realized she was in over her head. He'd often accused her of acting first and thinking later. This was a perfect example of her foolishness, but she had no intention of trying to get out of it. She wanted to know, and she wanted Alex to be the man to teach her. Slipping her arms into his discarded shirt, she wiggled to her knees behind him.

"Alex, listen!" she pleaded as she reached out to lay her hand on his back. He stilled. "All I'm trying to tell you is I . . . I don't want you to be disappointed." She was ready to explain she had no experience where men were concerned, despite what her wanton actions said.

Dropping the second boot, Alex turned. "I won't be disappointed, Breanna." He reached to brush back her hair. He smiled when he spied the white of his shirt. "I'm not looking to break in a virgin, nor do I care who else has had you." Her head began to shake. "You're mine now."

His hand circled her neck, drawing her mouth to his before she could protest.

Chapter 13

Kneeling on the mattress, Alex lowered Breanna's tense body down on it. He knew she wanted to object, but he didn't want to hear it. All he wanted was to feel her beneath him, moving, taking him inside her. Stretching out beside her, he placed a restraining leg over hers in case she decided to bolt. The moment he had her securely pinned to the bed, his mouth moved from her lips to her cheek to caress her ear.

"Don't," Breanna said, afraid of the feelings he was awakening.

"Don't what?" Alex's throaty question brushed her ear. "Don't do this?" His lips burned a trail of kisses down her neck to cease in the valley between her breasts. "Or this?" He pushed aside the shirt she wore and ran his fingers caressingly over the flesh of her breasts. "Or this, *querida?*" Cupping the fullness, Alex lowered his dark head. His tongue traced the hardening peak.

Breanna's eyes lowered when Alex ran his tongue across the peak and back, and widened with a gasp when he gently bit down. Her senses were completely at his command. Her eyes were open but she couldn't see. Her body was nearly bare to the night air, yet she couldn't feel the chill.

Breanna pushed at his shoulders, but he murmured for her to hold him and she responded like a puppet to his greater force.

He knew the resistance had left her. Slowly, he

186

released his hold on her to put his hands to better use. Long fingers ran the length of her and traced small circles on her sensitive hips. He heard her whimper softly when his rough hands met the tender softness of her inner thigh. His own passions were raging, his need painfully tense, but he would wait for her to become as passionate as he, before losing control.

Except for the one kiss she had offered him in the garden an eternity ago, she had only passively accepted the sweet torture he bestowed upon her. He wanted to push her to the level where she became an active partner. He wanted her to touch him, excite him purposefully as he was doing to her. If only she would . . .

Breanna's fingers slid over Alex's shoulder and found their way into the thickness of his hair. She pressed him closer to her breast while she kneaded the tense muscles in his neck before tracing his spine with her nails.

Alex trembled with rapture. She wanted him. No matter what she said, her body wanted his. He returned his questing lips to hers and was rewarded with a passionate kiss that promised greater pleasures to come.

He was ready and he wanted her ready to receive him. Moving his hand sensuously down her body, he sought the curls at the apex of her silken thighs. His fingers found the core of her throbbing pleasure and he heard her gasp.

"Easy, *querida*." His voice was a husky growl from deep in his throat. "I won't hurt you." She slowly relaxed with his promise and gentle ministrations. Soft purring sounds came from her throat, driving Alex nearly into a frenzy with his own need, but he refused to find his release until she had hers.

Breanna was entering an unexplored world of feeling. She could hear his raspy breathing but didn't know the agony that went with it. She was too busy feeling her skin growing hot and wet as an ache grew inside her. He moved to her side and she realized he was stripping away the last barrier between them. For a fleeting moment she was afraid, but the feel of his hot, hard flesh pressed to hers dispelled all fears. She wanted him to help her understand her restless need. She needed him to teach her the secrets of men that women only whispered about.

"Let me love you, *querida*," Alex moaned, anxious to feel her open to him. "Let me give you pleasure." When her only response was to wrap her arms about him, he slipped a hand between her thighs to part them.

Looking down at her face in the darkness, he could only detect her pearly teeth biting at her lower lip. If he had been less obsessed about possessing her, he might have suspected it was a gesture of fear surfacing. Instead, his eyes closed and he entered her.

A gasp of pain. Nails digging into the sinews of his back. Something was wrong. Alex groped for an answer and, when it came, it had the effect of ice water on his fiery desires.

Without looking at Breanna, Alex rolled from her and sat on the side of the bed, his back to her. Balancing his arms across his knees, he hung his head and tried to understand what had just happened. His rationale had been sound. Her independence, her travels alone, her plan to seduce Guillermo, everything pointed to a woman who knew and understood what went on between a man and a woman. Raking back his hair, he groaned. God! How could he have been so wrong?

Carefully, he rose and lit the bedside candle. Drawing a steadying breath, he turned to look at her. He felt a gut-wrenching ache when his eyes fell on her. She had rolled away from him. The shirt she still wore rode up around her waist, and his eyes were drawn first to her rounded hip, then to a dark smudge on her inner thigh.

Closing his eyes, he suffered his guilt in silence. He had hurt her, he knew it. She had been a virgin. That was why she thought he would be disappointed in her. That was why he had to make her moves for her. Berating himself for being so blind, he knelt on the bed and reached to place his hand on her shoulder. Her flinch cut through him like a knife, but he refused to let her be. He owed her more than that.

He eased down beside her, pulled a quilt over them both, and draped an arm across her waist to draw her firmly back against him.

Alex felt her shudder at his touch and tightened his hold, expecting her to bolt, but she merely released a sob and stilled. The silence that followed filled him with confusion. He was bombarded with self-loathing, yet his body throbbed with wanting her still. Guilt racked him, but he kept holding her to answer a sudden need to protect her. There was a tenderness welling in him that was hard to understand.

The emotions were new. They needed examining. For a moment he thought he felt so oddly because she had been a virgin, but he realized he hadn't really cared if she had been with other men. He suddenly knew that the past didn't matter. When she came to him it would be a new beginning for both of them. Unfortunately, it was totally new for her.

"I'm sorry, little one," he breathed while leaning to brush his lips against her hair. "Not for being the first. It had to happen someday, and I'm glad it was me." She remained still and silent. "But I'm sorry I hurt you. Had I realized what you were trying to tell me, I could have found an easier way." He moved to put his arm beneath the blanket to touch her.

Breanna tossed back the covers with a cry and

was about to flee when she whirled around to stare at him. In the low light of the flickering candle she was enchanting. Her hair was a glorious riot of burnished copper hanging about her like a cloak. The shirt she wore was parted enough to reveal the rising flesh of her breasts and only hinted at the treasures it covered. The sleeves fell over her hands, and she used one to brush aside a tear as it rolled down her cheek.

She was angry and terribly frustrated by what had happened, but her anger wasn't because of her lost virginity. He was right. It was bound to happen. Her agitation came from deep inside, from some mysterious desire, some need unfulfilled. He had made promises both verbally and with his body, only to roll away from her before they were kept.

She hadn't meant to cry out and drive him away, but she hadn't expected any pain, either. Now, to make matters worse, he was treating her like a child!

"Don't c-call me little one!" Her voice cracked. "I'm a woman! You've just seen to that!"

He smiled skeptically, raising his brow. He had expected tears, but once again Breanna was handing him the unexpected. She was angry, yet he wasn't sure what she was angry about.

"You're not quite a woman yet, *gatita*," he said, sitting up and leaning against the headboard. He saw her troubled eyes drop to his chest. Drawing up a knee, he balanced his arm across it. "What's the matter, Breanna? You seem perplexed."

"You talk in riddles!" she snapped. "How can I be not quite a woman?" His low, soft laughter at her ignorance made her cheeks burn. "Don't you dare laugh at me after . . . after what you've done!" Her clenched fists weren't visible beneath the long sleeves, but her stance was indicative enough of her rage. "Why, I . . . I could even now be . . . be pregnant!"

Alex was trying to contain his laughter when Breanna swung her fist at his cheek. She missed and fell across the bed. Before she could regain her footing, he grabbed her wrist and hauled her across his lap. His arms circled her struggling form and subdued her with little effort.

"You are not pregnant, little one," he whispered harshly. "I've yet to give you that part of me that could produce a child."

Breanna grew still and looked at him skeptically. "But you . . . we . . . I thought . . ."

"No, little one." His lips twitched and a nerve ticked in his cheek below his scar. "You are not quite a woman because, although you are no longer a virgin, you have not experienced the height of passion. His fingers wrapped in her hair and his lips moved toward hers. "But, I promise you, Breanna, before this night is over, you will."

Breanna's eyes fluttered as she struggled to wakefulness. The last thing she remembered was Alex's husky vow and his lips on hers. His kiss held a promise, yet he shifted her until she was comfortably at his side and stroked her hair until she fell asleep. She wasn't sure how long she slept. The room was dark again.

The warmth of Alex's chest pressed against her cheek. She could hear the steady rhythm of his heartbeat. Her arm was casually draped across his middle, and she snuggled a bit closer to enjoy his strength.

"You seem determined to keep me at my word, *querida*," Alex said softly as he wrapped his arms around her to draw her over his chest. Breanna could hear a touch of humor in his voice but could not see his face. "I try to be gallant and let you rest before . . . before I keep my promise, and you wake me with your fidgeting."

The night was shedding a layer of darkness, and dawn was preparing to make its entrance. Breanna thought she could feel his smile. "I wasn't fidgeting! I just woke up and—"

"I'm only teasing, little one," he interrupted while his hands wrapped themselves in the thickness of her hair. It had fallen across his chest and caressed him like silk each time she moved. "Why are you always going against me?" he asked, sighing and closing his eyes to await her answer. "Why do we always strike such sparks?"

Drawing a deep breath, Breanna rose up to perch her arms on the expanse of his chest, allowing herself to study his vague image. She could see his sooty lashes and the whiter skin of his scar as the sky lost one more degree of darkness.

"I don't know," she said.

Alex arched a brow, doubting her weak reply. "Don't know or won't tell me?"

Refusing to answer, Breanna pushed against his chest with splayed hands, trying to get away from his questions, only to find herself rolled over to her back with him above her.

"You're not getting away that easily, Breanna." Her name sounded like a caress on his lips. "I want my questions answered before we share that pleasure I promised."

Breanna turned her face away from his. "I suppose it's because we think so differently," she said, trying to give him an answer he would understand without antagonizing him. "You see yourself as California's savior, yet fail to see my worth."

"Oh, *querida*," Alex groaned. "Believe me, I do see your worth!" She glared at him. He knew instantly he'd said the wrong thing, but it couldn't be taken back. Instead, he would have to divert her attention. Rolling to her side, he parted the fabric covering her breast.

"Let's not talk now." He lowered his lips to gently kiss the hardening nubbin. "Let's work on that promise I made you."

He heard her ragged sigh of surrender and took

the fullness of her into his mouth to suckle. There would be no more words, he thought, as she ran her hands over his back. Carefully, he rose to his knees, drawing her up with him. Once they faced each other, he pushed away the shirt that covered her.

When she was as naked as he, he drew her close, her breasts pressing into his chest. Her name rolled from his lips as his kisses moved from her shoulder to her neck. He knew she enjoyed the feel of his hands caressing her. He could feel her satiny skin growing warmer.

"Let me love you, Breanna," he said raggedly, "and for God's sake, love me back!"

His plea was laced with lonely despair. Some element of it touched her soul, and she slid her hands up his powerful arms to hold him. A tremor ran through him, giving her a sense of power all her own. She turned her head, seeking his lips to convey her acquiescence in silence.

Alex's kiss consumed her. It branded and claimed her with its intensity. His arms were like bands of steel, holding her in desperate closeness and stirring the desires held in check the past few hours for the both of them.

Wishing to give as much pleasure as she was receiving, Breanna drew on her limited knowledge. Weaving her fingers in his hair, she tugged lightly to free her lips. Before he could misconstrue her actions, she placed tiny kisses at the corners of his mouth. Tentatively, her small tongue traced his lower lip and her teeth pulled gently at it.

Alex allowed her to play her tempting game a moment longer, but the ache in his groin was intense, and he had much left to teach her. Clamping his hands about her waist, he lifted her from her knees and settled her on the bed without breaking her hold on him. While she continued her assault on his mouth, his hands roamed over her silken flesh.

Breanna basked in his daring exploration. His mouth had left hers to gently attack and arouse. Her breasts, her thighs, the satiny skin at her waist and across her flat stomach, all received his attention. She was afire for something beyond her comprehension and slowly losing touch with reality.

Alex saw her drifting away and sought to draw her back. He withdrew his hands. Breanna moaned and arched her hips to follow them. When she could no longer keep contact, she breathed "Please, don't stop."

"It takes two to make love, *querida*." He swallowed hard, not immune to her plea. "You must touch me also, arouse my desires." His manhood pressed hard against her soft thigh belied the need for arousal, but he was counting on her innocence to add to his own pleasure and her experience.

Breanna closed her eyes to cover her awkwardness. "I . . . I don't know what to do." Taking a deep breath, she opened her eyes to find his watching her. "Help me."

Without a word, Alex took her hand and pulled it to his chest. He glided it over his muscled expanse and slowly, carefully, led her trembling fingers to the flat tautness of his stomach. She became so intent on the firm texture, the sensuous strength of him, she didn't realize his guiding hand had set hers free. Her fingers moved down to feather against his turgid staff.

Breanna shivered with a mixture of apprehension and the desire to know him, to know his body. Slowly, she allowed her curiosity to overcome her shyness. Her hand grew bolder as she discovered the power she had over this man. She could hear his breathing grow harsh. She could feel his body tense, the fine sheen that covered his body conveyed his great need. It was a heady sensation to have such control, to be the leader in this thing called passion.

Alex could stand no more. The silken strokes of

Breanna's hand were driving him beyond reason.
He knew he had to stop her caresses or bear the
shame of lost control. With a trembling hand, he
gripped her wrist.

"No!" Breanna cried when he stopped her.

"Yes," he growled, pushing her to the bed and
rising above her. "I can wait no longer." He braced
himself above her and pressed gently between her
thighs until he found that still virginal territory.
"It's time, Breanna," he rasped. "Time for you to
be a woman. Time to make you mine."

She was mesmerized by the possessive quality
of his words. He was laying claim to her very
soul. She'd been a fool to think she could dictate
to this man. He was the master and she a mere
slave to the passion he had awakened. For a moment she teetered between the desire to feel again
the quickening deep inside her and the fear that
she would no longer belong to herself if she did.

Alex saw only the fear, and it angered him. She
was his! Why couldn't she accept that fact? He
moved forward, thrusting true and deep to claim
her body in a single stroke. This time her cry
would not dissuade him. This time there was an
urgency to possess her.

Breanna began to struggle the instant he filled
her. He was so large, so hard, she thought he
would tear her apart. She closed her eyes and
thrashed her head about, but she could still see
him above her. His muscles rippled, the cords of
his neck bulged with each thrust. He was around
her, over her, in her, and she began to respond to
him.

Her hips matched the rhythm of his, and she
found herself caught up in the same pagan need.
She could feel the hot strength of him driving
deep, seeking and seducing some unknown part
of her. With a whimper, she reached with her body
to unravel the mystery.

Alex's best intentions to teach her the delights of

the flesh were close to being undermined by his weeks of abstinence. Agony filled his vitals, yet he held back. She had to come full circle! He had to keep his word to make her a woman, to teach her body the pleasures he had promised, but it was growing difficult.

She was near, he could sense it. *God, hurry!* his mind cried, and her body answered. He heard a guttural cry from her throat. He felt her hips arch tightly to him while her hands clutched his arms. She was on the brink of ecstasy. Gripping her hips, he quickened the pace.

"Now, Breanna! Now!"

They were one! She could feel the pulsing of him fill her and draw her beyond the sun. She gasped for air as her body trembled and pressed so closely to his, he could have absorbed her. She could not tell from whose mouth came the cries of passion until he whispered her name, and she knew the savage growls were her own.

The tension in his body eased slowly and he settled his weight over her. She listened to his heavy breathing restore itself to normal against her ear. Her hands absently kneaded the firm flesh of his hips while her own mind was restored to coherent thought.

The mysteries of her womanhood were solved. The fears for her destiny were just beginning. She knew and understood passion and desire. She had allowed a man to touch her and take her to a world of sensation, but what would it cost her? Her questions had once cost her kisses, her defiance this seduction. What would the price be if she lost her heart?

Breanna was afraid to examine that question. She was afraid it might already be too late. On the ship she had considered it but found it was a fool's errand to love him. He may have needed her to slake some desire, but only his dedication to his mission could hold his heart. He had put California before her once, and she had no doubts he could do it again. She reasoned that the only safeguard to salvage her pride was to treat this earth-shattering experience as something that would not permanently affect her.

Alex didn't know what she was thinking, he was too occupied with his own thoughts. He had made love to her. He had possessed her. It was what he had wanted to do, yet he still knew an ache, a need for more. She was quiet and passive beneath him now, but she had been a vibrant, willing partner in their carnal journey. Would it be like that each time he took her? Would what had just happened between them bind her closer to him or force her to flee?

The thought of her leaving caused a pain in his chest. He had found something unique in Breanna. What had been a natural act to ease himself had become a glorious union that touched his soul. He wasn't sure why he had never experienced such pleasure before. Perhaps because she was the first woman he had made love to, not just shared sex with.

In the dim light of predawn, he looked down at the woman at his side. Gently he brushed the wild curls from her brow. Her eyes were averted, keeping him from seeing her feelings. He saw her lips move to speak, then close again. He ran the tip of his finger down her arm.

"I kept my word, little one. It is not yet dawn and you are a woman. A glorious, passionate woman."

Breanna was thrilled by his words and the lips he brushed against her ear. It took all her self-control not to turn to him and seek a greater intimacy, but his seductive exploration was not conducive to coherent thought. To prevent him from going further until she could sort out her thoughts, she opened her eyes and stared at the ceiling.

"I'm new at this, Mr. King. Should I thank you?"

Alex stiffened. For a brief moment he thought he might have found someone to share his future with, but the dream disappeared in a red mist of fury.

"Christ!" he swore. "After what just happened, you can ask that?" He rolled away to sit on the edge of the bed in seething silence, until fury impelled movement and he stalked to the window, grabbing a handful of curtain and drawing it back. The sun was just appearing over the horizon, pink tinting the sky, but he could not see the beauty.

His ragged sigh reached Breanna's ears and she sat up, clutching a cover and drawing it to her breasts guiltily. Her cold tone was meant to ease any strain between them ... and protect her pride, she realized. What they had shared was incredible, yet she knew there was no guarantee for a future. All she was doing was making the inevitable parting easier. She prepared to tell him that when he spoke first.

"What do you want from me, Breanna?" he asked in a controlled voice. "Love? Marriage? Is that why you're pretending this meant nothing to you?"

Her eyes widened. What did she want? She had already admitted to herself she was beginning to care for Alex, but she believed there was no future for them. Was he telling her there could be?

Hope blossomed inside her. Pulling the sheet from the bed, she rose quickly and draped it about her body. Silently she stepped toward him, lifted her hand, and touched his arm.

"Don't!" he ordered and yanked away from her without looking down to see the hurt in her eyes. "I'm not used to curious virgins!"

Breanna's heart twisted. She wanted to tell him that she had no regrets, that she would take only what he could give if he would just treat her kindly, but he would not listen. He was taking away any chance for them.

"I'm no longer a virgin, Mr. King," she said flippantly, "and I am no longer curious!" She turned to leave the room, but his hand shot out, stopping her.

"Damn you, Breanna!" he said, seeing her toss her head defiantly. He saw the hurt she was trying to hide, and something in him softened. He was being cruel. His own fears were making him push her away when all he wanted was to hold her. He drew her resisting body into the circle of his arms.

"I'm trying to tell you I want you to stay with me." He struggled to get the words out.

Breanna leaned back and looked at him, stunned by his gentleness. "I . . . I don't understand," she stammered.

Pressing her head to his chest, he stroked her hair. "I don't understand it either, *querida*," he told her softly. "All I know is that I can't send you away." He felt her shiver. Was it the cool air, fear, or relief? "There is something between us. Something I never experienced before," he told her honestly. "If you would rather go, I won't stop you, but I want you to stay."

"You would let me go home?" she asked, surprised that their night together had caused such a change in him.

Moving back, he cupped her chin and made her look at him. "No, *gatita*." He grinned. "I may be crazy for wanting you, but I'm not fool enough to go that far." She frowned deeply. "I only want to know if you would like to go to Hilda's or would rather stay here . . . with me."

Pride and common sense told her to go, to get as far from him as she could, but the finger tracing her spine was convincing her to remain. Lowering her eyes, she said, "I'll stay, Alex, but only if—"

Alex pressed his fingers to her lips to silence her. "No conditions, Breanna. If you stay, it will have to be because you want to." Her eyes closed. "And we will see if together we can work out this thing that is between us."

He was asking her to live with him, to share a part of her life with him, but without making commitments. Could she do it? She knew it would mean sharing his bed. He was too virile for her to believe their relationship would be platonic. It was tempting, yet she had to consider the future.

If she stayed, she would be a fallen woman. No man would want her afterward, knowing she had belonged to another. But did *she* want another man after Alex?

"I'll stay," she whispered, her voice barely audible.

Alex hadn't realized he was holding his breath until she spoke. "You won't be sorry, Breanna," he said, tipping back her head to kiss her.

I hope not, she thought as she surrendered her mouth to his.

Chapter 14

Alex could not remember a sleep so sound. He struggled from its depths with visions of large brown eyes and coppery curls dancing in his mind. Breanna, soft and willing. Breanna, wild and demanding.

After she agreed to stay on Alex took her back to his bed and they made love until they were both limp. The memory of her silky hair being drawn slowly across his groin brought renewed life to his organ, and he reached for her.

Gone!

Damn! He'd believed she genuinely wanted to stay with him, but it must have been a trick, a ruse to put him off his guard. Ripping back the covers, Alex grabbed his pants and started for the door, donning them as he went.

"Bruja!" he murmured harshly, sure she had bewitched him. He stopped first to see if she had simply returned to her own room, and he found it empty. His anger blossomed as he headed for the front door, intent on finding her or someone who had seen her leave.

As his hand grabbed the knob, he paused. The clatter of pans in the kitchen made him sigh heavily. He cocked an ear and heard the soft lilt of a ditty floating out to greet him. Slowly his mouth softened, and he smiled.

Nearing the doorway, Alex stood in the shadows and watched her. She was standing at the stove in an apron and his shirt. Far from being amusing, the picture of her slender legs and softly rounded bottom in the silk covering was erotic. Her hair was hanging loose down her back, nearly reaching her waist, and each time she moved her head, it beckoned for him to come and touch it.

Breanna picked up a towel and bent to check the oven. The sight sorely tempted him. He clenched his teeth in a gasp, but she seemed not to notice. Silently, he eased up behind her and clutched her hips, pulling her back against his aroused hardness.

Expecting her to squeal, he was surprised when she leaned against him. She'd caught his movement at the door and decided to turn the tables on him.

"Did you think I had run away?" she asked, a wicked little grin on her face. At the guilty shake of his head, she grew more mischievous and turned in his arms. "I think you did, Mr. King," she said, tugging at a curl of black hair on his chest.

Alex winced but couldn't resist a smile. He was enjoying this playful side of her. "And I think you're getting to be a brazen little hussy, standing here dressed like that." Her cheeks pinkened. "You would tempt a saint, Breanna, and I think I've proved I'm far from that."

"Indeed," she agreed flippantly, pushing him away. "Now sit down. Your breakfast is ready." She leaned over to open the oven and get the biscuits, nearly dropping them when his hand swatted her bottom. "Alex!" she squealed.

Shrugging to let her know he hadn't been able to resist, he sat. She placed the biscuits on the table but stayed out of reach. She added a plate of scrambled eggs and slices of bacon, and poured coffee for them both.

There was a comfortable silence between them as they ate. It felt perfectly natural for her to be sharing his table. In fact, everything they did together seemed natural, he thought. It was as if they were destined to be two halves of a whole. She added spice to his bland world. She could give as good as she got, yet she could also curl softly in his arms and let him be her strength. She had enraged him and brought him to the height of bliss. Yes, he thought, Breanna Sullivan was like no woman he had ever known.

While Alex was listing her attributes in his mind, Breanna was assessing her feelings for him in hers. She was beyond feeling just fondness for Alex. He was beginning to become very important to her. In the night, she had tried to examine those feelings, to discover if she was falling in love, but she had no experience with love and could not come to any sane conclusion. By the light of day, it was no better. All she knew was that her life would be very empty without him.

Taking a sip of her coffee, Breanna thought of how she might bring them closer. Their mutual love for California might be the key.

"Alex," she said, toying with her cup. "I've been thinking."

His brow arched, but he remained silent. Was the time for recriminations at hand? Had she thought about the repercussions of staying with him and changed her mind? Placing his elbows on the table, he tented his fingers at his mouth and waited.

"You were right about Guillermo. It would have been foolish to try anything with him."

This was the last thing he thought she was going to say. To cover his surprise, he reached for his own cup. "I'm glad you see it my way," he said, not sure what was going on in that pretty head of hers. "He would have seen through your ploy, especially since he's suddenly begun to suspect me, and we gave the impression that we are . . . close."

"You gave the impression." She grinned. "As I recall, I was too busy trying to dissuade you."

Reaching across the table, Alex covered her hand with his. "Too bad you never had a chance," he teased. Her eyes lowered and he sat back, laughing at her shyness.

She waited for him to resume his meal before she went on. "I would be better able to get information from one of his subordinates," she said, gasping when he choked. "Alex! Are you all right?" she asked, leaping to his side.

Alex took a swallow of coffee to clear the lump in his throat. He drew several deep breaths, then turned to glare at her. "What the hell are you talking about?" he demanded.

"Me?" she asked, stunned by his anger. She took a step backward but it wasn't far enough. His hand gripped her wrist, preventing her from escaping.

"Yes, you!" He yanked her forward until she was standing between his spread thighs.

"I . . . I was just thinking that I could . . . could help," she stammered. "Now that we've settled things between us, I—"

"Settled things!" he growled. "You mean that just because I took you to bed you thought I would let you do what you wanted, didn't you?"

"No! I just thought—"

"Well, nothing's changed! I still think you're dangerous to yourself and could be a threat to us all."

Breanna tried to wrench her wrist from his grip, but he was too strong. She glared at him. "It has nothing to do with that! You just like bullying me and . . . and . . ."

"And making love to you?" he offered, hoping to make her forget her foolish notions.

"Is that all you think about?" she cried, wanting to do him bodily harm for considering her so inept.

Alex's eyes ran the length of her. They began to smolder when he reached out his free hand to stroke the bare flesh of her thigh. "Yes, Breanna," he told her, moving his hand upward beneath the shirt to caress the roundness of her buttock. She tried to pull away, but he dragged her to his lap.

Seeing the stubborn set of her chin, he sighed. "I care what happens to you," he admitted, but she didn't soften to him. "At first, it was only the mission that motivated my decision to bring you here, but somehow that's all changed now."

Breanna began to pluck at the hem of her apron. "At first, I hated you," she said softly. "And that's changed, too, yet I still feel the same about being a part of this endeavor to free California."

Alex was torn between thrashing her and taking her in his arms. The damned stubborn beauty was driving him mad. He needed to get away from her for a while, to settle his nerves and keep from losing his temper, and he lifted her from his lap and rose.

"Stay close to the house," he told her as he padded back to his room to finish dressing.

Breanna watched him go, feeling a cold emptiness in the pit of her stomach. Had she driven him away? Was her stubborn refusal not to give in on the issue of California going to cause an irreparable breach between them? If so, she didn't think it wise to remain.

Summoning her courage, she followed him. She had made her decision and she wanted to tell him now, before he had the chance to dissuade her.

Alex pushed his shirttail inside his pants with more force than was needed. He was angry, but some of the anger was turned on himself. He should have reacted less harshly. He might have convinced her that, at some future time, she could help. If he wasn't careful, he thought, yanking on a boot, he was going to make her angry enough to leave.

The thought struck him hard. He really had no power to keep her there. She only thought he did. In reality he had done no more than kidnap her for her own sake and the sake of those she could jeopardize. Or was that the only reason? Rubbing his neck, he tried once again to figure out his feelings for Breanna.

She excited him. She intrigued him. He found incredible pleasure in her arms. No matter what she did, he was enchanted. The only problem was that she did not belong to him, not really. If she chose, she could leave. There was only one way he would have authority over her—and that was if she was his wife.

Waiting for the shudder of disgust he expected the thought of tying himself to a woman to bring, he was surprised to find it didn't come. In fact, the idea held appeal.

He placed his hands on the bed behind him and tried to picture her there when he came home. She would smile and run to him, leap into his arms and cover his face with kisses. He would sweep her up and carry her to their bed. He would . . .

"I think it would be best if I go to Hilda's house," Breanna said from the door.

"I don't want you to go."

Breanna didn't want to hear him say that. She had made up her mind and refused to change it. Shaking her head, she went to her room and closed the door between her and the man she wanted more than anything.

She began to unbutton the shirt. It was time for her to dress and prepare to leave. Sighing as she thought of what might have been had they met at a different place and time, she jumped and spun when the door slammed back against the wall.

"I said I don't want you to go!" Alex said, his voice raised in anger.

"Last night you said I could if I chose to, and I do."

"Last night I didn't know I cared about you!" he shouted, moving threateningly close. "It didn't matter then."

She glared up at him. "I knew I cared!" she cried. "But I also knew it was madness to try to—"

"You care?" he interrupted, somewhat dumbfounded.

Breanna gasped and turned away from him. She hadn't meant to tell him that. "I . . . I didn't mean—oh!" she cried when his strong hands turned her to face him.

"Do you, Breanna? Do you care for me, even a little?"

There was such desperation in his voice, she could only stare at him. "Alex, I . . . I—"

He pulled her into his arms, holding her to him. "I want you to care, Breanna," he told her, his hands smoothing her hair over her back. "I want you to care enough to be my wife."

Breanna swayed against him. If he hadn't been holding her, she was sure she would have swooned. What was he saying? Was he trying to punish her with words that meant nothing?

"Y-your wife?" she mumbled against his chest.

"Yes, *querida*," he replied, suddenly wanting very much for her to belong to him and only him.

Carefully, Breanna eased away from his arms. He let her go. She walked across the room to the window to stare at the blue sea. It was almost the color of his eyes.

"Why, Alex?" she asked, her mind in a turmoil. "You don't love me. Why would you want to marry m-me?"

Alex sat on her bed but kept his eyes on her. "I've never been in love, Breanna. I'm not even sure if it isn't just something people confuse with lust, but I do know you're special to me." He stood and moved behind her. Without touching her, he went on. "You just said you care for me. I'll ask no more than that from you. It's enough, Breanna, enough for me to want to share my life with you."

Breanna bit her lip. During the night she had thought of what it would be like if she and Alex married. It seemed fitting since he had taken what was meant only for her husband. Now, with the possibility before her, she should be ecstatic, yet there was still something else to settle.

"And what about your mission, Alex? Where will I stand when you are called away to defend a cause we both believe in?"

He placed his hands on her shoulders and turned her to face him. "We'll work that out together," he said gently. Her eyes misted, and he saw something unexpected in them: a tenderness so pure it hurt to look into them. Pulling her into his arms, he kissed her brow.

"Say you will be my wife, Breanna." His lips traveled to her ear. "Many people have started with less than we are starting with and have succeeded. I know we can do as well together."

His arms had slipped around her waist, holding her scantily clad body against his. It felt so right to be in his arms, she wanted simply to accept, yet she had to be as sure in her mind as she was in her heart.

"What will . . . will everyone think?" she asked.

"Everyone who?" He smiled, knowing she was trying to find a reason to tell him no, but having trouble doing it.

"Papa, Heather . . . everyone!"

Moving his hand to the gaping front of her shirt, he gently slipped inside to cup her breast. "I thought you didn't care what anyone thought," he murmured. "I thought you did as you pleased." Finding the hardening little nipple, Alex rubbed it gently between his thumb and finger.

What she pleased was to have him make love to

her again. "I do." She sighed, reaching up to curl her hand around his neck. She offered her parted lips. "And I will."

It wasn't said the way he wanted her to say it, but he wasn't about to argue. Especially not when she was giving herself freely to him. He finished unbuttoning her shirt and began to move her backward toward the wall.

"You won't be sorry," he said, trapping her with his body. His hand slipped between them to search out the core of her pleasure. "We'll do well together, *querida*," he said, his voice growing husky with wanting her.

Breanna couldn't believe he was making love to her in broad daylight and standing! But he showed her it was more than possible. He unfastened his pants and bent low until he could enter her. Once embedded in her depths, he raised up, carrying her with him.

"Wrap your legs around me," he ordered huskily.

She obeyed and added the circle of her arms around his neck. "Alex, I—"

"Shhh," he hushed her. "Don't talk. Just let me show you what it will be like when we are wed." His own breathing grew harsh as he moved inside her. She was helplessly held between him and the wall, giving him total control over her. Her head began to thrash. He could hear her mewling like a hungry kitten, begging, wanting.

Alex felt the first quickening. "You're mine, Breanna," he said between clenched teeth. One more powerful thrust of his hips brought them both to a shattering climax. "This makes you mine!"

Breanna sat in the tub running the sponge over her shoulder. She was still struggling to shake off the lassitude that followed Alex's lovemaking. It was hard to believe she was bathing in preparation for her wedding.

He had ordered the bath only minutes after carrying her to her bed to let her rest. She wanted to sleep, but he seemed filled with an enormous energy that had him making plans as she dozed off. She was roused only minutes after drifting off by a beaming Hilda, who was delighted with the prospect. She settled Breanna in the tub, then went in search of something special for her to wear.

Alone, Breanna decided she just wanted to enjoy the luxury of her bath. She heard Alex's deep voice in the hall and smiled. He certainly had an unusually special way of convincing her to wed him. She would have had to be made of stone not to respond to his fervor, and he was fast teaching her exactly what she was made of.

A light tap at the door brought her out of her reverie. It was Hilda, her arms filled with ruffles and lace.

"These ought to do just fine!" she exclaimed, laying the bundle on the bed. She began to sort through the pile. "I knew I'd find something."

Breanna stepped from the bath and wrapped a large drying sheet around herself. Several petticoats, a silk camisole, a cream-colored lace blouse, a brightly colored skirt, and even a pair of leather sandals were spread out on the bed.

"Where did you get all this?" she asked happily.

"Several of Alex's men who live here are married," she explained. "Every one of their wives wanted to give something to Alex's bride." Satisfied that Breanna had everything she would need, Hilda turned to her. "Well, let's get you ready. He's waiting to ride to the church, and I've never seen him so anxious."

They got her dressed, and afterward Hilda began to arrange her hair. "He told me to leave it down," she said, spying the becoming blush on Breanna's cheeks. "But I think we'll tie it back like this." She had drawn up the sides, securing them with a ribbon. "Ain't right if he gets his own way in everything."

Stepping back to admire her handiwork, Hilda smiled. "No wonder he waited so long to find a bride," she said with tears in her eyes. "He was waiting for perfection."

Breanna rose and hugged the woman impulsively. "You've been so kind."

"I love Alex like a son," Hilda told her when she stepped back. "It ain't hard for me to be kind to the woman who loves him."

Breanna kept the smile on her face even though she wasn't sure how she felt. As Breanna was about to leave the room, Hilda called to her. She was holding a piece of exquisite lace.

"I thought this would be nice to wear." She unfolded a lacy mantilla and set it on Breanna's head. She arranged combs to secure it and arranged it around Breanna's shoulders. "There! Now you look like a bride."

Breanna's eyes filled with tears. Her wedding day! She was about to join herself to a man who had, in turn, driven her mad with anger and given her the greatest pleasure in her life. "I . . . I . . ."

"Shhh, you don't have to say anything." Hilda smiled, thinking it was bridal nerves. "Just go to him, Breanna. He's been waiting a lifetime for someone of his own."

Breanna found him in the courtyard at the front of the house. Dressed in a short Spanish bolero jacket of black with silver embroidery down the front, he had the look of a hidalgo. His arrogant stance in the fitted black pants enhanced the image of the nobleman.

He was talking with Hank and fell silent when he spotted her. Enchanted, he walked toward her, stopping only inches away.

"You look more beautiful each time I see you,"

he told her, bending to kiss her parted lips. Smiling at the glow in her eyes, he offered his arm. "Come, *querida*. The night is only hours away. I want to spend this night in my bed with my wife and not atop a horse."

Beside Satan, he donned a flat-brimmed black hat, then mounted. He reached down and circled Breanna's waist to lift her up before him.

"I hope you don't mind sharing my horse," he breathed near her ear. "Some of my fondest memories of you are on a horse." The crimson warmth of her cheeks brought rumbling laughter from his chest, and he gave Satan his head while the residents of the ranch waved and cheered.

They had been riding about fifteen minutes in silence. Occasionally, Alex would press a kiss to her shoulder where the loosely tied blouse had slipped to bare it, or gently run his hand down her side. It was as if he had to reassure himself that she was real.

Breanna enjoyed his touch and dreamily thought of the time she had told Millie she couldn't love a man like Alexander King. How foolish, she thought. There *was* no other man like him! But as to whether she loved him, that was still an unknown. Oh, she loved what he did to her. She even loved the strength of his convictions. But did she love the man himself?

"Look there," Alex said, pointing across to a small hillock.

The adobe mission sat at the top and could be seen from every direction. Its white stucco walls were topped by the brick-red tiles on its roof. A tall spire graced with a large white cross rose above the roof.

Children were playing in a nearby copse while men and women toiled in the fields that fed the small village nearby. A flock of sheep grazed on a hillside, and cattle meandered near the church-yard.

It was a serene picture that made Breanna won-der if she and Alex would work side by side. He'd told her they would settle the issue of her involve-ment in the California issue together. She wished it had been done before they were married, but she didn't see how she could insist now when they were only moments from the church.

"Scared?" Alex asked, sensing some nervous-ness.

"Yes," she admitted. "I've never gotten married before."

"That's all right, *querida*." He chuckled. "Neither have I."

"And are you scared?" she asked, tipping her head to see his face.

Alex looked down at her. In all honesty, he re-plied, "No, *querida*." He watched her eyes soften and placed a gentle kiss on her mouth. "Now let's stop wasting time." He grinned. "I want you wed to me before you change your mind."

It was a strange thing for him to say, but she shrugged it off as his own brand of teasing. His arms tightened around her, and he hastened Satan toward the church.

Father Francisco saw the rider approaching and shielded his eyes to try to identify him. A smile crossed his handsome dark face when he recog-nized Satan, and he arched a brow in wonder when he realized two people were atop the power-ful horse, and one was a woman. Brushing dust from his plain brown robe, he moved away from the mission wall to greet his guests.

Alex dismounted in one fluid movement and reached up for Breanna. The young priest was awed by the gentle exchange between his friend and the beautiful woman accompanying him. He waited until, hand in hand, they walked toward him.

"Alex, my friend!" He smiled broadly. "To what do I owe this unexpected pleasure?"

Clasping hands, the two met eye to eye and Alex grinned devilishly. "I've come to grant you a wish, Francisco." He reached for Breanna's hand. "I want you to marry us."

"Lord be praised!" Francisco laughed, shaking Alex's hand firmly. Turning to Breanna, he took her hands in his. "I am Francisco Parkins," he said kindly. "I've been friends with this scoundrel for a long time. I never thought I would live to see him settle down, and with such a lovely bride."

"Thank you, Father." Breanna smiled. "I'm Breanna Sullivan."

"Soon to be King," Alex interrupted, reclaiming her hand.

Francisco bade them follow him into the mission. He had wine served to them while he prepared the papers for their marriage and chatted amiably. Breanna was pleased to discover that Francisco knew her father. It made her feel closer to the priest. She also learned that he and Alex had been friends since they were boys. Eventually she had to ask him about his unusual combination of names.

"My mother was of Spanish-Indian descent," he told her. "And my father was an American whose people came from England." He went on to explain that as a half-breed, he had had few friends until Alex came along.

"I wasn't too kindly thought of, either," Alex said. "I was a loner with quite a chip on my shoulder. Only Francisco stuck around long enough to get through to me."

"And only you accepted me as an equal from the start."

They went on to talk about events in their

youth, leaving Breanna to enjoy the sound of their deep voices and their laughter.

Gentle brown eyes looked upon the newlyweds as they sealed their vows with a kiss. Francisco had been pleased with the strong, clear responses Alex made. There were no doubts, no fears in his promise to love and cherish Breanna. It had been a long time coming, but he knew it was worth the wait.

That Alex's love was well received and returned was evident in her eyes. Although her vows were gently whispered, Francisco was sure her feelings were no less powerful than Alex's.

"May God bless you, here and wherever you go," Francisco said as he blessed them. "And may your lives be long and fruitful."

He reached out his hands to congratulate the pair and offered them more wine.

"No, thanks, Francisco," Alex replied. "I'd like to get her home and work on the fruitful part."

"Alex!" Breanna groaned. "How can you say such a thing to a priest?"

Swinging Breanna into his arms, Alex claimed her startled mouth in a fiery kiss, leaving her breathless. "I spoke not to a priest, but to an old friend who will understand." Alex winked at Francisco. "Right, old friend?"

Francisco laughed. "Believe me, Breanna. I know him well. I am only pleased he wed you before thinking along those lines." Two faces immediately tinted different shades of red. "Well, anyway, he set the matter right quickly!"

Wishing to spend a moment alone with Breanna, Francisco sent Alex out to get the horse. Breanna made to follow, and he took her hand. "A moment, please," he said, waiting for Alex to be out of hearing range before he spoke.

"What is it, padre?" she asked.

"Breanna," he said. "I just want to share something with you." She gazed up at him, waiting. "Alex is a complex man. He is strong and sometimes stubborn to a fault." Breanna grinned shyly. "Ah, I see you have seen that part of him."

"It is a trait we both share," she admitted.

"Good. Then perhaps you can teach each other to bend." She nodded, and his smile faded. "And give him time to trust you, for it won't be easy for him. There are more scars than those you see."

Breanna suddenly wanted to question Francisco. She was sure he could help her find what was in her heart, but the fates decreed it would have to be another time.

"Ready, love?" Alex asked, reaching out his hand to her.

Breanna smiled at Francisco, then turned and clasped hands with her husband.

Chapter 15

A cacophony of sounds could be heard from the brightly lit ranch. In their absence Hilda had amassed the hands and their families and arranged an impromptu party for the newlyweds. Cheers could be heard the moment Satan crowned the hill almost half a mile from the house. Hearing them, Breanna smiled. She felt as if she was coming home.

Alex brushed a kiss against her temple and sighed. "There go my plans for the evening."

He sounded so dejected, Breanna laughed. "You would never make a priest. After this afternoon, I would think you are well satisfied for a while!"

His hands slipped up her sides until he cupped her breasts. Kneading them gently, he growled into her ear. "Are you well satisfied?" he asked, his exploration growing more sensuous as he spoke.

"I was," she replied, her own hand dropping to caress his thigh. "But it seems I have more stamina." Her lips twitched at her teasing. "I can wait until nightfall."

Entwining his fingers in her hair, Alex ground his mouth into hers until she was breathless. When he drew away, he could see the flare of passion in her eyes. "Then you can wait in the same condition I'm in!" He laughed when she wrinkled her nose and stuck out her tongue at him.

He slapped Satan's flanks and rode toward the

party, anxious to join the revelers and more anxious to see his wedding night arrive.

The sounds of two guitars and a fiddle mingled with clapping hands and stomping feet. Children, laughing and trying to tag one another, raced about the dancing couples. Hilda had worked wonders in organizing the party in so short a time. There was plenty of food for everyone, and Alex brought out the finest wines and blended whiskeys his home offered.

If not for a late September storm brewing off the coast, the revelers might have gone on until morning; instead, they were forced to start clearing everything away at dusk. The children were the first to leave, and Alex stood watching as Breanna bid each one sweet dreams.

The men were busy bringing in the lanterns as the breeze picked up. Hilda was organizing the cleaning up when she spotted Alex standing near the door watching his new bride. Her heart filled with happiness when she saw his eyes following Breanna's every move. Her most fervent wish had been granted, she thought as she walked to his side. He had found love.

"She's a beauty, that one," Hilda said softly, and saw him nod without taking his eyes from Breanna. He was silent, but it was not the silence of loneliness. He had a mate to share his life, and she praised the Lord that she had lived to see it.

A flash of lightning followed by the rumbling of far-off thunder heralded the arrival of the storm, scattering the remaining guests. Hilda placed a hand on Alex's cheek and drew his head down for a motherly kiss.

"Be happy, son." She smiled, glad for the rain on her face that disguised her happy tears.

Alex kissed her brow and hugged her tightly. "You'd better get inside," he said with a smile.

A second flash lit the sky and then they heard

the sound of another rumble. The rain was coming down harder as Breanna and Hilda paused in the yard for a quick hug before hurrying their separate ways. Breanna was soaked before she could reach the protection of the porch. Alex grabbed her hand and propelled her into the cozy warmth of the house. A fire had been set in the parlor, and Breanna headed for it, dripping as she went.

"Oh, God! I'm fr-freezing!" She laughed. Chafing her hands, she looked back at the dim hall to see Alex leaning against the closed door. "Aren't you cold?" she asked, trying to pull at the wet blouse that clung to her.

Alex moved from the shadows with pantherlike grace. "How can I be cold watching you play in the firelight like a temptress?" His hair fell over his brow and raindrops glistened on his lashes and dark skin.

"I'm not playing, Alex." Quivering laughter filled the room. "I'm tr-truly cold."

Pushing aside the desire caused by the vision of her standing there, her skirt plastered to her legs and the rigid peaks of her breasts visible beneath her wet clothing, he grabbed a blanket from the back of the sofa and went to her.

"You've got to get out of those wet clothes." He peeled off the clinging blouse and skirt while she kicked off her sandals. One by one, her petticoats went. When she was down to just her chemise, he rubbed briskly at her damp skin with the blanket.

"Wait here by the fire," he ordered as he left the room. He returned with several downy quilts and wrapped her in one as soon as he returned.

"What a storm!" Breanna shivered when the next roll of thunder shook the house. She dropped to her knees before the fire, seeking all the warmth it could give her.

Alex watched the play of firelight on her hair while he stripped off his damp shirt. He removed his boots and scooted her aside to spread the other quilt on the floor. The instant their makeshift bed was ready, he drew her across it.

"We might as well enjoy the fire awhile," he said, sitting with Breanna leaning against his chest. Breanna nodded and nestled between his thighs, sighing when his arms wrapped about her. "Warmer?"

"Ummm," she purred, her contentment complete. After a few minutes of silence, she tipped her head. "It was a nice party, wasn't it?"

He nodded and took the blanket he had used to dry her to rub at the long, wet strands of her hair. "Hilda is good at that sort of thing." He smiled. "I think she lives for the times she can help."

Wiggling around, Breanna knelt before him. "She's very special to you, isn't she?"

Alex leaned back on an elbow and patted the blanket at his side. Breanna climbed over his leg and settled beside him. They shared a moment of simply looking at each other before he replied. "She and Hank took me in when I was a boy."

"Where were your own parents?" she asked. For a while, she didn't think he was going to tell her. She knew the memory must have been painful. It showed too clearly on his face. "Never mind. I shouldn't have pried," she said softly, raising her hand to ease the furrows on his brow.

Taking her hand, he pressed a kiss to it. "It's all right," he said with a ragged sigh. "It was long ago." Dropping to his back, he watched the flames reflected on the ceiling. "My father died before I was born. My mother remarried," he began. "Her name was Sabrina. We lived back in Pennsylvania. Frank, my stepfather, used to like beating on us sometimes, mostly when he was drinking."

"Then why did your mother marry him?"

"A woman with a small boy has a hard time making it alone. Frank could be very charming. And he offered comfort and security." Crossing his arms beneath his head, he looked over at her and smiled. "Sometimes he wasn't so bad. At least not at first." The smile faded. "Then he started drinking more and more. The more he drank, the more he would hit my mother. I used to swear I'd kill him."

There was such savagery in his tone, Breanna shivered. Mistaking it for a chill, Alex rolled to his side and took her in his arms. His bare chest was surprisingly warm, and she waited to hear the rest of his story.

"Did you?" she finally asked.

"No," he said sadly. "I wish I had. My mother might still be alive." His voice quivered with the memory.

"Alex, don't!" she cried, rising up to press her fingers to his lips. "Don't tell me any more if it hurts."

Taking her hand, he kissed her palm. "It's okay. I want you to know." He drew her down to lie on his chest. When she was settled, he went on. "One night I tried. I drew a knife on him. He had no trouble disarming a twelve-year-old boy. During our struggle my mother grabbed his arm, trying to help me. He pushed her away and she fell. I tried to get to her but he backhanded me, forgetting he still held the knife."

She lifted her head and saw his fingers trace the scar. Her heart was breaking for the child he had been.

"It sliced across my cheek." The burning pain returned to haunt him, and he eased Breanna aside to rise and pour himself a drink. He stood looking into the fire. "I ran from the house and hid until morning. I managed to get to a neighbor's, and he discovered my mother had died that night, her neck broken in the fall. He patched up my face and helped me get on a ship sailing that day."

Breanna sat up, wrapping her arms about her knees. "Is that when you came to California?"

He sat down beside her, bending one knee to

drape his arm over. "No. I sailed for about a year, then signed with another ship to go around the Horn. I was fifteen when we landed in San Francisco, where I jumped ship. I wandered north with no destination in mind. That was when I stumbled on a small farm."

"Hank's place?"

"Yes." He grinned at last. "That was the best thing that ever happened to me." He turned to look at her. "That is, until you." He noticed the tears on her cheeks and leaned toward her. "As I said, Breanna, it was a long time ago." He brushed away the moisture from one cheek and kissed the other. "If things hadn't gone the way they did, we would not be here now." Although glad he had told her, he was tired of talking. "Still cold?" he asked suddenly.

"No, but what happened after—"

He rose to his knees. "Later," he said, carefully unfolding the sides of the blanket to reveal her scantily covered body. "It's time we remembered that this is our wedding night."

"I haven't forgotten," she breathed, reaching to run her hand over his taut body. He had given her some of his past; she would gladly give him something for the future.

For two days the rain fell. Breanna thought it was the most beautiful weather she had ever seen. It allowed them to keep the world at bay while they enjoyed discovering each other. Besides the hours of erotic exploration, he told her how he had built his empire, and she shared stories of her family and her voyages.

During one of her tales, he frowned. "It isn't too bright of you always to plunge ahead without thinking," he commented, his attention turning to the slender leg she had lifted in her tub.

"Maybe not." She grinned. "But it certainly is educational!"

He was perched on an elbow, the sheet draped over his hip and his hair hanging over his brow. "You leave your education to me. I'll teach you everything you need to know."

Still smiling, she tilted her chin. "Will you even teach me how to spy for you?" she asked playfully. Instantly he scowled, and she mimicked the look. "Alex, I was only teasing."

Tossing the sheet aside, he made his way to the tub, totally comfortable with his nudity. He dropped to his knees beside it. "Good thing," he said, taking the sponge from her hand. "I have no intention of letting you do anything so dangerous."

Breanna's frown didn't go away as his had. As he began to lather the leg she had lifted, she chewed her lip. "You sound as if you've made this decision already."

"I have," he said, more interested in bathing her than in talking.

"But I thought we were going to discuss it together."

Dropping the sponge, he twisted to face her. "Breanna, there's nothing to discuss. You're not going to get involved."

She sat up straight, the water not quite covering her breasts. "I am involved!" she said, her tone growing angry.

"You were involved until you married me." He felt that the matter was settled and rose to return to the bed. "Now get out of that tub and come back to bed."

Breanna couldn't believe her ears. He was treating her like some slave he had purchased for his amusement. "Not until we settle this," she said, gripping the sides of the tub to keep from throwing something.

Alex groaned. "It is settled, Breanna. When you married me, you relinquished your rights to me.

As your husband, I'm telling you I will not jeopardize your safety."

She stood and wrapped a towel about herself, climbed from the tub, and stomped closer. "What about the danger you're in? You go traipsing around Monterey like you own the place even though you think Guillermo is suspicious. What do you call that?"

"Necessary!" he snapped, sorry he hadn't been more careful with what he said to her. She was too clever. He could see she was not satisfied with his reply, and he sighed. "Listen, honey. I learned early in my life that people tend to ignore the obvious." He raked back his hair, hoping she would accept his explanation. "By working in the open, I convince them I have nothing to hide."

"By working in the open, you make yourself a target!"

Alex should have been upset by her arguments, but he found himself wondering about them instead. She was terribly agitated. He couldn't help thinking that she sounded genuinely worried. He decided to test the theory.

"What's the worst that can happen?" he said, rolling to his back.

Breanna shivered, and it had nothing to do with being wet. "You could be killed!"

Her anguish touched him. "I'd have thought that might seem a solution for you, Breanna," he said, glancing over at her. "You'd be a rich widow and free to get as deeply involved as you wish."

Breanna didn't know whether to scream at him or do him bodily harm. She was so distraught by the image his words conjured, she did both.

"You miserable cur!" she cried as she leaped on the bed to beat at him with her fists. "Don't you dare die!"

Alex grabbed her hands and tossed her over his hip to lie flat on her back, trapping her beneath him. "Why, Breanna? Why do you care if I die?"

Still feeling the pain of her thoughts, she closed her eyes and worried her lower lip. She didn't want to tell him why. She didn't even want to admit it to herself. It would leave her open to heartache, she was sure.

"Why, *querida?*" he asked more gently. She refused to reply.

"Could it be because you love me?" She sucked in a breath but remained silent. "Do you, Breanna? Do you love me?" He knew he could have admitted his own feelings for her then, but they were too new, too vulnerable to share yet.

"N-no," she whispered, shaking her head.

"No?" He sighed heavily and rolled from her. "Too bad. I don't think any woman has ever loved me." He reached for his pants. "I think I would have liked the idea."

Breanna saw him place one foot in his pants. Her heart was so filled with the love she denied, she had to share it. She had been a coward by denying it until now. "Alex," she called to him before he could go any further.

Looking back at her over his shoulder, he seemed only mildly interested, but if she could feel the pounding of his heart, she would have known how anxious he was to hear her words.

"Alex, I . . . I . . ." She lifted her arms to him. "Alex!"

It was enough for him. Twisting around, he drew her into his arms. His mouth took what she offered gladly. Frantic hands pushed away her damp towel. He wanted to touch her, feel her against him. He kicked away his pants and rolled with her until she was on top of him.

"Tell me," he said as he moved her astride him. "Say it, Breanna," he begged.

Breanna could feel his hardness probing for her depths. She realized what he was doing and wriggled until she could feel him sliding inside her. His breath caught, making her bolder. Splaying her hands on his chest, she sat up to take him fully. She watched his throat working to swallow.

"You are arrogant," she said, her own voice throaty with arousal. He opened his eyes and looked at her. She was nearly lost in the blue flame dancing in them. "You make me furious." She slowly began to rock her hips. His hands moved to her buttocks, teaching her a more satisfying rhythm. "I didn't want to," she said more breathlessly. "I never thought I would."

Her words, her breathy voice, her movements were driving him to the edge. Raising his hips to meet her, he watched her lips part and her head fall back. He lifted his hands to push aside her hair and expose her luscious breasts. "Tell me," he growled, his hands covering the soft mounds.

She couldn't! Oh, she wanted to, but she was beyond words. She felt his hands on her. She marveled at his thick maleness, filling her. She could feel her body reaching for the ultimate satisfaction. Nothing mattered but her growing need.

Alex desperately wanted the words, but she had aroused him beyond reason. There was no stopping now for talk. There was only pure sensation. He forced himself to watch her moving over him and saw the instant she reached fulfillment. The gloriously pagan shuddering of her body was enough to take him over the edge. He whispered her name harshly as she fell against him.

Breathing heavily, they were spent. Alex drew a cover over them and held her tenderly in his arms. She had proved her love more than any words could express, he thought, his arms tightening around her. The words would come.

Breanna knew it was true. She did love this complex man. She had no delusions about their marriage being all bliss. They were both too headstrong, but it would add spice to their already exciting life together. Gathering her courage to admit her feelings, Breanna drew a deep breath. "I love you," she whispered.

Alex closed his eyes and savored the sweet admission. He gently brushed her hair from her brow and kissed it. "I'm glad," he said, wondering if she was waiting for matching words.

He hadn't said them, she thought, a dull ache bringing tears to her eyes, but she hadn't really expected him to. She had no delusions that theirs was a love match. In fact, if she had not surrendered to him, she would never have married him, no matter how she felt. To her chagrin, she had given herself to him, body and soul. Now she would have to live with loving a man who did not—perhaps could not—love her.

"Hungry?" she asked, needing something mundane to get her through the awkwardness of the situation.

Despite his rumbling stomach, Alex shook his head. "No."

"Oh," she replied, wondering what should happen next.

There was no need for her to wonder. Alex was going to take care of it. Placing his hands on her shoulders, he eased her to his side. He wasn't surprised to find her eyes closed or to see the single tear escape her lashes. He felt he needed to explain.

"Breanna, I want you to know something." She didn't move, but he knew she was listening. "I've never had the chance or taken the time to find someone to share my life with. I never really planned to . . . until you came along." He gently ran one finger over her lower lip. "I'm committed to this thing with California and I can't quit now." Her eyes opened. They were filled with her love and the hurt he knew he was causing with his words.

"I don't want you to quit," she told him. "I only want to join you."

Alex groaned and lowered his head. "I know, *querida*," he told her, "but I want you here, safe, until I can come home to you and discover if I can love."

Breanna knew she could not change his mind. He was set on his course. She could either remain, feeling the abuse of her trust, or leave to experience a broken heart.

"I'll try to see it your way, Alex, but I make no promises."

Relieved, Alex gazed down at her, the love he couldn't speak shining in his eyes. "I'll make one," he said with a small smile. "I promise that every minute we have left will be something to remember."

It wasn't what she wanted to hear, but it was something she could believe. No sooner had he fallen silent than he began to keep his promise.

"Where's Alex?" Breanna asked Hilda when she came out to the kitchen.

"He's with Hank in the parlor." Hilda smiled as she stirred the stew in the cookpot. "A letter just arrived and—" She saw Breanna race from the room and chuckled at the energy of the young.

Breanna stopped at the door. Alex looked up and smiled at her unasked question.

"It's from John," he told her. He could see the apprehension on her face and shook his head. "No, he just had some news for us."

Relieved, Breanna entered the room to find him alone. "I thought Hank was here," she said casually. In the past few weeks, Breanna had begun to safeguard herself from the hurt that would come when he left, as he surely would. He had all but told her California came first.

"He had some chores to do." Alex knew she was keeping busy in the house to avoid him, but he also knew her curiosity would overrule any other plans she had. "He says your father was at Casa del Verde a few days ago."

"Papa," Breanna said sadly. "I haven't seen him in over two years."

"Well, you'll be seeing him soon." A light flickered in her eyes. "He'll be here in a couple of weeks."

Truly pleased, Breanna smiled warmly. "I'm glad. I'm anxious to see him."

Alex moved closer to her, wanting to hold her, but she stepped back warily. Pretending nothing was wrong, he said, "He's anxious to see you, too, and John adds that he's after my rump." She frowned in question. "It seems he caught Heather and Eric in a rather compromising position."

"Eric?"

"Eric Wilson, my foreman," Alex told her. He sat back on the edge of the desk and crossed his ankles. "I left him at Casa del Verde to keep an eye on Heather and make sure she was safe if Guillermo discovered you were gone." He shrugged sheepishly. "I guess I never figured they'd get on so well."

"And does Papa know about us?"

Alex shook his head ruefully.

"Then, if I were you, I'd be careful," she said, unable to hide the humor she was feeling. "Papa has quite a temper. He's liable to shoot first and ask questions later."

Alex enjoyed the return of her humor, even if it was at his expense, but there was something he had to ask her. Pushing away from the desk, he stood before her.

"Breanna, will you try to leave with your father?"

She paused to consider her reply. It would be a golden opportunity. She could salvage some pride, but it would cost her any possible chance that they could work out their difficulties.

"No, Alex," she told him honestly. "I won't leave with Papa." The relief on his face almost made her believe he might love her.

He watched her exit without another word. Would it have been so terrible to lower his guard and tell her how he felt? Yes, he nodded ruefully to himself. Breanna was clever. If he gave her that sort of power over him, she might use it to get her way. It was better if he waited until he could stay by her side with nothing else to contemplate but loving her.

"Ya damned pirate!" Patrick roared as he slapped his hand on Alex's shoulder. "I ought ta box yer ears, ya rascal!"

"How are you, Patrick?" Alex smiled broadly. "You're looking good for an old Irish warhorse."

"Don't try to sweet-talk me!" Patrick returned the smile. "The only way I'll tolerate talkin' ta the likes of you is if ya give me some of that good whiskey ya keep!"

Without another word, Alex led him to the parlor and poured out two drinks. "To your health, Patrick," Alex saluted.

"No, my friend, we better drink ta yours 'cause if you don't have the right answers, I'm gonna have ta knock yer block off!"

"Okay." Alex laughed. "You've been here only a few minutes and you've threatened me twice. Why don't you tell me what's on your mind." He motioned to a pair of chairs and they sat, then he offered Patrick a cigar.

"Tryin' ta soften me up?" he asked after lighting the cigar.

"Do I need to?" Alex retorted.

"Ya do if you're the one responsible for leavin' that skirt-chasin' Wilson boy with my Heather!" He took a swallow of his drink. "They were real cozy when I got home."

Alex chuckled. "Now, Patrick. You know Heather

wouldn't do anything she didn't want to do. If she's *cozy* with Eric, it's because she cares for him."

Patrick scratched the two-day growth on his chin and grinned. "I suppose you're right."

"And Eric's a good man. He'll do right by her."

Chuckling, Patrick rose and poured another drink. "Clever of ya ta figure it out. How'd ya get so sharp?"

Alex leaned back in his chair and grinned. "After living with Breanna for the last month I—"

"Living with her!" Patrick exclaimed, whirling to face the younger man. "And just how far has *that* gone?"

"As far as it can go, Patrick," Alex said, rising to face him. "I married her."

Patrick looked up to meet Alex's eyes. They were sparkling with mischief. "Well, I'll be damned! She's yer wife?" When Alex nodded, Patrick roared. "By God, King! John told me ya said you'd do what it took ta keep her from causin' trouble and ya did!"

"Listen, Patrick . . ." Alex tried to quiet the Irishman. "It may have started out like that but—"

"I gotta hand it to ya, lad, when you fight for a cause, you go above and beyond!"

"Damn it, Pat! Shut up and listen!" Alex scowled. "I married Breanna because I love her!" He paused, stunned by his own words. Slowly, a smile touched his lips. "I do. I love her."

Patrick wasn't surprised. "I never doubted it," he exclaimed, his hand landing solidly on his new son's shoulder. "Now let's go find that chit and see how she feels about it!"

With the back of her hand pressed to her mouth to prevent the scream that threatened, Breanna whirled about. She had just been ready to enter the parlor and greet her father when she heard the exchange with Alex. It all made sense! He had used marriage, even her love for him, to keep her out of the way!

She left the house, not wanting to hear any more, and ran into the thick foliage of the garden, her heart breaking. Alex had never told her he loved her because he couldn't. It had all been a joke. He had gotten her out of the way and made full use of her as a benefit to his mission. What a fool she'd been!

Dropping to her knees when she knew no one could see her, she wept bitterly. Alex called for her from the door, but she ignored him, recalling all the times he had patronized her. Even their marriage was only meant to give him legal power over her. He had never cared about her. Everything he did was self-serving.

"Oh, God!" she groaned, throwing herself to the ground to weep out her pain. What was she going to do? For long minutes, she let the hurt pour from her heart in tears, but eventually her pride began to rear its head. Alex had used her; now she would take what he had taught her and use it against him.

Sitting up, she sniffed and wiped her eyes. Alex had only married her to keep her out of the picture. There was never meant to be a future. She had nothing; she just didn't know it until a few minutes ago.

The only thing she did have was the knowledge of her ability to thwart his well-made plans. She could leave. She could go back to Casa del Verde, and there was nothing he could do to stop her.

She would need help, and there was only one man in the world she trusted right now—Francisco! She knew he would understand her need to leave once she explained the story. She would go to the mission and seek sanctuary until she could arrange her trip south.

Gaining her feet, she gave herself a few more minutes to dry her eyes and build her resolve. She had to make Alex think nothing had changed. It would not be easy, hurting as she was, but she knew she had to do it. Later, when she was free of him, she would cry over her love and what could have been.

Chapter 16

❦

Having bathed her face to wipe away any trace of crying, Breanna drew a deep breath and made her way around to the front of the house. She wanted to give the impression that she was returning from Hilda's.

"Breanna, my girl!" Patrick called, seeing her as he came out of the barn with Alex. "Where the devil have ya been?"

Keeping her eyes from Alex, she ran into her father's arms. "Papa!" she cried. "It's so good to see you!"

Patrick set her at arm's length. He saw something troubling in her eyes, which he thought required a more private moment to discuss. "Let me look at you, girl!" he said instead. "Why, ya look grand!"

Her eyes filled with tears again. "Look at me," she said, forcing a laugh. "I'm so happy to see you I'm crying like a baby!" Stepping back, she turned toward the house. "Let's go in and have a good chat," she said.

Patrick fell in beside her while Alex returned the horses to the stable. "You're lookin' fair ta bloomin'," he told her, dropping his arm around her shoulder. "Married life must be agreein' with ya."

"Yes!" she said too spritely to avoid looking at him with her lie on her face. "It's just fine."

"Good." Patrick smiled, wondering what was

234

bothering his daughter. He may not have seen her in a few years, but he still knew her moods well enough. She wore her feelings clearly, and she was trying desperately to hide them now.

They spent a few minutes talking about Heather and what she had been up to as Breanna made coffee.

"She'd better marry that boy," he declared. "I won't have no foolin' around under my roof."

Breanna smiled. "I'm sure she'll do what's right, Papa. You raised us both to do what was right." Recalling her surrender to Alex, she turned away so he wouldn't see her blush and changed the conversation to a safer subject.

"Papa, why didn't you tell Heather and me what you were doing?"

"What ya didn't know, daughter, ya couldn't tell."

Turning sharply, she stared at him. "We never would have told! You know how we all feel about the Mexicans running things."

"I know." He sighed. "But the fewer details you know, the less chance there is for a slip. It was better this way."

"Was it, Papa?" she asked, thinking of the price she'd paid for her ignorance.

Patrick rose and moved to her side. He placed an arm around her shoulders. "What's the matter, Bree?" he asked, sure she was troubled.

"Oh, it ... it's a silly argument Alex and I are having," she told him. "I want to be of some help, but he insists I stay out of it." She looked imploringly at him for understanding. "He wants me to sit here and wait."

Chuckling, Patrick rubbed his jaw. "That is the way of it, honey. The man fights and the woman stays home and waits."

"Why?"

"Well, 'cause that's just the way it is."

Breanna returned to her chore. "It's ridiculous,"

she snapped. "I could help. I could act as a messenger or maybe I could—"

"She wants to spy on Guillermo and his men," Alex said at the door.

"I'd settle for something else if you came up with it," she retorted, using their old argument as a reason to stay away from him.

"She could carry messages," Patrick said, trying to pacify his daughter and Alex at the same time. He didn't want to see their unyielding pride ruin their marriage.

"And if she's caught?" Alex asked, trying to make Patrick see the danger.

Breanna tossed her head. "I won't get caught. I'm smarter than that."

Alex laughed without humor. "If you're so smart, why did you come to me to investigate myself?" He saw her wince. "And how is it I've been able to catch you every time you thought to try something? No, Breanna. You're not as smart as you think."

Breanna thought of her plans. Soon he would see just how clever she could be. "All right, Alex," she said. "You've proven your point." She poured coffee for the two men and started to leave the kitchen.

"Where are you going?" Alex asked, not trusting her when she gave in too easily.

"To gather laundry," she replied. "Maybe I'm smart enough to do that."

Patrick blew out a whistle. "Got a real temper, don't she?" Alex only grimaced in reply. Patrick waited a moment, stirring his coffee, before making an observation. "She could help," he began. Seeing the denial on Alex's face, Patrick anticipated his outburst and curbed it abruptly. "Hear me out! She could keep track of any changes in the routine around Monterey. That would give her somethin' ta do without her gettin' too involved."

"No," Alex said firmly.

"Why the hell not?" Patrick snapped back.

"Because I won't be able to think straight if I don't know she's safe."

"Ah, the truth." Patrick grinned. "It ain't her helpin' what scares ya, it's what you'll be thinkin' when ya can't be with her."

"Yes," Alex snarled. "And I need to think clearly." He went to the door to look out. Leaning on the jamb, he said, "I never thought that doing my duty was going to cost me so much." He was referring to how difficult it was going to be to leave Breanna behind, but that wasn't what she thought as she stood in the kitchen door.

"Do you have any laundry, Papa?" she asked quickly to cover the pain his latest comment had caused. When he told her he didn't, she departed feeling she had made the right decision to leave Alex.

Alex woke and found Breanna gone. He smiled as he thought of her fussing in the kitchen as she had at dinner. He folded his arms beneath his head and stared at the ceiling. She had behaved strangely all evening. It had even carried over into their lovemaking. At first he attributed it to her father's presence in the house, but it seemed to be more than that.

She wasn't only agitated, she seemed almost afraid. She had clung to him in the aftermath of their exquisite lovemaking. He thought he had even detected tears, but she swore she wasn't crying. It took him a long time to figure that perhaps she was worried that he would soon have to leave.

Sighing, he thought it might even be a female thing bothering her. Women became emotional sometimes for no apparent reason. It would surely pass, he thought as he began to dress. He met Patrick in the hall and smiled, still recalling the magnificent night.

"Mornin', lad!" Patrick greeted him. "You're

lookin' pleased with yourself. Ya patch things up with Breanna?"

Alex shrugged with a devilish grin. "We didn't patch anything up but I have no regrets."

"I'm glad," Patrick commented, falling into step with Alex. "She was actin' strange last night. I was hopin' it was somethin' you two would work out."

Alex stopped and looked at Patrick in confusion. "I noticed it, too. I thought it might be something to do with you."

Patrick thought about his elder daughter for a moment. "No, not that she said. Did she mention she was angry with me?"

"No," Alex replied, sensing it was he who had upset her. "I thought it might be something more . . . natural. You know, like a female thing."

"Oh, yeah!" Patrick laughed. "Her ma was that way 'bout once a month as I recall." Alex only nodded, not exactly sure if he believed that was the problem. Patrick rubbed his growling stomach and chuckled. "I hope Bree has breakfast cookin'. I'm starved."

The two men walked briskly into the kitchen in search of food and came up short. The room was empty and there was no indication that anyone had been there since last night. The stove was cold. The back door was closed. There was no evidence of activity anywhere.

"I thought she was out here makin' breakfast," Patrick said.

"So did I." Alex threw open the back door. He called for his wife and received no answer. He went through the house calling her, but there was no reply.

"Where could she be?" Patrick asked in his wake.

"How the hell should I know?" Alex shouted, a fear growing in him as he went to check at Hilda's.

Patrick wasn't offended by his outburst. He was just as worried. After talking to everyone at the ranch, they soon realized that Breanna was gone— and the realization was tearing Alex apart.

"Want ta talk about it, lad?" Patrick asked when Alex fell solemnly into a chair.

"No," Alex said, staring across the room but seeing nothing. "I have to think about where she's gone . . . and why."

Breanna sipped the coffee Francisco had served her. "I'm sorry I woke you, but I didn't know where else to turn." She sighed heavily. "You're the only one I could trust."

Francisco had listened to her carefully as she relayed her story. He found it hard to believe that Alex had been callous enough to use her like that. He truly felt that Alex had married Breanna because he loved her.

"Breanna, are you sure of what you heard?"

Her head shot up, and new tears flowed freely. "My God! Don't you think I want to be wrong?"

Pacing the small confines of his office, he thought aloud. "He's been my friend for a long time. I never thought him capable of such a heartless charade."

Breanna stared at the rough wood on the floor. "He's capable of anything for his beloved California. Nothing and no one will stand in his way to see her free."

Feeling it was his responsibility to try to reunite the two, he asked, "Don't you think you and he should talk? I could send for him and—"

"No!" Breanna dropped to her knees before him, pleading. "Promise me you won't send for him." She gripped his hand and begged. "You're a priest. You must help me."

Francisco placed a hand on her cheek and nodded. "Very well, Breanna. I promise." He helped her to rise and gently held her. "But I wish I had the power to mend this thing."

Sniffing, she stepped back. "You don't, Father. No one does." She swallowed hard and squared her shoulders. "Alex never wanted a wife. At least not one like me." She settled on the bench and wrung her hands. "Perhaps if I had been empty-headed and adoring, we could have survived."

Francisco shook his head. Had she been those things, Alex would never have noticed her. He needed a woman filled with fire as he was. It wasn't the time to tell her this; she wouldn't have believed it.

"I'll make some arrangements," he told her as he turned to leave.

"Please, Father Francisco," she called after him. "Can you annul this marriage?"

"Knowing Alex, I doubt it," he said, trying to be as discreet as possible. Her red cheeks proved his point. "But I couldn't do anything anyway, Breanna. Alex is not a Catholic. The ceremony I performed was civil. Only a judge could separate the two of you."

She nodded in understanding and thanked him for his help.

"Don't thank me, Breanna. I do this against my better judgment. If I could make you go back to him, I would."

Within an hour, Breanna sat on the back of a small cart slowly moving south. Huddled in a bor-rowed shawl, she left her mind blank to avoid the sadness that threatened. When Francisco had lifted her into the wagon, he tried once more to get her to talk with Alex, but she told him everything was said that needed saying.

The old couple she was traveling with were fi-nally ready to leave.

"Breanna, if you need anything or want to keep in touch about . . . Well, remember, I'm here," Francisco said.

She nodded, her throat too tight to speak. The cart moved and she waved sadly. Francisco stood watching until they were out of sight.

Breanna could recall little of her journey. It was a vague blur of ride, stop, camp, and move on. She helped whenever she could, but spoke little. Her silent sadness kept the elderly couple from initiating any conversation.

It took them four days to reach Salinas, and when she bid them farewell, she was sorry she hadn't been more pleasant. They had been very kind, but her hurt was too new to think of anything else.

Without money, Breanna had some difficulty finding transportation for the remainder of her trip until a merchant hauling an empty wagon to Monterey for supplies offered to take her all the way to Casa del Verde after a promise of coin when they got there.

Again her ride was silent. She made no effort to talk to the spry old shopkeeper, and any comments from him were met with a curt answer.

The familiar lay of the land south of Monterey restored Breanna to life. Her home! Her sister! She would be safe there, safe and lonely. A sob caught in her throat as they turned into Casa del Verde. There were memories here she didn't know if she could bear to live with. If not, she reasoned, she might return to the East.

At least there she could lose herself in a sea of strange faces and not have to remember. There would be no memories of Alex in the garden, Alex at the beach, Alex in her room. Alex! Alex! Alex! Why did she have to love him so?

The wagon stopped. "Please wait," she told the merchant. She ran into the house and called for Heather. It was late, and the house was quiet. Without waiting for a reply, she opened the drawer near the front door and took out some money always left there for quick access. She returned to the wagon, placed the coin in the merchant's hand, and thanked him. Observing the generous amount, he tipped his hat and left her.

When Breanna returned to the house, she could hear activity overhead. She knew someone had been awakened by her call. She walked into the parlor and settled into a chair facing a dying fire. She felt drained, tapped of her life's energy. She almost wished she had entered quietly, avoiding any contact until morning, but it was too late now. Voices were coming from the hall and soon Heather would appear. If only she could keep her eyes open . . .

"I'm telling you, Eric," Heather whispered. "It was Breanna's voice. She called out to me." Spying the open front door, she gasped. "See! Someone is here!"

Eric eased past Heather and moved stealthily through the foyer, peering into the darkness of the library before moving into the parlor. Finding no one, he relaxed and looked at Heather as she crept up behind him.

"I told you, honey. It was just your imagination." He slipped his arm around her shoulders and tipped her chin. "Let's go back to bed."

"Imagination doesn't open doors, Eric! There was someone in here. I know—"

"What?" Breanna rose with a start and called out.

"Breanna!" Heather cried, running to her sister. "My God! What are you doing here?"

Before Breanna could answer, she noticed Eric standing near the door. He shuffled under her scrutiny. If he had only believed Heather, he would have at least donned more than just his pants. As it was, the way she looked from him to her sister and back, he knew she suspected that they were lovers. He was really in for it now. It was bad enough when their father had caught him with Heather in the barn.

Extending her hand, Breanna went toward him. "I hope you're Eric Wilson," she said, smiling.

"Yes, I am." Eric shook her hand, half-surprised there was no angry outburst.

With an audible sigh, Heather slipped into Eric's arms and smiled up at him lovingly. "You needn't worry, Bree. There is no one for me but Eric."

Feeling the burden of her long trip, Breanna started for the stairs. "And do you love my sister, Eric?"

"Completely," he replied clearly.

"Good. Then I'll leave you two and say good night."

"But, Bree ..."

"Not tonight, *chica*," she called from the stairs. "I'm too tired."

Heather had seen the fatigue. "All right, Bree," she said, but Breanna had already reached the second floor.

Patrick stood at the table and looked down at the sleeping man. He wanted to wake Alex and give him the letter that had just arrived from John, but knew Alex was exhausted and would sleep soundly, even with his head resting on his crossed arms.

Patrick had heard him pacing each of the five nights since Breanna had left. Even when Patrick assured him she would have returned to Casa del Verde, Alex merely glared at him. If only Patrick understood why Alex wasn't going after her.

When Francisco appeared at the ranch with one of Alex's horses, Patrick was sure that Alex would berate the priest for helping Breanna and then follow her, but it hadn't happened. Alex had thanked him and turned away. Catching Francisco before he left, Patrick tried to put some sense to the events occurring around him.

"All I can tell you, Patrick, is that Breanna left because of what I believe is a gross misunderstanding."

Standing in the door, Alex heard what he had said. "All right, Francisco, so you know how all this started," he said, moving out into the yard. "Now tell me what I can do about it."

"For the time being, nothing." He watched Alex's face darken. "In time, when she's hurting less, you might swallow your pride and go after her."

"It isn't pride keeping me here."

"Isn't it, Alex?"

Alex raked his hair, not wanting to examine the question. He'd spent the night doing that, but it needed an answer. "I've fought for everything I have. I'm fighting for something I believe in. I'm not going to fight to bring back a woman who doesn't want to stay."

Patrick had shared Francisco's surprise at the bitterness in Alex's voice. He was still dumbfounded by it four days later. He knew about Alex's childhood. He knew Alex found it hard to trust others, but he thought Alex's love for Breanna would change that. Apparently, it hadn't.

Restless mumblings drew Patrick's attention back to the lad. He was caught up in a dream. Jerking upright, he called out Breanna's name. It took a moment for him to shake off the residue of sleep and focus on his surroundings.

"You okay, boy?" Patrick asked.

Alex drew a ragged breath and rubbed at his eyes. "Yeah, I'm okay," he said, thinking about the dream. Breanna needed him and he was deserting her. She loved him yet he turned away from her. Blinking, he rubbed his hand over his bristled jaw.

"I've been a fool, Patrick," he said. "I should have gone after her. I love Breanna. I have to tell her that." He stood and shook out the stiffness in his arms. "I never have, and I can only hope I'm not too late."

"You are," Patrick said, handing him the missive. "We got ta go ta Sonoma."

Alex read the letter. "Damn!"

Patrick knew his mission would have to take precedence over his desire to go to his wife, and thought to ease the choice. "She'll be there when ya can get back, son."

It was all Alex could hope for. He'd nearly destroyed the best thing in his life. In fact, he might already be too late. His possessiveness might already have smothered his chances of salvaging her love for him.

"Let's go settle with John," he said. "I have a date with Breanna, and I don't want to keep her waiting too long."

Breanna heard the click of her door opening and sat up. Her nerves were stretched, and she had slept badly for all her fatigue. Heather's shy smile was welcomed.

Breanna smiled back weakly and patted the bed. "Come in, *chica* and sit down."

Heather, clad only in her nightdress, entered and crawled onto the bed. She was uneasy for a moment. Breanna seemed different, and she wasn't sure where to begin.

"You still look tired," she said. "Are you ill?"

Sighing, Breanna drew up her knees and wrapped her arms about them. She lowered her chin to one knee and stared at her toes. "No, I'm not ill."

"But you seem so . . . so different!"

"Different?" Breanna lifted her head and looked at Heather. "Yes, *chica*, I'm different. I'm a married woman." The sadness and hurt in her voice dispelled any pleasure Heather might have gotten from the news.

"Alex?" she asked unnecessarily. Breanna nodded. "You don't seem very happy about it."

Breanna thought of her wedding day . . . and the nights and days that followed. Then she dwelled for a moment on her humiliation and heartache. "I'm not," she said softly. She dropped her head to her knees and tried to keep the tightness in her throat from choking her. She was holding back the tears only with the greatest effort.

Heather placed a hand on Breanna's arm. "Do you want to tell me about it?" Breanna shook her head, and Heather sighed. "All right, but if you need to talk, I'll be here." Getting no response, Heather rose and quietly left the room.

Breanna sniffed. Talk! That was the last thing she wanted to do. The pain was too deep to reach her lips. It was bad enough that her mind was filled with it.

Dropping back on her pillow, she closed her eyes, praying sleep would come and give her temporary respite.

Ever since Alex had awakened that morning and decided to go after Breanna, he'd been scowling. Patrick thought his decision would have lightened his spirits, but it hadn't. He was, in fact, more surly.

"What the hell's eatin ya now?" he finally asked as they rode toward Sonoma, tired of treating the lad as if he were made of glass.

Alex blinked, unaware his brooding was so evident. "Sorry, Patrick, I was just thinking about *your* daughter." He grinned at the word he stressed. "It isn't going to be easy to convince her to come back."

"She's *your* wife. Don't take no for an answer."

"It's not the answer that worries me. It's the question."

"Listen ta me, boy," Patrick said, his voice gruff. "Do ya love my daughter?"

"Very much."

"Does she love you?"

"I think so." Alex shrugged. "At least she said she did."

"Then she does," Patrick assured him.

"So what's the point?" Alex asked.

"The point is, ya have ta make her come home, even if it takes the same sort of methods you used ta get her there the first time."

Alex laughed. "She'll be furious."

"Can't be much worse than she is now! What she needs is ta get pregnant." He saw Alex's eyes widen. "If she's pregnant it'll give her something of her own ta worry about, and she'll stay where she belongs."

Alex's laughter increased at the thought of Breanna bearing his child. "Come on, Patrick," he called, spurring Satan on. "I have two wars to win."

Patrick followed, his face aglow. It was a good thing he has happened to be there when the trouble started. This youngster needed his experience to handle his woman. "One war at a time," he called, racing to catch up with Alex.

Breanna had been home two weeks. Heather watched and waited, looking for some sign that it was time to talk, but it had not yet come. All Breanna did was walk trancelike about the house and garden by day and pace in her room long into the night. Her restless state was leaving its mark. Dark circles framed eyes that had once sparkled with mischief or flashed in defiance. Cheeks once flushed with high spirits were now pale and drawn.

Heather knew she had to convince Breanna to confide in her or watch her wither away. Finding Bree seated outside near the fountain, Heather seized the opportunity.

With a show of confidence she was far from feeling, Heather strolled across the patio. "Hello, Bree." She got only a nod for a reply. "Kind of cool out here, isn't it?" Breanna shrugged.

So much for small talk about the weather,

Heather thought. "Eric went into town on some errands, and I thought it would give us a chance to chat." She plucked at her skirt and grinned. "I don't get much time to myself when he's around." She saw Breanna glance up and smile weakly. Finally! A subject that had caught her attention.

"You should have seen the day he and Pa met." Heather laughed. "He caught us in the barn."

"However did you get yourself in such a spot?" Breanna asked, showing the first glint of interest since her arrival home.

Trying to fan the spark, Heather embellished her story. "The first time I saw Eric, I liked him. He liked me, too. Well, with him staying in the house and Rosa spending most of her time sleeping or praying, we sort of . . . we found we . . . oh, damn!" Heather's own embarrassment was proving to be an obstacle she hadn't anticipated.

"It's all right, *chica*." Breanna laughed. "I understand."

Heather beamed at the laughter and continued. "Anyway, Eric was working in the barn and I brought out his lunch." She shrugged playfully. "He never got around to eating it, and we didn't hear the barn door open in time."

Breanna's eyes sparkled. "You mean Papa caught you while . . ." At Heather's nod, Breanna's laughter bubbled forth anew. "Oh, *chica!* He must have been furious!"

"He was! There I was lying in the hay with my dress undone and Eric, bare to the waist, lying over me!"

With genuine interest, Breanna asked, "What did Papa do?"

"You know Papa. Swing first, ask questions later. He grabbed Eric and sent him flying. I tried to tell Papa that nothing had happened, but he wouldn't listen. Kept spouting that it would have. Towering over poor Eric, he demanded to know his intentions."

"And what did Eric say?" Breanna prodded.

"He said he wanted to marry me." She sobered and looked down at the toes of her shoes.

Breanna took her sister's hand and searched her face. "Don't you want to marry him?"

"Very much," Heather said. "I love him, Bree, but I don't know if he only said that to pacify Papa or if he means it."

"Didn't you ask him afterward?"

"No. I'm afraid, in case he doesn't really want to." Heather's desire to brighten Breanna's mood had darkened her own.

"*Chica.*" Breanna lifted Heather's chin to gaze at her. "I saw the way Eric looks at you. He loves you, honey." Hope welled on Heather's face. "I'm sure he really does want to marry you."

"Really?"

"Yes." Breanna smiled warmly. "And I know he'll make you happy."

Though she was unwilling to destroy the animation on Breanna's face, Heather knew she had to keep her talking. She simply had to expose her wounds to the healing light of day.

"And what about you, Bree? What will make you happy?"

Breanna rose and slowly paced the confines of the patio. "I don't want to talk about it now, Heather."

"You have to, Bree," Heather demanded as she followed and placed a hand on her sister's arm to still her. "It won't get better festering inside you. You know that."

"Yes, I know." She drew a deep breath, blowing it out slowly. "I just don't think I can handle voicing it."

"Try, Bree. Please, try."

Once the words started, they flowed freely. Breanna related all that had happened, beginning with the night Alex had taken her from her room and continuing until the last painful episode. Sitting quietly at her side, Heather watched the misery and anguish take over the glow that had been in Breanna's face.

When silence finally fell, Heather shook her head. "No wonder you're hurting." She spent a moment reflecting on some of what Breanna had said. "Are you sure he said he had married you only because of the mission?" she asked, having seen the look in Alex's eyes when he'd carried Breanna out. She was sure he felt something stronger than dedication to California!

Breanna clenched her hands in her lap and held back a sob. "Oh, I'm sure. I was a problem to be dealt with who could also be used for his personal satisfaction." The tears began to flow unchecked, and Heather placed her arm about Breanna's shoulders.

"But you still love him, don't you?"

Breanna wanted to cry out that she did. She wanted to hold on to the dream that he really had cared and it would all work out in time, but she knew it was a futile effort.

"N-no," she stammered out the lie. "I hate him."

Her declaration was whispered so softly that Heather knew it wasn't true. Her mind began to go over the situation that had sent Breanna running home. At that instant, she knew there was more to it and she had to try to set things right. Alex was every bit as stubborn as Breanna. He could not be forced into something he didn't want to do, not even for the land he loved so much. If he had married Breanna, it was what he wanted.

Without another word, Heather rose and left Breanna to herself. Her wounds would begin to heal now that she had opened up, allowing Heather to work on something else. Tapping her finger on her chin, she smiled secretively. Maybe, just maybe . . .

Chapter 17

"**T**hank you for meeting me, Captain Frémont," Heather said a week later as she dismounted on the hillside overlooking the stormy surf. "I know how difficult things are becoming for you, and I appreciate your time."

John smiled and took the reins of her horse. "Don't you think you can call me John? After all, I gather from your note that we are about to become conspirators."

Heather laughed. "John it is!" She waited while he tied the horses before she began to explain the purpose of her visit. "This may seem as though I'm interfering in Breanna's personal life, but ... how much do you know about her and Alex?"

John stopped and looked over the water. "I've known Alex for a few years. Breanna I've just met." He knew that wasn't what she was really asking. "Heather, I make it a point not to get involved in anyone's personal life unless it affects the mission we're on." He saw her frown. "In this case, however, it might."

"The kidnapping?" she asked, her cheeks turning pink as she recalled her part in it.

John nodded. He picked up some pebbles and rolled them in his hand. "I'm afraid I'm partly responsible for that. I thought there was something brewing between them and that Alex could use his interest in her to keep her out of trouble." Sighing

251

heavily, he added, "I heard things didn't work out too well."

"Oh, they worked out better than any of us expected," Heather told him forlornly. "Breanna is in love with Alex."

Frowning, John indicated a rock where Heather could sit. "Then why did she run away?"

"Pride and something she overheard." Heather went on to explain that Alex had never taken Breanna's skills and desire to help seriously. "So she left, hoping to find a way to help fight for something she believes in."

"I can understand them arguing over it, but leaving?"

Heather plucked at her skirt. "She also heard him tell Papa about marrying her to keep her from interfering."

John released his breath in a whistle. "I don't know her well, but I'm sure that wasn't something she could let pass."

"It wasn't, and that's why I wanted to see you. I believe Alex was right in his way. Breanna doesn't always think of the repercussions when she acts. I think she's going to try to do something for the cause, despite the risk."

"And you think that if I can get Alex back into the picture, he'll be able to prevent it?"

Heather grinned. "He has the best chance of anyone."

John considered her request. "I can't just call him back, Heather. I need him where he is for the time being."

"Then can you find something to keep Breanna occupied?"

"I'm going to have to leave that up to you for a few weeks," John told her seriously. "I have some things I have to take care of, including a meeting with Guillermo. I'm sending for Alex to join me in Monterey for that."

Heather chewed her lip. "Well, with Christmas

only a few weeks away, I guess I can distract her well enough."

John smiled. "Good. With Breanna occupied, I'm sure things will work out. Once she and Alex get together again, I don't think we'll have to worry about her causing problems." He extended his hand and helped Heather to her feet. "Alex is not only a good friend, he's been a big help in this operation. The least I can do is see him happy when it's over."

"Thank you, John." Heather smiled up at him. "I'm sure playing Cupid was never part of your orders, yet I know the two of them will appreciate it."

"Perhaps. But they can't be my main concern. You have to understand, I'll do what I can, but the rest is up to them."

"A rider just brought a message from John," Patrick said as he sat next to Alex before the campfire. "You're ta be in Monterey in two weeks. He's meeting with Guillermo. You're ta be watching from your room at the hotel. He'll signal ya when it's over." Reading the missive, he went on. "If he takes off his hat and looks skyward, everything is okay and he's got his orders ta start mappin' California as a U.S. territory. If he don't, the Mexicans are refusing to sell the land, and you're ta meet him at Hawk Hill that night."

Alex nodded but continued to stare into the fire. After a moment, he asked, "Any news about Breanna?"

"Yeah, he says she's with Heather at Casa del Verde." Patrick poured a mug of coffee. "Says Heather is keepin' an eye on her."

Alex raked his fingers through his hair and tossed the remains of his cigar into the fire. "It'll be a great way to spend Christmas, won't it, Pat? Here I sit sharing a plate of beans with an old Irishman while my wife ... my wife ..." His words drifted off in anguish.

"Here." Patrick pushed a bottle into Alex's hand. "Drink this. It may not cheer ya up, but it sure can't hurt."

"Thanks," Alex said, taking a full swig of the liquor. Sighing as the warmth of the drink spread through him, he handed it back. "I owe you. Ask and it's yours," he bantered lightly.

Patrick grinned. "Grandchildren. I'll be wantin' some grandchildren." He chuckled at Alex's frown. "I'll not settle for less!"

"And how the hell am I supposed to manage that with my wife a couple of hundred miles away?" Alex snarled.

Arching a brow, Patrick leaned back. "Ya can take on the whole Mexican army, ya get everybody together to fight for a new republic, ya build an empire alone, and ya say ya can't figure out how ta get one wee lass pregnant? I don't believe it!"

Deep, rumbling laughter broke the silence. "Wee lass, indeed! She's the most stubborn hellcat I've ever tangled with. Why, she's—"

"Careful, lad," Patrick teased. "That's me girl you're talkin' about."

Alex's spirits had risen with the bantering. With luck, he would soon be close enough to get a chance to see her. Reaching for the coffee, he grinned. "Aye, Patrick, and my woman!"

How could they have so grossly underestimated Guillermo, Alex thought as he headed south toward Hawk Hill. He'd covered over thirty miles to make the meeting on time and he was weary, but more riding was ahead of him if he was to meet John. His plans to squeeze in a visit with Breanna were thwarted by the signal he had hoped not to see.

He had arrived in town that morning and had

gone straight to his room, as was his practice after being away. He hadn't wanted to do anything out of the norm, in case Guillermo had taken to watching him as he had every other American. Standing in the window, he waited for John to emerge from Guillermo's office.

He had watched as John stepped outside. It had been impossible to read his face, but the signal had been clear. No luck. Alex had merely marched into the dusty street and mounted his horse, setting into motion plans that had been laid months before.

There would be a war. There had never really been any doubt about that. Word had come from President Polk that war was inevitable since Mexico was still refusing to sell the land that sat between the United States and the Pacific Ocean. The silent message sent that morning only told him it would be soon. There would be no more time to prepare.

John was somewhere inside the small abandoned fort which was just becoming discernible in the dim light of dawn. Having decided to see Breanna on this trip, Alex was extra cautious in his approach. He eased into the dark interior and realized no one was there, not even John.

He drew his saddle from his tired steed and tossed it to the ground along with a blanket. He might as well try to get some sleep until John arrived. There was no way to tell what was ahead, and he felt he'd better take advantage of the opportunity for sleep.

He stretched out on the ground and looked at the soft pink sky growing ever deeper until the first rays dissolved the colors into full light. His thoughts turned to Breanna. Images of her sleeping flashed into his weary mind. Her hair would be spread across her pillow with long tresses curling about her shoulders and circling her firm breasts. Her lips would be soft and parted in slumber, and her long lashes would fan over her cheeks.

"God!" Alex groaned as the conjured image brought an ache to his groin. Rolling to his side, he clutched the blanket as if he were strangling it. He had to draw deep, slow breaths to calm himself.

"Is that you, Alex?" came a voice from beyond the arched doorway.

Rolling to his feet, Alex raked back his hair from his brow. "Yes, John."

John led his horse within the walls of the small fort and tied it to a post. He started toward Alex and stopped to shake his head ruefully. Alex's dark, handsome face was etched with pain. His eyes seemed to reflect his repressed passions.

"You okay?"

"Yeah, I'm fine," Alex said, his tone unconvincing. He withdrew a cigar from his vest and lit it. He'd been foolish to dwell on Breanna until he could do something about her.

John would have liked to comment on the reply. His friend wasn't looking fine at all. But there was something far more important he had to discuss.

"My men and I have been ordered out of California," he said simply.

Alex stared, stunned by the news. "Damn! I was hoping it was just another one of Guillermo's games to prove his power." He drew on his cigar, blowing out the blue smoke harshly. "So now what do we do?"

John picked up a small twig and began to twist it. "I want you to join my men when they leave Monterey. They'll head east as if they are following Guillermo's orders. Once you're sure no one is following, take them north."

"What about you?"

"I have something I have to do, then I'll join you."

"You won't know our route," Alex said, wondering what was holding John back.

John could read the question on Alex's face. "I won't be joining you overland. I'm going from here to San Francisco to send in my resignation to Polk."

Alex was stunned by the reply. "Damn it, John! You can't quit this mission when we're so close. You're the one who got us organized in the first place."

John laughed. "I'm not resigning from the mission, Alex, only the army. I can't implicate the president in this. It was an understanding before I left that if the situation escalated to the point of war, I would disassociate myself from the army and continue to direct the mission."

Relieved, Alex sighed. "So when do we leave?"

"Let's get some sleep," John recommended. "You look like you could use some." Alex nodded. Settling on his own blanket, John perched himself on an elbow and glanced at Alex. "After that, you can go see that wife of yours." He saw the surprise on Alex's face. "It is why you were so anxious to get down here, isn't it?"

Falling back on his saddle pillow, Alex grinned. "It had crossed my mind."

John grew serious. "You won't have much time, Alex, but it's the least I can do for you." Lying down, he placed his head on his crossed arms. "I don't know what's going to happen, but I'm sure it will be a while before you have the chance to see her again."

Thinking of her, Alex closed his eyes. He had missed Christmas with his wife, but he had something for her. "I only need enough time to tell her how I feel and convince her to stay out of trouble."

Covering a chuckle, John rolled to his side. If he knew anything about Breanna, it was that Alex didn't have enough time to do what he wanted, not even if he had a lifetime!

Breanna felt a sudden warmth beside her and turned to it. Anxious hands separated the buttons down the front of her nightdress, and she moaned when moist lips kissed the peaks of her breasts. Too many nights she had lain in Alex's arms, only to discover it was all a dream. This night, however, was different. This was real!

She had stirred, her eyes fluttering. He had already been touching her. It would have been easy to stop him, yet she realized she didn't want to. It was a moment he had somehow managed to steal. Nothing else mattered. Her young body needed him. Her heart wanted him.

She could feel the texture of his skin beneath her hands as she moved them over his strong back. There was an urgency in them that prevented questions. The only words were husky pleas and whispered declarations of mutual desire.

"Yes, Alex," she breathed as he removed her gown. His weight shifted and she reached for him. He was over her, seeking her aching depths. She rose to meet him, marveling at the heat that filled her. Slowly they began to move in the age-old rhythm of lovers.

He called her name, urging her ever closer to the wondrous fulfillment his body promised. She responded with waves of ecstasy that ignited the ultimate fire within him. Their bodies strained to enjoy every nuance of a mutual climax.

Alex knew Breanna would soon begin to ask questions once the lassitude of their union wore off. To avoid speaking, he covered her parted lips with his own while reaching for something he'd left on the nightstand. Without disturbing their passionate kiss, he managed to clasp the chain about her neck.

"I'm a little late, darling, but Merry Christmas,"

he whispered against her parted lips. She was losing the struggle to stay awake, and he knew he had only moments. "I love you, little one. Remember that." He wasn't sure she had heard his declaration until a satisfied smile touched her lips.

Breanna yawned and stretched languidly. She could hear activity from somewhere in the house and didn't care to bother with it. She had slept well for the first time in weeks. Nothing else seemed important enough to disturb her after that. She preferred to dwell on the night just past.

He had come to her. How or why had never been discussed, and it really didn't matter. All that was important was the tender passion they shared. By not asking him questions, she was relieved of answering why she had run or what her true feelings were regarding Alex. Of course, questions would probably haunt her in the light of day, but she preferred to think about his whispered words of love instead.

Slowly, she slipped her fingers to her throat. Proof that he was more than a dream hung about her neck. Tossing back the covers, she sighed. If she needed more proof, it was in her state of undress and the reddened areas about her breasts where his unshaven chin had brushed her tender flesh.

Blushing, Breanna gazed down at the gold medallion nestled between her breasts. Holding the pendant in her hand, she turned it. A shiver raced down her spine. An elaborate single letter was etched into the golden surface.

Tears began to fill her eyes, blurring her vision until the letter evaporated into a sparkling sea of gold. A brand! A mark of ownership! He had not come as a husband and lover, but as a thief in the night to steal her resolve to hate him.

"Oh, Alex," she cried. "Why?"

Holding the charm tightly in her hand, she

sniffed when she recalled the last words he had spoken. Did he love her? Had she been wrong? Closing her eyes, she prayed there was a chance he spoke the truth. Unfortunately, the past came back to haunt her when she remembered her other prayers.

The weeks since leaving Alex were filled with prayers that he would come to her and explain what she had overheard that fateful day. He had come, but not to explain. Instead, he had used the darkness to enjoy her body. Warmth suffused her and she tightened her jaw. Her traitorous body had gone over to the enemy without the least bit of struggle.

Breanna grabbed her nightgown and wriggled into it. She was beginning to feel more like his whore than his wife. The medallion tapped her breast, and she reached to remove it, feeling it was only a reminder of what a fool she could be. A soft knock at the door halted her and she hid the necklace beneath her gown before calling out.

"Yes?"

"It's me," Heather answered. "May I come in?"

"Of course!" Breanna replied too cheerfully as tears still filled her eyes.

"I didn't mean to bother you but . . ." Heather saw the tears and the forced smile. "Breanna! What's wrong?"

Breanna shook her head. "Nothing, really." She brushed away the threatening tears. "I'm all right. Just a bad dream," she said with a weak smile.

Not convinced Breanna was telling the truth, Heather decided to let it go for the time being. "Captain Frémont is downstairs. He wants to speak with you."

Breanna hoped that he had heard she was willing to help and might have something for her to do. With Christmas past and Millie married to Paul, there was little to occupy her time except listening to Heather discuss her own marriage plans.

"Very well. Tell him I'll be down shortly." Heather smiled and left without another word as Breanna began to dress.

"Captain Frémont," she said crisply at the door to her father's den. "What can I do for you?"

John rose and extended his hand. He had to admit he could better understand Alex's desires when he saw her. Deciding to further Alex's cause, he smiled. "Mrs. King," he addressed her, noting the slight wince at the use of her married name.

"Brandy, captain?" she inquired out of duty and poured him a glass when he accepted. "Please, sit down." Breanna had taken a chair and did not wish to give him the advantage of standing over her.

"Thank you, Mrs. King," he said, fully aware she preferred he not use her wedded title.

"Call me Breanna," she stated tersely.

John grinned into his glass. She seemed rather annoyed this morning. He could only assume Alex had not been successful in seeing her.

Uncomfortable with his reticence, Breanna broke the silence. "I'm curious to hear why you have come from Monterey to see me, captain."

"I didn't come from Monterey, Breanna. I spent yesterday at Hawk Hill with Alex." So, he thought when he saw her frown, Alex had seen her. "I've been asked to leave Monterey."

Breanna's head lifted. Something was wrong. "Guillermo?" John nodded and she sighed. "So it begins in earnest."

"It seems so," John said, wondering what was facing the many men who had united for this very possibility.

After absorbing the impact of his words, Breanna leaned forward. "Is that why you're here? Are you warning us that there will be trouble?"

"Yes, there's bound to be trouble, but I'm here to make sure you realize how very important it is now that you stay away from Guillermo and his men." He saw her frown in disappointment. "I mean it, Breanna," he added sternly. "There is much at stake. I can't afford to let you do something that might require assigning men to help the women we've left behind."

"Honestly!" Breanna snapped, rising to glare down at him. "You men think that just because we're women we can't—"

"Whoa!" John interrupted with a raised hand. "I'm not saying there isn't going to be something you can do. I only mean you have to wait until we're ready to move." He paused, hoping she would believe him. With luck, Breanna never would get her chance, but she didn't need to know that. All he cared about was keeping her from interfering for a little longer.

"You mean I can help?" she asked skeptically.

John nodded. "Yes, but only when we're ready, and only if you receive orders from me." He watched her return to her chair to think over his words. "Breanna," he said seriously. "This is all too real. People are going to kill and be killed. The men involved will be in enough danger without worrying about their womenfolk." He saw her raise her chin to look at him. "That includes your father and . . . your husband."

Pain crossed her face. "Alex and I are married, but I am his wife in name only. I know the truth, captain. I know he only married me to keep me from interfering in this rebellion."

"That's not true," John said, wondering if Alex had been unsuccessful last night after all.

"Please, I don't care to dwell on it." She rose, indicating the meeting was over. "I won't jeopardize your mission, captain. I, too, believe in what you're doing, but I still think I can be valuable."

John rose also. "I don't doubt it." He smiled, taking her hand. "But remember, Breanna. Lives can't be replaced. If we are to succeed with as little

bloodshed as possible, there has to be discipline."
He was ready to depart when she called to him.

"John," she relented at last. "Be careful and ...
and take care of ... everyone." Touching the brim
of his hat in a salute, he turned away, leaving
Breanna with her thoughts and Alex's gift
clutched in her palm.

It took John two weeks to arrive at the camp in
Sonoma. He'd sent his men out of Monterey, written to Polk, resigned from his official post, and assigned Eric the task of keeping an eye on Breanna.
He was free to take full charge of the Americans
ready to fight for an independent California. The
tide of complacency had turned. It was time to act.

"Great security you have here, Alex," John said
as his friend exited a tent and walked to where he
was dismounting. "I rode in without so much as a
challenge."

"You were spotted two hours ago." Alex put out
his hand in welcome. "The men know who you
are."

After shaking hands, John brushed off some of
the accumulated dust from his uniform, then went
to join Alex for some coffee. En route to the fire
and the blackened pot, he spoke with several of
the men sitting around, who teased him about giving up his commission but vowed they would
obey his orders regardless.

Once Alex and John were seated, a comfortable
silence ensued while they drank their coffee. Alex
could sense John's fatigue and allowed him time
to gather his thoughts. He enjoyed the quiet as
well; it gave him time to reflect on his wife.

The night he had gone to her, he had hoped to
explain all the things he thought troubled her. He
had had no intention of making love to her, but
the moment he saw her sleeping so beautifully before him, he was lost. Expecting her to wake and
fight him, he found her turning to him willingly.

What had started out as a stolen kiss became a passion-filled frenzy.

He thought of the necklace he had clasped about her lovely throat. Had she torn it off in anger when she realized how easily she had succumbed to him, or did it still lay nestled in the warm, soft valley between her breasts?

"Alex!" John tapped his friend's arm and finally drew his attention. "Where are you, *amigo?*" he said. "I've spoken to you twice and you never heard a word."

"Sorry, John. I was thinking about Breanna. I guess I got carried away."

"I saw her the morning after we met," John told him, noticing the interest on his face. "I wanted to be sure she gave us the time we needed before getting into trouble."

"And did she agree?" When John nodded, he continued, "Then maybe you ought to think about a career in politics. You must be able to charm anyone."

There was a note of sarcasm in Alex's voice. Obviously, he was unhappy with the fact that she listened to him when she wouldn't listen to her own husband. "It wasn't charm, Alex," he explained. "It was common sense. Breanna is not stupid. I could hardly have fooled her unless she was distracted." He grinned at Alex. "I guess I have you to thank for that?"

"Yes," Alex said. "I saw her the night before."

"But she wouldn't listen to you."

"Actually, we didn't get a chance to talk."

Chuckling, John poured more coffee. "I suppose that was best, especially since she won't believe you." He could see the questions on Alex's face. "She thinks your marriage was meant to keep her from doing her part in the revolt."

"She has no part in the revolt!" Alex snapped.

"Sure she does," John said assuredly. "She believes in it and she wants to see all the Mexican injustices ended." He watched Alex fidget with his cup. "Breanna is a passionate woman, Alex."

Alex snorted. "You think I don't know that?"

"I'm referring to her feelings about this campaign," John said. "She's bright and courageous. She doesn't like being considered a hindrance."

Alex thought about what he was saying. Alex truly had made her sound inept. His lip twitched with the hint of a smile. "I suppose I should be glad she ran off and didn't try to prove her point with that damned whip she's so good at using."

"Perhaps you should be, my friend," John said. "Just remember how good she is the next time you meet."

His tone implied something Alex needed to clarify. "So she's still angry even after . . ."

"Yes, she is," John replied to save Alex the need to explain what had gone on that night. "In fact, Alex, she doesn't really consider herself your wife."

"What?" Alex demanded harshly, his head snapping around to face John.

John shrugged. "That's what she told me."

Alex rose, his hands fisted. "I don't care what she said! She's my wife whether she likes it or not!"

"I'm only telling you what she said," John repeated to cover the laughter that threatened. He found he was enjoying the battles raging between Alex and Breanna. It was a relief from his worries about the real battles ahead.

"What else did she tell you?"

Scratching his chin, John considered. After he had spoken with Heather, he knew the trouble between Alex and his wife was nothing more than a struggle of wills. Once, he had avoided the same thing with his wife by accepting missions that required they spend a lot of time apart. He didn't want the same for Alex. He shrugged.

"She figures you only married her to keep her out of things."

"That's rot."

"Said she heard you admit it."

Suddenly it dawned on Alex that Breanna must have overheard his conversation with Patrick. It was the only explanation for her misinterpretation of his feelings. Alex thought of that conversation. If it hadn't been for Patrick and his bizarre sense of humor, none of this would have happened. Prepared to say as much, he was interrupted by none other than the culprit in this whole mess.

"John! I heard you were back and—ugh . . . !" Patrick hit the ground before he knew what had happened.

"You son of a bitch!" Alex roared at the downed man. "From now on, keep your damned mouth shut!" He stomped off before Patrick could gain his feet.

"What the hell's wrong with him?" he asked as John helped him to rise.

John couldn't resist laughing when Patrick rubbed his jaw. "It's a long story, Patrick. Since you're in no shape to talk, I think you'd better sit down and listen."

Chapter 18

The ceremony would be small and quiet. With family and friends spread far and wide during these trying times, Eric and Heather had only Breanna, Millie and Paul, and the few hands left at Casa del Verde to serve as witnesses.

Eric had arrived with the priest right on schedule and stood nervously awaiting his bride. Breanna came in and smiled. Eric glanced up from his fidgeting hands and was stunned by Breanna's beauty. If only Alex could see her at that moment, he thought, he would be unable to resist her.

She was clad in a gown of deep burgundy that made her skin shine like polished ivory. The deep square cut of the neckline hugged her shoulders and dropped straight down until it cut across her full breasts. The long sleeves were snug on her slender arms, and soft ecru lace circled her wrists, trimmed the full skirt, and formed a band around her small waist.

Her auburn hair was drawn up and severely twisted into a bun at the back of her neck. Surprisingly, rather than detracting from her beauty, the style only enhanced it. Her eyes took on an exotic slant no man could ignore. Not even if the man was a bridegroom.

Breanna caught his wandering eyes and glanced down at her attire. "Is there something wrong with my dress, Eric?"

"What?" He'd been caught staring and stam-

267

mered. "No. You . . . you look great." Reaching to take her hands, he smiled. "I just never realized what a beautiful sister-in-law I was getting." His smile was charming and bespoke only an admiration for her beauty.

"And may I say you are looking very handsome yourself?"

"I want to impress my bride," he said. "She deserves better than a cowboy with a small spread and little money. I don't want her to realize that until after we exchange our vows."

Breanna leaned to kiss his cheek. "I don't think she could do any better, Eric." He shrugged, and she excused herself to greet Father Timothy.

While she stood with the priest discussing the upcoming ceremony, Eric noticed the gold chain around her neck. It was the only jewelry she wore, having since removed her wedding ring when she came home. Possibly the band hung from the chain, but it was tucked beneath the burgundy velvet. Still, he had to wonder, since she seemed unconsciously to touch it frequently. Eric was still wondering when a knock at the door summoned her.

Assuming the few guests were beginning to arrive, Breanna opened the door with a warm smile, then stiffened. She couldn't move or speak. She could only stare at the splendidly black-clad figure casting his shadow over her.

"Hello, little one." Alex smiled and devoured her with his eyes.

Breanna's hand rose to her throat to stifle a cry. After all the times she had thought of him since the night they made love, she'd never dreamed he would come to her like this. "Alex," she breathed, stunned. Fighting to regain some composure, she straightened her spine. "What are you doing here?"

A devilish grin crossed his face and a light danced in his eyes. Catching her unaware, he had seen the desire leap into her eyes before she masked it.

"I'm here to give Heather away. When we got Eric's message, we couldn't find your father." Of course, the truth was he hadn't looked. Patrick had avoided him after his surly attack, choosing to ride circuit on the men rather than stay too close. It had been advantageous, allowing Alex to come in Patrick's stead. "May I come in?"

Without a word, Breanna stepped back so he could enter. Her eyes scanned his broad back, the width of his shoulders, and the lean firmness of his hips as he spotted Eric and went to greet his friend. They were clasping hands when she realized she was still holding her breath. He was here! He had walked back into her life as if nothing had ever happened!

She had often imagined their first encounter after their stolen night of love. Never did she think it would be like this. Anger and accusations, possibly. Passionate embracing and longing kisses, probably, but never this apparent disregard.

His rich, deep laughter at some shared joke with Eric echoed in the room, and she began to tremble. A desperate desire to run came over her, and her eyes darted about for an avenue of escape. Muffling a sob with the back of her hand, Breanna ran up the stairs to rid herself of the sight and sound of him.

Breanna flew down the hall to Heather's room. Without knocking, she entered and leaned against the door the moment it clicked shut.

"Good Lord! Bree!" Heather draped her veil across the bed and ran to her sister. "What's wrong? You look like you've seen a ghost!"

As she blinked back the tears that threatened, Breanna's voice caught in her throat. "I . . . I have. Alex . . . he's . . . he's downstairs." Her eyes darted frantically. "He's here to . . . to give you away."

Gently, Heather's arm circled Breanna's shoulder and she led her to a chair, sitting her down and kneeling beside her. "Bree, I'm sorry this had to happen today." She gathered Breanna's cold hands in hers. "But, Bree, it's my wedding day. I know you're upset, but please, don't ruin it for me."

Heather's plea reached though the numbness engulfing Breanna, and she looked up into the lovely face before her. Heather had never asked much of her. She couldn't let her down. Despite the agony of facing Alex, she knew she would do as Heather asked.

"We'd better finish getting you ready then." She tried to smile and failed. "It will be all right, *chica*. I promise you." She took Heather in her arms. "Nothing will ruin your day."

Breanna was drawing from the last of her reserve when she waved farewell to Heather and Eric. She knew Alex was standing behind her, and it took every ounce of determination not to run. The last few hours had been difficult.

While she helped Heather finish with her toilette, a surge of self-confidence flowed through her. She had nothing to be afraid of! After all, it was Alex and his games that had forced her to leave. She had only stood up for herself to survive his cruel hoax. She praised herself for her resolve which had quickly dissipated when she found him waiting at the foot of the stairs.

A terrible wave of longing had swept through her, squelching her decision to remain aloof. His eyes were afire as they scanned her, and she had to clutch the banister to avoid swaying. He placed one foot on the stairs, and she hadn't been able to ignore his strength as his chest pressed against the black silk of his shirt with each breath. If Heather hadn't come up behind her, she might have stood there watching him forever.

Spurred on to movement, Breanna had floated

down the stairs and walked past him without a glance, but she had known he watched her. She had felt his eyes on her back as she went into the parlor, just as she felt them now while she watched Heather and Eric ride away.

After that initial moment of shock on the stairs, the day had been a blur. Vague images of Heather on Alex's arm, the ceremony, a guest here and there, floated through her mind. The only concrete part of the day was Alex. They never spoke, yet huge volumes could have been written about the communication they shared in thoughts and gestures.

He never took his eyes from her, and when she chanced to look at him, he would salute her with a silent toast or a raised brow. Now, it was over. Her promise to Heather had been kept at great expense, and her nerves were stretched to breaking. Her body cried out for relief from the tension.

Drawing a shaky breath, she turned back to the house without a word to those standing in the yard. She could hear muffled conversation, but it didn't register in her tired mind. All she could think of was Alex and how she could make him leave. She spotted his hat on a table in the foyer and the coat he had thrown over a chair. Breanna gathered his things and turned toward the door to find him standing there.

She swallowed hard. It would be over soon, and she would muster one last display of bravado. Staring at his belt buckle, she pushed his things toward him.

"Here!" She drew back sharply when he took them to avoid touching him. "Thank you for helping Heather and Eric." Where were the others? she wondered when he didn't move. Millie should have come in to help clean up by now. She tried to look past him, but he blocked the door effectively with his broad shoulders.

"They're not coming, little one," he said, and offered her a twisted grin when her wide eyes met his. "I've sent them all away."

"You had no right." Breanna backed up slowly.

Never taking his eyes from hers, he tossed his hat and coat on a small table before moving stealthily toward her. She felt like a small animal trapped in the hypnotic gaze of a great predator. His pantherlike movements stalked her, and she grew frightened of the power he exuded over her.

"Go away!" she demanded, inching ever closer to the door of the library. If only she could get inside, it had a sturdy lock and would give her time to—

"I'm not going anywhere, Breanna. We have some unfinished business, you and I." He wanted to tell her that what she'd heard between Patrick and him was not what she thought. He wanted to tell her he loved her.

Breanna's thoughts were suddenly filled with the memory of the night he had crept into her room and made love to her. There had been no time for explanations then, no plea for forgiveness. There had been just a slaking of desires. These memories drove away the fear and allowed anger to replace it. Her hurt and humiliation grew to a seething rage.

"No!" Breanna cried and spread her hands before her, breaking the spell he was weaving. "Enough! I won't listen to your lies anymore!" To her surprise, Alex paused to stare at her. "I know, Alex! I know the truth!"

Alex took a step toward her, and she flinched. "What the hell are you talking about?" he shouted.

"I won't let you use me anymore!" she screamed and turned to run. She entered the library and tried to lock the door, but before she could secure it, Alex pushed into the room, throwing her back with the force of his entry.

Breanna lost her footing and landed on the floor in a flurry of skirts. She would have scurried to her feet, but Alex was towering over her before she could move. His legs were braced for battle.

"Damn you, woman! If you hadn't run off you would have known I told—"

"Get out!" Breanna interrupted before he could finish. "Just get out of my house!"

Alex grabbed her flailing arms and yanked her to her feet. He pulled her up against his chest. "This is *my* house, Breanna, and I'm tired of fighting with you!" He tried to lay claim to her lips, but she fought like a wildcat. Gripping a handful of her hair, he forced her to still. "You're my wife, love," he told her more gently. "And it's time you remember that."

His mouth possessed her startled one. He was able to delve slowly into its warm wetness. She held herself stiff in his arms, but he continued to pursue a response. He heard her whimper softly and eased his hold. She was surrendering.

The ploy would work, she thought. Alex was too filled with his power over her to suspect she was using the ruse of surrender to execute her escape. It was not easy. His kiss was tantalizing and seductive. A big part of her was ready to give in to him, yet her mind ruled. She was not about to go back to more hurt. Moving carefully, she positioned her arm and, with all her strength, drove her fist into his stomach.

"Ugh!" he groaned, releasing her.

Without pity, Breanna drew back her hand to bring it soundly to his cheek. "Keep your hands off me!" she ordered. She should have taken the opportunity to run while she had it. The resounding crack snapped her out of her tirade, and the magnitude of what she had done began to sink in when she saw the rage on his face.

Alex's hands snaked out to grip her upper arms. "Don't ever hit me again, Breanna, unless I deserve it."

"You did deserve it!" she retorted, her head tilting back so she could glare at him. "You used me, and I won't let you do it again!"

Angered further by her stubborn accusation, Alex shook her. "You're my wife, Breanna! I can *use* you whenever I see fit!"

"No!" She tried to break away. "It's over!"

Sweeping her struggling form up into his arms, Alex carried her to the nearest chair and sat down. He held her trapped in the circle of his arms. "It will never be over until I say so," he told her while dropping her back to expose her throat. He saw the chain and smiled. "You wear my brand, Breanna," he said to her as he reached inside the neck of her gown to withdraw the medallion. Looking at the intricate "K," he held it up for her to see. "You are mine, body and soul."

"I belong only to myself!" she cried, renewing her struggle to get off his lap.

Alex sat back, cradling her to his chest. "Don't fight it, Breanna," he breathed near her temple. "You are mine, and I will not settle for less than your love."

Breanna stilled, too exhausted to continue. "You had my love, but you used it against me."

Closing his eyes, he tightened his arms. "You're wrong, *gatita*." He wanted to say more, but her hurt was too raw. She wouldn't believe him yet; she wouldn't let herself trust him. "I've always wanted you," was the only thing he could say that she would believe.

Drawing back from his embrace, Breanna stared at him. There was pain in her eyes. "And what about what I want, Alex?" she asked softly. "Doesn't that matter?"

"What do you want, Bree?" he asked, his voice growing tender.

She closed her eyes and returned her head to his shoulder so he wouldn't be able to see her face. She knew she was vulnerable, yet didn't wish him to see it. "I wanted you to take me seriously," she began. "I am not a child to be humored, yet you always make me feel as if you think I am."

Alex smiled over her head. Did she realize how small and defenseless she sounded now? Sighing, he brought his hand to her hair and brushed it back. "Believe me, love, I never dreamed of trifling with you."

Hearing the humor he made no effort to hide, she tried to sit up, but his arm tightened. "You're doing it now!" she exclaimed when she couldn't move.

Lifting her slightly, he made her face him. "No, Breanna," he told her sternly. "What I'm doing now is telling you how much I love you!"

Stunned, she felt her jaw drop. After working it a moment, she grew skeptical. "You are?"

Alex nodded and let a smile touch his sensuous mouth. "Yes, love. I think I have from the first time I saw you sitting in the hotel dining room." He watched her eyes soften. "You were all fire beneath that frigid facade. I knew you'd be more woman than any man could hope for."

"But what about what you told Papa?" she asked, afraid to believe him.

"You only heard part of it, kitten," he said. "You missed the part about your being stubborn, opinionated, hot-tempered and a brat." He watched a smile flit across her mouth. "And you missed the part when I told him you are the woman I love and always will."

Tears filled Breanna's eyes. "Oh, Alex!" she breathed as she fell against him to offer her lips. He loved her! It had all been a terrible mistake! His arms circled her and held her close. It was a glorious rebirth, a new beginning with all the passions held captive deep inside let loose in a savage storm of want and need.

Alex marveled at the urgency of her kisses. She was so much woman, so much a daughter of Eve, he wondered for the first time in his life if he was man enough to handle her many facets. With each kiss, each caress, she was becoming more a purring kitten and less the tigress that had faced him so boldly, but she was no less exciting. Matching wits with her was like playing with fire. It could be warm and captivating or it could burn, but it was something he could not live without.

Caught up in his driving need for this woman, he swept her up into his arms as he rose. He carried her urgently through the foyer and up the stairs, pausing at her door to gaze down at her.

"Are you sure?" he asked, waiting until she nodded. "I don't want another sin laid upon my head now that we have cleared the others."

Reaching back for the doorknob, Breanna opened it. "I'm sure," she told him, no trace of shyness in her voice.

All thoughts of the past and the future dissolved in a mist of sensation. Their mutual love wrapped them in a cloak of desire that shut out the rest of the world.

There was tenderness in the way Alex undressed her. His fingers fairly trembled as he unfastened the hooks of her gown and brushed it off her shoulders. Tentatively his hands went to her hair, withdrawing the pins until the thick mass cascaded down her back. He felt her sway when he drew it aside to feather tiny kisses beneath her ear. The heat from her satiny skin urged him to move on. He ran his hands over her hips and pulled the ties of her petticoats until they, too, fell away.

Breanna could hardly hold herself erect. She arched toward him, wanting him to hurry and at the same time reveling in the exquisite torture of his slow seduction. His hands had set her afire with a few simple touches, and his lips were fueling the flame. She couldn't resist a throaty purr when his mouth found her breasts and suckled them through the thin fabric of her shift.

Driven to give as much pleasure as she was receiving, Breanna reached out to touch him. She could feel his thundering heart beneath the cool silk he wore. Suddenly needing to feel his flesh, she eased her hands between them to release the buttons of his shirt.

Alex stood and let her remove his shirt. He watched her eyes caress him an instant before her hands began their own exploration. Her dainty fingers slipped through the dark mat there and paused to tug teasingly at a curl.

"I've been a fool," she whispered, looking up at him. His brows furrowed questioningly. Breanna's eyes sparkled. "I placed such little faith in our love. I should have known you are your own man, Alexander King. No one and nothing could make you do what you didn't want to do." Slipping her arms about his waist, she rubbed her cheek against the soft hair on his chest. "Can you forgive me?"

A single finger touched her chin and tilted her head. "I should be the one seeking pardon. If I had only realized sooner that I love you, I would have saved us both a great deal of heartache."

Alex's dark head lowered tenderly to kiss her trembling lips, and she felt a great need to consummate their love. Her hands went to his belt buckle, releasing it to fall to the floor. Her fingers managed to open the fastenings on his pants. She could feel his hardness pressing to escape the fabric that held it captive. A deep groan escaped his throat when her fingers found him.

Trying to sound in control when he was near to bursting, Alex took her hand to still her seductive caresses. "It has been too long, love," he explained huskily. "If you would be with me to the finish, you'd best stop now."

Filled with the power of her femininity, Breanna drew back. "I would, indeed," she whispered, her hands going to the ribbons of her shift. She watched him struggle to breathe. She saw the muscles on his chest tighten. A nerve twitched in his cheek beneath his crescent scar. With inexorable precision, she slipped the last of her garments down over her hips.

Alex looked at her, transfixed. Like Venus rising from the sea, she stood before him. The only thing gracing her exquisite form was the gold of his medallion. Worshipfully, he knelt before her. His bronzed hands caressed the pale skin of her hips and moved to circle her waist while his lips placed tiny kisses across her stomach. His tender reverence tore at her heart.

In rapturous wonder, Breanna's fingers entwined in his ebony hair and drew his head to nestle beneath her breasts. She leaned to press her cheek against his thick hair. Surprisingly, tears filled her eyes and fell silently until a small sob escaped her. Alex scooped her up into his arms, and sat on the bed holding her.

"Breanna?" His voice was gentle. Her head was buried beneath his chin and there was no answer. "Won't you tell me what's wrong?" His voice seemed etched with pain. His hand pushed back the curtain of her hair and brushed at the tears on her cheek. "Please, love," he coaxed, needing to know what caused her grief.

The agony in his voice made her lean back over his arm. Breanna slipped hers about his neck and drew his face close to hers.

"I love you so much, Alex," she whispered. "And I'm so filled with that love it . . . it welled up inside me." She felt his tension easing beneath her hands. "I simply could not find the words to—"

His lips stopped the flow of her words most effectively and dissolved her need to say them.

What manner of man had she fallen in love with? Breanna wondered. Lying on her side, she could feel the strength of him pressed to her back and marveled at the exquisite union they had shared in the night. With every kiss, every caress, he had drawn her deeper into the vortex of his overpowering masculinity. How did she ever think she could walk away from him? Her fingers toyed with the chain about her neck, and she sighed.

"Regrets, my love?" His deep, throaty voice broke into her thoughts. Her silence kept him from enveloping her in his arms.

Breanna smiled to herself. For all her declarations of love throughout the night, he was still as insecure as a schoolboy. It was no wonder they had difficulties. Despite his worldly experiences, he was a novice at being in love, and it was up to her to reassure him.

Rising to her knees. Breanna clutched the sheet and tucked it beneath her arms. Settling back on her heels, she tossed her head to whip back the long tresses that had fallen over her shoulder.

Alex rose up to balance on his elbow. He beheld the siren before him. She was so like an ancient bride kneeling before her master, yet there was a quality of strength and pride in the way she sat before him. He had to wonder how often in history a woman sat in apparent subjugation when, in fact, she was bringing her master to his knees.

"Is it so difficult for you to answer me?" he asked, his finger tracing her bare arm.

Breanna sighed and reached to caress his handsome face. Gentle fingers tried to ease away the deep furrows on his brow as he awaited her reply.

"Not difficult," she whispered, letting her fingers trace down to his lips.

Alex gripped her wrist and turned it aside to press kisses to her pulse. When she still sat mute, he drew her toward him until she leaned across his chest. "Then answer me," he ordered, his patience suddenly short.

Breanna leaned closer and kissed his throat. She

felt the quickening of his heartbeat and let her lips play up the corded column to his ear. "Don't be so bossy," she whispered, and bit gently on his earlobe.

Alex's arms quickly wrapped around her, trapping her to his chest. "Answer me, vixen, or you'll rue the day."

It was impossible to tell if he was playing with her by the stony expression on his face. There was no hint of amusement, nor was there the familiar flash of anger in his clear blue eyes.

Breanna chewed at her lip. "Is that a threat to beat me?"

"Breanna," he warned, one eyebrow arching.

Pushing away from him, she returned to her knees. A grin flitted across her mouth, and her eyes sparkled mischievously. "Then I suppose I can tell you." Never taking her eyes from him, she stretched her arms high over her head, freeing the sheet to fall about her hips. "Ummm," she purred, and lowered her arms. Seeing the gleam in his eyes, she wiggled to the edge of the bed. "No, Alex." She shook her head. "I have no regrets."

Amusement twitched at Alex's mouth. "Then why are you sneaking away from me?" He threw back the blankets and started to ease toward her.

Shrugging playfully, Breanna slid from the bed and scurried behind the footboard. "Because you grow too sure of yourself, Mr. King. If I let you know how much your touch thrills me or how the way you call my name turns my legs to jelly, I can never be my own mistress."

Alex was slowly creeping closer, enticed by the way her voice had grown softer and seemed to purr. "And is it so important that you be your own mistress?" he asked, easing within reach of her.

Breanna picked up Alex's discarded shirt. She slipped into the black silk and covered herself provocatively. Pushing up the sleeves, she turned to the bed and sat with her back to him.

"It used to be," she mumbled, and stretched her bare legs out beside him.

"And now?" Alex ran his hand up and down her leg, gently kneading her thigh. "Are you adverse to sharing your life with me?" He turned to place his head in her lap.

Slender fingers brushed through his hair. "No, I'm not afraid to share my life with you, Alex. I'm only afraid of being left behind to wait while you live so recklessly."

Alex looked up into her eyes, gleaming with unshed tears. "I'm a man, *querida*. I cannot change the way I live, nor can I ignore my allegiance to my country." He slipped his hand around her neck and drew her lips to his. "Any more than I can cease loving you." Sure she was convinced, he lay back and smiled. "I don't want a slave, Breanna. I want a woman. One who will wait when necessary and ride with me when possible."

Breanna pondered his words. She wasn't sure it was enough to only wait. "But—"

"No buts, *gatita*." He sat up and cupped her chin in his large hand. "I'm a man. You're a woman. We *are* different." He pulled apart the shirt she wore and lowered his lips to her breast. "And I love the difference."

"But, Alex—"

"Shut up, *querida*," Alex growled and drew the peak of her breast into his warm mouth, teasing the tip with his tongue.

"Yes, Alex," she said softly, forgetting what they had been talking about.

The rain beat heavily against the windows, but the lovers within did not notice. Stretched out before the warmth of the fire, Alex held Breanna across his lap. They had made love half a dozen times in the twenty-four hours since his arrival, and he still felt he could take her again. Prepared to prove his point, he was distracted by a thumping at the outside door.

"Someone's here!" Breanna, startled, sat up. Before she could gain her feet, Alex had set her aside and was at the door.

There were no lamps burning in the house. The only light was from the fireplace. Only someone intent on coming to Casa del Verde would have ventured toward the darkened structure. Cautious, Alex called out.

"Who's there?"

"Damn it, Alex! Open up! I'm drowning!"

Alex opened the door wide and threw back his head and laughed loudly. "John! You rogue! Come in! What the devil has you out on a night like this?" Before he could reply, Alex was dragging him toward the warmth of the library. "Come on, there's brandy and a fire in here."

Breanna was waiting to see who their caller was. When she saw John, she smiled. "Sit by the fire," she ordered, spying his soaking cloak. "Alex, tend the hearth while I get John some brandy."

"Is she always this bossy?" John teased, leaning toward the heat and spreading his hands.

Alex grinned and shrugged. "Only when I let her be." He laughed and received a healthy kick to his shin. "Ow! Breanna, why did you do that?" he asked, rubbing his sore limb.

"You great oaf! Sometimes I wonder what chance California has in the hands of the likes of you!" She handed John his drink and winked playfully

John chuckled and took a warming swallow of the amber liquid. "Mmm, good." He sighed, relaxing in the chair closest to the fire. He saw Alex sit and pat his lap, but Breanna shook her head, opting for the ottoman at his feet.

"Well, John," Breanna broke the silence. "What's brought you out on a night like this?"

John held his glass in both hands and rolled it back and forth. He stared at the fire a moment to reflect on the couple awaiting his reply. He was not so much a soldier that he didn't know the glory they were sharing. Although his own wife preferred the society of the East to being at his side, he knew Breanna was different. Part of the reason for his visit involved that difference.

"I'm here for two reasons," he finally said. Looking at Alex, he sighed. "I'm sorry, Alex, but I need you up north. There have been some skirmishes that might get out of hand." He saw Alex nod resolutely even as Breanna reached to take his hand.

He watched the loving exchange and hoped the rest of his purpose didn't do anything to ruin it. "And you, Breanna," he said, drawing their attention. "I want you to see if you can find out about any troops leaving Monterey during the next few weeks."

Chapter 19

"**O**h, John!" Breanna exclaimed, thrilled that at last she was being given a part in the revolt. "I'll do whatever you need me to do!" Excited by the prospect, she failed to see the scowl forming on Alex's face. John did notice, even as she questioned him about how to get the information.

"Perhaps I should try to get someone else," he offered, sorry he hadn't talked to Alex first about requesting Breanna's involvement.

"Don't be silly!" Breanna laughed. "This is perfect. No one will be expecting a woman, and I can—"

"No!" Alex said harshly.

Breanna whirled around, only to be amazed at the anger on his face. It was not only unexpected, it was completely devastating after the time they had just shared.

"*No?* What do you mean, *no?*"

Furious with both John and Breanna, Alex directed his anger toward the one over whom he had the greater power. "I mean what I said, Breanna. You're not going to do this."

Trying to keep her temper in check, Breanna glared at him. "And who will do it, Alex? Can you think of someone else better qualified?" She glanced back at John to force him into the discussion. "Is there, John? Is there someone else who can get close enough to gather the information you want, someone you can trust as much as me?"

John looked at Breanna, then at Alex. "No, there is no one else." He saw Alex's jaw clench. "She is known by Guillermo. He is attracted to her," he admitted honestly despite the deepening of Alex's color. "She can get close without raising suspicion."

"You see!" Breanna exclaimed, laying her hand on Alex's arm in pleading. "Please, Alex. Don't make me defy you in this."

Alex lowered his eyes to stare at her. He knew she would never let this opportunity pass, and it riled him that he could not stop her. When he left, she would do it anyway, but he didn't have to like it. Drawing a steadying breath, he made one more effort.

"I don't want you involved, Breanna." He saw her spine stiffen. "You are my wife, and I want you to obey me in this."

Breanna bit her lip. She loved Alex, but this was a way for her not only to help California, but to help him. "I can't, Alex," she said softly, praying he would understand. "You, my father, all the men who are risking their lives for what they believe in, can use this information I gather." He closed his eyes as if he were refusing to hear her.

"Alex!" she cried, gripping his arm. "It's possible that my small part could save a life!" She threw her arms around him. "What if that life is yours?" There was no reply. "I love you, but I have to do this. Please, Alex. Give me your blessing and wish me luck."

Alex glared at John. He knew it was necessary or John would never have asked, yet it was too difficult to deal with. Placing his hands on her arms, he set her from him.

"You have neither if you defy me in this," he announced coldly. The defiance in her eyes was answer enough. Stepping away from her, he faced

John. "I'll see you in Sonoma." He turned and headed for the door, but paused to look back at Breanna.

She was crying softly but stubbornly refused to comply with his wishes. His heart felt like cold lead in his chest. She was beautiful and proud. Part of him wanted to open his arms to her, but part—the part that had known the pain of losing someone he loved—remained stony. He wanted to lash out and make her hurt as much as he was hurting.

"I never really cared about having children, but I should have made sure I got you pregnant," he said, his eyes raking over her when she gasped. "Obviously, what I want means nothing. Perhaps a child would have kept you home!"

Breanna stood frozen as he left, not moving until she heard the door slam. A tender hand touched her shoulder, and she looked up to see John, his eyes filled with concern.

"I'm sorry," he told her gently. "I never thought he would be so against it." Thinking of his other limited options, he sighed. "You don't have to do this, Breanna."

Recalling her words to Alex about saving a life, she wiped away her tears. "Yes, John. I do."

Breanna stood at the doorway that led into the ballroom of the hotel. She was delighted she didn't have much longer to wait to begin her assignment. The two weeks since Alex had stomped out were altogether too long, and she was glad they were over.

Not only had she spent hours going over the details and instructions John had given her, but she had taken ill. Sure it was only a bad case of nerves made worse by a breaking heart, she struggled through each morning. Fortunately, she only felt ill in the early part of the day, and she reasoned it was her sleepless nights that were the cause. She was relieved that Guillermo's party was an evening affair.

With luck she would discover something helpful, and she would exhaust herself so she could sleep. Sleep had been elusive since her parting from Alex. His image haunted her. She could hear him demanding she forget this escapade, yet she knew she had to go through with it. It was very possible what she learned could make a small difference.

She was thinking of what she was to do should she glean any information when she heard someone say the general had arrived. She pasted a smile on her lips and made her way inside.

The room was almost full, and she spotted several local landowners she recognized. Many were Americans. She couldn't help wondering if any of them were rebels, but she knew it would be too risky to pry. John was preparing men to arm Hawk Hill in an effort to draw troops away from Sonoma. It was possible she could find out if there actually would be a need to divert Guillermo's attention.

The soft strumming of guitars began. Smiling at those close to her, Breanna began to move around the room. It seemed she was still considered a heroine. Many of the couples stopped her to praise her actions against the drunken soldiers who had threatened the old man. She had hoped Guillermo might have forgotten the episode, but she soon realized it would have been impossible.

"You really were very brave." A matronly woman Breanna had never met before smiled at her.

"Very brave," a deep voice echoed from behind her.

Breanna turned and was once again impressed with the tall good looks of Felipe Guillermo. He towered over her, and instinct made her want to draw away. Instead, she smiled up at him.

"General, how nice to see you again."

Felipe could not resist enjoying the plunging neckline of her gown as he took her hand and bowed to kiss it. "My pleasure, señorita," he said huskily.

Breanna breathed a sigh of relief that Guillermo thought she was still unmarried. Her marriage to Alex could very well ruin any opportunity she might have to gain his trust. So far, Alex was still in the general's good graces, but there was no telling if that would change.

Keeping Breanna's hand in his, he tucked it in the crook of his arm. The gesture was meant to lay claim to the beautiful girl. He was not pleased with the company she kept, but he did appreciate her womanly curves enough to overlook it.

"I have not seen you since my last party," he said as he led her toward his private table. "Have you been hiding from me?"

"I assure you, general," Breanna said sweetly, "I have not. It's just that my voyage was long and I rather looked forward to the peace and quiet of Casa del Verde for a while."

Felipe quirked a brow. "But you have been home for months! Surely you are ready now to go out into society." When she only shrugged lightly, he leaned toward her. "I rather thought you were merely too busy with my friend Alex."

Breanna fought the urge to swallow the lump that was forming in her throat. She had the impression Guillermo was fishing. Remembering John's warning that this man was no fool, she calmly shook her head.

"No, general. I have rarely seen him since your party. It seems he is away quite a lot."

"True," he said with a smile that never touched his eyes. "One would think he was involved in something he wanted to hide."

"Perhaps, but let's not bother talking about him when I would rather hear about you." She leaned to press her breast provocatively against his arm. She was learning about womanly wiles, and she would not hesitate to use them.

Distracted by the lushness pressed against him, Felipe suddenly didn't care if there was a connection between Breanna and Alex. His suspicions could wait. If, by some chance, she was Alex's woman playing at intrigue, he would use her both for his own pleasure and as a weapon against Alex.

"It would be my pleasure, señorita." He smiled, this time with desire dancing in his dark eyes. "What would you like to know about me?"

Careful! she thought to herself. This was too good a chance to ruin by being overanxious. "Well, to begin, do you like to dance, general?"

Rich laughter filled his corner of the room. She was no frivolous female, this Breanna Sullivan. If she was playing a game with him, he looked forward to each match.

"Indeed!" he exclaimed, and motioned for the musicians to play.

Breanna had a headache. She was tired of the verbal banter she and Felipe had engaged in all evening. There was no doubt in her mind that he was baiting her. She found it exhilarating at first, but it soon paled. Uneasy fencing with him, she only wanted to leave. Unfortunately, she had learned nothing, and that kept her from slipping out.

Excusing herself from one of the couples who had trapped her into a conversation, Breanna sought a moment's respite. Felipe had gone off with one of his soldiers, allowing her to wander about freely, but there was nothing of interest being discussed among those in attendance.

In search of the women's salon, she stepped into the hall behind the ballroom. Catching a glimpse of Guillermo and several other Mexican officers entering a room, she stepped soundlessly into the shadow of a drapery. Fortunately, no one saw her. The door shut, and she inched closer.

Standing before the door, she whipped her head back and forth to be sure there was no one around to notice her eavesdropping. Finding herself completely alone, she pressed her ear to the door. The thick portal muffled every bit of sound. Clenching her fists, she knew she had to find out what was going on inside.

She gathered her skirts and quickly sought the back door that led out to the gardens behind the hotel. Making her way unseen around the building, she counted windows until she saw the one she sought. Easing along the shrubbery skirting the building, Breanna stepped behind a bush beneath the open window.

"But do you trust her, generalisimo?" an unknown man asked.

"Of course not, Juan," Felipe snapped. "I am merely amusing myself with the pretty gringa." Breanna heard his footsteps as he spoke and noted the sound of liquid being poured. "I thought her involved when she used that whip on my men but have since decided she is only a spoiled child." Breanna bristled as she listened to him sip his drink. "Should she prove to be otherwise, I will delight in seeing her duly punished. Until then, I will simply play with her."

Breanna felt her face grow hot. Spoiled child! she fumed, wishing she could go in and scratch his eyes out. But she clenched her teeth and turned back to listen.

"Then you will not tell her we are looking for King?"

Felipe grunted. "No, Martinez. As I said, I will be cautious. Alex would not come strutting into town if he knew we were after him. I prefer to catch him here where I can use him as an example to those foolish enough to think they can fight us and win."

Impulsively, Breanna shifted her position so she could peer into the room. She saw one man shrug his shoulders. "We do not know for sure they are looking to fight."

Glaring at the little man, Felipe sniffed in disdain. "You are a fool, Juan. This man Frémont, I don't believe he is here to make maps. Those imbeciles in Mexico City will see I was right. These Americans are going to make war. They want California, and they are foolish enough to think they can win it."

The third man in the room impressed Breanna as a man of greater authority, which he soon proved. "You best beware how you speak to those in power, Felipe," he warned. "If you are wrong, and word gets back, you may find yourself sent off to Spain in disgrace."

Felipe lifted his head arrogantly. "I am not wrong, Martinez, but even if I should be, I will still have King and all the lands he has amassed." Raising his glass in a mock toast, Felipe laughed. "To Alexander King and his capture!"

Stifling an angry gasp, Breanna stepped back and cringed as she felt a twig dig into her side. She let out a small yelp before she could prevent it.

"What was that?" one of the men asked, moving quickly to the window. He leaned out, looking left and right.

To her relief, there was no moon. Her gown was dark and blended with the foliage where she pressed herself back into it. Holding her breath, she sighed softly only when the man returned to the room.

"You are getting nervous, *amigo*," Martinez remarked. "Perhaps you should leave these plans to Felipe and me."

"I'll stay," Juan announced. "I would like my share of glory to be as healthy as yours."

"Then let's decide how we want to disperse the extra men you've sent for."

"You two handle it," Felipe said. "I think I shall go find the delicious gringa and try to convince her to warm my bed tonight."

Breanna's eyes widened. She hadn't thought he would leave the room so quickly. She could hear the others discussing new troops, but she couldn't risk getting caught. She had to warn Alex that a trap was being set for him. It wasn't exactly what John wanted, but it would have to do.

Easing along the wall, Breanna was almost at the door when she heard it open. The last person she wanted to see stepped outside and called her name. Afraid he would suspect she had been spying, she whirled and bent low, moaning a reply.

"Breanna!" he called again, hearing her misery. "What's wrong?" His hands circled her waist and felt the spasms she forced.

It hadn't been easy, but Breanna managed to simulate the violent retching she had experienced that morning and numerous others. The memory brought a clamminess to her skin and made her tremble, adding substance to her claim to illness.

"I ... I'm sorry, Felipe," she moaned again. "I fear I ... I am ill."

Disappointed that he would have to search elsewhere for companionship that night, Felipe sighed heavily. "Would you like to go home, *querida?*" he asked, annoyed with her.

Wanting to cry out that she was not his love, Breanna weakly nodded and allowed him to assist her inside. To her relief, there had been no further talk coming from the room, or he might have suspected she was listening. Felipe briskly saw to getting her wrap and led her to her carriage, where Millie's husband, Paul, was ready to take her home.

"Thank you," she said, falling back into the seat. "I should like to repay you for your kindness when I am feeling better."

Encouraged, Felipe took her hand. It was trembling, and he hoped it was because she was thinking of what they would be missing that night. "I look forward to it, *querida*," he said as he bent to kiss her hand.

Breanna forced herself to reach out with her other hand and to gently run the backs of her fingers down his cheek. "No more than I," she breathed. Felipe stood quickly. Too quickly. She was afraid she had extended too tempting an invitation. Gasping, she clutched her stomach, and the fire in his eyes died.

"Until we meet again, *querida*," he said and turned to leave her in her misery.

"Get us out of here!" she whispered harshly to Paul. The carriage bolted forward and she blew out a held breath. She wouldn't have been so relieved if she had seen Guillermo beckon to a soldier.

"Follow her," he ordered before returning to his party.

"Where to?" Paul called back to her when they were on the edge of town.

"Home, Paul! I have to change so I can get my news to Hawk Hill."

Paul frowned. "But, Breanna, I'm supposed ta carry any messages, and I thought you were sick."

Scrambling to kneel behind him, Breanna shook her head. "No, I'm fine and I have to go myself this time." She knew Paul wanted to argue, but he wisely accepted her decision. The carriage bounced and Breanna turned to go back to her seat. A distant movement caught her eye.

At first, she thought it was merely the shadows of the night dancing about the landscape, but then she realized it was a rider.

"Paul! We're being followed!" she cried, gripping his arm to make him turn around and see.

"Damn," Paul groaned. "That Guillermo ain't easy ta fool." He reached for the whip and snapped it over the horse's rump to encourage more speed.

Thrown back into her seat, Breanna began to chew on her thumbnail. She had been so sure Guillermo believed her! As the carriage jostled, she began to think the man following them might not be one of Guillermo's men, but she had to be sure.

"Paul! When you go around the bend ahead, stop!"

"But Breanna! Why would—"

"I said stop!"

Grumbling beneath his breath about stubborn women, Paul drew the carriage to a halt the instant they were out of sight. Unassisted, Breanna scurried out.

"Hand me the whip!" she ordered. "Now move on, but more slowly. I don't want him to lose sight of you. And watch for my signal." She stepped back and watched Paul grudgingly obey her orders. The sound of hooves striking the ground made her turn around. She was only going to have one chance to catch her pursuer. Coiling the leather whip in her hands, she stood ready.

The carriage made its way inside the walls of Casa del Verde. A groan from the floor brought a smile to Breanna's lips, and she raised a small foot to place it on the center of the Mexican soldier's chest.

"Just a few more minutes," she said sweetly, grinning down at him. She was still filled with the exhilaration of making the capture. Her timing had been perfect. He had ridden around the bend, rearing back when he saw her standing there. Before he could escape, she cracked the whip and brought it around his neck, yanking him from his horse.

Paul had returned in minutes to find her wrapping the whip around the man's wrists. He was out cold from the fall. In awe, Paul tossed him into the carriage. They were on their way before he said a word, and that one was only an expletive.

"Keep him in the barn under cover," she told Paul when they arrived. "I'll find out what John wants us to do with him when I see him." She started for the house. "And saddle me a horse," she called back, missing the admiring smile on Paul's face.

"Millie!" she called the instant the door was opened. "Come help me change!"

Millie ran from the kitchen, surprised to see Breanna in such high spirits after days of moping. "Change for what?" she asked as she ran up the stairs behind her.

"I have to get a message to Hawk Hill," Breanna answered over her shoulder.

"Now! But it's the middle of the night." She saw Breanna struggling to unfasten her gown. "For heaven's sake, Bree! You can't go traipsing about the countryside now."

"Yes, I can." Breanna bubbled with excitement. "Now hurry!"

Shaking her head, Millie did as she was asked while Breanna told her what had happened that evening.

"Let Paul go," Millie finally said while Breanna buttoned her riding jacket.

"I need Paul here to guard my prisoner," Breanna explained. She heard Millie groan and saw her roll her eyes. "Don't worry, Millie. I'll be all right."

Millie would have loved to argue with her, but Breanna was already halfway down the stairs. Throwing up her hands impotently, she made her way down to locate her husband to see if he would have better luck in keeping Breanna home. To her chagrin, she was only able to watch as Breanna rode off.

The outline of the small fort shimmered before her and Breanna sighed deeply. The cold night air stung her cheeks as she rode, but it helped to keep her from falling asleep. The events of the last few hours had exhausted her, yet she still had one more thing to do before returning to her bed.

She slowed her horse and ventured forward carefully. Try as she might, she could see no signs of life. John had told her a man would be there at all times. Surely now, when she had important news, someone would be available to send it on.

Ready to quit her search, Breanna saw a shadow separate itself from a thicket and move toward her. Before she could distinguish the features of the unknown man, she heard him swear.

"Damn it all, Miss Bree! Where the hell is Paul?"

Breanna slipped off her horse and ran toward the familiar voice. "Smitty?" she called, identifying one of the old hands from Casa del Verde.

"Yes'm, it's me," the disgruntled man replied. "What I don't know is why it's you!"

Drawing her horse into the shadows, Breanna said, "I have a message for John, and it was too important not to carry it myself."

Still not pleased that she had come instead of Paul, he led her inside, where he had a small fire burning and a pot of coffee steaming. He offered her a cup and pointed to a log she could use as a seat.

"So what's yer message?" he asked, handing her the coffee.

Breanna relayed everything she'd heard, including the mention of more troops and what Paul had learned from her captive. When she came to the end of her tale, she knew she had done well.

Smitty scratched his head. "Ain't good news, but I bet John'll be damned glad to get it."

"And I'm damned glad I was of help," Breanna said, feeling she would be vindicated when Alex heard it.

John pulled back the tent flap and poked his head in. Alex was engrossed by a table full of maps and charts. Only the chilly wind ruffling them made him notice his solitude had been invaded.

"Come in or get out, John, but close that damned flap!" he roared, shivering with the cold wind.

"We have a visitor," John said, ignoring the bad temper that had followed Alex since he'd left Breanna. He stepped aside and ushered in their guest.

"Francisco!" Alex's mood brightened at the sight of his old friend. "What brings you here on this godforsaken night?"

"Alex, my friend!" Francisco took Alex's hand. "Nothing is godforsaken, not even you." If he didn't know Alex so well, he would have doubted his own words. "But you look terrible, *amigo*. Are you not well?"

Alex raked his fingers through his too-long hair, then ran his knuckles over a few days' growth of stubble. "No, I'm all right." He shoved some gear from his cot and sat among the rubble. "It's just this damned waiting. I'm not known for patience," he said, trying for a laugh and failing.

Francisco found a chair under a pile of clothing and sat. "Are you so anxious to fight?"

"It's not the fighting I want. It's to have it done with. Sitting around, waiting for the first shot, that's worse than any battle." Alex lowered his head into his hands and sighed. "It seems my life has become a waiting game."

Francisco could see his friend's pain and knew

the cause. He'd spoken with Patrick before coming to see Alex. He knew about the trouble between him and Breanna. Smiling to himself, he was sure that she was the real cause of his impatience.

"How about some coffee?" Alex finally asked.

"Sit," Francisco ordered. "Patrick is already brewing a pot and promised to send it in as soon as—ah, here it is now."

A young man entered, placed the pot on the top of the maps along with two cups, and left with little more than a nod. Francisco stood and poured out the hot coffee, adding something from a flask. Handing a cup to Alex, he smiled.

"Thought you might need it." He picked up his own cup and returned to his chair. "So, now are you going to tell me what is really bothering you?"

After taking a large swallow of his coffee, Alex looked better able to cope. "Having a priest for a friend doesn't mean I have to make a confession."

"Then think of me as a friend who happens to be a priest," Francisco answered. "I do it all the time. To me you are a friend, not a spy, soldier, kidnapper . . . Shall I go on?"

Alex couldn't resist chuckling. "All right, you've made your point. I'll forget you're a priest if you'll forget some of my less than admirable traits."

"Agreed!" Francisco exclaimed, raising his cup in a salute. The two relaxed and enjoyed the hot brew for a few moments before Francisco broke the silence. "Now would you like to tell me what's really troubling you?" He saw Alex's reluctance. "It's Breanna, isn't it?" He chuckled at Alex's surprised look. "No, I'm not endowed with mystic powers. I just talked to Patrick."

Alex nodded slowly. "And he told you Breanna and I are still at odds."

Francisco thought of the beautiful woman Alex had wed. "I had hoped you two would have worked things out by now."

"We did," Alex said. "Then she got John to give her an assignment." He took another drink, wishing it was straight whiskey. "She's trying to get some information for him from Guillermo."

"I see nothing wrong with that, Alex," Francisco told him. "Many of the women are trying to help."

"Many of the women aren't as beautiful as Breanna."

Francisco smiled. "So it's jealousy eating at you."

Alex stood and paced. "You're damned right I'm jealous!" he roared. "Jealous and worried sick!" He was ready to continue pouring out his anguish when John entered with a look on his face that stopped him cold. "What is it, John?" he asked, afraid it was bad news concerning his wife. "Breanna?"

John shook his head. "No, she's fine, but she did get us some news." He took a deep breath. "She found out that Guillermo has set a trap for you."

"Damn!" Alex swore, knowing his usefulness to the Americans had gone up in smoke. No longer could he get information or move freely to contact those still remaining superficially loyal to Mexico.

"She also heard that more troops were being brought in to Monterey. Fortunately, she was able to find out when and how many when she captured one of Guillermo's men."

"Captured! How the hell did she manage that?"

"Smitty didn't give me the details," John said, "but I would imagine it was something to see."

Alex rolled his eyes. "I knew it! I knew she'd do something stupid."

John glanced at Francisco and shrugged. Alex was beginning to pace, and there was no way of knowing what was on his mind.

"Assign me to Hawk Hill," he finally said.

"But Alex! Guillermo would like nothing better than to catch you there."

Alex grinned devilishly. "He won't catch me. I'll

get out before they even know I was there. I just want to see Breanna. I want to make sure she doesn't do anything else. She was lucky this time. I'm going to make sure her luck holds."

"Alex," John said firmly. "She might well have saved your life in this. Make sure you remember that."

"I'll remember," he said softly. "But I'll also make her remember her vow to obey."

Chapter 20

❝It's so good to be home," Heather said, sipping her tea. "San Francisco was exciting and it was wonderful sharing it with Eric, but I'm glad to be back."

Breanna tucked her feet beneath her and smiled. "It's good to have you back. It's been too quiet around here with you gone."

Heather laughed. "I must say I didn't expect that, especially since Alex was here when we left." She saw her sister frown. "I take it things didn't go well with the two of you."

"Not exactly," Breanna admitted. "At first it did," she said, thinking of the glorious intimacies they had shared. "Then John came and gave me an assignment. Alex hated the idea."

Leaning forward eagerly, Heather wanted to hear all the details. "And what happened then?"

Breanna rose to pour herself more tea. "Then we had another argument and he stomped out."

Heather could hear the pain in Breanna's voice, despite her attempt to hide it. "But you still love him."

Breanna whirled about. "Of course I love him! It's just that we don't seem to get along!" Resuming her seat, she plopped her chin on her hand. "I think it was a big mistake, our getting married."

"You mean because he did it for the cause?"

"No." Breanna shook her head. "We cleared that up. I was wrong, Heather. Alex married me be-

301

cause he wanted to, but I don't think we can stay together. We're too similar."

Heather thought of the stubbornness and the pride that burned in them both. She almost chuckled when she thought of the sparks they ignited. "Maybe you could learn to bend," she finally said.

"Maybe he could!" Breanna retorted fiercely. She saw Heather's brow arch and sighed. "You see, we don't even agree when we're apart."

"So what are you going to do?" Heather asked, sure Breanna had some solution in mind.

"Do? What can I do? I love the arrogant, stubborn man! All I can do is hope that someday he'll understand that and it will be enough."

Tapping her chin with one finger, Heather shrugged. "Would it be so hard to be the wife he wants, Breanna?" She saw her sister thinking over her words. "Could you maybe see it from his point of view?"

"His point of view is to dominate me!"

"Maybe that's because he loves you, too, and is worried he might lose you."

Breanna thought of her wedding night and the story Alex had told her about his mother, Sabrina. He had loved her and he had lost her. Was he being overprotective because he feared losing again?

"You're awfully headstrong, Bree," Heather added. "You often act before thinking when you feel you're right. Maybe you should step back and think this through. You might discover you're risking an awful lot to have your own way."

"But Heather, if I hadn't insisted on helping John, Alex might already be Guillermo's prisoner. He was wrong. I did help."

"Yes, Bree, you helped, but you were lucky. You might have ended up a hostage to bring Alex to his knees. Did you ever think of that?"

Heather's words struck a chord. Hadn't she heard Guillermo say something similar? Sighing,

Breanna leaned her head back and smiled at her sister.

"Married life has made you very wise, Heather, but give me time to sort this out."

Heather nodded slowly. "As long as you stay out of trouble, all we have is time now, Bree."

Breanna thought of the weeks which had passed and those still to come. It seemed she was relegated to waiting after all. Aware that it was exactly what Alex had wanted all along, she smiled ruefully. "Yes, *chica*. Only time."

The days seemed to drag for Breanna. She paced her room for hours, then moved out to the patio to pace some more. There had been no word from her father, John or, most importantly, Alex. It was as if, when he walked out on her, she had ceased to exist for him. That made it difficult for her to consider what Heather had said. How could she see things from his point of view when she was so busy feeling sorry for herself and simmering over his neglect?

Several times she thought she might go into town, but common sense restrained her. The night she had gone to gather what information she could, she had all but promised Guillermo that she would see him again. The last thing she needed now was to have to keep that promise.

There was no doubt that he only intended to use her. He'd said as much to his compatriots. The thought of his touching her the way Alex did made her shiver with disgust. Both men were handsome, but she loved only one. The other was merely a means to an end.

Ready to lie down and take a nap, she felt her stomach growl. She realized she was no longer sick each morning. In fact, she was feeling quite well. It was probably because she no longer was under the pressure of being involved in espionage.

Deciding to find something to eat to tide her over until dinner, Breanna left her room.

Almost at the bottom of the stairs, Breanna heard voices in the parlor. She immediately recognized Heather's voice, then Eric's. Smiling, she was ready to leave them to their privacy when she caught Alex's name mentioned. All thoughts of hunger disappeared as she made her way toward the open door.

"But they'll need all the men they can get, honey," Eric said emphatically. "I have to go."

"No wonder Breanna fights to be a part of this," Heather snapped. "It's better than sitting here worrying."

"Breanna wants to be a part of this because she's stubborn. She wants all the benefits of being a woman and the power that belongs to men. Your father made a big mistake teaching the two of you to think for yourselves."

"Eric! That's a terrible thing to say."

There was a moment of silence. Breanna was sure Eric was trying to corral his temper. "Look, honey," he finally said. "All I'm saying is I'll be more careful if I don't have to worry about you."

Breanna heard Heather cry, then it was silent. It was obvious her sister was going to comply with her husband's wishes. For some strange reason, Breanna was glad. She had made a mess of her life by fighting with her man. She turned from the door and slipped across to the library.

The room was as dark as her thoughts. She sat and leaned forward to let the tears flow down her face. Eric was right. She was too stubborn for her own good, but he was wrong about her father. He had made his daughters strong-willed to help them survive. She'd been foolish enough to turn that strength against the only man she would ever love.

"Oh, Alex," she whispered. "I've been such a fool!"

She heard Heather and Eric enter the foyer and she stopped her tears to listen to them once again.

"Be careful, my love," Heather said softly. "And hurry back."

Eric chuckled. "I'm only going to Hawk Hill. John wants us to make a ruckus so Guillermo will send troops. Before they arrive, we'll be gone."

"Then why go at all?" Heather asked, unable to resist one more attempt to keep her husband close.

"Because Guillermo needs to think we're going to fight there when, in truth, our main force is in Sonoma. By drawing some of Guillermo's troops to Hawk Hill, our men in Sonoma may gain the edge we need to win this war."

"I hate that you're leaving, but I love you!" Heather cried.

Breanna covered her ears. She didn't mean to eavesdrop on their private moment. It reminded her too much of the moments she and Alex had shared. Thoughts of Alex made her drop her hands and sit up. Would he be at Hawk Hill? Was it possible that he was only a few miles away this very minute?

She rose and went to the door. The foyer was empty. A sound from above made her smile. They were saying good-bye in the age-old way of lovers. Little did they know their interlude would give her the time she needed.

The small fort at Hawk Hill had come alive. There were campfires and men everywhere. No longer was it a dark encampment used to hide a courier or two. It was the starting point for a war of independence. Eric had said enough to make her realize the greater fighting would be up north, but this would be the first of it.

Crouching down in the brush, Breanna strained to see if she could spot anyone familiar. She was taking a big chance, but she was sure it was worth it. She had to let Alex know she understood his desire to safeguard her. She had to promise him she would gladly wait for him before he went into battle.

"Hold there!" someone said sharply from behind her.

It was useless to ignore the order, even fool-hardy. Slowly, she rose and lifted her hands in surrender.

"Well, I'll be damned!" the man said breathily. "A woman!" He shook his head in surprise. "Jesus, lady! What the hell are ya doing here?"

Breanna looked up at her hands. "May I lower them?" He nodded, and she dropped her hands and hugged herself against the chill of a damp March night. "I wanted to see if . . . if someone was here."

The man settled back on one leg, relaxing the other while he listened. "Who?" he asked, feeling as if he should know the little lady.

"Alexander King," she told him, suddenly hoping Alex wasn't there. He was sure to be upset by her foolishness once again.

The man blew out his breath. "I shoulda known! We've all heard about ya, Mrs. King." Breanna grimaced. "Why, that thing with the soldiers, it was a right brave thing for ya ta do."

"Please," Breanna said, hating the reminder. "Could you please just tell me if my . . . my husband is here."

"Yes'm, he sure is. And I'll be real pleased ta take ya to him."

But will *he* be pleased? Breanna wondered as she followed the soldier across the cleared space between the trees and the fort. Silence fell around the camp as she approached a small cluster of tents. She kept her head lowered, trying to appear less conspicuous, but it didn't matter. Every man there spotted her, including the one she had come to see. To her relief, he wasn't the first who greeted her.

"Breanna?"

It took a moment to recognize the man. "Father Francisco!" she finally cried, running into his extended arms. "Oh, Father Francisco! I didn't recognize you."

Holding her at arm's length, he smiled. "It's the absence of my robes. It always amazes me how many don't know me without them."

He was dressed the same as all the other men. She frowned. "You're going to fight, aren't you?"

Francisco smiled. "Priests have been fighting injustice and tyranny for a long time, Breanna. I can do no less." He saw her doubt. "I assure you, I am both capable and ready to do my part."

"I know," she said sadly. "It's just that I hate to see any of you fighting." Shivering, she gazed at him with wide eyes. "It scares me, Father Francisco. Men are going to die in this. I pray it isn't you."

"Or Alex?" he asked, seeing the object of her search quietly moving up behind her.

"Did I hear my name?"

Breanna spun about to come face to face with Alex. He was magnificently dressed in black from head to toe. She wanted to leap into his arms but remembered all the men watching. She also remembered their parting and his anger. It wasn't possible for her to read his face, cast as it was in shadow. Drawing a breath, she nodded.

"I . . . I need to speak with you," she stammered.

Without a word, Alex took her arm and steered her toward one of the tents. She almost had to run to keep up with his long strides, but she refused to lag behind or beg him to slow down.

Alex knew he was being rough, but it was the only way he could keep himself from throttling her for putting herself in peril. No matter the reason, he was furious. It was one more example of how irresponsible she could be. When they reached the tent, he pushed her roughly into the dark confines.

"All right, talk!" he ordered when they were alone. "And it better be good!"

Not caring for his tone, Breanna lifted her chin daringly. "Is that any way to talk to me after I saved you from Guillermo?" she asked, momentarily forgetting why she'd come.

"If you're going to act like a child, Breanna, I'm going to yell at you like one!"

She was ready to snarl something in return, but noticed the weariness of his stance. She lowered her chin and gazed down at the dirt floor. "I shouldn't have come," she said softly. "I only thought . . ."

Alex stilled. "Thought what?" he asked, his tone less threatening. She shook her head and made her way toward the flap. His hand reached out, grasping her arm to draw her back close. "What, Breanna? What made you come?"

She looked up at him. In the dimness she was sure he could see the sparkle of her tears. "I . . . I . . ." She never had a chance to tell him. With a groan, he took her into his arms.

"Oh, God!" he breathed harshly, his lips seeking hers frantically. She called out his name, but it was lost in his mouth before he could hear it. His kiss was savage. His anger became a burning desire to possess her. His tongue delved into her moist mouth. And he gloried in her response.

Words could never convey the meaning of their kiss. Their bodies strained to get ever closer. Their hands caressed and explored, needing to touch to know they were truly together.

Sounds from outside the tent penetrated Alex's frenzy. He swore raggedly. Breanna mistook it for renewed anger and tried to push free of his embrace. "No, love," he groaned against her ear. "It is not you who makes me stop." He sat on the cot, and pulled her into his lap. "It's this place."

Breanna was still struggling to stop the dizziness from his kiss. "This place?" she asked, her voice quivering.

Alex chuckled ruefully. It was obvious she was oblivious to where they were and why. Drawing a steadying breath, he nodded. "If I continued to kiss you, *querida*, I would not stop."

She was suddenly glad it was dark. Realization dawned, and she felt herself turning red. "I . . . I wasn't thinking," she said shyly.

"Neither was I," he admitted with a deep sigh. For a moment, he nestled his head against her neck, but it only increased his need for her. "Breanna," he groaned, lifting her to sit at his side. "I'm afraid I can't keep touching you without . . ."

"Oh!" She nodded, leaping to her feet. More voices came from near the tent, and she glanced around. "Could . . . could you light a lamp?"

Alex rubbed his thighs to tamp down his raging desire, and rose to do as she asked. The tent was suddenly bathed in light, but it didn't help. All it did was reveal the depths of their desire the darkness had hidden.

"Damn it!" he snarled, wishing she hadn't come to tempt him with her nearness. "Why are you here?"

His anguish was all too apparent, and Breanna thought to say what she had to as quickly as possible so she could leave. He was too close and she craved him too much.

"I came to tell you I'm sorry," she began. "I . . . I should have done as you wished."

Her apology gave him pause. She seemed upset, and it made him wonder. "Breanna, did something go wrong that you haven't told anyone?"

"No!" she exclaimed, not sure she cared for the way he was looking at her. "I just realized you were right. It was my duty to wait for you."

Alex thought of the information she had garnered and from whom she had gotten it. Suddenly, his mind was filled with images of Breanna seducing Guillermo to get what she learned. He could see her moving sensuously toward him, enticing him. The vision burned into his brain.

Breanna saw something in his eyes that frightened her. She took a step back defensively. "Alex?" she said, trying to snap him out of his dark thoughts. "Alex? What is it?"

He heard her fear and mistook it for guilt. He scowled fiercely at her. "Did you kiss him?" he demanded.

"What?"

"I said, did you kiss Guillermo?"

Stunned, Breanna slowly shook her head.

Alex wanted an answer. He yanked her close. "What did you do to get the information?"

"Nothing!" she cried, trying to pull free. When she knew it was futile, she went limp. "Would I fight you, the man I love, only to give myself to him?"

Alex felt like a fool. Her words rang true. His arms loosened, yet she did not move away. "Breanna," he said harshly. "I'm sorry."

He would have stepped away, but she wrapped her arms around his middle. "Don't be sorry, Alex," she told him fiercely. "Just hold me." His arms embraced her, but this time they were gently holding her captive against his heart. He looked down at her and gently brushed away her tears.

"I love you," he said softly. "You'll probably drive me mad, but I do love you." His lips were drawing closer, and he could feel her breathy sighs, but it was not to be. Someone called his name, and he closed his eyes to hide his frustration.

"Enter," he said, setting her free.

"Sorry, Alex," Francisco said, sensing the tension. "But it's time to start moving the men out."

Confused, Breanna turned to face the two men.

"Out? But I thought—" She was going to say she thought Eric's words were only to calm Heather.

"That's what we want Guillermo to think, too, *querida*," Alex smiled, still struggling to rein in his desire for her.

"Then there will be no battle?"

"Not here. Not now."

Instead of being relieved, Breanna discovered she was upset by the news. "You mean I've been worried sick about nothing?"

"It isn't nothing, Breanna," Alex explained. "There is still the danger that Guillermo will get his troops here before we can vacate the camp."

She wasn't pacified. "And where do you go from here, Alex? Do I need to worry about the next campaign, or should I simply sit and wait until you tell me to worry?"

"For God's sake, Breanna!" Alex wished they were anyplace but here. "Let's not go back to bickering."

"Why not?" she demanded. "It seems to be the only thing we do well."

Rumbling laughter filled the tent. His eyes raked her full breasts and moved down to her hips suggestively. "It's not the only thing, Breanna." Francisco's cough, and her indignant gasp, reminded him they were not alone. "Damn!" he swore to cover the awkwardness of the situation.

"Father Francisco," she said, ignoring her husband's crude remark, "would you have someone get my horse. It's tied to one of the trees." Francisco was glad to have a reason to leave, but he was surprised when she stepped out of the tent with him.

"Breanna!" Alex called, not through with her yet.

She stopped and turned back to him. She could sense his anger and felt it was directed at her. It hurt. She had come to lay her heart at his feet, and he had trodden upon it. She wanted to hurt him back.

"Take care of yourself, Alex," she said flippantly. "When this is all over, come to see me. Maybe we can work something out." She turned and started to walk away, but paused. Glancing over her shoulder, she raised her chin. "Then again, maybe not."

She heard him curse and closed her eyes, but he didn't follow. She felt Francisco take her trembling hand and forced herself to keep moving. Thankfully, he did not speak to her until she was in her saddle.

"Breanna," he said gently, taking her hand in his. "Give him time. He has never loved before. I think it scares him more than he will admit."

"It scares me, too, Father Francisco," she said sadly. Leaning down, she kissed his cheek. "Take care of yourself." Straightening in the saddle, she paused. "And take care of him, too." Francisco nodded and she let the man holding her reins lead her away.

"Alex King," he said beneath his breath. "You're a damned fool."

"Don't you think I know that?" Alex said from his side.

Francisco was confused. "What do you mean?"

Alex turned to walk back toward his tent. "I was a fool to fall in love when there was a good chance I wouldn't live through this. What just happened was for the best. She'll hate me, but she'll get over it."

Francisco stopped short and grabbed Alex's arm. "You did that on purpose?" Alex nodded. Looking skyward, Francisco whispered, "Forgive me!" the instant before he landed a solid blow to Alex's chin, knocking him to the ground.

"What the hell did you do that for?" Alex asked once he could draw a breath. He ran the back of his hand over his mouth and found blood on it.

"For Breanna!" Francisco snapped. "She should have hit you but couldn't because she loves you. Right now, I don't have that problem."

Alex watched his long-time friend stomp away. He lifted himself from the hard ground and dusted himself off. He started to call after Francisco but stopped to rub his sore jaw.

"If you're done making a spectacle of yourself," John said as he drew up beside him, "we have men to move out."

"You, too?" Alex asked, hearing the censure in his tone.

"Me, too."

Alex shook his head in confusion. As soon as he had time, he was going to think everything through. Maybe then he could figure out what the hell was going on!

Breanna saw a horse and carriage outside the house. It was the first thing she had noticed since leaving Hawk Hill. Her eyes were too filled with tears to focus on anything. She had humbled herself and gone to him, but he had pushed her away.

Thinking of the kiss they shared when they first entered the tent, she sniffed. Well, he hadn't exactly pushed her away, she reasoned, but he had refused anything else she had offered. All he seemed to want was her body, and that wasn't enough for her!

Hurt and angry, she dismounted. The lad standing ready to take her reins must have sensed her heartache because he didn't greet her in his usually friendly manner. Brushing some loose strands of hair from her face, she went inside. With luck, she could avoid whoever was calling.

"Breanna!" Heather said from the parlor before she could slip past.

"Give me a minute to freshen up, *chica*," she answered as she made her way to the stairs.

"I've seen ya in worse shape, honey," a voice called to her.

Breanna froze. Slowly she turned to see who had spoken. "Hilda!" she cried, racing down the steps to open her arms to the woman she thought of as Alex's mother.

"Hello, child," Hilda smiled after they stepped apart to look at each other. She could tell that Breanna had been crying but decided it wasn't the time to ask why.

"What are you doing here?" Breanna asked, still surprised.

"Alex sent me." She saw Breanna scowl. "He thought I'd be safer here and—"

"How thoughtful," Breanna said disdainfully.

"—and he thought I could help you out," Hilda finished.

After the way he had just treated her, Breanna found it difficult to give him any credit for kindness, but she was thrilled to see Hilda. "No matter," she said with a wave of her hand. "You're here and that's all that counts."

Hilda didn't try to hide the concern in her eyes, but Breanna wished to ignore it for the time being. "Has Heather settled you in a room yet?" Hilda shook her head. "Then let's do it now. I think the one overlooking the garden will suit you. Besides"—she forced a smile—"it's across from mine."

Breanna continued to babble as she showed Hilda the room. She asked about everyone at Alex's ranch and seemed to be interested in her replies, but Hilda knew otherwise. Taking Breanna's hand when she went to turn down the bed, Hilda looked deeply into her eyes.

"What is it, child?" she asked kindly. "What has you so upset?"

Breanna tried to fight the tears and the pain, but Hilda's gentle concern was her undoing. "Oh, Hilda!" she sobbed. "I've ruined everything!"

Together they sat on the bed and Hilda heard the whole story. It was obvious that the girl loved Alex, and Hilda suspected Alex was also in love, yet he would have more trouble accepting it.

"There, child," Hilda said, holding the sobbing Breanna in her arms. "I don't think it's as bad as you think."

Breanna sat up and stared wide-eyed. "Not bad! All he wants is my . . . my . . ."

Hilda shook her head. "It's more than that," she said with a smile. "Oh, he's a lusty lad, but I believe he loves you."

"I wish I believed it," Breanna said, rising to her feet. She paced back and forth before the astute eyes of the older woman. "He says he does, but then he seems to purposely push me away!"

"Even when you told him about the child?" Hilda asked.

Breanna froze. Slowly, she turned to face Hilda. "Child! What child?"

Hilda chuckled. "You don't know, do you?" She saw the blank look on Breanna's face and put an arm around her. "The child you're carrying, honey. Alex's child."

Slowly, Breanna lowered her hands to her abdomen. There was a roundness there she had not noticed.

"When was your last monthly?"

Chewing her lip, Breanna thought back. "December," she breathed. "The middle of December."

Hilda frowned. Breanna had been at Casa del Verde then, and she had no idea where Alex was. "Did you see Alex anytime that month?" she asked, praying the child belonged to him.

Slowly, Breanna nodded. She was thinking about the night he had sneaked into her room. They had made glorious love that night, and it seemed he had given her more than a necklace as a present. A small smile softened her eyes.

"A baby," she whispered. "He gave me a baby for Christmas."

Hilda calculated the child would come in September, and she told Breanna.

There was a hint of spring in the air. The long, hot summer was fast approaching. When it passed, she would be holding Alex's child in her arms. No matter what happened between them, she would always have that part of him.

"September," she repeated, her face glowing with happiness.

Hilda hugged her. "Shall we go tell your sister?"

Breanna nodded and started to laugh. "She's going to be an aunt!"

"And you're going to be a mother, honey," Hilda said, "and Alex will be a father."

The thought of Alex holding a small infant in his large hands brought a twinge to her heart. "Will he be glad?" she asked, afraid of the answer. "He once told me he had never thought about having a family. Maybe he doesn't want children."

Hilda thought of Alex as a boy and his terrible loneliness. "He'll want *this* child," Hilda said as she tenderly laid her hand on Breanna's tummy, "because it's yours."

Tears filled Breanna's eyes. "I hope you're right, Hilda," she said, apprehension in her voice. "But whether he does or not, I want it with all my heart."

Chapter 21

The majority of the men had slipped away from Hawk Hill under the cover of darkness. Only a handful remained to keep the fires burning, making the Mexican troops think it was still occupied. All others evacuated the area in small numbers and gathered again at a designated spot north of Monterey, Alex among them.

He rode alone in the column. It was not difficult to see that a number of the men were upset with him. He could only assume it had to do with the incident between him and Francisco. They all knew he was a friend of Alex's and a priest. For Francisco to throw a punch in anger, he had to have just cause.

As they moved ever farther north, Alex realized he was going to have to clear the air or suffer their silence. For many miles, he chose silence. It gave him a chance to think about Breanna and how hard he'd been on her.

He hadn't meant to be. When he first saw her at the fort, his heart soared. She had come to him. She had tried to bare her soul and offer him exactly what he told her he wanted. Almost losing control in her arms, he had realized that it was possibly the last time he would hold her. Hawk Hill was a ploy, but Sonoma was going to be the real thing.

Thoughts of leaving her a widow put him on the defensive, especially when he considered she might find someone else if he was no longer in the picture. That led to imagining her with Guillermo. Before he knew it, he was furiously jealous.

When she challenged him before she left, he withdrew behind a wall of indifference to protect his own vulnerability, and to help harden her heart should he fail to return. He could have explained that to Francisco but he hadn't, preferring his censure at the time. However, after miles of silence, he was beginning to rethink his choice.

Not having the opportunity to talk with Francisco during the ride, Alex resolved to settle the problem in camp that night. There would be no fires, but the men would gather around in small groups for dinner and conversation. It was the same every night, and he was counting on it.

Gazing at the men scattered across the hillside, Alex sighed. It was now or never. Stepping over some men and moving around others, he located the gathering he sought. Stopping on the perimeter of their circle, he slowly looked at each one.

"All right," he began. "Spit it out. I got the message, and I'm sure each one of you is dying to say something."

For long moments, the men remained silent. A few threw him sidelong glances, but none spoke. None, that is, until Patrick dropped back on an elbow to look up at him.

"You're a fool, lad, for not trustin' her. I know my girl, and I know it was hard for her ta humble herself to ya. She would only do it if she loved ya."

Alex was ready to tell him he knew that when John sat up. He draped his arm over a bent knee and spoke without looking at Alex.

"You're a good man in a fight, Alex, but you've got a lot to learn about women. Your first lesson is, don't throw away the best thing in your life for pride's sake. It's a damned cold bedmate."

Alex dropped down on his haunches to explain

he had already discovered that when the last of his three friends began to speak.

"We've been friends since our youth, Alex. I suppose I know you better than anyone." Francisco looked across the small circle at his friend. "You've spent enough time alone. I know you've been hurt and the prospect of it happening again scares you." He saw Alex close his eyes to cover the pain of his memories, but he wasn't finished. "But you'd better be more afraid of being left alone or you're going to lose her."

Alex was at a loss for words. He needed some time to think over what each had said. He nodded and wandered off to find some solitude.

"Suppose he understands all that?" Patrick asked no one in particular.

"He understands," Francisco said. "Now all he has to do is decide whether to take our advice."

Alex stood in the darkness. He thought about everything his friends had said. They were right. He was playing a risky game where his wife was concerned. No matter that his rationale was to protect her as well as himself, he was in jeopardy of ruining the best thing in his life.

Sitting on a rock, he leaned forward to brace his arms on his thighs. Images of Breanna in her myriad moods filled his mind. God, but he loved her! If only he could feel secure in that love. He remembered the emptiness left by his mother's death. He was so afraid that if he gave his heart completely to Breanna, he would someday have to face the agony of loss again.

Breanna was not a quiet, soft-spoken woman who would passively see to his needs. She was feisty and strong-willed. She would always keep him on his toes. There would be no peace, but, then again, he knew he would never tire of her. It was this impetuous streak that scared him the most.

She was a survivor. Should he push her away, she would stand on her own two feet and salvage her life. He, on the other hand, needed her to make his life complete. When she ran from his ranch, his world had nearly crumbled. Bitterness filled him, and would have destroyed him, if he hadn't realized it hurt because he loved her.

Looking up at the ebony sky, alive with the sparkling lights of a million stars, he said, "What should I do?"

He thought of the impending war and the time they would have to be apart. He considered the fact that he might die. He tried to look at every possibility and came to only one conclusion.

He made his way back to the camp and strode directly to the men he wanted to see. They seemed to be ignoring him, yet he knew they were anxiously waiting to hear what he was about to say.

"As soon as we're done here, I'm going back to see my wife. We have some things to clear up, and one of them is that I want her to remain my wife."

"Good for you, boy!" someone shouted from another group to his left.

"Knew you were a smart lad!" came another voice.

"Yeah!" called a third.

Alex had never been so glad for darkness. He was sure his face was a deep red now that he realized all the men scattered about had been listening in on his personal life. Prepared to find a secluded spot where he could sit and hide for a while, he was stopped by a hand on his arm. He turned to see Smitty, smiling at him.

"I watched that girl grow up. Always thought she was something special. Glad you've finally realized it."

He walked away and Alex sat, shaking his head. Had he known Breanna had so many champions, he would never have worried about her antics. Well, almost never! She would always be in his mind and his heart. Now all he had to do was convince her of that.

It wasn't going to be easy, especially since he had tried to keep her at arm's length even as he claimed her. He knew she was confused by a declaration of love one moment and condemnation of her abilities the next, but he was going to succeed. He had to. Their future together depended on it.

Breanna fairly glowed since discovering she was going to have a baby. The few left in the household were bustling over the news. Hilda and Millie and Heather starting a layette, and Paul was busy redoing a room for a nursery.

Overseeing everything, Breanna found herself too busy to think about Alex. It made her mood lighter and offered the escape she had so desperately needed. Too many nights had been spent wondering if they would ever find common ground.

After their last encounter, she was sure of only two things. She loved Alex and, for some reason, he was afraid of that love. She reasoned it had something to do with what he'd told her about his childhood, but that had happened long ago. Surely by now he would see that only death could make her leave him. Perhaps, when it was all over, she could go to him again and present him with his child and her heart. Maybe then he would be able to accept them both.

"Bree!" Heather called from the door.

Breanna smiled and waved her closer. There seemed to be a sparkle in Heather's eyes that she hadn't seen since before Eric left. "What is it, *chica?*" she asked.

Heather shrugged, trying to contain the joy she was feeling. "Nothing really, just that Millie wants to see you down in the barn."

"And that has you looking so happy?"

Shaking her head, she replied, "No. My happi-

ness must still be left over from hearing your good
news."

"It is good, isn't it?" Breanna beamed.

"The best," Heather said. "Now why don't you
go down there and see what Millie wants."

Breanna started for the barn. There was a spring
in her step she couldn't resist. She might have a
battle with her husband ahead of her, but there
was no denying the child was going to be nothing
but joy for her.

The door to the barn was closed. She inched it
open and stuck her head inside. "Millie?" she
called into the near darkness. "Millie, are you in
here?" She took a step inside, then another.
"Millie? Heather said you—oh!" she cried when
hands gripped her shoulders from behind.

"Millie isn't here, love," Alex whispered warmly
against her ear. "I sent for you." She tried to turn
to face him, but he held her tightly. "Not yet,
Breanna," he told her, his lips brushing her temple. "I don't want you to look at me until I tell you
that I love you. I've said the words before, but
they never meant what they mean now."

"Alex, I—"

"Let me finish," he interrupted, his hands moving up and down her arms. When she leaned her
head back against his chest in silence, he sighed.
"I've been hard on you, Breanna, because I was
afraid to let you get too close to me. The fear of
losing you forced me to drive you away with my
demands."

His arms wrapped about her waist to hold her
closer. "I've been jealous and possessive, hoping to
make you what I thought I wanted, but I was
wrong. I finally realized the only way you would
truly be mine was if you were free to go but chose
to stay. Will you stay, Breanna? Will you be my
wife forever?"

Breanna's eyes were tightly closed. She was so

filled with love for this man, it was impossible to speak. But her silence was misconstrued.

"I know I'm asking a lot after all I've said to you," Alex said, hoping he wasn't too late. "And I'm not promising things will always be rosy in the years ahead, but I want us to try. We have to try!"

"Alex," Breanna breathed, turning about in his arms. She looked up into his eyes. They were the tumultuous blue of a stormy sea. Her hand rose to his cheek, and she smiled.

"My darling Alex. There are no guarantees in life, but I promise you this. I will always love you. I'll try to be a good wife and obey you, but—"

Alex didn't want to hear any more. He was being given a second chance with this woman, and he wasn't going to waste time. Scooping her up into his arms, he carried her to a blanket covering a pile of fresh hay that he had prepared earlier. Gently, he laid her down.

Suddenly he felt young. Despite the imposed brevity of his visit, he felt as if they had forever. A sensuous smile touched his mouth as he gazed at her. He wanted to tease and tempt her the way she had often done to him.

"So you want to be a good wife?"

Seeing the humor dancing in his eyes, Breanna cocked her head and smiled. "Yes, my love," she purred.

"And you will obey me?"

Breanna sat up. Slowly she moistened her lips with her tongue. "When it suits me."

Alex felt his body harden with her gesture. His smile faded. "Then, if it suits you, let down your hair, Breanna." He watched in fascination as she lifted her arms to remove the pins. Her breasts rose provocatively, as a curtain of russet curls tumbled wildly about her shoulders.

Alex found a tempting curl and wrapped it around his hand. He tugged her ever closer. "Now unfasten your gown," he said before their lips touched.

With shaking hands, Breanna reached behind her back and hastily unhooked her gown. She was burning with her need for him. Her task would have been more quickly accomplished if he was not playing at her mouth with his tongue, but eventually her bodice slipped forward.

In the dimness of the barn, Alex could see the rosy circles of her nipples pressing against the lawn of her shift. He lowered his head and captured one in his mouth.

Breanna called his name softly, her hands slipping around his head to hold him closer. She could feel him suckling, and the pull reached to her most feminine parts. A whimper escaped her throat, and he eased her back until she was lying beneath him.

Lifting his head, Alex knew she was aroused. He leaned back and began to shed his own clothing, never taking his eyes from her body. When he was wearing only his pants, his hands moved to her disheveled attire. Slowly he began to remove each piece, stopping occasionally to sample the parts of her exposed. When his hands unfastened her pantalets, she gripped his wrists.

"Someone might come in!"

Alex chuckled gruffly. "No, love. They know I'm here."

Sighing, Breanna raised her hips and let him draw away the last of her clothing. "Then let's not waste a moment, my love." She watched his hands tremble as they opened his pants and, as he pushed them down over his hips, she reached for him. He rasped her name when her fingers gently stroked him.

He was hot satin in her hands. She felt him draw a breath and saw his jaw tighten. Realizing this was the greatest adventure she could experience, Breanna drew him down over her.

She was ready for him. Her body quivered with delight as she felt him exploring her. Without reservation, she reached between them and guided him. A spasm of pure pleasure shot through his body when he eased into her depths.

Through clenched teeth, he growled softly the instant he felt himself touching her womb. She lifted her hips to cradle him and he began to move.

There was no pending war, no California. There was only this euphoria that was Breanna. She held him, she nurtured his soul, and she gave him the greatest pleasure a man could endure. How could he ever have dreamed she would be so totally his?

The barn grew warmer. Breanna could feel the hot moisture of his skin where they touched. The pleasant pressure of him moving in and out of her was taking her beyond reality. She held him tightly, wanting to draw him completely inside her, but she had to settle for that throbbing part of him that filled her at this moment.

Alex was fighting to keep himself from exploding in her depths. He wanted this union to be more perfect than ever. He could hear her breathless moans and knew she was nearing the ultimate climax. Her head began to move from side to side and she called his name, pleading for fulfillment.

"Wrap your legs around me!" he ordered, and she immediately complied. Gripping her waist, he rose up and sat back on his heels. The deep thrust that followed brought her over the edge and she cried out. The feel of her breasts rubbing his chest and the clenching spasms inside her were enough to bring him explosive relief.

"Oh, God!" he groaned, wrapping his arms tightly around her. He felt her go limp in his arms, and he couldn't resist moving his hands down to cup her rounded bottom and hold her against him to enjoy the aftershocks of their lovemaking.

"Am I obedient enough?" she whispered breathlessly against the sinews in his neck.

Alex leaned back to see her face better. Her eyes were soft, and her mouth held only a hint of a smile. She had the look of a woman well loved. He brushed back her hair and smiled down at her.

"You are enough of everything for me, Breanna." Unable to resist, he tenderly lowered his mouth to hers.

Nestled in his arms, tasting his mouth on hers, Breanna knew happiness, but the world was not going to let it continue. Sighing, she returned her head to his shoulder.

"How long can you stay?" she asked softly, hating to be the one to inject reality into their blissful moment.

"I have to leave tonight," he told her, his hands caressing her spine. "It was hard enough getting in with the troops all around."

Breanna's head snapped up. "Alex! You were crazy to come here!"

Alex grinned and bent to rub his chin across the rise of her breast. "It's your fault, *querida*. You make me crazy." He lowered her back to their makeshift bed, falling beside her to draw his fingertips playfully across her waist. "But I would risk the fires of hell to be with you."

Cupping his handsome face in her hands, she smiled. "And I would rather you be careful so you come back to me when this is all over."

Chuckling, he dropped a kiss on her nose. "I had to come this time, *querida*. I was ordered." She frowned in confusion. "It seems that when I was so rude to you at Hawk Hill, the men took your side. It was either come here and make amends or become an outcast with the troops."

"Poor Alex." She grinned. "Forced to see to the needs of his wife." He nipped at her shoulder and she squealed. "Would that I could order you so!" His teeth moved lower to graze her breast.

"It would be an order I would rush to obey," he said as his head moved to settle on her stomach. He turned so he could look at her. "You see *querida*, we all have to take orders. Some we enjoy; others are most distasteful."

"Like when you ordered me not to spy on Guillermo," she said as she rose to balance on an elbow.

Alex nodded. "I did not want to see you harmed, love. I thought you understood that."

Breanna reached for a piece of straw and began to draw circles slowly over his chest. "I thought you felt I was not capable," she admitted honestly. "That's why I fought you on it."

"And I was afraid of losing you," he replied, gripping her wrist to pull her close. "That's why I insisted."

"And now you're not afraid anymore?"

Alex kissed her palm and sighed. "I'm still scared, Breanna, but I'm not going to let it deny me the pleasures of you. I was a fool not to take advantage of the moments we had because I was angry and scared. I don't plan on becoming a lunatic now that I know I can have the best of you waiting when I return."

Breanna wasn't quite satisfied with what he was saying. She rather thought it sounded as if he was only interested in the physical side of their relationship. It made her wonder how he was going to take the news of her pregnancy. She decided to test him.

"And what if I am round and filled with a child when you return?"

Alex shrugged, missing Breanna's serious tone. "Then I shall have to bite the bullet until you whelp." He heard her gasp and thought he understood why. "Don't worry, love. I took my vows seriously. I have no intention of seeking relief elsewhere."

It took all of Breanna's determination to keep

her face from showing the anxiety she felt. "And what of the child when it does come, Alex? How will you feel about it?"

Sighing, Alex eased his head back to its soft pillow. He thought of how much he worried about his wife. A child would only complicate matters. The last thing he felt they needed was the responsibility of a baby. Should anything happen to him, it would be hard enough for her. Being a widow with a child would be even worse.

"I told you once before, I've never really given children a thought. I suppose it would be all right once everything is settled." He didn't see her bite her lip. "But now that you've come around to see the foolishness of taking chances, I don't see a need to spoil things with a child."

Breanna wanted to cry out that she already had his child growing in her, but she held it back. They had only hours before he left again. If there was one thing she had learned, it was that she hated parting from him when they were at odds. Not trusting her voice, she relied on her touch to change the subject.

Alex lifted his head to look at her when her hand began to caress his chest. He couldn't see her clearly with her hair shielding her face, but he sensed something was wrong. He was ready to ask her what it was when he became distracted by her growing boldness.

He thought he needed more time to recuperate from their earlier lovemaking, but he underestimated his wife and her effect on him. In moments, he was thick with desire, fairly bursting with need. She had bewitched him and he was beyond words.

"Do you want to slip back to the house to get something to eat?" Breanna asked as she stepped into her petticoats.

Alex paused to watch the siren he had married.

"I don't want to risk being seen," he told her. "Besides, if I am to delay my leaving it will be to ravage you once more."

The heat of a blush touched her cheeks as she recalled the last few hours. All they had done was make love and doze in each other's arms. In her wildest imagination she had not realized there were so many ways for them to come together.

"I shall have difficulty enough explaining my long absence," she said with a small grin.

He stood and looked at her. Her hair was a wild mass of glorious curls. Her lips were slightly puffed from his kisses. There was no denying the limpid quality of her eyes. He pulled a piece of straw from her hair and held it up for her to see.

"I don't think you'll need to explain," he teased.

They finished dressing, and Alex went to saddle his horse. Breanna found herself wondering whether she should tell him about the baby. She didn't wish to ruin the beauty of what they had shared, but she felt he had a right to know.

"How long will it be before I see you again?" she asked, moving to place her chin on the stall to peek over.

"I don't know, honey," he told her truthfully. "Things are beginning to happen. We got word that President Polk was moving troops toward the border in Texas. If we know, so does Guillermo. It could escalate things here."

She watched him efficiently finish readying his horse. They had only a few more minutes. "Alex," she called to him softly.

He could hear distress in the way she said his name. He moved around the stall to take her in his arms.

"It'll be all right, honey," he soothed, running his hand over her hair. "Soon it will all be over."

Now! She had to tell him now! Wrapping her arms tightly around his waist, she pressed her face against his chest. "Alex, I'm going to have a baby."

She waited, but he stood quietly holding her. Slowly, she leaned back to look up at him. "Alex? Aren't you going to say anything?"

Alex had made light of what was ahead to relieve her mind, but he knew the truth. There were going to be casualties in this war and he could be one of them. It was not going to be an overnight event; it could go on for months, even years. Wars brought out the jackals to prowl the land, looting and pillaging. It was bad enough for a woman, but a woman with child?

"What can I say, Breanna." He sighed. "The deed is done."

"Yes, it is done," she said softly and stepped away from him. She watched him gather his things and take his horse's reins to lead him to the door. Carefully, he checked outside. Seeing no one, he reached for Breanna with one arm and dragged her resisting body against his. His mouth claimed hers, branding her with his kiss. As quickly as he took her, he let her go.

"At least you will have something to remember me by if I don't make it," he said before disappearing in the night."

It was another hour before Breanna returned to the house. She'd waited and watched apprehensively until she was sure he had gotten away safely, then fell on the straw bed they had shared and cried.

He didn't want the child! He couldn't have made it clearer! Dropping a hand to her stomach, Breanna cradled the precious burden she carried.

"I don't care!" she sobbed. "I want you!"

"Breanna!" Heather called into the darkness when she heard the sobs. She held up a lantern and saw her sister. "Bree! Are you all right?" she cried, dropping down beside her. The last thing she expected after Alex's surprise visit was tears!

Sniffling, Breanna sat up and pushed back her

unruly hair. "I'm all right," she said, but her tone denied it.

Heather sat back on her heels. "What happened? I thought that once you two—"

"He doesn't want the baby!" Breanna exclaimed, fighting a new flood of tears. "He wants me, my body, but not the baby!"

Heather was stunned. She couldn't believe the same man who had stood inside this very barn, his eyes filled with love for Breanna, could not want the child that was the result of their love. Shaking her head, she sighed.

"You were wrong about his reasons for marrying you, Bree. You could be wrong about this. He might just be so surprised, he has to adjust to the idea."

Breanna shook her head slowly. "No, Heather. We talked about children and he doesn't care for them."

"Could it be because it's one more thing for him to worry about when he already has so much on his mind?"

It was possible, but Breanna wasn't in the mood to consider it. "All I know is he thinks of the baby as a souvenir for me in case he doesn't come back."

Heather's jaw dropped. "Did he tell you that?" Breanna nodded. "Why the dumb ox!" She heard another sniff and put her arm around Breanna. "Come on, honey. Let's go back to the house and get you and the baby something to eat. You'll need your strength to clobber that fool when he comes home."

Chapter 22

"Six weeks!" Breanna stormed. "Six weeks and we haven't heard a single word from any of them!"

Heather had suffered the same pain of not knowing, but hearing it voiced made it worse. "Do you think you have a monopoly on worrying, Bree?" she asked sadly.

Breanna's attention turned to her sister. Heather's head was lowered, but Breanna could see the tears and the frantic twisting of her handkerchief.

"I'm sorry, *chica*. Sometimes I forget I'm not the only woman waiting for news."

The sisters shared weak smiles and seemed to relax back in their chairs, resolved to get through another day. After a few moments of private thoughts, Breanna spoke.

"I suppose carrying this babe has shortened my temper."

Heather couldn't resist laughing lightly. "It's not the child, Bree. According to Papa, your temper was short from birth!"

"I do seem to have a short fuse, don't I?"

Heather nodded in total agreement and poured them each more tea. "And you jump to conclusions too easily," she added. "You're sitting there sure you haven't heard from Alex because he doesn't care to write, but Eric and Papa haven't written, either. It's possible, they can't get a message to us."

"I know." Breanna sighed forlornly as she reached for the sugar. "It's just that patience isn't one of my virtues."

Taking a moment to sip her tea, Heather plopped her chin in her palm. "Millie was in town this morning with Hilda. She said it's buzzing with rumors about the war, but no one has any details." Watching Breanna shift to a more comfortable position, she added, "I guess we have to believe in the old adage that no news is good news."

"I suppose, but it would be nice if—"

Breanna's voice broke in a gasp and she pointed to a spot behind Heather, who spun around and clutched her throat in shock and fear.

"Sorry, didn't mean ta scare you ladies none, but nobody answered the door, so I let myself in."

Breanna stood stiffly to avoid trembling. "Who are you and what do you want?" she demanded, gripping Heather's hand to draw her close and present a united front.

The tall, rangy stranger, clad in dusty buckskins and clutching a beaver hat, scratched his shaggy beard and shuffled awkwardly. "I reckon I better clear this up and set yer mind ta ease. Ya see, Alex sent me here ta—"

"Alex!" Breanna cried, her entire demeanor changing. Scurrying around the table, she took his arm and pulled him toward it. "Come in! Sit down! Heather, get Mr.—?"

"Merritt, ma'am," the stranger replied. "Ezekiel Merritt."

Smiling brightly, Breanna nodded. "Get Mr. Merritt something to eat and drink."

"Thanks, ma'am. I could use somethin'. I've been travelin' straight from Sonoma and—"

"Sonoma! Is that where Alex is?"

Ezekiel watched her sit on the edge of her chair to await his reply. "Yes ma'am, he sure is." Smiling, he braced his arms on the table. "Now why don't ya set back and relax, and I'll tell ya all the news soon as I git my wind."

Anxious, Breanna nodded, but she never moved. Heather charged back into the dining room with a tray bearing coffee and a large dish filled with warm bread and jam.

"I hope this is all right. I've put stew on to heat but it will be a few minutes."

"Um, looks great! Been eatin' cold beans for nigh on a month. Anything but them will be fine." Merritt began to eat the moment the tray was placed before him. Between bites he managed to learn the names of the young women and who belonged to whom. He wasn't surprised to find out the fiery lass was Alex's woman.

"Mr. Merritt—"

"Call me Zeke," he interjected before filling his mouth again.

"Zeke," Breanna said impatiently. "I hate to be a poor hostess, but could you please tell us the news you have now?"

Shoving the last of a piece of sweetened bread into his mouth, Zeke wiped his chin with his sleeve, belched, apologized, and sat back to relay what he knew.

"Well, now, where ta start," Zeke pondered, rubbing his bearded chin.

"Mr. Merritt!" Breanna cried. "I don't care where you start, just start!"

Zeke chuckled at the anxious lass and nodded. "Yea, okay. Let's see . . . back in May . . . four or five weeks ago . . . them Mexes got our declaration of war. That bein' the United States," he explained. "Got it right on time, too, and I heard they was mad as hell!" He took a swallow of coffee. "Most of the fightin's been down there but we had some here in Californy, too. Nothing big though, 'ceptin' it was enough ta cost us a few good men." He shook his head ruefully. "Damned shame." An audible gasp drew his attention to a pale Breanna. "Sorry, ma'am. Didn't think ya was squeamish."

"Alex?" she breathed, hoping he would understand her question without her asking it.

Zeke immediately caught on. "Misled ya, did I? Nope, he's fine, same as Eric and yer pa." He saw Heather's slump of relief and felt for her. He wasn't much at polite conversation. He'd spent most of his life trapping game in the high country and didn't have the polish necessary to talk with ladies. He'd questioned Alex's decision to send him, but orders were orders.

"Two days ago, we got us our own flag. It was somethin' ta see, I'll tell ya," he said proudly. "White it is, with a red band 'cross the bottom and a red star in the corner. Got a bear walkin' in the middle. Heard tell they picked a bear 'cause he always stands his ground and so will we."

Tears glittered on Breanna's lashes. She could visualize the men watching their new flag raised high for all to see.

"Got writin' on it, too," Zeke went on. "Says *California Republic* in big letters. Ain't nobody who won't know we're free after readin' it, 'ceptin' if they cain't read!" He chuckled. "Then we'll just tell 'em!"

"And our men?" Heather asked. "How are they?"

"Proud and strong as that there bear." He beamed. "Holin' up at Sonoma. Got a real fort now. Frémont's not there, though. He's leadin' his troops all over the countryside. Doin' good, I heard."

Breanna could not contain herself any longer. She simply had to have more details. "Zeke, you said Alex and Eric and Pa were fine, but what exactly does that mean?"

Zeke finished his coffee and smiled. "Well, ma'am, you can both be right proud of yer men. Alex's in charge at Sonoma and Eric's with him."

Seeing their relief, he was glad Alex had insisted that he sidetrack to Casa del Verde on his way to join John. "Yer pa is ridin' with John. I'm headin' to meet up with him from here. If'n ya got any messages for Patrick, jot 'em down and I'll deliver 'em."

Breanna looked hopefully at their guest. "Did Alex send any message to me?"

"No, ma'am, he didn't." Seeing her disappointment, he added, "He's right busy, but he did take the time ta make sure I stopped here ta see ya." He fumbled in a pouch hanging over his shoulder. "Got a letter here for you, though, Miss Heather."

Taking the precious letter, Heather clutched it to her breast and stood. "Excuse me. I'll go read this and ... and write something for you to take to Papa."

As soon as Heather left, Breanna turned her attention back to Zeke. "Didn't Alex even give you a verbal message for me?"

"Yeah, he said ta tell ya he was doin' fine and he should be back for ya soon."

"That's all!" Breanna fumed. Her temper brought her to her feet and Zeke followed suit, recalling that small bit of manners. For the first time he noticed her condition and smiled to himself. Alex had definitely left his brand on this filly before leaving.

"Yes, ma'am. That was all he had ta say."

"Damn him!" Breanna swore, drawing a suppressed chuckle from her guest. "That's just like him! That miserable bastard!" She paced back and forth, speaking more to herself than to him. "He sneaks back here, gets me pregnant, and can't take a moment to write me so much as one sentence! He's too busy! Damn him! I sit here waiting, and nothing!"

Realizing she was causing quite a scene, Breanna blushed. "Oh, I'm sorry. I ... I sometimes get carried away."

"Don't worry yourself over it, ma'am." He shifted uncomfortably before the fury in skirts. "I understand, I think, but don't be too hasty in judgin' him. He's got a lot of men ta see ta and it's a big responsibility."

Ashamed of her outburst, Breanna nodded. "You're right, of course." Trying to salvage some dignity, she smiled weakly. "Would you like me to pack some food for you to take with you?"

"That'd be right fine, ma'am," he said. "I'll just set right here and have some more of that good coffee while I wait for ya and Miss Heather."

"We won't be long," Breanna said, heading for the kitchen.

Within minutes, Heather returned with a letter for her father and Breanna followed her, carrying a small bundle of food for the mountainman. He took both and stuffed them into his leather pouch. He thanked them and picked up his hat.

"Thank you for coming, Zeke," Heather said softly, still holding the letter from Eric.

"My pleasure, ma'am." He smiled. "Been a long time since I've had the company of a lady, and havin' two's been right nice." Heather returned his smile and excused herself with wishes for his safe journey. Zeke extended his hand to Breanna. "Thanks for the grub, ma'am."

"It's the least we can do," Breanna said and took his hand. It dwarfed hers, and she suddenly felt close to the man. On tiptoe, she kissed his cheek. "Godspeed, Ezekiel Merritt."

Reddening slightly, he merely nodded and walked away, a good feeling lightening his steps, but Breanna didn't share that feeling. Her heart was heavy with doubt and anger. How could Alex not send her some private word after that night in the barn? Was it possible he was so adverse to the idea of her pregnancy that he couldn't bear to write?

"Damn you, Alex King!" she cried, stomping

her foot. "You'd better make it back to me so I can
... can ... Oh!" She whirled and pounded up the
stairs to her room to vent her fury in a flood of
tears.

It had been just over a week since Ezekiel
Merritt had visited, and nothing seemed to lighten
Breanna's mood. Heather decided the only thing
left to try was some physical labor that wasn't too
taxing. Only after considerable coaxing, Breanna
agreed to sort out her closet, but after an hour, she
flounced down on her bed in a huff.

"Nothing fits!" she complained, and drew a
chuckle from Heather.

"What did you expect? You're six months pregnant!" Heather sat beside her and patted her on
the back.

"I know," Breanna said, rubbing her growing
roundness. "But I've let out every seam, and even
my loosest clothes don't fit over this."

"It can't be helped, Bree." Heather saw her nod
reluctantly. Enthusiastically, she continued. "I have
an idea! Let's raid the fabric chest and create a few
new fashions just for you." Breanna's interest immediately peaked. "We can design something
comfortable and attractive."

"And cool," Breanna added, tapping her lip as
she thought what she wanted. "There was a soft
pink silk and a lovely yellow fabric as I recall."
Moving quickly from the bed, she grabbed Heather's hand. "Come on. Let's go see what we find
and make some sketches."

It was a soothing way to pass the time, and both
women needed to be occupied. They didn't know
how long their men would be gone or how long
the war would last. They only knew they had to
fill the hours until they were reunited.

"It's really quite lovely, considering." Breanna
smiled and fingered the yellow gown she was

wearing. It met the criteria of being cool and comfortable, yet still managed to be a lovely addition to her wardrobe.

"Are you sure you want to take so much sun?" Heather asked as she adjusted the ribbon tied beneath Breanna's breasts.

Turning to examine the soft folds down the back, Breanna nodded her head. "Yes, it'll be wonderful!" Simple in design, the dress was fashioned after an old-style empire gown. It was sleeveless and the neck was scooped low over her full breasts. A white ribbon had been woven around the neckline and tied in a small bow in the front. Another ribbon gathered the fabric beneath her breasts and fell halfway to the floor down her back.

"Perhaps." Heather examined her sister. "You'd better not wear it on an outing. Eyebrows are sure to raise when they see you aren't wearing petticoats. You'd stand out for sure."

Breanna chuckled and patted her round form. "I'd stand out no matter what I wore." Their shared laughter was suddenly silenced by a commotion below stairs. Millie's high-pitched squeal could be heard above the din, and the sisters could only stand and stare momentarily. Spurred by curiosity, they moved toward the door.

"Whatever could be—" Heather's words caught in her throat. The door was thrown wide and in its frame stood Eric. She could hardly believe her eyes and didn't trust herself to speak even his name. She simply threw herself into his arms and gulped down great sobs.

Breanna's heart skipped at the sight of her sister raining kisses on her husband's face, and her thoughts shifted to who else had come home. Moving silently past the pair, she walked slowly to the head of the stairs. Apprehension grew with each step until she found herself halfway down.

Before her stood Millie and Paul each trying to

tell the other everything that had happened during the three and a half months they were apart. Gear was piled haphazardly in the foyer. The lilting brogue of her father's voice added gaiety to the small group, but with a sinking heart, Breanna realized the deep timber of Alex's voice was missing.

"Breanna, lass!" Patrick called when he spotted her on the stairs. "Just look at ya! You're more lovely than ever with the babe comin'!"

She descended into her father's waiting arms. "Papa!" She sighed and rested her head on his shoulder. Heather and Eric came down as well and the entire family gathered for exchanges of welcome. Patrick draped an arm around the shoulders of his daughters and led them into the parlor. The three sat on the sofa together.

Eric poured out sherry for the ladies and healthy drafts of brandy for the men before sitting on the arm of the sofa beside his wife.

"How long can you stay?" Heather asked, pressing her cheek to the hand Eric rested on her shoulder.

"How long do you want me?" Eric smiled down at her.

"You mean . . . ?"

Nodding his head, Eric looked from Heather to Breanna. "Yes, it's over."

Patrick could no longer contain himself. "We won, lass! We are a free republic!" The next few minutes were filled with the telling of the last big stand at Sonoma and the surrender of Mexico to the Republic of California.

Alex had been in charge at the fort. Breanna clung to each word about his leadership and heroics but the question still remained, where was he? Suddenly it was more than she could stand.

"Where is he, Papa? Why didn't he come with you?" she blurted during a lull in the narrative.

Patrick's eyes shifted to Eric. They seemed to be

uneasy all of a sudden. She looked from one to the other, but neither would meet her eyes. "Papa?" He lowered his head to look at his clasped hands draped over his knees. "Eric?"

The task seemed left to him, and the glistening tears in her dark eyes made it increasingly difficult. Kneeling before her, Eric took her hands in his.

"Honey," he began. "Alex was wounded the day before the surrender." There was no easier way he could tell her, and he watched her close her eyes and sway. "He took a bullet in the thigh."

"Wh-where is he?" she questioned, holding back the tears that threatened to spill.

"Francisco had him taken home."

Breanna rose sharply. "I have to go to him!"

Taking her arms in his hands, Eric held her before him. "You can't, honey. He made us promise not to let you."

"But—"

"No buts," he said firmly. "Alex said you stay, and so you stay." The fire of defiance was crackling in her eyes. "He's worried about you." His eyes lowered to her stomach. "And the baby."

The baby? He was worried about their baby? Sitting back down, she asked, "How bad is it?"

Sighing with relief that she was not going to argue, Eric dropped down to his haunches before her and held her hand. "He lost a lot of blood, but the worst of it was the damage done to the bone. Francisco said it was going to take a long, painful time to heal."

Breanna attempted to smile with relief, yet the tears rolled down her cheeks just the same. She looked around the room, happy to see them all where they should be. Slowly, she got to her feet with Eric's help.

"If you will all excuse me, I think I'll lie down."

No one tried to stop her, and when Heather

made to follow, Eric reached out and held her back.

"Let her go, honey. She needs to be alone for a while."

Reluctantly, Heather agreed, but asked, "Will Alex really be all right?"

Eric sat next to his wife. "We told her the truth, honey. It's just hard to think of Alex down after knowing him all these years. Breanna will come to grips with it, just like we did."

And come to grips, she did. After a good cry filled with worry and some self-pity, Breanna slept. Several hours later she woke, freshened herself, and rejoined the family to begin the weeks of further waiting yet to come.

Alex had survived! He would come back to her, and she would welcome him with open arms, just as soon as she gave him the tongue-lashing of his life! Having decided that being angry at him was easier than worrying, she listed all the reasons. They'd been parted four months and he hadn't sent a single word. He'd been wounded and still nothing. He was full with a child she wasn't even sure he wanted, and he kept her away.

If she could just stay angry, she might forget the agony of knowing he was in pain. She might overlook her own growing discomfort and level out her mercurial moods. But it was a big *if* that the passing weeks would continue to test.

The day was uncomfortably warm and Breanna's temper was sorely pressed. She was denied even the pleasure of riding due to her growing shape. Only the greatest efforts were holding her natural energies at bay. She had paced the house and moved to the patio in search of some cool shade or a breeze.

It was more bearable in the garden where it was cooler and she could find something to do. She spotted some weeds among the last blooms of late summer and decided to set herself the task of clearing them. The family was scattered around the ranch, and she prayed no one would catch her and insist she stop.

She fastened an apron beneath her breasts and tied a scarf around her head to keep her hair from falling forward. With considerable effort she lowered herself to her knees and began. In moments beads of perspiration formed on her brow and in the valley between her breasts. A dull ache began in her lower back. She sat back on her heels to ease it. The child, unhappy with its mother's endeavor, kicked hard.

"Easy, baby." She smiled and lovingly cradled her burden. "You will be free soon enough."

"How soon?" A deep voice filled the garden.

Breanna closed her eyes and caught her breath. Fearing it was a dream, she turned slowly, ready to be disappointed, but thrilled when Alex was actually standing there. She breathed out his name.

"Hello, little one." He smiled his devastatingly crooked grin.

Breanna watched him move carefully toward her as if each step caused him great pain. He was using a cane, and his limp was pronounced. She noticed his pallid complexion and the dark smudges beneath his blue eyes. He'd lost weight, but it only made him appear taller.

That she had been denied sharing his pain made her eyes flash the moment she realized he was over the worst of his injuries.

"Don't you dare call me that, Alex King!" she scolded and tried clumsily to gain her feet. She had to relent and take his offered hand to rise. The moment she was standing she yanked her hand from his. "Why didn't you write? Don't you know how worried I've been?"

Alex understood her reaction. It was one of relief, and he let her rant while he took stock of her. A dirty smudge marred her cheek, and her hair was struggling to escape the scarf restraining her riotous curls. She was wearing an unusual peach gown that enhanced the golden tan she had acquired over the summer. The light in her eyes crackled, and he would have liked to watch the myriad of emotions they revealed, but his eyes were drawn to the rise and fall of her breasts above the deeply cut neckline of her gown. He almost smiled when he saw the gold chain that nestled there. Pregnancy and fury certainly agreed with Breanna. She had never looked more beautiful.

"I love you, Breanna," he said firmly when she would have gone on with her tirade.

Breanna ceased. She realized suddenly that she could have lost him forever. Tears filled her eyes, and she threw herself into his arms sobbing his name. The strength of his embrace belied his weakness, and her world soared when their lips met. They might have gone on rediscovering each other forever, but Alex drew back.

"Can we sit, *querida?*" he asked.

Breanna noticed the white line about his lips. "Oh, Lord!" she paled and led him to the nearest chair. "I'm sorry, darling. I wasn't thinking." She helped him settle and fussed over him. "Can I get you anything? Food? Brandy?"

Gripping her wrist, Alex pulled her toward him. "Nothing except you." He patted his good leg. "Come, sit here. I want you close to me."

Breanna tried to pull free. "But you're hurt!"

Alex grinned. "You aren't going to make me chase you? For as God is my witness, I will."

Sure that he would, indeed, Breanna let him draw her to his lap. Her arm circled his shoulders, and she played with his too-long hair. "Does it pain you greatly?" she asked when he set the cane aside and straightened his injured leg to ease the ache.

"It did, but it's getting better."

"You should have let me come to you. I wanted to."

Spying the stubborn set of her chin, he ran his finger across it and smiled. "There was nothing you could have done, *gatita*. When Hilda returned to the ranch, she fussed over me. And besides," he said, "Francisco loved having me as a captive audience. He was able to list all my sins, and I could do nothing but listen."

Breanna laughed. "I'll bet you loved that!"

"It was great fun." Alex rolled his eyes. "But he only thought he had my attention." Growing serious, he moved his hand to her neck. "The whole time my thoughts were actually filled with you."

Trying to resist the desire to turn and kiss his hand, Breanna tipped her head. "Then why didn't you just send for me?"

Alex sighed deeply. He knew she would not rest until he explained. He really didn't want to go into the details, but he figured he could touch on it sufficiently to satisfy her.

"A lot of Mexican soldiers have scattered. They're hungry and scared. It wasn't safe for travel, *querida*. It still isn't." Gently he moved his large hand to cover her swollen stomach. "I couldn't bear to think of you or the child in danger."

Breanna's face fairly glowed with his words. "Then you want this child?" she asked hopefully.

"God, yes!" he said, bringing her into the full circle of his arms until her breast was pressed to his cheek. "I only told you those things to lessen your hurt should I not return." He lifted his head and gazed into her eyes. "Now that I know you're stuck with me, Mrs. King, I can tell you I love you both."

Breanna had never known such pure joy. Touching his jaw with her hand, she lowered her head to offer a kiss. Alex was anxious to accept it, but the baby had other plans. A strong kick hit Alex's hand, and his eyes widened. His attention immediately shifted to the strong movement in wonder.

"Does that hurt?" he asked.

Breanna shook her head with a smile. "No, love, though it has taken my breath away from time to time." She watched as his hand continued to move gently in awe over the roundness that held his child. She could not resist covering it. When he looked at her, she could see he still needed reassurance. "I feel wonderful, Alex." She kissed his cheek. "Especially now."

Spying the dirt on her cheek, he cocked a brow and ran his thumb over it to show her. "But I doubt you are supposed to be working out here, are you?"

Wrinkling her nose, Breanna tried to ignore his question, but he took her chin in his hand and made her face him. "Not exactly," she said finally. She saw his amusement and laughed. "All right, so I'm not supposed to, but I thought I'd go mad if I had to sit idle for one more minute!"

Alex relaxed. "Ah, my Breanna! You are still a pure delight!" His hand moved to her breast and held it tenderly. "I've missed you. There was not a day that went by that you were not uppermost in my mind."

Covering his hand with her own, Breanna leaned her head against his shoulder. "Is that why you were wounded?"

"No, love. Rest easy, it was not your fault. Francisco's horse was shot out from under him, and I rode back to get him. We were nearly at the fort when several men rode at us, firing wildly." He grew silent a moment. "It's funny. I didn't even know I'd been hit until I dismounted and my leg would not bear my weight."

Breanna didn't think it was funny at all. She was about to say so when he continued.

"Anyway, Francisco felt responsible and insisted

he had to help nurse me back to health. His own penance, I think."

Breanna hugged him closer. "I'm glad you were in such good hands."

Ready to resume the kiss their child had interrupted, Alex bowed his head to kiss the rise of her breast. "Not as good as the ones I'm in now."

Breanna was surprised that her body could still burn so, but his tender kisses were setting her afire. A soft moan slipped from her parted lips as she begged for his mouth on hers.

Anxious to comply, Alex heard voices in the house and cursed. "Damn!"

Amused by the depths of his frustration, Breanna gave him a quick kiss and laughed when he growled at her. "Later, my love. We have forever to share that kiss and more."

It was the perfect time to tell her there was no forever. At least, not yet, but he preferred to let her have her moment. Kissing the palm of her hand, he turned his attention to the others who were quickly joining them.

Chapter 23

⌒◯◯⌒

Dinner was ready. Heather went out to the patio to call the men when she noticed they seemed less jovial than she expected. In fact, they were downright serious about whatever they were discussing. She walked straight toward them.

"Well, are you going to tell me what's going on?" she asked, her hands on her hips as she gazed at each one in turn.

"Nothing," Eric said too quickly. He immediately slipped his arm around her waist to distract her.

Heather stepped away and stomped her foot. "Don't tell me that! I'm not so easily fooled!" She whirled to face Alex. "Are you taking Eric away from me again?"

Amused by the stance that was so like Breanna's, Alex shook his head. "No, Heather," he sighed. "I assure you, he is definitely going to be around."

Sensing something foreboding in his tone, she moved beside his chair and laid her hand on his shoulder. "But something is wrong, isn't it?"

"Might as well tell her," Patrick said as he moved closer to the group. "She could be of help."

Heather frowned. "Tell me what?"

Alex had Eric check that Breanna was not within earshot. Satisfied, he motioned for Heather to sit down, then he leaned close and spoke softly.

"A lot of Mexican troops are moving around

348

trying to get back across the new border. We've caught several stealing what they could en route."

"Yes." Heather nodded. "We've heard about some incidents."

"But have you heard that Guillermo is in hiding? Did you know he was still after my neck?" Heather's gasp was answer enough. "Well, he is."

"But it's over! Surely he doesn't think he can—"

"He thinks he can vindicate himself for everything that happened by destroying me." He braced his chin on his fist. "There were hundreds of men involved in all this, but he feels I alone must pay."

"Probably because you were right under his nose through most of it," Eric added.

"Maybe," Alex agreed. "And I have to say that under normal circumstances, I'd look forward to facing him, but circumstances aren't normal." Locking eyes with Heather, he said, "There's my injury and Breanna to consider."

Heather paled. "Good Lord! You don't think he'd—"

"It's possible," Patrick commented, placing a hand on his daughter's shoulder for support. "That's why Alex came back instead of finishing with John first. He wanted to warn us to be careful."

"And just in case something does happen, we'll need you to help keep an eye on her." Alex took her hand. "Can I count on you, Heather?"

"Absolutely," Heather said softly. "But you'd better stay close, too," she added to Eric.

"I'll be close, honey," he said. "In fact, you'll probably get tired of falling over me."

Alex picked up his cane and stood slowly. "Then, if that's settled, let's go in. I don't want Breanna suspecting anything."

Stepping alongside him, Heather had one more question. "How are you going to explain leaving again?"

"The best way of all, Heather." She tilted her

head, and he smiled. "I'll simply tell her the truth."

Heather was terribly curious about the explanation Alex was going to make. All through dinner she waited for it, but conversation among the men seemed to center around the recent battles and the aftermath. Breanna seemed content simply to listen to the men, until they began to speak of the future of California. Alex seemed to grow evasive.

"You know something, don't you, Alex?" she finally asked.

"Indeed," he said, reaching for her hand. "I had hoped to save my news until after dinner, but my astute wife has seen fit to force the news early." Turning his attention to those at the table, he began in a serious tone.

"Ladies, gentlemen, our republic was short-lived." The startled expressions made him pause a moment longer than necessary to add impact to his next statement. "The United States claimed California as a territory two weeks ago."

Patrick thumped his fist down on the table. "Well I'll be damned!"

Stunned, Eric stared. "It worked! By God, it worked!"

It took a moment for the women to realize this was the goal they had been fighting for all along. Getting caught up in the enthusiasm of the men, they smiled at one another.

Alex let them enjoy the news of their success a moment longer. He gently squeezed Breanna's hand and laughed at her confusion. When Patrick demanded to know everything, he began to explain.

He relayed the bits of information concerning the American troops outside of Mexico City and the rush of Mexican soldiers trying to get there. And he clarified what still had to be done.

"Since President Polk has asked John to set up

the territorial government, I think everything will settle down quickly." Knowing this was the perfect time to make his announcement, he turned to Breanna. "He's asked for my help."

Breanna straightened in her chair and withdrew her hand from his. "When must you go?" she asked, her voice chilled.

"I have to leave for San Francisco in two weeks," he replied simply. Hoping to soften the news, he added, "I was supposed to be there already, but I begged John for time to come and see you."

"How thoughtful of you." Her honeyed sarcasm didn't elude him. "And I don't suppose you would consider taking me with you?"

Aware she thought he was deserting her again, Alex shook his head. "Be sensible, Breanna. What could you do there in your condition, and who would help you when your time comes?"

He was right, of course, yet she was still upset with his decision. "Very well," she said softly and stood, her eyes scanning the family. "If you will excuse me, I'll retire." Alex made to stand, but she held out a hand to stop him. Once he resumed his seat, she exited.

Alex watched her go, torn between the desire to follow and explain, and the belief that she was better off not knowing. His indecision must have shown.

"Don't worry, lad," Patrick said. "It's her condition. It makes them get a crazy idea ya think them unappealing. Once she's slender again, she'll forget all this nonsense. Never could convince her mother I loved her just as much when she was pregnant."

Alex rose and ran his hand over his stiff thigh. "If you'll excuse me," he said, taking his cane, "I think I'll go try."

"Alex?" Heather stopped him. "You could just

tell her the truth—the real truth behind your visit."

Considering it, Alex shook his head. "She'd want to do something to help," he concluded. "And I'd prefer her to think of herself and the child this time, not me."

Heather sat and watched him make his way to the stairs. He was right. Breanna was sure to want to try to act as a distraction for Guillermo, perhaps even going so far as to become bait for a trap. It might be painful for Breanna, but it was better that she did remain in the dark.

Alex stood at the top of the stairs and wiped beads of perspiration from his brow. He had been foolish taking the stairs, but he had to see Breanna and talk to her. He paused long enough to restore his breath and went to her door. He thought of his two previous visits to this bedroom and chuckled.

He had never knocked before and didn't intend to this time. He pushed the door open. His tall, dark form filled the doorway. He stood there until she turned her head slowly to acknowledge his presence.

She had known he would come. Some instinct prepared her, and she was not surprised. "What do you want, Alex?" she asked, her tone brusque.

He limped to the side of the bed and marveled at how beautiful she was, and how desirable. He was shocked to discover he wanted her. That they were both physically at a disadvantage was the only thing that cooled his blood, but it took effort.

"May I sit?" he asked, lowering himself to the edge of the bed when she nodded. His breath came out sharply when he took the weight off his injured leg and he paused a moment to relax. "I shouldn't have tried the stairs yet."

Pushing aside her anger and hurt in the face of his discomfort, she said softly, "It pains you greatly, doesn't it?"

"Yes, it hurts." Facing her, he frowned. "But not as much as when you doubt my love."

Turning away from him, Breanna let out a long sigh of self-doubt. "How can you love me when I'm so ... so ..."

"So filled with my child?" His hand moved to cover her rounded stomach. "This babe is proof of my love." She turned back to look at him and searched his eyes for the truth. "To my knowledge, little one, this is the only child of my loins."

Breanna couldn't resist teasing him. "You mean you were a virgin before I came along?"

Alex chuckled deeply. "Hardly, my love. Surely you don't think I came by my expertise naturally?" Her reply was simply a loving touch to his cheek. Covering her hand with his, Alex drew her palm to his lips. "Do you think we'll cause a scandal if we don't go back down?"

Breanna shook her head. She moved over on the bed and patted an empty spot. "I don't think so. Besides, what kind of trouble can a fat, pregnant woman and a wounded gentleman get into?"

"Oh, Breanna." He chuckled, removing his boots and coat. "In a day or two I'll show you." Easing down beside her, Alex found a comfortable spot for his leg, then lay back to take her in his arms.

Breanna snuggled against him and reveled in his warm strength. Her fingers began to play with the buttons of his shirt until his hand clamped over hers.

"Please, Breanna. Don't make it more difficult for me than it already is. Just holding you like this is wreaking havoc on me."

She was delighted with the knowledge that even pregnant, she was desirable to him. "I'm sorry, Alex." She settled quietly at his side. "I'll be good."

"That's the problem, honey," he said forlornly. "It's always been good."

"Go to sleep, Alex," she ordered, and chuckled when he groaned.

The next few days were the best and worst of times for Breanna. The days were long and hot and she was restless with inactivity. On top of that, Alex was being terribly attentive. It simply made matters worse. She knew he would be leaving again. She couldn't help thinking that his actions were the result of a guilty conscience.

"Why don't you take a walk in the garden!" she snapped when he got in her way for the dozenth time that morning and they had yet to leave her room.

"Would you like that?" he asked sweetly. "My leg is sore, but I—"

"Not us!" she said. "You!"

"But, honey, why would I want to go alone?" He heard her make some throaty sound that almost made him laugh.

"Because I need some peace and quiet," she said between clenched teeth. "First it was just Heather. Then Eric and Papa. Now, it's you, too!" She tried to whirl away from him but less than gracefully bumped into her vanity chair. "I can take care of myself," she said.

"Poor Breanna," Alex consoled, taking her into his arms to hold her while she brooded. "Pursued by a scoundrel, set upon by a rogue, then married to the same."

She enjoyed the security of his arms and was ready to apologize for her outburst when he ruined everything.

"If you would simply realize I know what is best for you and listen to me, you would feel much better. You should have learned by now that I only have your best interests at heart."

Holding her breath, she eased out of his arms and made her way to the vanity.

"We have so little time, love. I want to spend as

much of it with you as—ow!" he yelled when her hairbrush struck his chest. "What the hell did you do that for?"

"Get out!" she screamed. "Leave now!"

"What did I say?" He took a step toward her.

"Go! Go to San Francisco now and leave me alone!" When he didn't move, she whirled to pick up a vase, prepared to throw it.

"All right!" Alex snarled as he backed from the room. "I'm going!" Before he got to the top stair, she slammed her door. The ruckus had drawn Eric halfway up the stairs.

"What the hell is going on?" he asked, seeing the confusion on Alex's face.

"Damned if I know!" Alex roared as he pushed past him and made his way down the stairs.

Breanna heard the shout and stomped her foot in fury. If she had listened to him he could well be dead! she thought. If he wanted only what was good for her, he wouldn't leave her behind again! And, as to her best interests, he wouldn't have married her in the first place!

Going to the bed, she lay down and wept.

"If she doesn't get over this mood, and soon," Alex complained, "I'm going to wring her lovely neck!" He slammed down his cup and Heather thought about the china he was bound to smash. "For two days she's been brooding, and every time I try to talk to her she throws something at me. Christ! I was safer on the damned battlefield!"

Heather had to laugh. "This house has been a battlefield since she came home. I'm used to it."

"Well, I'm not," he said, leaning back in his chair. "I want back the woman I married!"

"That is the woman you married, Alex," she reminded him. "She's always been a tempest. She just wasn't a pregnant tempest."

Thinking of how she had fought him at every turn since they met, he smiled. "I suppose you're right, but what can I do to get her over this insane rage she's going through?"

"Do you really want to know?" Heather asked.

"God, yes! If you can stop this, Heather, let's hear it. This can't be good for her or the baby."

"Leave," she said simply. "Go to John now." She saw him scowl. "I know it hasn't been easy for you, either, but maybe being apart will help you both."

Her words made sense. "But what about Guillermo? What if he somehow knows I've been here and comes after I've left?"

"You were going to leave in a few days anyway. You came back to warn us, and now we're ready. Go, Alex. Settle everything, then come back. By then she will probably have had the baby and you two can . . . work on things."

She could see he was considering her solution. "Breanna's proud," she added. "Right now she sees herself as a burden to all of us. Loving you the way she does, she feels she is less of a woman because of her condition."

"Less!" Alex gasped. "She's more woman right now than most!"

"Then be man enough to give her the privacy she needs now."

Silently, he thought about all she had said. "All right, Heather. I'll do as you suggest, but first I have to talk to her one more time."

"She isn't going to let you," Heather warned.

Alex grinned crookedly. "I don't intend to give her a choice."

Breanna wasn't aware anything was amiss until her mouth grew dry and she seemed unable to moisten it with her tongue. She roused herself from a deep sleep and suddenly realized something was wrong.

A lamp had been lit in her room and her eyes darted from one side to the other. Her first instinct was to rise and solve the small mystery, yet, when she tried, she found herself securely tied to the bed frame, a gag in her mouth. The door to her room swung open and a smiling Alex entered with a tray bearing a decanter and two glasses.

"Ah, you're awake." He grinned and saw the flash of fury in her eyes. "Now calm down," he soothed. "This will be over in a few minutes if you behave." She grumbled something and dropped her head back on her pillow. "That's a good girl."

Placing the tray on the nightstand, Alex eased his hip to the bed and settled down. Ignoring Breanna for a moment, he poured himself some brandy and drank a healthy swallow. Balancing the tray and navigating the stairs on a cane had been no easy task. He needed a moment to recuperate.

"There," he said. "That's better." Turning slightly, Alex looked down at Breanna. "I'm sorry about this, honey, but you forced me to take drastic measures." Her murderous glare proved his point. "You might as well behave and listen to what I have to say or you'll remain like this all night." His eyes challenged hers, and she finally nodded. "If you promise not to scream, I'll remove the gag." Again she nodded, but more vigorously.

"You bastard!" she choked out the moment the cloth was removed, but she quickly turned her head when he moved to replace it. "Don't! I . . . I'm sorry!"

Alex tossed the cloth aside. "Very well." He poured some water into a second glass and held it while Breanna drank until her thirst was quenched.

"Thank you," she replied, but refused to look at him. "Now will you untie me?"

"Oh, no!" He laughed a bit harshly. "I'm tired of having you throw things at me. Your damnable temper is a little more than I can handle right now." He placed one hand over her full stomach and the other rubbed his thigh. "Under other circumstances I would have turned you over my knee and beaten you black and blue."

Breanna gasped. "You wouldn't dare!"

"Oh, believe me, Breanna. Right now I would take great pleasure in doing just that!"

"Sure! Use physical force!" she snapped. "That's your solution for everything, isn't it?"

"What the hell do you think you've been doing the last few days!" he shouted back at her. "Christ! At least with the Mexicans I knew if I got hit it would be a bullet. With you, God only knows!"

Breanna suddenly recalled the startled look on his face the few times she had thrown something at him and began to laugh.

"What's so damned funny?" he demanded, bringing greater peals of laughter from her.

"You!" she struggled to get out. "And me!" Her laughter was contagious, and Alex realized the tension was dissolving.

"God, Breanna, but you're going to drive me mad!" he said, loosening her wrists.

The first thing she did was brush the tears of laughter from her eyes, then she pushed herself upright. She sat back on her heels, still chuckling. "I'm sorry, but when I think of the lengths you and I go to, to express a point, it just seems so funny!"

Alex slipped his hand beneath her hair and gently rubbed her neck. "We are a pair, aren't we?" Breanna's eyes softened as she nodded in agreement. "And I don't suppose either of us will ever change."

"I doubt it."

"Good," he said, drawing her mouth to his. He marveled at the warmth of her lips. He felt her small tongue shyly seeking the heat of his mouth and knew he could get lost in her seduction. "Easy, honey," he said, moving his lips to her cheek. "I'd hate to have our child meet his father prematurely."

She nodded reluctantly and scooted to rest against the headboard while he took another drink. He gazed back to see her toying with his medallion.

"Want to tell me what has you so upset?" he asked, turning to sit beside her and slip his arm around her.

"No," she said softly, suddenly ashamed of herself. "But I do want to tell you I really don't want you to go."

He nestled her head beneath his chin. "I have to go, honey. You know that."

Slowly she shook her head. "Yes, I know."

"In fact, I came here tonight to say good-bye."

She pushed back and looked up at him, her eyes sparkling with unshed tears. "But I thought—"

"The sooner I go, honey, the sooner I'll get back." He gently kissed her cheek, then held it tenderly. "I just didn't want to go with us at odds."

"When will you go?" she asked, her hand moving lovingly over his chest.

"First thing in the morning."

"And how long—"

"Long enough that when I get back you'll be ready for me to chase you around the house." He saw her cheeks pinken. "We have a lot of time to make up for."

"I won't make it easy for you, Alex," she said with a weak smile.

He laughed. "You never do!" He slipped away from her for a moment to turn out the light, and in the darkness, he lay down and took her in his arms.

"I love you, Alex," she whispered.

"And I love you, *querida*," he said, with a kiss on her brow.

* * *

He wanted to leave without waking her. Carefully he rose and picked up his boots. He paused beside the bed and looked down at her. He had to smile. She was sleeping as soundly as a child, yet she was more woman than he'd ever dreamed existed.

She stirred, and he backed away. If she opened her eyes now he would have a difficult time leaving her. As quietly as possible, he turned, opened the door, and walked out without looking back.

A lamp was burning downstairs, and he suspected either Patrick or Eric was up waiting. He entered the kitchen to see Patrick pouring coffee for him.

"Thanks," he said, sitting down to pull on his boots.

"Thought you might want a cup before ridin' out." He sat at the table across from Alex. After a few moments of silence, Patrick spoke. "The men are all aware there could be trouble."

"Good," Alex said. "I'll feel better knowing she's being guarded."

"And what about her?" Patrick asked. "What do I tell her if Guillermo is successful with you?"

Alex felt a tightness in his chest. "You tell her I've always loved her and I always will," he replied in a husky whisper. Reaching into the pocket of his coat, he withdrew an envelope. "And you give her this." He handed it to Patrick. "It signs over everything I own to her and the child."

Patrick's head shot up. "You sound as if you don't expect ta come back."

"I'm coming back," Alex said firmly. "It's just a precaution in case I don't."

Cramming the envelope in his vest pocket, Patrick shook his head. "I was hopin' that once the war was over . . ."

"Yeah, me too," Alex added before he gulped the last of his coffee. Alex rose and shook Patrick's hand in farewell. "Take care of her for me," he said.

"I will, boy," Patrick replied, but Alex was already gone.

At last his luck was changing. As he sat in the heavy brush on the road to Monterey, he couldn't believe his nemesis was riding only a few hundred yards away. Carefully, he raised his rifle and took aim.

Just a few more moments, and the man who had made a fool of him would be dead. His hand shook and he wished he had been able to find something to eat before now, but he would eat later.

Yes! he thought. He would dine at Casa del Verde with the lovely Breanna at his side. The lovely bitch who had warned Alex and prevented him from returning to Mexico City with the traitor in tow.

One more moment. He rubbed the sweat from his brow with his sleeve. *Ready* . . . He blinked and knew the moment was at hand. *Aim* . . . He lined up the barrel with his victim. *Fire!* Laughter rolled over the countryside. Laughter that spoke of madness and revenge.

"Now for Breanna!" the hysterical voice called out, but only the prancing horse that danced around the sprawled form of Alexander King heard it.

Alex was gone. He'd left exactly as he had planned in the early morning without waking her. She knew it was easier just to fall asleep in his arms and wake to find him gone, but she was sorry she hadn't been there to hold him one more time.

Rolling off the side of the bed, she stood and rubbed her back. The babe was beginning to settle lower and lately made her uncomfortably awkward. She went to her vanity and brushed out her hair.

She wanted to fill her day with mundane chores so she could avoid thinking about Alex and the lengths he'd taken to bridge the gap between them. It wasn't going to be easy. His image was everywhere. Even the brush she held made her smile when she thought of how she had flung it at him.

Still smiling, she donned her yellow gown, tied back her hair, and started slowly down the stairs. The house was surprisingly quiet. She wasn't sure if it was still early or very late, but she did expect to find someone in the kitchen.

"Heather?" she called as she reached the kitchen door. She peered inside to find it empty. Making her way through, she went to the back door and looked out onto the patio. A smile touched her face. She could see her sister's head over the back of one of the chairs. The coffeepot was on the table and Heather was obviously waiting for her.

The warm sun touched her face. She wanted to enjoy it, but another catch in her back made her pause. So she was ready to call out to her sister, but the spasm passed, and she moved forward.

"Good morning, *chica*," she said, walking around the table. "It looks like—"

Breanna gripped the back of a chair to keep from swooning. She couldn't believe her eyes. Her sister wasn't waiting for her to have breakfast. She was gagged and bound to her chair!

"Heather!" she gasped, and started toward her. There was a frantic plea in Heather's eyes, but Breanna ignored it in her haste to free her sister. She eased herself down on her knees at the side of the chair and began to work on the knotted rope binding her.

"Who did this?" Breanna cried. "Who tied you up?"

"I did, señorita. Now move away from her."

Breanna's head swung around. For a moment she did not recognize the man standing there waving the pistol. Then, when a sinister smile twisted his mouth, she brought her hand to her throat to stifle a scream.

Chapter 24

~~~OC~~~

"I said move!" Felipe ordered. Breanna took one shaky step away from Heather, and he calmed. He reached behind Heather and took a sweet roll and shoved it into his mouth.

"I had hoped to dine with you properly, *querida*," he said while chewing, "but I have not eaten in three days." Taking another roll, he paused. "You will forgive me for my poor table manners, won't you?" He saw her frightened stare and laughed harshly as he continued eating. "Of course you will!"

Struggling with a rising hysteria, Breanna wrung her hands and glanced at her sister. Heather was as white as a sheet and perfectly still. Both were aware that their only hope was that someone would come in and see the danger. Until then, she had to make sure Guillermo did nothing to harm them.

"W-would you like coffee with your . . . your breakfast?" she asked, hating the quiver she couldn't quite control.

Felipe smiled coldly. "So you can throw it at me, *querida*? No, I think not." Wiping his mouth with his sleeve, he moved toward her. When he was standing close, he looked down at her. For the first time he noticed her enlarged shape.

"So Alex was riding you after all," he sneered. "And I thought you were a lady. It's a shame I didn't know you were a whore when I met you."

He raised his hand to cover her breast. "I could have tasted some of your charms myself."

Breanna flinched but remained rooted to the spot. Somehow she knew if she resisted, he would become violent.

"What are you going to do?" she asked with more control than she felt.

"Do?" Felipe asked as if the question surprised him. "Why, Breanna, I'm going to take you to Mexico with me." He moved away but turned to watch her as he added, "Now with Alex gone, my superiors will have to settle for you."

Breanna felt the blood drain from her face. "G-gone? What do you mean, gone?"

"Oh, didn't I tell you?" He smiled at her. "I killed him before I came here."

"No," she whispered. Another cramp clutched her, and she brought her hands to her stomach. "Nooo!"

Guillermo frowned. He didn't like the way she seemed to be in pain. As she was recovering, he realized they were standing out where anyone could see them. Grabbing a knife, he cut through Heather's bonds.

"Help her!" he ordered.

Rubbing her wrists, Heather ran to her sister. "Bree? Is it time?" She fervently prayed it wasn't. She was several weeks early!

"I . . . I don't know," Breanna said breathlessly.

"Inside!" Guillermo ordered, shoving Breanna when they were slow to react. "I've taken care of the guard posted out here but I do not wish to be seen by any others."

Breanna winced, hoping Guillermo didn't mean he had killed the man left behind to protect them.

"Be careful!" Heather demanded, too worried about her sister to be afraid of him. She took Breanna's arm and led her inside. With each step, she prayed Eric and their father would return from investigating the report of soldiers just north of the house, while at the same time she hoped they would stay away. Guillermo was crazy enough to kill anyone who got in his way.

Once inside, Felipe seemed to relax. He gazed around the foyer almost as if he were a guest. It lacked the opulence he was accustomed to, but it did have a certain style he liked.

"I would have enjoyed living here, I think," he told them. "It suits me." He came up behind Breanna and wrapped his hand in her long auburn tresses. "It would have been a perfect place to house my mistress."

The pain had passed, and with it Breanna's fear. Heather was free. It was possible that together they could overtake him. A small smile touched her mouth, and she turned slowly to face him. She leaned forward so that he would not miss the cleavage at her neckline and tilted her head provocatively. With luck, Heather would understand what she was doing.

"Felipe," she breathed, placing her hand on his chest. She felt the thundering of his heart and wanted to be ill, but there wasn't time. "Felipe, I'd rot in hell first!" She brought her knee up sharply into his groin as Heather grabbed for his hair.

It seemed they were going to succeed in besting him. He was doubled over, clutching his throbbing groin. Heather was pulling his hair fiercely while Breanna reached for the pistol in his hand. She had the barrel and was beginning to yank it free when another spasm struck.

She cried out, distracting Heather. Felipe took advantage of the lull in their attack and brought the pistol down across Heather's head, sending her to the floor where she lay unconscious. Breanna called out her name, but the only response she got was Felipe's hand across her mouth.

"*Puta!*" he roared, still trying to recover from her attack.

Stumbling backward, Breanna hit a small table. It teetered and they both went over. Breanna pushed back her hair and tried to crawl toward her sister. Guillermo's hand gripped her arm and hauled her roughly to her feet.

"Leave her," he said calmly. "We have to get ready to go."

Breanna knew that if they left Casa del Verde, her chances of ever seeing it or her family again were frighteningly slim. Tasting her own blood in her mouth, she asked for some water.

Suddenly, the bedraggled man before her seemed once again to become the gracious Spanish don in whose home she had danced. He seemed confused by his surroundings. Running his hand through his hair, he shook his head.

"Water. Yes. I . . . I need to clean up." He took Breanna's arm and led her back toward the kitchen. "It won't do to have my superiors see me like this."

Breanna was more terrified of this Guillermo. He was surely insane. She tried to figure out how to deal with him, but his earlier words were making her reckless. Then she remembered his words. *I killed him!*

"Hand me that towel *querida*," Guillermo told her. It was only then that she realized he had released her and gone to the sink. He was pumping water into the basin, his back to her. As she picked up the towel, her eyes scanned the area. There was a large knife on the table.

She carefully slid the knife off the table while his back was turned and hid it in the folds of her skirt as she moved toward him with the towel outstretched. "Here," she said softly.

Felipe shook the excess water from his hands and turned to accept the towel. "*Gracias, querida*," he said with a smile.

He appeared so like the man she had known,

she almost didn't use the weapon she clutched in her hand. *"I killed him!"*

"Bastard!" she screamed, and drove the knife into his shoulder. She heard his cry of pain but did not wait to see how much damage she had done. She ran as quickly as her rounded body allowed.

Heather hadn't moved, but she could not risk stopping to check on her. She could only hope Heather was just knocked out momentarily. Filled with terror, she had her hand on the front door-knob when she was grabbed from behind. She whirled around toward Felipe like a savage cat, her nails reaching for his eyes.

She knew that if she let up at all, Felipe was prepared to do something terrible to her, and she struggled more fiercely. Each time he groaned or grunted, she struck again, but the exertion was taking its toll on her. She was exhausted. Her swollen shape made her awkward. In all too short a time, she knew it was useless. She kicked out at him once more and felt a gripping pain deep in her womb.

Gasping for breath, Felipe saw her fall back against the wall. He had fought men who did not have the tenacity of this one small woman. For a moment, he felt a certain respect for her. Despite the pain she had inflicted, he could almost forgive her. Almost.

"You lose, *bruja.*" He panted, wincing with the burning pain in his shoulder. He took a cautious step closer. "You warned Alex about my trap, but now he's dead." She didn't flinch, so he took another step. "You thought to thwart me, but now you will be totally in my power."

Breanna knew he was talking but there was such a ringing in her ears, she couldn't hear the words. All she knew was that something was wrong. A tightening started again but this time it was different. This time there was warmth and wetness. Gasping, she looked down at the floor.

Felipe's eyes followed hers to the puddle at her feet. Harshly, he swore in Spanish. She was ready to deliver the child of that bastard lying dead in the dirt. He knew she would not be able to ride, but he couldn't let her stay. Perhaps they might make it in a carriage. He looked for Heather but she was gone! The bitch was gone! Sometime during his struggle with Breanna she had crawled silently away. Panic gripped him when he realized she would bring help.

"Come on!" he ordered, grabbing Breanna's arm.

Breanna stumbled forward, losing her balance. "Felipe, please!" she cried. "Let me go!" He continued to pull her and she fell to the floor. "You can get away if you leave me!" She sobbed, but he kept moving forward, dragging her behind him.

A contraction made her clutch her stomach. Felipe was yanked up short and was prepared to strike her, only to hold back when he saw the reason for her resistance.

"Get up, *querida*," he said almost gently.

"I . . . I can't." Breanna sobbed.

"Get up!" he yelled, grabbing a handful of her hair.

Breanna struggled and managed to get to her knees. At that moment she realized Heather was gone. "Please," she prayed for someone to rescue her. "Please."

Some bit of sanity surfaced in Felipe's brain. Perhaps it was a survival instinct, but he looked down at Breanna and knew that he would never escape if he took her with him. He remembered his pistol in the kitchen and, sure Breanna could not get away, ran back for it. In seconds, he was once again standing over her.

"I had thought to take you to Mexico City, *querida*," he said with a touch of regret. "Unfortunately, I am forced to change my plans." He slowly lifted the pistol until it was pointed at her.

Breanna knew she was facing her own death. Strangely, she was not regretting it for herself. Alex was dead. Her only reason left for living was, at this moment, fighting to be born, but it was a fight an infant could not win. Refusing to look at the man responsible for destroying everything she loved, she lowered her head to the floor to wait for the final moment.

"*Adios, querida,*" Felipe said casually, pulling slowly on the trigger.

The front door crashed open.

Felipe glanced up, his face turning white. "You!" he snarled, convinced he was looking at a ghost.

Breanna struggled to turn her head toward the door. "Alex!" she cried, sure she had already died, until her body spasmed. Her cry distracted Alex. There was blood on his face, but he had never looked better. Time froze for the lovers, as Guillermo shook off the shock of seeing his nemesis risen from the dead.

"At last I am blessed!" he said, his voice high and crazed. "I will have the pleasure of watching you die, again!"

Without thinking, Breanna reached for the pistol he had raised to aim at Alex. She ignored Alex's frantic call. Her hand circled the barrel, and she yanked it hard toward herself.

There was an explosion, then another, and her body was racked with pain. She thought she heard someone cry out her name, but she couldn't fight the blackness that beckoned.

"Breanna! Wake up! You have to help, damn it!" Breanna's thrashing ceased and her eyes fluttered. "That's it, honey. Come on. You can do it! Fight like you fought me!"

The deep, demanding voice reached through the pain-filled darkness and slowly drew Breanna back to consciousness. There was a burning in her shoulder and a deep drawing in her abdomen. It would have been so easy to slip into the blackness again.

"Fight, Breanna!" Alex glanced at Patrick, who prodded him on. "You don't want me to think you've become a coward, do you?" Her eyes started to close, and he shook her carefully. He had to make her wake up and help with the birth of their child or they would both die!

Trying one more approach, he placed his hand on her face. "You don't want me to have to find another woman to raise our child, do you?" She frowned in her twilight world. "Think about it, honey. Me, in the arms of another." She began to struggle. "If you love me, Breanna, for God's sake, fight!"

Her head began to roll back and forth. Alex and another woman . . . never! "Nooo!" she cried out weakly at last and opened her eyes. Alex was the first person she saw, and she reached out a shaky hand to him.

Between laughter and tears, Alex clutched it and drew it to his lips. "Oh, darling! We're going to make it!" A new contraction started. "Patrick, get Millie!" he called out as Breanna squeezed his hand.

"Alex!" she cried, biting down on her lip so hard she drew blood.

Brushing back her damp hair, Alex felt his insides twist. "Go ahead, honey," he rasped. "Scream!"

Breanna rose up to clutch her stomach but remained silent. The contraction eased and she fell back, gasping. Her body was soaked in perspiration. Taking a moment to catch her breath, she saw the most precious of faces hovering over her.

"Alex, he . . . he said you were dead."

"Shhh, love." Alex began to bathe her face with a cool cloth. "It's over. I'm fine." She was beginning to doze off but he knew it was a natural sleep, one her body would not let her enjoy for long. Their child wanted to be born, and soon.

"How is she?" Millie asked the instant she came through the door.

Without taking his eyes from her, Alex replied harshly, "How the hell should I know!" He realized he was taking out his fear and frustration on the wrong person. "I'm sorry, Millie. I didn't mean—"

"Don't worry about it," Millie said gently. "You've been through a lot." She bent over Breanna to check on her, then turned to Alex. "You'd better have Heather dress your wound."

Raising his hand to the deep crease along his temple, Alex winced. "Later." Millie tried to insist. "I said later!" He rubbed his throbbing head. "I won't leave her, Millie. I'll never leave her again."

A new pain woke Breanna. Millie didn't have time to worry about Alex. She thought he should leave them to the birthing, but was sure he would refuse. Rather than waste time, she began to do what needed to be done as if he weren't there. Much to her surprise, he turned out to be useful.

"Lift her up," Millie instructed as she slid a clean sheet beneath Breanna. Breanna moaned, and he blanched. "I need to take care of her wound," she said more calmly than she felt. "Help me get her gown off."

Alex didn't want to move Breanna again. It hurt each time. Reaching for the top of her gown, he ripped it in half from the neck to hem, and drew back the side that was bloodsoaked.

Millie couldn't resist an amused shake of her head. But she sobered the instant she saw the dark hole beneath Breanna's bloodied shift. Gently, she tore apart the gauzy material to examine the bullet wound.

"Thank God, it went through." Efficiently she began to cleanse the wound.

"Will ... will it harm the babe?" Alex asked, keeping his eyes on Breanna's face.

Millie smiled. "No, Alex. They'll both be fine."

Breanna began to moan. She was gripping Alex's hand tightly as the pain intensified. After what seemed like an eternity, she eased. And so it went on for hours.

"How much longer can she endure this?" Alex asked, sure his wife was going to die if she had to take much more.

"I don't know," Millie said raggedly. "I think everyone is different, and I've only helped my brother's wife."

Alex rolled his eyes.

"Why don't you go downstairs!" she snapped, her own nerves strained.

"I told you, I'm not leaving her!"

"Then be quiet! I'm doing the—"

"Alex!" Breanna screamed unexpectedly.

The two stared at each other and blanched. It was time.

"Push down," Millie ordered, moving to check Breanna's progress. "I see the head!" she cried, bringing Alex to his feet. "Push, Breanna!"

Breanna had never experienced such pain. Her body felt like it was being torn apart. She thrashed her head and gripped Alex's hand and the headboard with more strength than she ever dreamed she possessed. Digging her heels into the mattress, she arched her back off the bed.

"Do something!" Alex roared.

"She has to do it!" Millie yelled back.

Dropping to his knees, Alex wrapped both his hands around hers. "Breanna! Push, Breanna!" he begged. "For the love of God, get this over with!"

"Does it always take this long?" Eric asked Patrick as he entered the library where the old man had been sitting alone for hours.

Thinking of the two births he had witnessed,

Patrick sighed. Two daughters. He had been blessed with two beautiful daughters, and in the past day, he had almost lost them both.

"How's Heather?' he asked in lieu of an answer.

Pushing back his hair with trembling fingers, Eric sank into a chair. "She'll be all right." He leaned forward and braced his head in his hands. "But God, I was so scared!"

Patrick thought of how pale and weak Heather had been when she stumbled into the barn. None of them had known what was going on or how she had been hurt. Blood had matted her hair on the side of her head, but she would not let anyone attend to her until she told them what was going on in the house.

Patrick left her with Eric and had run to help Breanna. She was in more immediate danger. He didn't think he would ever forget the sight of Guillermo ready to shoot as the front door crashed open. The scene would forever be etched in his mind.

Breanna on the floor. Alex looming in the doorway. Guillermo's gun being pulled down. A shot! A scream from Breanna, and that savage cry from Alex. There was a second shot, and Patrick realized he had pulled the trigger.

"I know, boy," Patrick said in a subdued voice. "I was scared, too." He blew out a breath. "I ain't never shot a man in the back before."

"Don't think about it, Patrick. You didn't kill a man. You killed a wild animal that needed killing."

The room grew silent as the two men took to waiting again. Eric couldn't stand the inactivity and poured a couple of drinks. Handing one to Patrick, he tried to think of something to say.

"I wonder what kind of child Breanna and Alex will have," he finally said. "I suppose it will have the devil's own temper."

A small smile touched Patrick's weathered face. "And be damned stubborn, too."

"Probably a fighter."

"Definitely a fighter!"

"No, I don't suppose we'll be blessed with a sweet, obedient child." Eric chuckled. "With a devil for a father and a hellion for a mother, we'd better check to see if it has tiny horns."

Patrick grinned. "Might even have a—"

A terrible scream brought them both to their feet.

"Christ!" Eric swore. "What's happening?"

Patrick paled, knowing his daughter's time had come. "The babe," he said nervously.

Eric's face was ashen, too. "Good Lord! Is . . . is it always like this?"

"It ain't easy, boy," Patrick mumbled, moving slowly to the door.

Eric fell back into his chair, and his breath came out in a whoosh. "My God! I . . . it . . . Jesus! I hope Heather never gets pregnant!"

Footsteps beat a rapid tattoo on the stairs and drew the attention of the two men. Millie ran across the foyer, beaming. "It's a girl!"

Alex looked down at his wife and daughter. He had never seen anything more beautiful. Breanna was exhausted, yet there was a loving smile on her lips. His heart was so filled with love and pride, he wanted to shout his happiness to the world.

"She's perfect, isn't she?" Breanna asked, reaching to take his hand and draw him to her side.

Alex smiled. "As perfect as her mother," he replied, bending to kiss Breanna's brow. "Thank you, *querida*," he breathed, pressing his cheek to hers.

There was a shuffling in the hall, and Alex knew the others would be coming to see his wife and daughter. Placing one more kiss on Breanna's lips, he rose. "Don't let them stay too long," he told her. When she tried to keep him beside her, he shook his head. "I better go get cleaned up. I'll be back soon."

Her eyes fell to the dark head cradled in her arms, and he left. Without a word, he paused before Patrick. The two exchanged looks that spoke for them. Breanna would be all right. The child was healthy and whole. The nightmare was over.

Patrick placed his hand on Alex's shoulder and smiled. "Get some rest, boy," was all he said.

Alex's leg was aching but his heart was so full, it didn't matter. Slowly he made his way outside to discover it was dark. He breathed in great gulps of the cool night air. Once he felt the tension draining from him, he made his way to a chair and sat down.

He held out his hands before his eyes. He had never realized how large they were until they held the precious bundle of his child. He had been the first person in this world to touch her, and he would never be able to thank Millie enough for making him take the child as it came from his beloved wife's body.

"It's a girl!" he announced proudly, unashamed of the tears that ran down his cheeks. "Breanna! We have a daughter!"

Millie cut the cord, and he carefully carried the child to Breanna's waiting arms. Together they checked her. If he lived forever, he would never forget the soft laughter they shared when they knew she was perfect.

"What shall we name her, love?" he asked, smiling at the way the babe sought to suckle her own fist.

"Sabrina," she replied softly. "Sabrina King."

Alex felt new tears burning his tired eyes. He had told her the name only once, and she had remembered. Gazing at the fading stars in the first rays of morning, he let the tears fall.

"You have a granddaughter, mother, and she's been named after you."

Heather looked down at Alex's slumped body. He was dirty and there was dried blood on his temple. She thought back to when she had decided he would be a perfect mate for her sister. Never had she dreamed their courtship would be so tumultuous or their marriage such an adventure.

"Alex," she called gently, shaking his shoulder. His eyes opened and reflected the blue of the morning sky. "I think you'd better come in and let me see to that wound now." She smiled down at him. "And get you something to eat. You're probably starved."

Alex sat up, blinking. "Breanna? The baby?"

"They're fine. In fact, they are both sleeping and you need to get cleaned up if you're going to see them when they wake up." She wrinkled her nose. "You'd scare them both if they saw you now."

Alex stood and worked out the kinks in his body that came from sleeping in a chair.

"Are you all right?" he asked, remembering Heather had also been involved in the ordeal.

Gingerly, she touched the cut on her head. "Just a slight headache," she said, stepping in beside him as they walked to the house. "My biggest problem is Eric. After listening to Breanna give birth, he's sure I shouldn't have to go through it." With a grin, she glanced up at Alex. "Of course, it's too late for him to do anything about it now."

Alex paused and took her hand. "You mean . . . ?"

Heather nodded. "Early next year," she said.

Smiling warmly, Alex kissed her cheek. "He'll live through it," he said. "I did."

"Oh, you men are so big and brave!" she teased.

Alex could feel the heat of a blush when he thought how he had almost fainted several times during Breanna's labor. "In facing the wrath of God, we're brave," he said. "It's only childbirth that does us in."

They entered the house to find the family seated at the table, which was filled with platters of food. The aroma of fresh coffee drifted up, making him realize how hungry he really was. The table was alive with chatter about the newest member of the family, until everyone slipped into silent thought.

A number of tragedies had been spared the day before, but the past was best forgotten and buried, like the Mexican general.

To break the somber mood, Patrick spoke. "When do ya think you and my daughter will be going home?"

Alex thought of Breanna at his ranch. "I suppose as soon as she can travel."

"And what about that business with John?" Eric asked. "You said he wanted you to help him."

"John will just have to find someone else to take care of it," Alex announced solemnly. "I've given all I can afford to give to this cause. I'm going to take a bath, then see to my . . . my family." He smiled. "They are all the business I mean to take care of."

Breanna couldn't take her eyes off the dark head nuzzling at her breast. She was so beautiful, a tiny replica of her father. Breanna knew that if she had lost him, she would still have had Sabrina.

"But now I have you both," she breathed, kissing the little head.

"And both of us love you," Alex said from the doorway.

Breanna's joy shone on her face. Alex knelt beside her and kissed her tenderly.

"How do you feel?" he asked as he placed a finger within his daughter's grasp. Sabrina pulled it tightly against the breast at her pursed lips. Breanna's skin was like warm silk, reminding him just how long it had been since he last had held Breanna in his arms as his lover.

"I'm feeling fine." She saw his eyes fall to the bandage on her shoulder, and shook her head when he frowned. "It's over, Alex." She tenderly touched the raw crease on his brow. "We have survived and hold the future here."

"I want us to go home, honey," he told her.

"Then let's go home."

Author's Note

The United States government under President Polk, not a handful of Californians, actually instigated the Mexican war. The doctrine of manifest destiny was responsible for the desire to see the United States stretch "from sea to shining sea."

Although Hawk Hill and Sonoma were battle sites, most of the fighting took place in Mexico, including the capture of Mexico City before the end of the war. As a result of this war the territory that included the current states of California, Nevada, Utah, Arizona, and parts of Colorado, New Mexico, and Wyoming became a U.S. possession that added over five hundred and twenty-five thousand square miles to the United States.

John Griffiths, John Frémont, and Ezekiel Merritt were actual persons and played their respective roles in my story as factually as I could tell them with my fictitious Breanna and Alex. After the peace treaty with Mexico was signed in February 1848, it took California less than three years to become a state. On September 9, 1850, the Golden State became the thirty-first to join the Union.